MAD, BAD, AND DANGEROUS IN PLAID

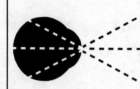

This Large Print Book carries the
Seal of Approval of N.A.V.H.

Mad, Bad, and Dangerous in Plaid

Suzanne Enoch

THORNDIKE PRESS
A part of Gale, Cengage Learning

GALE
CENGAGE Learning·

Farmington Hills, Mich • San Francisco • New York • Waterville, Maine
Meriden, Conn • Mason, Ohio • Chicago

GALE
CENGAGE Learning

LIBRARY OF CONGRESS CATALOGING-IN-PUBLICATION DATA

Enoch, Suzanne.
    Mad, bad, and dangerous in plaid / by Suzanne Enoch. — Large print edition.
        pages cm. — (Thorndike Press large print romance)
    ISBN 978-1-4104-7909-9 (hardcover) — ISBN 1-4104-7909-9 (hardcover)
    1. Highlands (Scotland)—Fiction. 2. Large type books. I. Title.
PS3555.N655M33 2015
813'.6—dc23   2015010775

Published in 2015 by arrangement with St. Martin's Press, LLC

Printed in Mexico
1 2 3 4 5 6 7 19 18 17 16 15

For Jack —

The best nephew an aunt
could ever ask for.
I'm so proud of the young man you are,
a gentleman in every sense of the word.

PROLOGUE

"What do ye think, Lachlan?"

Her heart pounding, Lady Rowena Mac-Lawry pirouetted in the middle of the Glengask House morning room. All the way from Paris, this gown was. It practically floated on the air, mauve and a deep gray she knew precisely matched her eyes, because she'd spent hours holding up swatches of material to her mirrored reflection until she'd found the perfect charcoal hue.

"What do I think aboot what?" Lachlan MacTier, Viscount Gray, returned from the corner of the room.

"My gown," she added, trying not to sound plaintive.

He looked up from the game of cards he was playing against her older brother Munro. "Oh. It's fancy. Are ye having a costume ball fer yer birthday, then?"

Rowena frowned, dropping the folds of the skirt she'd held to show off the lace hems. "This isnae a costume. It's my new dress. Ranulf willnae tell me if he's bought me a gown, so I had this one made. I cannae be withoot a new dress fer my eighteenth birthday."

Munro chuckled. "Gads, Winnie, ye know ye could torch half yer wardrobe and still nae wear the same gown twice in a month."

"Oh, be quiet, Bear," she countered, using her brother's rather appropriate nickname. "A lady must have gowns."

" 'A lady,' " Lachlan repeated with a snort. Pushing to his feet, he walked over to tug on her long, midnight-black ponytail. "I dunnae think a lady has burrs in her hair."

She tried to ignore the responding tingle running down her scalp. "I dunnae have burrs in my hair."

He tugged again. "Nae today."

"I'm going to put it up fer the party, anyway. Ranulf said we could have four waltzes. Four!"

"Aye?" Lachlan sat again, a strand of his dark brown hair falling across one light green eye as he looked at her. "Best of luck in finding four lads willing to brave the Marquis of Glengask glaring at them like the devil himself."

Three. She only needed to find three lads, because he would be the fourth. That was how she'd imagined it for months and months. Rowena kept her expression carefully amused. "Ranulf's my brother; nae my jailer. And he likes *ye*, Lach. We could waltz."

"Aye, he likes me. I'm a MacLawry clan chieftain, and I agree with where he's guiding the clan. And we cannae forget that I bring all the MacTiers to clan MacLawry, and he's the MacLawry."

Yes, and Ranulf had become both the chief of clan MacLawry and the Marquis of Glengask at age fifteen, back when Rowena had only been two. The clan was as it had been since her first conscious memory of it. And Lachlan was . . . Lachlan, eight years her senior and her brother Bear's closest friend. Handsome as sin and destined to marry her. Except that lately she'd begun to wonder if he realized that last bit.

"It's more than that, and ye know it." Rowena gave an exaggerated sigh. "I've a mind to go fer a walk through the glen. Would ye care to join me?"

"Nae while Bear owes me five quid," he returned, picking up another card and then setting it down faceup. "Where's Arran?"

"In the library, I'd wager," Bear put in. "He'll go with ye."

But she didn't want to go walking with

9

Arran; yes, he had a better grasp of fashion and proper, gentlemanly behavior than either Munro or Lachlan, but in the end he was her brother, set midway between Ranulf and Munro. The ladies down in An Soadh and Mahldoen whispered that Arran was devilish handsome — though they said that about all three of her brothers — but the simple fact was that he wasn't Lachlan. "I'll go on my own," she announced, and turned on her heel.

Oh, it was so aggravating! There she was, a week shy of her eighteenth birthday, a young lady of both wealth and good education, and fairly bonny if she did say so herself. And the man she meant to marry found playing a dull game of cards more interesting than taking a walk with her. She could likely say she was going to the kitchen pantry to escape through the Jacobite tunnels below Glengask, and Lachlan would only tell her to take a lantern with her. He was supposed to be chivalrous and attentive, not . . . not interested.

"Ye shouldnae chase him so hard." A low brogue came from the library doorway as she stomped past it, and Arran emerged to join her march down the hallway. Or *she* was marching, rather; with his tall frame and long gait it was merely a leisurely stroll for him.

"I'm nae chasing anyone. I'm off fer a walk, and I asked if Lachlan would care to join me." She scowled. "And why should-nae he want to? I'm a charming lass, am I nae?"

"Aye, ye are," her older brother returned. "Ye're also . . . familiar."

"I am nae familiar!" she protested. "I've nae even kissed him."

"If ye had, he'd likely be dead, ye being nae but seventeen." The glance he sent her was both assessing and serious. "I dunnae mean to say ye've behaved inappropriately. I mean he's known ye since ye were born, and ye've been pestering him since ye learned to talk."

"It's nae pestering. It's flirting."

"That's a fine line, *piuthar*."

"I'm nae a fool, *bràthair*," she retorted. That was just ridiculous. Of course she knew the difference between flirting and pestering. But Arran was the cleverest of them. He'd even spent time in the English army and had seen Prince Georgie. Ignor-ing what he said would be unwise. "Ye mean to say he's accustomed to me. That I'm nae but a . . . piece of furniture he's learned to walk around."

"Aye, I sup—"

"Then I have yet another reason to go to London fer my Season. So Lach will see me as a lady. So I'll learn how to be more than just a Highlands lass."

"Dunnae pin yer hopes on that, Winnie," her brother returned, stopping in the foyer to pull on a coat and hand her a heavy wrap. "Ye ken that Ranulf willnae allow it."

She pulled on the cloak and tied her bonnet beneath her chin. She'd only begun wearing a proper lady's hat over the past few weeks, and the ribbons still scratched at her. "I've asked him to give me a Season as my birthday gift," she said, nodding at Cooper as the butler pulled open the front door. "And ye know he'd nae deny me a thing if it's fer my eighteenth birthday."

"I know that, and I know Ranulf," Arran commented, offering his arm to her.

A glance up the hallway told her that both Lachlan and Bear seemed perfectly content to let her go walking alone. Either that, or they'd heard Arran join her. Whatever she would have preferred to think of their ungentlemanly ways, the latter explanation made more sense. Everyone knew she was never to go outside without an escort. Not with Campbells and Dailys and Gerdenses lurking on the borders.

What Arran had said — everything he'd

said — made sense, as well. Lachlan Mac-Tier was accustomed to her, and he clearly still saw her as the wee lass who tagged along with the lads to catch frogs and hunt rabbits. To alter that, she needed a Season in London.

Their own mother had had a London Season, but of course she'd been English. The odds of Ranulf agreeing that his only sister should follow in their unfortunate mother's footsteps were abysmal. They barely even spoke Eleanor Wilkie-MacLawry's name, and they hadn't since she'd swallowed poison rather than remain widowed in the Highlands with four rambunctious children.

But none of that altered the fact that Rowena wanted — needed — to go to London and that Ranulf would likely forbid it. Well, she supposed she had a week to make her plans. And to convince herself that the consequences would be worth the trouble likely to come her way as a result.

And if Lachlan didn't appreciate the young lady she meant to become, surely she could find a handsome, titled Englishman who would.

CHAPTER ONE

Three Months Later

"Infatuation. That's what it was." Rowena MacLawry flipped her hand at the pair of young ladies seated opposite her. "I mean, for heaven's sake, I barely knew anyone else."

Lady Jane Hanover kept her gaze aimed out the coach's window. "I think I would be more convinced that you've set aside your feelings for Lord Gray if you spent less time talking about how you don't give a fig about him."

"Don't be rude, Jane," her older sister commented. Lady Charlotte smiled at Rowena. "Talking through a complication often does wonders for untangling it. And considering that you spent your previous eighteen years viewing Lord Gray in a particular way, I expect it will take some time to see him differently."

Rowena nodded, reaching across the

15

coach to squeeze the hand of Viscount Hest's older daughter. "Just so," she agreed, carefully burying her brogue beneath the cultured English tones she'd spent the past three months perfecting. "It's a new way of thinking about things, is all." Shifting, she looked south out the window to catch a glimpse of the long tail of coaches behind them. Civilization on the hoof, as it were.

The contents of those vehicles was the result of three months spent learning how to be a proper lady, of reminding herself that gentlemen looked only with amusement on ladies who conversed about shearing sheep and fishing and bathing in a loch like some sort of heathen. Well. She wasn't a heathen. And she had the friends and admirers and wardrobe and manners now to prove it.

"We all have to find a new way of thinking, don't we?" Jane commented, shifting to sit beside Rowena. "You and I are about to be sisters-in-law. And we're in Scotland, of all places! Do all Highlanders wear kilts? I never thought to ask."

As much as she could appreciate a finely shaped man in the black and red and white colors of clan MacLawry, Rowena continued to be surprised at most of her English friends' infatuation with the garb. "Today

16

everyone will be in kilts and clan colors. Ranulf will want his betrothed to see Glengask at its best."

Color touched Charlotte's cheeks, and that was rather heartening. Rowena didn't think Lord Hest's older daughter could be as calm as she'd been pretending over the past few days. Not when she was about to set her eyes on what would be her new home. Her new life.

She stifled an abrupt grimace. Charlotte was traveling north to a whole new life with a man who adored her. All *she* was doing, though, was returning to her old life after three glorious months in London. Nothing had changed for her, *except* for her, of course. How long would that last, though, back in the Highlands with her brothers? She didn't belong here any longer. She belonged in wonderful sophisticated London.

"However you feel about Lachlan Mac-Tier and however he feels about you, I would imagine he is going to be very surprised at seeing you again, Winnie." Charlotte grinned. "And what . . ." She trailed off as a musical, high-pitched wail drifted over them. "What is that?"

Finally Rowena chuckled. Whatever else might trouble her, the four MacLawry siblings were about to be reunited. Together, at Glengask, they were unstoppable. And Glengask, however much she wished it was several hundred miles to the south, was where she'd been born. "That is 'A Red, Red Rose,' " she said, "played on at least half a dozen bagpipes, from the sound of it. It's a love song, for you, I'd imagine. We're here."

Her own heart sped, so she could imagine Charlotte's must be pounding. She could say she felt eager to see Bear again after three months, and that she wanted to throw her arms around clever Arran and his new wife after they'd spent a fortnight on the run from Campbells and MacLawrys. She could tell herself that when Ranulf had left London a little over a week ago and ordered them all to follow, she hadn't been ready yet to leave. What she never wanted to admit was that part of her hesitation at returning to Scotland had been that niggling day-dream — the one where Lachlan MacTier swept her up in his arms and kissed her. It was annoying that she couldn't stop being such a fool, even over a man who clearly didn't deserve her. Infatuation was a stupid, embarrassing thing, and it should be done away with entirely.

The timbre of the wheels changed as the

coach left the rutted dirt road for the hard-packed gravel and crushed oyster shells of Glengask's shallow, curving front drive. Charlotte and Jane both pressed up against the windows and chatted excitedly, but Rowena wasn't ready to look. Not yet. However much she adored her brothers, southern England called to her. Or perhaps deeper down she dreaded her own reaction to seeing Lachlan again, and she was simply a coward.

"Oh, look, Charlotte! It's Lord Glengask!" Jane exclaimed, practically bouncing in her seat. "And there's Arran and Mary Campbell!"

"Lady Mary MacLawry, now," Charlotte corrected, sending another glance at Rowena.

Was she supposed to be ill at ease or jealous? Rowena wondered. Yes, she'd been the sole female at Glengask for the past eleven years, and yes, she wished she'd had an opportunity to make Mary Campbell's acquaintance before Arran fled London with her, but honestly the idea of having a sister — two of them, once Charlotte and Ranulf wed — filled her with glee. That house had been too full of hot-blooded Highlands men for far too long.

"That very large man with them — is that

Bear? Or is he the other one? My goodness, he's very . . . muscular."

"Stop pestering, Jane. We'll find out in a moment."

Immediately Jane left the window and seized Rowena's hand. "I'm so sorry, Winnie," she said. "I forgot you left here angry."

Rowena squeezed back. "You mean I slipped out the back door and ran away to London angry," she said with a brief smile. "I know they've forgiven me, and if they hadn't I would only point out that Ranulf wouldn't have met Charlotte, and Arran would never have met Mary, if they hadn't followed me. As for the rest, my eyes have been opened."

As she finished speaking, the coach rocked to a halt. The door swung open so hard it nearly came off its hinges, and before she could even squeak Bear leaned inside, grabbed her around the waist, and lifted her out onto the Glengask drive. Then she was engulfed in large, strong arms and surrounded by the familiar smell of leather and mint soap.

"Bear, I can't breathe!" she gasped, but hugged him back. If Munro MacLawry was happy to see her back home, then all was right with the world. Or nearly everything was, anyway.

Finally he released her and took half a step back. "By God," he drawled, the Highlands brogue thick in his voice, "I think ye're taller. And look at yer hair, Winnie — it's prettier than raven's wings. Do ye nae think so, Lach?"

She barely had time to mentally square her shoulders before Viscount Gray stepped into view. Like her brothers he'd donned his kilt of white and black and red, but that was where the similarities of appearance ended. Where her brothers were tall and broad-shouldered and all muscle, Lachlan was leaner and more narrowwaisted. His hair was a deep mahogany rather than the midnight black of the MacLawrys, even if he had adopted Bear's tendency to avoid a barber. His eyes had always reminded her of lush springtime — but that had been before. Now, they were simply green.

"Aye," he said, looking like he wasn't certain whether to offer her a handshake or a hug. "Very fashionable. Welcome home, Winnie."

She stuck out her hand to spare him the dilemma. It likely wasn't his fault he hadn't a romantic bone in his body, she decided. "You're no doubt surprised I don't have burrs in my hair," she said with a practiced smile in her practiced new accent.

His brows knitted. "What happened to yer voice?" he asked.

"Nothing happened to my voice," she returned, retrieving her fingers as swiftly as she could. He was her silly, youthful past. That was all. And she'd brought her future with her in those other coaches, so she needed nothing from him at all. "It's the proper way of speaking. Now if you'll excuse me, I would like to meet my new sister-in-law."

With that she turned her back on him and let out a long breath. What had she been so worried about? That she would abandon her common sense and try to kiss him? Ha. He was merely a man — albeit a very handsome man — and he was no longer the only potential suitor whose acquaintance she'd made. Nor was he even the only one present.

And because of that, she still needed to do a bit more maneuvering. Halfway to her new sister-in-law, she angled over to where her oldest brother stood with his betrothed. "Thank you for allowing me to invite some friends, Ranulf."

His expression unreadable, the marquis inclined his head. "I require a Sassenach witness or two at my wedding, so we'll say this is mutually beneficial. Though I think ye had yer own plans more in mind than mine when ye sent oot the invitations."

"Nonsense, Ranulf. I've brought along representatives of the finest English families." For the most part, anyway.

He glanced from Charlotte to her parents approaching from one of the following coaches. "I suppose we'll find oot," he returned, then took a half step closer to her and lowered his black-haired head. "Just ye keep in mind that this isnae London. I'll bury any lad who steps too far, Rowena."

"I don't think any of them would dare," she said truthfully, as the small horde of English began exiting coaches and traipsing noisily up the drive. "This is your kingdom."

"Aye, it is," he agreed, taking Charlotte's hand and gazing at his betrothed as though it had been far longer than a week since he'd last set eyes on her. "Welcome to Glengask, *leannan,*" he murmured, kissing her knuckles.

"It's beautiful," Charlotte returned with a warm, excited smile. "Just as you described it."

"It's more bonny with ye here." Ranulf tilted his head. "And did ye know we favor beheadings in the Highlands?" he asked, raising his voice.

"Since when?" Rowena put in, frowning.

He was going to frighten everyone away before a single piece of luggage could enter the mansion.

"I ken ye're all aware there're different rules in the Highlands than these soft English lads are accustomed to," he continued levelly. "Fer instance, here we dunnae bother turning our backs on someone if they do something improper."

"Nae," Bear took up, looking from his brother to the dozen coaches still spitting out ladies and gentlemen and servants. "Here we'll bloody yer nose and set ye on yer arse."

"And then we'll find ye a nice, deep bog to rest beneath," Arran said finally, clearly understanding the direction of the pronouncement.

Rowena's cheeks warmed. "That's quite enough," she hissed. "My friends are not accustomed to threats and violence. And if you want to be seen as gentlemen," she went on, stopping just short of jabbing a finger in Ranulf's direction, "you can't bellow at people who haven't done anything wrong."

Ranulf lifted an eyebrow. "I can be a gentleman," he rumbled in his deep Highlands brogue. "I have eyes, as well. Ye have a great number of Sassenach men with ye, *piuthar.* I dunnae think they're all here to witness my wedding. I'm nae acquainted with most of them, fer one thing."

"That isn't —"

"And they'd best keep in mind that ye're my only sister," he pressed, "and that I've nae spent this long looking after ye to see someaught . . . unacceptable happen now." Releasing Charlotte's hand, he took one long step forward. "Nor do I mean to let ye ferget yer heritage, however prettily ye choose to talk," he continued in a much lower voice. "Are we clear, Rowena Rose MacLawry?"

It took a great deal of will to look up into his stony blue eyes. "Aye. Yes. I understand."

"Good."

Ha. This from men who wagered over the quantity of whisky they could consume. Well, her brothers *and* Lachlan had best behave themselves, too. Because she had a good idea that her new friends were not going to be the problem. After all, they'd all had governesses and tutors and dance instructors. They all knew how to conduct themselves at balls and formal dinners and house parties. And whether Ranulf realized it or not, she was very close to preferring *that* life to the one with which she'd grown up. It wouldn't take much more to tip the balance. In fact, the right man could do it fairly easily. With a flounce of her skirts she continued on to where Arran and Mary stood a little apart from the crowd at the front doors.

Lachlan MacTier took a step backward to avoid having a trunk set on his toes. "Did ye know she was bringing half of London north with her?" he muttered at Bear beside him.

"Nae," Munro growled back. "Ran said his Charlotte's family and a few of Winnie's and the Hanovers' friends are to attend the wedding. Nae this horde." His brows lowered. "They're all so . . . pretty. And breakable."

"Aye." Lachlan gazed after a tall, spindly lad with high shirt points and blond hair that looked so smooth and shiny it could likely reflect the sunlight. "Breakable."

Whatever Bear said, this frilly lot didn't look like the sort of folk Lord Glengask would befriend, much less invite beneath his roof. And given that bit of speech a moment ago, this seemed to be the youngest MacLawry's idea. Lachlan shifted his gaze sideways. Black-haired Winnie MacLawry slid her hand around the arm of one of the taller fellows, smiling as she said something and gestured at the grand gray and white sprawl behind them.

She'd invited these people — or at least a good share of them. Did she truly feel connected enough to the Sassenach after only three months in England that she needed to bring London back with her to the Highlands? Or was the lass who had traipsed after him for nearly two decades in her pigtails and too-lacy skirts trying to make him jealous?

Perhaps he was rating her estimation of him too highly, but then perhaps he wasn't. Both Arran and Bear blamed him for her flight to London in the first place. If gifting a lass with a pair of fine riding boots on the occasion of her eighteenth birthday could cause her to leave her lifelong home and her family, then he supposed it *was* his fault, but it all seemed very silly and overly dramatic. She'd thrown a tantrum, and now she was home. Nothing else had changed, except for the way she talked, apparently.

"I hope we dunnae have to remember all their names," Bear muttered.

"They're nae all men, Bear," he pointed out, offering his friend a brief smile. "And here we are, two strapping bachelors standing aboot while we wait fer yer brother's wedding."

"Ye're nae a bachelor, Lach."

27

"I *am* a bachelor, and I'm fairly certain of that fact. I've nae wife, and nae a woman in mind fer one."

"Maybe so," the big man mused after a moment, then angled his chin at his sister. "But does she know that?"

"Fer Lucifer's sake, Munro. It takes two to make a marriage, and I've nae made anything of the kind with yer bairn of a sister. Leave off. It's bad enough with her writing me poetry all the time. Dunnae ye begin it again, too."

"Is she still writing ye poetry, then?" Arran asked as he joined them, his new bride, Mary, at his side.

"Nae. She was too busy with shopping in London, I wager. Ye know she stopped a few weeks ago." It had actually felt a little odd, at first, to not have a letter waiting for him each day, close-written lines telling him everything about her first days in London. He'd almost felt like he was there with her. He hadn't written back, of course, because her brothers watched like hawks, and he was not going to be trapped into something simply for being kind. And so he'd been relieved when she'd stopped. Just as he was relieved that she hadn't tried to throw herself into his arms when she left the carriage a few minutes ago.

28

"Then I suppose ye are a bachelor," Arran continued, clapping him on the shoulder. "Just keep in mind that Ranulf's marrying the first Sassenach lass he set eyes on in London. Ye dunnae want that happening to ye, I reckon."

"Hm," Mary put in, leaning into his shoulder. "If I recall, didn't you swoon after the first *Highlands* lass you met in London? And wasn't she a Campbell, of all things?"

The middle MacLawry brother grinned. "I didnae swoon, lass." He leaned down and kissed her cheek. "But ye do stop my heart."

She put her palm over the front of his left shoulder. "I saw you get shot, Arran," she whispered. "No jesting about your heart stopping."

"Aww, the two of ye are making me weep," Bear commented. "Come along, Lach. Let's be bachelors and introduce ourselves to the lovely, delicate lasses."

"Just dunnae roar and frighten them all away, Bear."

That sounded like something he would say, anyway. Truthfully, the last thing Lachlan wanted was to find himself tangled up with some foreign lass who'd likely blow over in a stiff breeze, and who might turn out to be related to the MacDonalds on her father's side or something. Sweet Saint

29

Andrew. That said, the younger sister of Glengask's betrothed was pretty enough, and obviously Ranulf had already approved her family bloodline. She might suit for a kiss and a giggle, as the Sassenach said, anyway.

"Dunnae say I didnae warn ye, lads," Arran called after them.

By the time everyone, guests and servants, had found bedchambers and been reunited with their luggage, Lachlan had managed a rough head count — though the servants dressed so finely he wasn't entirely certain he'd put everyone into the correct category. Seven gentlemen, five lasses, four Hanovers including Lord and Lady Hest and both their daughters, and seventeen servants including an English valet named Ginger who'd been acquired by the Marquis of Glengask. For the first time . . . ever, Sassenach outnumbered the Scots at the Mac-Lawry seat of power.

Lachlan wasn't surprised when Glengask hunted him down in the library, where he'd retreated with a glass of whisky. Bear might enjoy the turmoil, but Lachlan preferred conversations where he could actually make out what the other party might be saying. "Do ye hear that?" he asked, from the chair by the low fire. "The walls are humming with noise. More noise than usual, I mean."

"Aye." Ranulf poured himself a glass and took the opposite chair. "And half the Mac-Lawrys buried oot by the loch are spinning beneath the stones. All of Glengask could be swallowed up by a bog at any moment."

Chuckling, Lachlan glanced toward the closed door. "Was this invasion yer idea or Winnie's, if ye dunnae mind me asking?"

"The wedding in the Highlands was my idea," the marquis returned. "I left the guest list to Rowena, since I had to ride ahead." He didn't elaborate, but Lachlan knew that he'd galloped north with one groom and a wolfhound for company and protection, and that he'd reached Gretna Green just in time to save Arran and Mary and prevent an all-out war between the MacLawrys and the Campbells.

"They seem very . . . English," Lachlan offered.

"That, they are. And they expect us to be an English household. Which we arenae." Ranulf sat forward. "I mean to see to it that they have a taste of Highlands hospitality, but at the same time I dunnae want us to be embarrassed here. I need to borrow some of yer staff."

Lachlan wasn't surprised at the request,

but coming from the marquis directly, it did seem unusual. However things proceeded in the south, up north of Fort William, Glengask's word was law. His clan had the largest population — and the largest standing army — in the Highlands. Requesting servants seemed a bit trivial for him. "Whoever ye need," he returned.

"Thank ye. I'll be hiring some cooks from the village, and more lads fer the stable, but I dunnae want Robert the miller's lad dumping haggis on someone's lap."

"Winnie should've sent ye word that she had half of Mayfair riding north with her."

Deep blue eyes sent him a speculative look. "I dunnae ken this was meant to surprise *me.*"

Hm. "She stopped writing me letters weeks ago, Ran. And she barely shook my hand earlier, she was in such a hurry to greet Arran's lady and her new friends."

"Even so, I think it's time we had a chat, Lachlan."

That didn't sound promising. Evidently the trap that had been hanging over his head practically since Winnie's birth was about to be sprung. There was nothing as aggravating as a predestined life. And he didn't want one. "Ran, I had naught to do with her tagging after me," he protested. "I've nae given her cause to think anything. I mean, Bear and the rest of ye are closer to me than my own cousins, and I've nae brothers and sisters of my own. Nae but fer the lot of ye." Not even that seemed clear enough for comfort. "Ye are my brothers. And she's my sister."

"Very well, then." Ranulf took a slow swallow of whisky. "Ye're a good man, Lachlan, and I'd nae have an objection if ye'd decided to pursue Rowena. But I'm glad ye've made up yer mind aboot her, because I'll nae see her dragging aboot hoping fer someaught that'll never come to pass." He finished off his drink and stood. "I do want to hear ye say it — that ye've nae intention to offer fer my *piuthar*. Because I have plans to make if I dunnae want her to wed some Sassenach lord with property at the opposite end of the kingdom."

Lachlan stood, as well. "I've nae intention of offering fer Winnie," he said aloud, wondering now if escaping what had seemed inevitable had always been that simple. He didn't think so, but he wasn't about to let this one chance pass him by. "She's already my family."

"She may be yer sister in *yer* mind, but I can guarantee that she's nae thought of ye as a brother. Ever. But I'm nae one to meddle." With a heavy nod Glengask walked to the door. "I'll tell her. I dunnae want any misunderstandings."

"I'll tell her," Lachlan countered, though he wasn't entirely certain why he felt the need to speak up. Generally he avoided womanly hysteria and tears at all costs. "She'll believe me. I hope."

"See that she does. And tell her today, if ye will. I'd prefer to keep any foolishness to a minimum."

"Agreed." He hesitated, then set down the glass and craned his head to look over his shoulder at the marquis in the doorway. "I have told her before, ye know."

"Nae. Ye've talked around it. Say the words, and spare us all some mischief." Glengask's shoulders rose and fell. "And some grief."

Once Glengask returned to the chaos of the rest of the house, Lachlan finished his whisky. Over the years he thought he'd made it clear enough that he could never feel . . . romantic toward the bairn he'd had following him about like an eager puppy since she could toddle about on her own wee legs.

He thought he'd danced on the edge quite well, really, rebuffing her girlish advances and at the same time keeping from breaking

34

her heart. Apparently no one appreciated his subtlety — though in clan MacLawry subtlety had never been a prime weapon in the arsenal.

But now, and for the first time, he felt like his future was his own. It was a giddy feeling, almost. No one had any expectations of him. Well, almost no one. Ranulf did expect one thing of him. Blowing out his breath, he stood. Best get it over with, and hope she didn't begin weeping. The last thing he wanted was Bear breaking his nose because he'd made the granite mountain's little sister cry.

He found Winnie in one of the upstairs sitting rooms. She'd put on a pretty cream and blue gown, though he hadn't seen anything wrong with the one she'd been wearing when she'd arrived. She was pretending to be English, though, and everyone knew the Sassenach changed clothes more often than a deer flicked its ears.

She sat in the middle of her fluttery new friends, all of them laughing about something the tall fellow with the shiny hair had said. Lachlan couldn't recall his name, but doubted the scrawny fellow could so much as lift a caber — much less toss one.

"Might I have a word with ye, Winnie?" he asked, wondering why he abruptly felt . . . uncomfortable. He'd spent nearly as much time in this house as he had in his own, but with these people, the sounds and scents they brought with them, he couldn't help the sensation that he didn't quite belong.

"Certainly, Lord Gray," Winnie said cheerfully, rising. "Jane, don't let Lord Samston begin another of his stories until I return." She flashed a grin at the yellow-haired man by the window.

"I wouldn't dream of it, Lady Rowena," he drawled, sketching a bow that likely would have looked fancy even in a royal court.

Lachlan followed Winnie into the sunroom at the end of the hallway. A handful of wooden benches and chairs lay scattered amid potted roses and lilies — plants too delicate for the changeable Highlands weather. "That lot's like the monkeys in a menagerie," he commented with a loose smile. "All chattering at once and being cozy with the top brute in the herd."

"And who is the top brute, do you think?" Winnie strolled over to one of the large, south-facing windows.

"That Lord Samston. Nobody talks when he does."

"Very observant of you," she returned,

leaning her spine against the window and folding her arms over her chest. "But considering that he was introduced to you as the Earl of Samston, you already knew that."

"Nae," Lachlan returned, though he knew he should likely be getting to the point of this conversation and not provoking Winnie. He'd teased with her for her entire life, though, and unlike those prissy lads down the hall, he had no fear of her temper. "It's nae aboot rank. Nae completely. Samston's the fellow to watch."

"I'll keep that in mind." She lifted a graceful eyebrow. "Thankfully he's very easy on the eyes."

"Him? He's too shiny."

Winnie tilted her head. "I'm a bit confused, Lachlan. Which word did you want with me? To tell me that Lord Samston is powerful, or that he's shiny?"

"Neither. And I still dunnae why ye feel the need to talk like a Sassenach," he said, frowning. "Ye can fool whoever ye like in London, but ye're home now."

She turned her back on him, ostensibly to gaze out at the sharp-peaked mountains around them. "Is that what this is about, then? You don't like the way I talk? Because that's really none of your business."

"I dunnae suppose it is. And nae, that's

nae the word I wanted, either."

"Then tell me what you want, Lord Gray, so I can return to my duties as hostess."

Lachlan frowned at the back of her head and her gracefully coiled black hair. A few months ago Winnie MacLawry would have gone to great efforts to prevent him from leaving a conversation. Once she'd even pretended to sprain her ankle so he would carry her from Loch Shinaig back to the house. He'd told Donald the stableboy to do it, and she'd abruptly recovered.

But that was neither here nor there. And the sooner he could make his intentions — or lack thereof — clear, the sooner he could stop worrying that he would be trapped into something simply because Ranulf couldn't refuse his sister anything she truly wanted.

He took a breath. "Face me, will ye?"

Her shoulders rose and fell, and she turned around again. "This sounds serious," she mused, her expression still a bit annoyed. With him — which was unusual in itself.

"I ken that fer a long time ye've had yer heart set on . . . on things being a particular way, lass, and I ken that I was one of the reasons ye scampered doon to London — so I'd see ye as a lady rather than a wee girl."

"You n—"

"But what ye do doesnae matter, Winnie," he continued over her interruption. "I'll always see ye as ye are, and that's the bairn with the scraped knees I taught to fish. What I mean to say is, I'll nae — never — marry ye, Winnie, so whatever ye have planned in that head of yers, dunnae trouble yerself. Have yer fun with yer friends, help Lady Charlotte with her Highlands wedding, but dunnae expect anything to come of us. Do ye understand?"

For a long moment she gazed at him while he waited for her pretty blue eyes to overflow with tears. Bear would likely attempt to bloody him, but Ranulf had practically ordered him to do this. It wasn't as if he *wanted* to see her cry.

Winnie smiled. Then a chuckle burst from her chest. "Oh, dear," she managed.

That did not sound like heartbreak. Lachlan frowned before he could remember that that was a good thing. "What's so damned amusing?"

"You looked so serious. I'm so sorry," she returned. "Poor Lachlan. You must've been terrified every time you saw me appear."

"Nae. I wasnae terrified. And I'm nae afraid of ye now. I just want ye to ken that there'll be no marriage between us."

"Of course I understand that. You were a childhood infatuation. I'm certainly not a child any longer."

This was not what he'd expected. "It's been three months. Ye've changed yer accent right enough, but yer heart? That's nae so simple, I think."

"Now you're confusing me. Are you jealous that I've realized what I want, and that it isn't you?"

"I'm just doubting the truth of yer words, lass."

"Oh, pish. Until three months ago, I'd barely spoken with a man who wasn't my brother. I'd never waltzed with anyone but the four of you, and no one had ever complimented me without me first having to ask them to. And so I'm sorry I was so relentless in my pursuit, but you can hardly blame me for it."

"I dunnae blame ye fer anything. I just want to have an understanding between us."

"There is one. But this conversation is unnecessary. My time in London allowed me to open my eyes," she returned, still cool and composed. "I wrote you letters and you never responded. Since my first memory I've been asking you for flowers and dances and poetry, and you couldn't be bothered. Not once." Stepping forward, she put a hand on his arm. "I don't want you any longer. You're not worth my time."

Then she leaned up and kissed him, sisterlike, on the cheek. "But I do thank you, for showing me precisely the sort of man I do *not* want in my arms. It's a lesson I've learned quite well." With that, her fingers walking up his shoulder, she strolled past him, humming, out the door again.

Lachlan stood where he was for a long moment as he tried to keep his head from spinning. *What the devil?* Nearly eighteen years of her pursuing him, and suddenly he wasn't worth her time? Ha. The day he couldn't please a woman — any woman he chose — was the day he would strap stones to his waist and jump into Loch Shinaig.

Of course he hadn't *been* pursuing Winnie MacLawry, so what did she expect? It was ridiculous. She'd been after him, changed her mind, and then decided she could insult him because of it? He'd done nothing wrong. Hell, he'd done nothing at all. On purpose. If he *had* wanted her, he would have had her, and that was that.

But to say he wasn't the sort of man she wanted — that was insulting. He was as fine and charming as any of those scalawags in the other room drinking tea with their pinkies stuck in the air. He might not be an earl, but he was a damned viscount. And he'd wager any number of her pretty, delicate Sassenach lasses would be pleased to receive his attentions. That would show her.

All this from a child with burrs in her hair. She could play the adult if she chose, but he might just decide to show her that this was not a game for children. "Ye've done it now, lass," he muttered. "Dunnae throw down yer wee glove unless ye're ready fer someone to take up the challenge. We'll see who's worth wanting. And having." It wouldn't be her, but she could damned well watch.

CHAPTER TWO

"Ye truly should be wearing a bonnet or one of yer brothers' warm hats today, m'lady," Mitchell said, as the maid tucked a hairbrush and extra hairpins into a drawer of the dressing table. "This isnae London. A brisk wind could freeze yer ears off."

"I grew up here, Mitchell," Rowena returned, taking a last turn in front of the full-length dressing mirror to admire her red and black riding habit and the rakish red beaver hat perched atop her black coils of hair. "I haven't forgotten the weather, for goodness' sake." She picked up her riding gloves and headed for the door. "But I cannot wear a bonnet with this outfit, or all the English will laugh at me. If I wore one of Bear's floppy hats . . ." She gave an exaggerated shudder. "If I did that, I might as well save everyone some trouble and join a nunnery."

"No one's marriage prospects have ever

been ruined by a hat," the lady's maid insisted stoutly.

"Not yet, perhaps. But I will not be the first."

"Saint Bridget protect us all, then."

Rowena left her bedchamber and descended to the first floor. Around her the house was already well awake, and she smiled at the sound of one of the upstairs maids humming as she opened curtains and cleaned out rooms abandoned for the morning. Glengask had always been a loud, lively place, filled with visiting chieftains and allies and cotters and pipers and multiple men she'd thought were footmen until she'd eventually realized they were Highlands warriors, members of clan MacLawry brought in by Ranulf to help watch over the family. To protect them.

Today the old, fortified sprawl boomed and shook with the noise of an additional two dozen Englishmen and women and servants — Sassenachs, all of them. She'd arranged that, and however put out her brothers might feel, making English friends could only benefit them. Even better, they might decide they approved of whichever man she decided to marry. At the least her brothers couldn't be supporting Lachlan any longer — and if they were, she needed to set them straight. Why he'd felt the need to inform her they wouldn't suit she had no idea, since she'd realized it months ago. And he'd clearly never thought of her romantically at all.

She'd made it halfway through the long portrait-lined gallery upstairs when a strong hand grabbed her shoulder and yanked her sideways into the armory. "What the —"

"Ye've ambushed us, ye know," Bear rumbled, releasing her. In his left hand a claymore swung loosely, and from the look of the tree stump they'd somehow dragged into the room while she'd been away, he was annoyed at something. Her, apparently.

"Ranulf got here three days before we did," she returned, smoothing the sleeve of her new riding habit. "And since he ordered us to pack up and follow him north, you can blame him." She narrowed one eye. "Or blame Arran, since he's the one who headed north when we still had three weeks before the end of the Season."

"Dunnae ye try to fancy up the tale, *piuthar*. Ran didnae invite half the Mayfair fancies to join him at Glengask. That was *yer* doing."

"Yes, it was."

"Ha! Ye admit to it."

She put her hands on her hips. "Do you

know what they call women your age who haven't married?"

He cocked his head at her, a lock of his too long black hair falling across one gray-green eye. "Desperate?" he suggested.

"That, too. They call them 'spinsters,' and say they're 'on the shelf.' You're only six years older than I am, Munro."

"Dunnae ye worry, Winnie. Lachlan'll get through his h—"

"Lachlan MacTier is not going to marry me," she cut in, ignoring his frown. "Yes, I know we all assumed it would happen, but Lachlan didn't. And I was stupid to think my wishing for it would make it so."

"I'll talk to him, then."

That would be a disaster. "I already did. Or he came and found me, rather, to tell me I've been wasting my time and that we would never be a match." She shrugged, a part of her still surprised that it had hurt as little as it had. Evidently a lifelong dream *could* be set aside as if it were nothing. Because it had been. She'd done it. "And don't go punching him for being honest."

"Ye seem to be taking this bit of news fairly well," the brother closest to her in age mused, studying her face.

"I gave him up a week after I left here," she returned. "I'm a fine lass, Bear, and I have better things to do than pine after a man too . . . thick to appreciate me." She gave a twirl in her fashionable habit. "He had his chance, and given his complete lack of passion and romance, I'm glad nobody means to hold me to something I thought made sense when I still believed in unicorns."

She'd told just that to herself multiple times, and the more she repeated it, the more she remembered just how little regard Lachlan had ever had for her, the more sense it made. And saying it aloud now only served to put an official end to the story of Lachlan and Rowena, the fairy tale of a naïve young girl who'd finally grown up to see that her prince was a stupid block of wood.

Bear regarded her for a long moment. "So these fancy lads are here fer ye to assess?" he finally asked. "Ye'd marry a Sassenach who'd take ye away from the Highlands?"

That was the one thing that troubled her. As much as she'd wanted to escape Glengask three months ago, as tired as she was of how set in their ways everyone was, how sophisticated she felt with her careful accent and clothes from Paris, she would miss her brothers. "I don't know," she answered truthfully. "For love, I think I would."

He cursed in Gaelic. "I dunnae like that," he said unnecessarily. "Are ye certain ye didnae invite those pretty lads here just to make Lachlan notice ye?"

"Oh, for Saint Bridget's sake. Don't be absurd, Bear." Perhaps she wasn't above demonstrating to Lord Gray that other men found her intriguing, but that was just pride. "These people are all potential allies for Ranulf. You don't drag an aristocrat a thousand miles to make someone jealous; there would be repercussions. And why would I invite female friends if I were looking to make a man notice me?"

"I suppose we'll see aboot that." He glanced past her shoulder, toward the depths of the house. "So that means the lasses are fair game, nae?"

That made her frown. "They're my friends. I tried to match Jane Hanover with Arran, and that didn't turn out well. And don't you go breaking her heart, too." She eyed him, suspicion tightening her shoulders. "I thought you were wooing Bethia Peterkin."

He shrugged, a grin touching his mouth. "Wooed and won, Winnie. A man needs new lands to conquer."

"Conquer away, then. Try not to begin any new wars, though; Ranulf just ended the last one."

"Aye, and left us with Arran wed to a Campbell." He shook his shaggy head. "A Campbell, living at Glengask. And she's a fine lass. Odd times we're in, and that's fer damned certain."

She definitely agreed with that. "If you're finished with chewing on my ear, then, I'm going riding with my friends."

Bear snorted. "Those English ponies they brought up will be dead by the end of the day if ye dunnae keep to a walk. At least we'll have fresh meat for dinner."

Rowena laughed before she could stop herself. "That's enough, Bear. Most Sassenach already think we're devils and barbarians. If they hear you talking about eating their mounts, they'll flee into the wilds."

As she turned around, he caught her hand, turning her to face him again. "Ye're still a Highlands lass, then. I'm glad to know it."

Before that could begin a whole other conversation and argument, she left the armory and its rather impressive array of weapons behind. She had been born a Highlands lass, but she'd learned better. She didn't have to be crass or naïve or go about with burrs in her hair. Rowena scowled. She really needed to stop conjuring that conversation. It had been three months ago for one thing, and for another it only reminded her of how foolish she'd been until such a short time ago.

She couldn't be surprised that Bear — and likely Ranulf and Arran, as well — thought she'd invited handsome young men to Glengask in order to antagonize or lure Lachlan. A few months ago she might have done such a thing. The idea of him being jealous had so often entered her daydreams that there were moments she'd almost thought it real.

But it wasn't real. Nothing she'd imagined between them was real. These men here were real, and they said flattering things to her and complimented her eyes and her wit and her dress and certainly didn't see her as a nuisance. They made her heart beat faster. In fact, all she could do at this point was be thankful she'd realized how very uninterested Lachlan was in her before she'd somehow forced herself into a match with him. She would have spent the rest of her life in misery.

"You, Lady Rowena," a low, cultured voice drawled as she entered the foyer, "are a vision. Diana the huntress brought to life."

No, her only regret where Lachlan was concerned was that she hadn't realized earlier how hopeless her pursuit had been. She smiled as Adam James, Lord Samston, doffed his hat and then offered his arm. "If you begin the day with such flattery," she returned in her practiced tones, "by afternoon you'll have nothing kind left to say."

The earl chuckled. "Nonsense. I have two directions in which I may proceed. Loftier, or . . . more intimate."

Cooper the butler pulled open the front door, somehow nearly cracking Lord Samston's head against the solid oak as he did so. "I beg yer pardon, m'laird," the old Scotsman intoned. "I didnae realize yer melon was so grand."

Adam frowned. "I do hope they don't allow you about sharp objects," he said crisply, gesturing for Rowena to precede him out the door.

"Nae, m'laird. I favor the musket, or a good, solid club."

"Don't mind Cooper, Lord Samston," Rowena broke in, half pulling the earl over the threshold and out to the drive where a dozen horses waited, their breath fogging in the crisp morning air. "He's overly dramatic."

"My brother-in-law has an estate just outside Edinburgh, you know," he commented as he put his hands around her waist, smiled down at her, and lifted her into the sidesaddle of her white mare, Black Agnes. "He brought in servants from London just so he could understand what they were saying."

"Cooper's been with the family for ages," she returned, noting that Jane was already outside, along with Lady Edith Simms and her brother Lord Victor. "Ranulf would never replace him — or any of them — if that's what you're implying."

"Well, I'm not going to admit to any such thing now, am I?" The smile still on his face, he swung up onto his chestnut gelding, King.

The Edinburgh connection was one of the things she favored about Adam James, actually. Even if it was only through marriage, the earl had Highlands acquaintances. Highlands geographically, anyway; from what she'd been able to discover, his brother-in-law Lord Lewis had barely an ounce of Scottish blood — but he *had* had the good fortune to be the sole surviving heir of the old Lord Lewis.

"Ah, more rivals," Adam mused, and she looked up as Arnold and William Peabody left the house, followed by John, Lord Bask, and his cousins Sarah and Susan Parker.

"We're all friends here," she commented,

though if Lord Samston saw her as a desirable prize she certainly had no objection.

"Are we?"

When Rowena glanced over at him, seated comfortably on King, his gaze was directed at the low hill beyond the drive. A big bay stallion came into view, the man riding him hatless and bent low over the beast's neck as it galloped toward them. Even with the sun behind him painting him into silhouette, she recognized Lachlan MacTier, his longish brown hair flying about his lean face and Beowulf blowing beneath him. However finished she was with him, she did enjoy watching him ride. Anyone would admire a skilled horseman, she supposed.

He galloped up the drive and stopped neatly beside her. "Is there trouble?" she asked, drawing Black Agnes in when the mare began to fidget.

"Nae," Lachlan returned, sending Beowulf in a tight circle around her. "Heard ye were going fer a ride this fine morning. Thought I'd join ye."

She eyed him. He seemed very chipper for a fellow who'd thought he'd broken her heart. "Why?"

He grinned. "Because ye've some lovely lasses with ye, and it wouldnae be a true holiday in the Highlands if they didnae meet

53

a Highlander."

If she'd needed any further proof that this man did not carry some hidden infatuation with her, that provided it. But she had known him for eighteen years, and he could be charming when he wanted to. So, rather than point out that with three MacLawry males in the house and a bevy of Glengask and Gray servants about, her friends were literally surrounded by Highlanders, she nodded. "Do as you will."

"I'm glad we can still be friends, Winnie, even after your — the — misunderstanding."

She beckoned him closer, and he obliged, sidling up so they were only a foot apart. "We all make mistakes," she muttered. "All I ask is that you not begin something with Jane Hanover if you're only playing. She's very romantic. And very . . . young."

Lachlan lifted an eyebrow. "Are ye nae the same age?"

Back when she'd arrived in London she would have said yes. But she'd seen their London house set on fire, seen Ranulf and Arran antagonized and challenged simply for being Highlanders. She'd been shielded by Arran when George Gerdens-Daily drew a pistol on them. "Not any longer," she said with a short smile, then turned Black Agnes to greet the latest arrivals.

The shiny fellow, Lord Samston, trotted beside Winnie as the group set off toward the gorge that carried the runoff from Loch Shinaig. Lachlan watched them from his place toward the back; it would never do if one of the Sassenach got lost among the cairns, never to be seen again.

"So you're Lord Gray," a sweet voice commented from his right, and he turned his head. A pretty lass with honey-colored hair rode beside him on one of Glengask's spare mounts.

"I am," he returned. "And ye would be Lady Jane Hanover, aye?" he said, deciding Winnie's rules didn't apply to him.

"Aye," she answered, and giggled. "Is it true you're . . . unattached, then?"

So Winnie had been talking, then. This could be tiresome. "Aye. I'm free as a bird, lass. Always have been."

Oh. I thought . . . Well. Never mind. "I certainly don't wish to intrude on your privacy."

She was polite, but clearly his so-called connection to Winnie had been discussed, and he seemed to be the injured party. Blast it all. But then again, he supposed the misconception could work in his favor, if all the lasses wanted to offer him comfort. But not if they thought him some wilted, dour flower. "There was nae an understanding between Winnie and me," he retorted. "I'm eight years older than she is, fer Saint Bridget's sake."

"Oh. Of course."

When she blinked at him, Lachlan blew out his breath. Being linked with Winnie MacLawry was certainly nothing new. It wasn't Jane Hanover's fault. And at least he and Winnie had straightened it out between them. The news would reach the house-guests and the rest of the clan before long — hopefully. "As a matter of fact," he went on, putting on a smile, "I may well be long-ing to meet a likely lass."

Her nose crinkled as she smiled back at him. "I think you may be a bit of a rogue, sir."

"Aye. All Highlanders are rogues. Have ye nae learned that?"

"I'd been wondering if the MacLawrys were the rule or its exception."

Lachlan laughed. "Both, I ken."

A higher-pitched, sweeter echo of his own laugh drifted back to him along the trail. At the front of their herd shiny Samston pointed at a pair of foxes scampering through a patch of heather, his commentary evidently clever enough to amuse Winnie.

The fellow then reached out to catch Black Agnes's bridle and guide the mare around a fallen tree limb.

Well, that was ridiculous. Winnie had walked and run and ridden this path for eighteen years. She could certainly navigate a downed branch. Aside from that, Black Agnes had a temper, and the fool might well find himself without a pinkie to lift in the air when he drank his tea.

"Who is this Samston?" he asked, frowning as Winnie thanked the fellow for his unneeded assistance, actually using the word "chivalrous."

"The earl?" Jane returned, following his gaze. "His name is Adam James. He has four properties in Somerset and Derbyshire, and they say his income is somewhere in the vicinity of eight thousand a year."

That told him almost nothing, but that was how the Sassenach measured a man — by his property and his money. "But what sort of man is he?" Lachlan tried again. "What do his friends think of him? Does he have friends?"

"I . . . Yes. He's considered to be quite the catch. For the past few weeks he's been paying particular attention to Winnie. I think she likes him, but she said he keeps asking about her dowry. That's made her quite cautious, I think." She drew in a breath beside him. "If I may ask, why do you care? I mean, if you —"

"Her brothers are nae too keen on having Winnie wed to a Sass . . . an Englishman who'll take her away from the Highlands," he broke in, before she could jump to the conclusion that he was jealous or something. "I'm curious over whether Samston'll pass muster."

"Oh. That makes sense, I suppose."

"Aye." Of course it did. He would have to tell Bear about the dowry nonsense. Winnie could certainly do better than a fortune hunter. Lachlan cleared his throat. He was here to prove something to Winnie, not to talk about her. "So, Lady Jane Hanover, what do ye think of the Highlands so far?"

Her smile reappeared. "It's breathtaking. Winnie says the weather can turn ferocious in a heartbeat, but at this moment it's lovely."

"It's never the same twice," he responded, nodding to himself. It was the sort of place that dug itself into the bones and sinew of its people. He, for one, found it vital to be here.

"Jane, you mustn't keep Lord Gray all to yourself," another female chirped.

Now this was more like it. A lad could

enjoy having several pretty lasses brawling over him, even if they were delicate and English. Winnie could say that she found him disappointing, but in his experience she was the only one to do so.

"We're having a conversation, Edith," Lady Jane returned, her expression more amused than annoyed. "You're welcome to join in."

Edith slowed the dainty black mare she'd brought north with her. She'd be lucky if the beastie didn't break a leg just descending to the bottom of the gorge. "Whatever are you conversing about, then?" she asked, with a too bright smile.

"Aboot the lovely day with which we've been favored," Lachlan drawled. She wouldn't do for a tumble; Edith seemed entirely too desperate for a man, and he'd likely never escape if she got her hands on him. "A fortnight ago we had snow flurries."

Edith nodded, as attentive as if he'd been telling the location of hidden gold. "Are you a clan chief? Like Lord Glengask?"

"Nae. I'm a chieftain."

Her smile remained fixed in place. "What's the difference?"

"I have say over the MacTier sept — branch — of clan MacLawry. I have relations and cotters who answer to me, and I answer to Glengask." And he could argue with Glengask over some disagreement, though that happened only rarely. Ranulf had a vision for his clan, and Lachlan highly approved of it.

"Oh, so you're his lieutenant."

It was far more complicated than that, but clearly the Edith female with her tightly pinned brunette hair only wanted to know how much power and influence he held. Which was a great deal, but not in as obvious a fashion as the Marquis of Glengask. "Aye," he said aloud. "Someaught like that."

"And Glengask's brothers are chieftains?"

"Nae. They enforce Glengask's law."

"Law? Goodness, that sounds very fierce."

He glanced forward again. Now that they'd entered the gorge they found themselves among trees and a splendid set of rocky falls running down the center. The trail curved around boulders and glades, and at the front of the group Winnie and the yellow-haired lord slipped from his sight.

That wouldn't do. However he felt about her romantically, the one thing her brothers and he knew above all else was that Rowena was to be protected. And that meant both her physical safety and her reputation. "Excuse me," he said, and nudged Beowulf in the ribs.

The big bay picked up his pace, and in a moment he was directly behind the two lead riders. The other men present kept themselves occupied with the other lasses; evidently they meant to let the earl have a go at Winnie first, before the next fellow moved in. Very civilized, it was.

The pair in front of him slowed, and he drew Beowulf in to match their pace. He could only make out one in three or four words Winnie spoke, but that was enough for him to decipher that she was telling Samston about the local myth surrounding the gorge, how the wives of Highlands warriors killed in battle could be heard at night wailing, how their tears had formed the steep-sided valley.

Lachlan moved in a bit closer. He'd heard the story countless times, but Winnie had a way of telling it that could make him wonder whether the distant wailing sounds he heard some nights were bagpipes or long-dead, mourning Highlands lasses.

"You are quite romantic, aren't you?" Samston commented. "And you pretend to be so practical."

"I'm both, I think. At least, I don't think that being one precludes the other."

"Precludes," was it? Since when had she begun using such fancy words? Clearly it

was something she'd learned in London, along with her new accent. For a lass who'd thought romance meant throwing flowers at the back of his head, that was quite a statement.

It was odd, though, seeing her lowering her eyelashes at the earl, turning her head just so in order to best show off her lovely neck. This was a play that he'd become accustomed to acting in himself. But not once as they rode deeper into the gorge did she even send a glance in his direction. She'd said that she was finished with chasing him about. Now, abruptly, he believed her.

He should have felt relieved, he supposed, that he no longer had to tiptoe so carefully among the MacLawry males, that he didn't have to watch what he said, be careful not to compliment her, in order to avoid waking up married. If she hadn't said that she found him disappointing, he likely *would* be feeling relieved now. But she'd insulted him and his manliness, and he didn't much like that. If he'd ever so much as tried to be charming to her, she'd be singing a different tune right now.

The Earl of Samston didn't seem to find the notion of Winnie being romantic as threatening as Lachlan did, because the shiny fellow only inclined his head and edged his grand English horse closer to Black Agnes. For a moment Lachlan hoped the feisty mare would take the chestnut's right ear off, but she only snorted and tossed her head. Even the lass's horse was turning Sassenach.

"How far from here is your estate?" one of the Parker sisters, Susan, he thought, asked him brightly, drawing even with him.

So much for the proper English rule of not speaking to a man unless a lady had been formally introduced. He had met most of them in passing over dinner, though, so perhaps that counted. Or perhaps the rules had changed in the nine years since he'd visited London.

"Gray House is two miles south and west of the main house at Glengask," he answered.

"But I thought Lord Glengask owned all this land."

More talk about the English obsessions with power, property, and wealth. "He does. His property curves about mine and goes on north and east. My property is more westerly."

"Oh. It's fortunate that you're all allies then, isn't it?"

Allies and fourth cousins. "Aye," he answered non-committally.

"Are you a clan chief, like Lord Glengask?"

He narrowed one eye as the beginnings of a headache began pushing at his skull. "Nae."

"Oh. What about Lord Munro? Bear, I think you call him? Is he a chief?"

For all that the Sassenach viewed Highlanders as devils and barbarians, the lasses seemed eager enough to know which of them was more marriageable. "Some-aught like that," he said. Bear might have come along this morning, after all. The fact that he hadn't — well, every man for himself.

Finally they all reached the lower end of the gorge, just above where the stream danced over a series of weather-flattened boulders and plunged down to the lower slopes past the village of Mahldoen, the more southerly of the two main Glengask villages. It was a picturesque place, and he wasn't surprised that Winnie had chosen to show it off to her new friends.

He swung down from Beowulf, but before he could reach Winnie to help her down, Samston slid his arms around her waist and lifted her out of the sidesaddle. The earl set her down, but didn't release his grip. Instead the two of them stood looking at each other as if the rest of the landscape had ceased to exist.

Whatever the devil Samston was about, Lachlan didn't like it. Her brothers wouldn't, either. Men didn't paw at their wee sister, especially Sassenach men who asked about her dowry. If she wasn't still trying to make him jealous — and it certainly didn't seem that way — then she was in well over her head. She knew how to play at wooing, how to pretend to faint at a lad's feet or to trip and fall into his arms, but those were only girlish tricks for attracting attention. Once she had that attention, she would have no idea what to do next.

Samston would know, though, and that was the problem. "We should've brought fishing poles," Lachlan said loudly, and stepped forward to push between the two of them. He could pretend to be thickheaded and oblivious if it served him to do so. "We might've caught dinner fer the house."

"We'll be here for several weeks," the earl commented from behind him. "Perhaps the gentlemen might go fishing another time. As for today, I much prefer spending it in fairer and gentler company."

"Very prettily said, Adam," Winnie put in, a smile in her voice.

Lachlan snorted, this time not covering

65

his annoyance at the smooth-talking Samston. "Aye. Declaring a lass to be more bonny than fish is gallant, indeed."

When he turned around, though, the look Winnie sent him wasn't the amused, exasperated one with which he was familiar. Rather, she looked genuinely and deeply annoyed. He half expected her to slap his face and order him to leave.

Instead she faced her new friends and spread her arms. "This is one of my favorite places," she said, "and I'm so pleased to be able to share it with all of you. Please don't mind Lord Gray; he still thinks gas lighting is magic."

Everyone laughed. In fact, they seemed to find it all a bit more amusing than the comment warranted. He'd been teased before, and he was generally good-humored about it. After all, he gave as good as he got. But this didn't feel like teasing. It felt like an insult, and she'd never done that to him before.

He stood back as the Sassenach made their way to the edge of the fast-moving stream. When they were all occupied with the view, he edged up behind Winnie. "So we're nae to be friends either, are we?" he murmured.

Her shoulders stiffened, but she didn't

turn around. "Stop insulting my friends," she whispered back. "You're not as charming as you seem to think you are, Lachlan. I apologize if I damaged your pride by not being in love with you, but that's your own fault."

"Ye didnae damage my anything," he retorted, just remembering to keep his voice down. "Ye're behaving like a simpering sheep. Did ye lose yer wits along with yer Gaelic?"

"I'm trying to present the fair side of the Highlands to influential peers. And you're being a big, brawly . . . you." She shifted, then stepped backward to stomp on the toe of his boot. Hard. "Go away."

"I'm guarding ye."

"My brothers didn't find it necessary to trail after me today, so there's no reason for you to be here, either."

"Those four lovely lasses with ye give me a pound of reasons, lass."

Finally she faced him, her chin lifted and her arms folded over her chest. "Then why are you standing here refusing to stop talking to *me*?" she enunciated.

He glared back at her, his gaze lowering to her soft-looking lips as they flattened in obvious annoyance. Or was it some kind of cynical amusement, because she thought

67

she'd bested him? He'd always been able to decipher her moods without any trouble at all. Why couldn't he do so now? And why *was* he arguing with her when a handful of lasses stood just a few feet away waiting to be charmed?

It was the first time she'd ever stumped him, the first time she'd ever stood toe-to-toe with him as if the consequences didn't matter to her — because they didn't. Her stormy gray eyes practically crackled with . . . something. Something fiery and not at all simpering or fainthearted. Or English.

Lachlan took a step closer to her before he'd even realized it. Then a hand touched Winnie's shoulder from behind, sweeping down her arm to catch her hand. "Come, Rowena," Lord Samston drawled, turning her back toward the water. "Tell me what these flowers are called."

Blinking, Lachlan caught himself up again. The earl didn't treat Winnie — Rowena — like a child. No doubt she found that flattering, but it was fairly obvious that Samston sincerely didn't view her as a bairn. None of the Sassenach gentlemen did. To them she was a lovely young woman of title and privilege and wealth, the only

sister of the most powerful man in the Highlands.

Were they seeing her inaccurately, or was
it him? Given the way his gut had reacted
to her just then, he had a good idea that it
was him. That perhaps — just perhaps —
he'd made a mistake in turning her away
before he could become acquainted with
the lady she'd claimed to be.

He could tell himself that it was for the
best, that going after her and then deciding
they weren't compatible would cause an ir-
reparable rift between him and the Mac-
Lawrys. At this moment, though, the fore-
most thought in his brain was that he didn't
like seeing another man touching her. Not
at all.

CHAPTER THREE

Ranulf paced.

Rowena stopped in the doorway of her brother's office to watch him for a moment, walking in measured steps from the bookcase to the window and back again. With him thirteen years her elder and their father dying when she was too young to remember anything but a thick black beard tickling her cheeks, her brother had been more of a parent than a sibling to her. And seeing him any less than completely composed was both rare and disconcerting.

"You wanted to see me?" she asked.

Turning in mid-step, he nodded. "Aye. Have a seat, will ye?" he said, continuing past her and shutting the door, closing them in.

Her uneasiness rose another notch. "Everyone's been behaving themselves, I hope. I chose very carefully which friends to bring north with me."

"I know ye did; Charlotte and Lord Hest hadnae an ill word to say aboot any of the Sassenach. Thank ye fer that, *piuthar.*"

She sat in one of the two chairs facing his sturdy desk. "You're welcome. Bear hasn't killed any of them then, has he?" Or perhaps she should be asking about Lachlan's behavior. He'd certainly been rude and unfriendly yesterday. It was very unlike the image of him she'd carried about for most of her life.

A brief smile touched Ranulf's face as he moved to the window. "Nae. Everyone's still alive. I ordered Munro to behave himself, though I am somewhat inclined to send him away to Edinburgh, just to be certain."

"You can't force him to miss your wedding," she protested. "I only invited the ladies to make a balanced party, so it wouldn't look like . . ." She trailed off, blushing.

"So it wouldnae look like ye were bringing suitors to Glengask to see who best fit the family?" he finished, lifting an eyebrow. "Ye think I didnae see that the second ye arrived?"

"I —"

"Ye spoke with Lachlan, aye?" he interrupted, before she could conjure an alternate story. "He told ye that — well — he —"

"Lachlan told me that he would never offer for me," she finished, touched by his obvious reluctance to cause her pain. "You needn't worry about sparing my feelings, Ran. I truly have none to injure where Lachlan is concerned. I was young and silly, and he was . . . present, I suppose." And handsome and tall and lean, of course, but he was far from the only man who could fit that description. She knew that now.

Ranulf blew out his breath and finally took the chair on the far side of the desk. "I'm relieved to hear it. I would have welcomed a match between ye, but only if ye both wanted it."

"He isn't worth the tears I wept over him, my *bràthair.*"

"If he couldnae see ye fer who ye are, then he didnae deserve ye." He sat forward, dark blue eyes assessing her. "I've someaught to tell ye, and I dunnae want ye to hammer at me until ye've listened to it all."

Oh, dear. "I agree," she said slowly. If he was going to tell her that none of the English lords were acceptable before he'd bothered to become acquainted with any of them, they were definitely in for an argument.

"A few weeks ago I meant to have Arran marry Deirdre Stewart, to give us an alliance with clan Stewart. Then our brother went and lost his head over Mary Campbell, and I thought we were aboot to step into open warfare again."

"But we have an alliance with the Campbells now, do we not?" she asked. "Her grandfather declared peace, and you agreed to it."

"Aye. I agreed to peace. I'd nae call it an alliance. More of a mutual decision to leave each other be." He scowled, then wiped the expression from his face. "I have people to watch over. Cotters who've fled the MacDonalds and Campbells and need homes and employment, education fer the young ones, mills to run, a hundred other things. What it comes down to is . . . I've three lads in mind fer ye. Lord Robert Cranach and James MacMaster of clan Buchanan, and Niall Wyatt, Viscount of Cairnsgrove, from clan Watson."

Her heart thudded sickly in her chest. "An arranged marriage? But —"

"Nae. Not in so many words, anyway. Fer most of yer life I thought ye'd be marrying Lachlan. There was naught to consider aboot it. Now, though, I ken ye're looking fer a love match. If ye're willing to consider all those Sassenach lads, could ye nae consider a Highlander or two, as well?" He looked down at his hands for a moment. "I didnae pick their names oot of a hat. All of them have spent time in London. Two of them have houses there."

That touched her deeply. A few months ago he'd all but sworn that he would never allow her to set foot outside the Highlands, and now . . . this. "I'm listening," she said aloud.

"I'd nae force any of them on ye, *piuthar,* but clan Buchanan is missing some prime opportunities to expand their presence, and the Watsons could grow their shipbuilding with a bit more money and manpower."

He was asking. Ranulf wasn't ordering or dictating, or forbidding her to do as she pleased. That in itself set her off-kilter, as did the way he'd just spoken to her — like she was an equal. An adult. "Do you have a preference?" she asked, pleased that her voice remained cool and level.

Her brother cocked his head. "Honestly? Or so ye can kick him in the man parts?"

That made her grin. "Honestly, if you please."

"Lord Robert Cranach. He's four-and-twenty, and from what I hear more progressive-minded than most of his clan."

Rowena nodded. "I won't promise any-thing, but other than admiring Lord Samston's manner and his fine dancing, I've no real attachment to any of these gentlemen. Not yet, anyway. So I've no objection to meeting Lord Robert or any of the other men you named."

For a long moment he gazed at her. "Ye continue to surprise me, Rowena," he said finally, "even when I've come to expect more of ye."

She'd never received a better compliment. "Thank ye — you — for saying that."

"I'll say one more thing, *piuthar,* that I should have said weeks ago." Abruptly he stood and moved around to the chair beside her, where he took one of her hands in his. "I thought I had the right of it, keeping ye away from London. I worried that ye'd prefer that soft life and the pretty, pampered men there. Ye both proved me wrong, and led me to Charlotte. Ye're nae a wee bairn any longer, Rowena, and I'm pleased and proud of the true Highlands lass ye've become. That ye are."

But that wasn't who she was. She *did* prefer London. But she'd looked up to this man for her entire life, and to hear him say he was proud of her . . . "Bring me your bonny Highlands lads, *bràthair,*" she managed, her voice shaking a little. "I'm ready to be swept off my feet."

Ranulf lifted her hand to kiss her knuckles. "Just keep in mind that there'll nae be sweeping withoot my consent or permission." With a grin he released her again. "Now off with ye."

"We're walking down to An Soadh today, if you want to join us. Arran and Mary are coming. And Bear." She sent him a sly smile. "And Charlotte asked to be introduced to some of our cotters."

"And ye saved that fer last, did ye?" Blowing out his breath, he rose and strolled over to pull open the office door again. "I'll join ye. And *I'll* be introducing my lady to our people, thank ye very much."

Now she only needed to go tell Charlotte that Ranulf wanted to go down to An Soadh with them, and she would have the entire London party joining her. And to think, she'd never hosted anything before. She was beginning to believe she had a knack for this sort of thing.

She turned up the hallway — and slammed into a broad, hard chest. Staggering backward, she looked up with an apology on her lips as two strong arms grabbed her shoulders to steady her. "I'm sorry, I didn't . . . Oh. Good morning, Lachlan."

He looked down at her, his hands still on her shoulders. "Good morning, Winnie. I hear ye're leading yer herd into the village today. I thought I'd join ye."

If he meant to misbehave as he had yesterday, she didn't want him along. She didn't want him along anyway, because it was much easier to ignore someone when they weren't present. But telling him that would only widen the chasm between them. "You don't need my permission."

"Well, I thought I'd ask ye anyway. We did have a few words yesterday."

"Did we? I've had so much to see to lately. It must've slipped my mind."

"Has it, then? How fortunate fer me."

When he didn't show any inclination to move, she shrugged out of his grip. "Yes, I suppose so. Because if I *did* perchance remember, I'd likely be annoyed that you were behaving like a petulant child." She walked past him. "Just try not to embarrass me again."

Before she could even blink her back was against the wall and his finger jabbed between her breasts. "Look at me," he murmured, his voice low and angry.

She lifted her gaze to meet his long-lashed green eyes. Whatever had happened to his usual good humor, this version of Lachlan MacTier — the one she'd encountered over the past two days — left her . . . unsettled.

77

Nothing like the sweet, pillowy, giggly feelings she'd always had around him before. "I'm looking at you," she retorted, keeping her voice flat.

"I'm nae a fool, lass," he continued in the same hard tone. "I'm nae a dog ye can pat on the head and send off to the kennel. If ye dunnae want me aboot, then say so, and I'll decide if I agree with ye. But I will speak my mind, and I will say someaught when one of yer Sassenach beaux acts in a way that's unworthy of ye."

Her heart skittered a little, and she didn't like the sensation. "Since you are the very portrait of someone not worthy of me, you'll have to expect that I am not going to take your opinion into consideration."

With a half growl he leaned a breath closer, looming over her like a living statue of granite, hard and heated. Then he turned on his heel and strode down the hallway.

Rowena sagged against the wall. When Lachlan had finally told her what she already knew, that they had no future together, she'd thought they could remain friends. After all, they had eighteen years of mutual history. She knew him to be good-humored and affable. Perhaps, though, that had only been when he considered himself to be a fourth brother to her.

As she'd said, she didn't need another brother. She'd certainly never seen him that way. What had just become clear, however, was that he truly had viewed himself as just that. And now he'd altered the way he looked at her, and whatever indulgence he'd felt seemed to have vanished. Lachlan Mac-Tier wasn't quite who she'd thought him — and that in itself rather upended things. If her own perceptions were wrong . . .

She shook herself. Ranulf had just handed her three new suitors, and she had to herd fifteen Sassenach about An Soadh while keeping them all entertained and happy. If Lachlan meant to make trouble, she would put a stop to it. It didn't seem they could be friends any longer, and if he meant to make himself an enemy she would be sad, but she would treat him as one.

"Did I hear Lachlan?" Ranulf said, making her jump as he emerged from his office.

"Yes. He headed toward Bear's bedchamber."

"Good. I've nine chieftains coming fer the wedding, and nae the inclination to allow my celebration to turn into a brawl because I've nae enough whisky to hand." He grimaced. "My head's already pounding at the thought of all the pipers competing to wake us in the mornings."

"Perhaps you and Charlotte should have followed Arran and Mary's example and eloped," she suggested, forcing a smile. If there was one thing Ranulf didn't need added to the plate it was her feud — if that's what it was — with Lachlan.

"Dunnae tempt me, lass," he rumbled, and kissed her on the cheek as he passed.

Still trying to shake off the idea that she didn't even know the man with whom she'd been obsessed for nearly two decades, Rowena went to find Charlotte Hanover.

"Ye look like thunderclouds," Bear Mac-Lawry commented.

Lachlan glanced sideways at his friend, then returned to glaring at Loch Shinaig as they walked the path along its shore. "Yer sister ordered me nae to embarrass her," he said stiffly.

"She warns me aboot that at least once a day," her brother said with a shrug. "That Sarah Parker keeps sending me looks. What do ye think?"

"It doesnae trouble ye that she's ashamed to be aboot ye?" Lachlan persisted.

"She wouldnae let go of my arm last night. I dunnae think that's shame."

"Yer sister, ye *amadan.* Nae Sarah Parker."

"Keep yer damn insults to yerself. Winnie's a lady now, Lach. She curtsied to the queen to make it so. Ye're only rattled because she's done nae but sigh over ye until now. Ye'll have to get accustomed to being nae better than the rest of us."

Perhaps that was the rub; yesterday she'd surprised him for perhaps the first time ever. And the way Samston kept putting his hand on her arm, like he bloody owned her or something — no, he didn't like it, and he didn't want to become accustomed to being . . . catalogued and dismissed as someone unworthy of her time.

He could parade former lovers in front of her, he supposed, and show her just how much her opinion of him mattered. But over the years he'd been so careful not to let her know he had lovers, or anything else that might needlessly hurt her, that it seemed cruel to shove it at her now just because she'd annoyed him.

A hand wound around his arm, and he just barely kept from flinching. Instead he took a breath and glanced sideways. "Lady Jane," he drawled, an odd combination of relief and disappointment running through him.

Jane Hanover smiled up at him. She definitely seemed less inclined to go about with her nose in the air than the other Sassenach lasses, which spoke in her favor as far as he was concerned. She'd become Winnie's dearest friend, which made him wary, but he'd also been warned to stay away from her, which today made him feel contrary.

"Everyone seems so excited by Charlotte and Glengask's wedding," she said, gesturing toward the front of the group where the couple walked arm in arm. "When was the last grand wedding held up here?"

Lachlan had to think about it for a moment. "The Stewarts had quite a to-do aboot eight years ago, but I cannae recall another where the MacLawrys would have been invited to attend. We've had smaller gatherings, but there's nae a thing like the clan chief marrying."

"It's to be very like a royal wedding, isn't it?"

"Aye. Here, Glengask *is* royalty. None of the other clans can match him fer power in the Highlands." He took a breath, brief uneasiness running through him. "And fer this wedding we'll have two clans here — the MacLawrys and the Campbells. The Duke of Alkirk himself, and his retinue. *The* Campbell."

"Goodness. I had no idea any of the

Campbells were coming. One of them shot Arran just a week ago."

"Ye dunnae have to remind me of that, lass. But Ranulf wants a lasting peace, so we'll help him forge it."

She lowered her lashes a little. "That sounds very brave."

A very different warning began sounding in his skull. He shrugged. "If it goes well, it'll be a fine gathering we'll all be too drunk to remember."

"Oh, but I want to remember this. The Highlands are magnificent."

"Aye, they are. They say ye can walk oot yer door every morning and never see the same sight twice. To —"

Someone bumped him from behind, sending him a step sideways. "We'll have to find you a wrap or a scarf with the MacLawry plaid, Janie," Winnie broke in, moving between them and taking her friend's arm. "Charlotte will be presented with our clan colors."

"My father said Ranulf wants him to wear a kilt," Jane returned, giggling. "He's prepared to be mortified."

"There's naught embarrassing aboot wearing a kilt," Lachlan protested. "Ye Sassenach are beyond sense."

Even as he spoke, though, his attention

was on Winnie. Was she trying to protect Jane from his evidently irresistible conversation? Or despite what she'd now informed him on several occasions, was she jealous that he was chatting with her friend? If it was the latter, someone needed to figure out what they wanted. And he wasn't entirely certain that confused someone was her. It was damned annoying; she'd never occupied his thoughts like this before. Trouble. That's what she was. Trouble.

"Lachlan," she said, her voice cooling, "did Bear tell you we're holding a gathering the week of the wedding? Ranulf approved; he thinks it'll keep everyone too occupied to cause trouble. I asked Bear to make the arrangements, as I'm occupied with my guests and the wedding events."

"Aye, he told me." Though he had his doubts that putting cabers and claymores and hurling stones in the hands of Highlanders was a way to avoid trouble.

"You should go tell him you'll help. Or do you prefer tagging along with the lasses while we go shopping?"

He narrowed his eyes. Perhaps it had been indigestion rather than a momentary confusion. His head cook was on loan to Glengask, after all, and the cook's helper had developed an obsession with lard. He straightened to look over Winnie's head at Jane. "I enjoyed our conversation, lass," he drawled. "Anything else ye wish to know aboot the Highlands, I'll be pleased to tell ye."

"Thank you, Lord Gray," she returned, blushing prettily. "I shall likely take you up on that very kind offer."

"I look forward to it." He sketched a shallow bow, then deliberately glanced at her clearly annoyed companion. "Winnie."

"Lachlan."

Before she could come up with some other task for him, he lengthened his stride to put some distance between himself and the two women. Going directly to Bear felt too much like being ordered about, so he slowed beside Arran and his Campbell bride where they walked close to the middle of the group. "Yer sister is damned annoying," he rumbled.

"This is her first time playing hostess," the middle MacLawry brother said with a faint grin. "And since the occasion is Ranulf's wedding, it'll also be her last time playing hostess. Here, anyway. Have a wee bit of patience. Or bite down on a twig. That works, as well."

"Rowena is doing remarkably well, I think," Mary Campbell MacLawry put in.

"To be only eighteen and balancing foreign guests, a wedding, a clan gathering, and an influx of my kin — I'm not certain I could manage all of that at her age."

" 'At her age,' " Arran mimicked in his deep brogue. "There's nae but three years difference between ye. And ye made me a Campbell lover. I've nae doubt ye could manage a wedding and a gathering."

She leaned closer against his shoulder. "I'll help her as much as I can, but I'm still glad not to have all this on my shoulders."

Lachlan took a breath, trying not to vomit at all the excessive sweetness. "Whatever's on her shoulders, I'm nae going to have her bellowing and ordering me aboot like I'm some drover."

"She's been ordering all of us aboot," Arran returned. "Yer kilt's twisted because she's nae cooing and fawning over ye any longer. Ye're just one of the lads, now, Lach."

That couldn't be it. Winnie had never been so aggravating or unpredictable as she had been since she'd returned from London. All those soft days and compliments from soft-handed men had changed her. Of course Arran didn't see it, because he'd been seduced by London, as well. And so had Ranulf, even; a few months ago the marquis would have burned his own house down before he'd see any Sassenach sleeping beneath his roof. Now, he was marrying one of them.

"Ye've lost yer senses, Arran," he grumbled. "Ye're in love, so everywhere ye cast yer eyes ye see naught but gold and rainbows. I'm going to talk to Bear."

Arran snorted. "If Munro's yer last hope fer logic and evenhanded discussion, ye might as well throw yerself into the loch."

Ignoring that and the chuckles continuing behind him, Lachlan made his way forward through the herd of padded shoulders and impractical shoes to find Bear escorting not just Sarah Parker, but her sister Susan, as well. The big man did like a challenge, but two English lasses with their cousin present seemed a mite dangerous, even for Munro.

He would have to find a better time to warn the youngest MacLawry male that his sister needed to be reined in. Instead, all he could do at the moment was keep an eye on her. With the extra rooms for chieftains and other, less friendly, guests being readied, all it would take would be Winnie giving someone the wrong quarters because the room color matched their eyes or something, and another war would break out in the Highlands.

Samston and the narrow-chinned fellow,

Arnold Peabody, had joined Winnie and Jane. They walked four abreast with the men on the outside, effectively walling her off from him whether that had been their intention or not. Whether he even wanted to approach her or not. Which he didn't, except that she needed to realize that he wasn't her pet wolfhound. She had Fergus and Una, presently padding along behind Ranulf, for that.

"Winnie says there are two villages on Glengask land," another female voice said, and he turned his head to see another of the English lasses, Lady Edith Simms, with her skirts gathered in her hands as she hurried to catch up to him.

Ah, the desperate one. The brown-haired lass couldn't have been more than five feet tall, wee compared to his two inches past six feet. But she was smiling, and she wasn't telling him that he was disappointing and only good for caber-tossing. Nor had he been warned away from her, as he had been from Jane Hanover. At the least she wouldn't be announcing that he was an idiot.

"Aye," he returned, offering his arm. She wrapped her wee fingers around his sleeve, and he couldn't help feeling something like a hulking giant beside her. Winnie was at least half a foot taller, and he didn't feel like he towered over her — especially when she was angry.

"Where is the other village?" Edith asked.

He shook himself. This wasn't about Winnie. This was about him enjoying himself and these visitors despite the youngest MacLawry's exasperating behavior. "It's aboot two miles to the south from here," he answered. "The stream ye rode along yesterday falls down to run by Mahldoen. And there are other settlements, but they're smaller and more scattered."

"It must be so lonely up here," she said after a moment. "Do you live at Gray House all by yourself?"

"Aye, except fer the servants. I suppose that's why I spend most of my spare time at Glengask. We were all practically raised together."

"Ah," she said, nodding as if he'd answered some question of hers. That was curious.

"Did I solve some riddle fer ye, lass?"

"Winnie told us all about Glengask while we traveled north. She said you were a cousin, but nearer to a brother."

"A third or fourth cousin, or someaught. My grandmother was a MacLawry, a cousin to the chief." Every time in the past he'd tried to point out that they were family, Winnie had taken pains to point out how distantly they were related. Now it was him doing so. "And Winnie didnae think us family when she went aboot calling herself Lady Gray."

Edith giggled. "I can hardly blame her. You are what we would call in London a well-favored man, my lord."

Lachlan smiled. "Call me Lachlan, lass. I dunnae sit in my castle and watch the world through my windows."

"Lachlan, then."

While he and the MacLawrys might prefer to spend their days out-of-doors, that clearly wasn't true of the London lot. Halfway to the mile-distant An Soadh they were already sweating and blowing like spent horses. The conversation dwindled, and he was fairly certain half of them would have given up and turned back if the way forward hadn't been shorter than the way back.

This high in the mountains he wasn't surprised, but how irresistible could Winnie find a blotchy-faced man rolling on the ground and gulping for air? Arran's arm had just come out of a sling two days ago, and he wasn't even breathing hard.

"You're smiling," Edith pointed out from beside him, her tone somewhat breathless, as well, and her grip on his arm seeming more for support than any reasons of flirtation. "You must tell me what's so amusing."

Aye, he could do that, and have Winnie bellowing at him again. Lachlan smoothed his expression. "We've had four days of sunlight in a row," he drawled. "That's enough to make any Highlander smile."

That seemed to satisfy her, because she grinned and nodded at him. "Oh, yes. Winnie says we're seeing the countryside at its best now. She and Samston are going riding in the morning to see a valley where the walls and floor are simply covered in bluebells." She sighed and leaned still closer against him. "That sounds romantic, doesn't it?"

"Aye," he rumbled, pinning the back of the earl's head with another glare.

"Do you know where this valley is, Lachlan? Perhaps you could take me riding there."

"I dunnae recall it," he lied, unwilling to be dragged into a romance simply because his attention was elsewhere.

Someone needed to warn Ranulf that his sister was making a fool of herself with a Sassenach lordling fortune hunter. The marquis would put a stop to that quicker than a gunshot. Or *with* a gunshot, if Samston didn't watch himself.

What the devil was Winnie up to, anyway? She'd managed to have the London Season she'd wanted, but that was no reason for her to be telling old friends she was done with them or to parade herself in front of these English fools like some lass playing dress-up. That tactic hadn't worked on him, but the Sassenach men didn't view her the way he did.

When they reached An Soadh he kept an eye on her, as her brothers were all obviously preoccupied with females. Someone had to try to keep her from looking — or being — foolish. As the cotters realized Lord Glengask and his betrothed were on foot in the village they began to appear from everywhere, and the London crowd broke into smaller groups to tour the rather picturesque village.

The London ladies would no doubt laugh at the dress shop's limited selections, but he'd never found a fault with anything from Mrs. Todd the baker. And of course Ranulf was already discussing the wool manufacturer where they wove MacLawry plaid as well as a handful of others to be shipped to America and the northeast, and the pottery mill that he'd arranged to build because of the surprising market they'd found for items bearing images of thistles and heather.

Glengask had begun several businesses whose main purpose was to sell goods to uprooted Highlanders forced to move to the cities or even abroad. Most of the facilities were located in Edinburgh, though a few had sprung up around the river Dee and boasted their own villages to house the employees.

He'd heard all this before, and had helped with both the logistics and with convincing suspicious and hostile Highlanders that changing their present didn't require them to erase their past. It was the most difficult part of being a clan chieftain, finding ways to preserve Scottish traditions while laying pathways for a more comfortable future. And when successful, it was also the most rewarding thing about being Lord Gray.

"I'm near to breaking into song every time I hear this tale," Bear said, shedding females as he approached. "Do ye think the Sassenach give a damn aboot any of it?"

"Nae. There's nae a man among 'em who's seen a family burned oot of a cottage to make way fer sheep. I'd nae be surprised to find that they've ordered it, though, from their cozy houses in the south." His gaze went to Samston — except the earl was

93

nowhere to be seen. And neither was Winnie.

"Ye're a cynical lad, Lach."

He shook himself, looking back at Bear. "Aye, I suppose I am. I'd rather be cynical than disappointed."

Bear's eyebrows dove together, but before he could comment, Lachlan left the crowd. It would serve Winnie right if he told everyone that she'd gone off somewhere with Samston, and he couldn't even explain to himself why he was instead walking in the other direction. Stupid thin-blooded men who looked down their noses at everyone and thought it made them clever — how could anyone find one of them attractive? How could Winnie do so, when she had her own brothers, and him, as examples?

He spied her and Samston leaning on the fence that corralled Mr. Addie's pair of Highlands cows. No doubt the earl saw fit to comment on their long-haired shagginess, and to compare them to the sleek black and white Herefords of his fair country. And Winnie would giggle and bat her eyes and not care what he was saying, as long as he paid attention to her.

Samston faced her, touching her elbow with one hand and then drawing his palm

94

down her arm to grip her fingers. And Winnie — *Winnie* —reached up to cup his face in her palm. The gesture was sensual, and intimate, and not at all the sort of flirting in which a high-spirited girl would engage.

But then Winnie — Rowena — wasn't a wee bairn any longer.

Lachlan took her in all over again. Her lush black hair coiled into a pair of braids that her maid Mitchell had looped partway down her back, strands escaping to caress her oval face in the cool breeze coming off the mountains. A jaunty, useless straw hat half shadowed her eyes, deepening their color to the soft gray of a Scottish wildcat's pelt. He well knew she had a temper to match. The green and white walking dress was undoubtedly the latest London fashion, and the way it pressed against her curves and slender form with the pulsing of the breeze . . .

He swallowed. Good God. When had this happened? He was fairly certain that she'd been but a child three months ago. When she'd returned and he'd told her once and for certain that he would never offer for her, and she'd practically laughed as she'd agreed with him — she'd been a child then, hadn't she? A petulant girl biting back at him because she'd been denied her favorite obsession?

The Highlands, the world, flipped over on its ear. The portrait of her that he'd held in his mind of the little girl with a rip in her too-frilly skirt and burrs in her hair no longer existed. Rowena MacLawry was a stunningly attractive young woman, and he hadn't even seen it until another man put his hands on her.

Lust, jealousy, anger pushed at him, warmer than the late summer sun, and he backed away before either of them could notice him and see it on his face. Clearly he'd made a mistake in turning her away. And now he needed to set things right before shiny Samston put a ring on her finger.

It shouldn't take much. After all, she'd been in love with him for nearly all of her eighteen years. And once he reminded her of that, and informed her that he saw her now as the lovely lass she was . . . Well, things were about to change.

CHAPTER FOUR

"However splendid your Highlands, Rowena," Adam James murmured, gazing at her with his pretty brown eyes, "they cannot possibly compare to you."

"The —"

"Hush," he interrupted. "I'm going to kiss you now."

It seemed an unnecessary announcement, given the way he'd led her off behind Mr. Addie's house. She wasn't certain she knew or trusted him well enough for them to be kissing, but someone needed to be her first kiss. Before he became too attached to her, Rowena also needed to inform him that Ranulf had selected three other men she'd agreed to meet. But a first kiss was a first kiss, and she felt disinclined to discourage him. If nothing else, it would be one more item she could tick off her list of things Lachlan hadn't done for her.

His mouth lowered over hers, warm and

soft and not at all wet (as Jane had warned her about). She pressed her lips back against his and remembered to bend one knee and lift her foot a few inches off the ground as she and Jane had practiced in the mirror at Hanover House all Season. All in all, it was very well done if she said so herself.

He started to back away, then with a swift glance beyond her shoulder, closed on her again, clutching her even closer. Her lips felt squished, and her nose dug into the side of his cheek. Rowena lifted a hand to push him away. This wasn't at all romantic, for Saint Bridget's sake.

"There you are," Jane's voice came, followed by a feminine squeak. "Goodness!"

Adam stepped back from her, a slight grimace crossing his features. "I apologize, Lady Rowena," he said. "I have overstepped the bounds of propriety. And Lady Jane, I must beg your discretion."

It all seemed so overblown — and so . . . rehearsed. Rowena frowned at him. "Did you mean to have someone see us kissing?" Clearly her propriety was not overstepped, because she hadn't even forgotten the proper accent she'd adopted.

"I . . . I would never do something so underhanded," he protested, flushing.

He hadn't flushed when he'd kissed her.

That was what his grimace had been about — he'd wanted someone other than Jane to discover them. "Well, you needn't worry, then," she returned, disappointed to her bones. How simple and naïve did he think she was? Especially after his repeated "polite inquiries" about what Ranulf would grant her upon her marriage. "Jane will keep our secret." She walked away from him without a backward glance and took her friend's arm.

"I mean to do right by you, my lady. We erred, drawn together by our mutual pass —"

"Do stop talking," she shot back. "I'm not fooled."

Jane sniffed at him. "And if I might make an observation, Lord Samston, you have no idea how lucky you are it was I who saw you. Telling any of her brothers that you kissed Winnie, particularly when no one else will corroborate that statement, will be much more likely to result in them killing you than in them offering you Winnie's hand and her dowry."

"I have no idea why you feel the need to attack me," the earl said stiffly. "All I did was ask for your discretion."

"That, and kiss me a second time when you realized someone was coming. That isn't mutual passion, my lord. That is your greed. Come with me, Jane. I want to show you the bakery."

With a flounce of her skirts, she towed Jane around the corner of the cotter's shack. "Did you know he meant to kiss you?" her friend whispered.

"I thought he might. I'm not sure he even liked me, now, though." And she'd had quite enough of that.

"I think he liked you. If he hadn't been so desperate for your money, he might have won you both." Jane wrinkled her nose. "Perhaps it *is* a good thing that he behaved this way."

"I won't argue with that." Rowena tried to muster a laugh, but as it occurred to her that she'd now had her first kiss and that it had been not out of passion but because Adam wanted money or power or something, she didn't feel terribly amused.

As they returned to the village center and the rest of their group, she sent a cautious look at Ranulf. Her oldest brother wore an easy, amused expression, his gaze on Charlotte, and she relaxed a little. Arran seemed likewise occupied with Mary, and Bear was caught up again with the Parker sisters. They hadn't noticed her departure from the party, then — something both highly unusual and, under the circumstances, very welcome.

"May I ask you a question?" Jane released her arm, but stayed close by. "But you mustn't get angry. It's only a question."

"You can ask me anything, Janie," she returned, immediately curious. "Of course I won't be angry."

"Lachlan. Lord Gray."

Oh, dear. Blast it all, she'd ordered Lachlan to stay well away from Jane. And yet, every time she turned around the two of them were chatting. Given the new tension between herself and Lachlan, she had to blame the viscount for intentionally flouting her request. "That's not a question," she said carefully.

"It was an implied question, I suppose," Jane said, her cheeks turning pink. "I mean, now that Samston's out of the running, so to speak, you're not . . . you won't change your mind about Lord Gray, will you?"

Almost against her will Rowena turned her head to glance at Lachlan — to find him gazing directly back at her. However she didn't feel about him, she could objectively say that Lord Gray was a damned handsome man. Out-of-doors like this, with his broad shoulders and wind-tossed brown hair, and in a kilt or in buckskin trousers and boots as he was today, he was the image every young, romantic girl took to bed with her when she dreamed of wild, untamed Highlanders.

She'd grown up with those dreams. Perhaps it made sense that she had tamer, more manageable, less unpredictable expectations now. Ones where the man both appreciated her interest and returned it. Rowena sighed, looking back at Jane. "I have no attachment to Lachlan. I'm not even certain we're friends, any longer. If you like him, I will only warn you that you will be wasting your efforts and your heart on someone who doesn't possess one, himself."

"He's been very nice to me."

"He *is* nice. He's even charming. But he's like that with everyone. Don't fool yourself into thinking his smiles are meant just for you."

Her friend nodded. "My eyes are open. I've seen how frustrated you were. I made a mistake in falling for Arran, thinking he had a tendre for me when he was just being polite, but I do understand that now."

Rowena had her doubts that Jane's eyes were open as much as her friend thought, but as she'd only recently realized her own mistake where Lachlan was concerned, she could hardly refuse to give Jane credit for her own epiphany. "Then do as you will, my dear. Just please, please don't let him break your heart."

"I won't. I promise."

"Winnie, is this the bakery you've been telling us about for a fortnight?" Edith asked, breaking into the conversation. "It looks very . . . plain."

"That's because the biscuits speak for themselves," Rowena returned with a smile, shaking herself. "I suggest we go in and see if Mrs. Todd has baked any honey biscuits today."

As she led the way across the dirt street, she caught sight of Lord Samston rejoining the group headed for the pottery manufacturer — and saw the look Lachlan abruptly sent the earl. The venom in his expression startled and unsettled her in equal measure, both because Lachlan was so rarely out of countenance, and because there was no reason she knew of for him to feel such vitriol.

"Excuse me a moment," she said, quickly giving Mrs. Todd a smile and a request for two dozen honey biscuits before she slipped back out of the shop.

Of course Lachlan was no concern of hers, his moods no longer influenced her own, and his likes or dislikes were nothing she adopted for her own. But he still stood alone at the rear of the group, and he still looked like he wanted to pummel the Earl of Samston senseless. Adam James had disappointed her, but no one was to bash visitors who'd come north to attend a wedding.

"Did you swallow a bee?" she muttered, stopping beside Lachlan.

"Nae. But I've a mind to punch that smiling fop in the teeth," he returned in the same tone.

Oh, no. Had Lachlan seen the kiss? No, that didn't make sense; if he had, he would either have told Bear, or already begun a brawl with the earl. "And what prompted this urge to violence?" she asked anyway, just to be certain.

"He has a smug look aboot him. I dunnae like it."

She glanced sideways at the object of her decades-long infatuation. "I could ask you what's changed between this morning and now, but honestly, Lachlan, I don't care. Leave him be. Leave all my guests be, and take your sour looks somewhere else."

He faced her, the glint in his light green eyes sharp enough that she took an involuntary half step backward. "I think we already discussed that I'm nae yer dog, lass. Yer

Lord Samston doesnae belong in the Highlands, and he doesnae belong with ye. If he doesnae take care, he may find he has enemies here."

The Lachlan she knew didn't threaten people for no good reason. But until the last five or six minutes one or the other of the two men had been in her sight all morning. What had she missed, then? "No, you're not my dog, of course," she retorted, still keeping her voice down. "And you're not a fool, either. Whether you dislike Lord Samston or not, you know better than to make trouble. If you damage a Sassenach lord for no reason, you'll cause a disaster that'll make our feud with the Campbells look like a soiree."

Lachlan gave a derisive snort. " 'A soiree'? Someone needs to remind ye that ye're a Highlander, lass."

She frowned. Whoever this man was, he felt . . . unpredictable. That was new, and she wasn't certain she liked it. Not that that mattered, of course. "I don't need to be reminded of anything."

"Aye, ye do, if ye think any of these soft, fortune-hunting lads can make ye happy."

Now he sounded jealous, and that made even less sense. "We've had the discussion where we established that you don't need to be concerned about my happiness. If that's why you're glaring daggers at Adam, stop it. It's none of your business."

"Ye're wrong aboot that, lass."

She glared at him. "What makes you think he's a fortune hunter, anyway?"

"Ye keep yer counsel, and I'll keep mine."

Well, that was enough of that. "I don't know what you're angry about," she stated, planting her hands on her hips, "but since you seem to be growling about Samston and me, all I can say is that you're too late. I have plans, and they dunnae involve ye. You."

It felt oddly satisfying to say that, and to be able to let him know through her tone that she was angry. More than likely, he disliked the fact that she wasn't agreeing with his every word or hanging on his every breath, and that had caused all this. If he felt neglected, though, well, he could just find someone else to fawn over him. Jane seemed a likely substitute. Because after three months of reminding herself daily, hourly, how much time and effort and pieces of her heart and her future she'd wasted on him, she wasn't about to give him one more minute.

"Mayhap my plans *do* involve ye."

"Now you're being ridiculous. Shut up."

Lachlan didn't look like he was finished with this conversation, so before he could say something that would destroy the one or two threads of friendship that remained between them, she stalked away, stepping off the street and onto the main floor of the pottery manufacturer. No one looked terribly interested in learning how the plates and teacups were made, but as far as she was concerned that meant they'd missed the point. Because Ranulf didn't care overmuch about the how of it, either. It was far more impressive that he'd managed to build the business in the first place, and that two dozen cotters earned an income from working there.

"Ranulf?"

Her brother turned around, a pretty serving platter decorated wih thistles in his hands. "Aye, *piuthar.* Have ye shown yer friends the bakery?"

"Yes." More or less, anyway. "Have you sent word to those . . . men you mentioned?"

He lifted an eyebrow. "Ye havenae changed yer mind, I hope."

"No, not at all." Rowena took a breath. "I was just wondering when we might expect them."

The marquis continued to eye her curiously. "Cairnsgrove may be here as early as tomorrow afternoon. The other two will take another day or so. Why do ye ask?" He glanced beyond her to where she knew Samston and a few of the others stood.

"No particular reason," she said carefully, keeping her expression neutral. This wasn't so much about Adam James, anyway, as it was about the past eighteen wasted years. The sooner she found someone, the sooner she could stop thinking altogether about Lachlan MacTier. "I'm anxious, I suppose, to get on with things. With my life."

"Ah." He handed the platter to a worker and took Rowena's arm, guiding her a few steps away from the group. "And did someaught in particular prompt this anxiety of yers?"

She could tell Ranulf that Samston had kissed her as a ruse to get hold of her dowry, or she could say that Lachlan seemed to be much more angry and intense than she remembered him, but either answer could cause far more trouble than she wanted. And Lachlan was still Bear's dearest friend, and the chieftain Ranulf trusted above all others. "We're planning your wedding," she improvised with a smile. "Shouldn't a lass be thinking of her own?"

"Aye. I suppose so."

Tomorrow afternoon. She would no longer be riding out to Madainn Srath with Samston in the morning, but surely she could avoid trouble until then. At that moment, though, Jane walked up beside her, as if one of the old gods had read her mind and was laughing at her.

"Lachlan asked me to go riding with him in the morning," her friend said, handing one of two honey-dipped biscuits over to Rowena and grinning excitedly. "I didn't even have to flirt with him first."

"Oh. Splendid," Rowena returned, keeping the smile on her own face. Either Lachlan's last conversation had only been to try to make a fool of her, or he had asked Jane to go riding in order to aggravate her. "There are an abundance of picturesque trails about."

"He mentioned Madainn Valley. Is that the one with all the bluebells?"

"I . . . Yes, it is. And an old castle ruin. Arran says it's haunted."

Jane shivered. "Goodness."

"Don't worry. I'm certain Lachlan will protect you."

Oh, she sounded like a bitter old spinster, even to her own ears. She hadn't meant it that way. It was only that her friend required very little urging to fall headlong in love, and Lachlan was a poor target for a young lady's heart. And even worse — perhaps — *he'd* asked *Jane* to go riding. Did he mean to cause trouble? For Jane? For her? For the clan?

She frowned. Evidently she would be going for a ride herself in the morning. Lachlan wasn't allowed to wound anyone else. Especially not her dearest friend.

"Is that the old castle?" Jane asked, her breath blossoming in the chill morning air. "The one Winnie says is haunted?"

Lachlan lowered his gaze from the tree line and reined in Beowulf. Where the devil was Winnie? Yesterday Jane had told him they would be in just this valley — her and Samston. And whatever the earl thought to attempt in this notoriously romantic setting, Lachlan meant to put a stop to it. Except that they didn't seem to be there.

"Aye," he said aloud, twisting in the saddle to look across the pond at the base of the high cliffs. "Teàrlag Castle. They say old Lord Teàrlag sent his wife away on a visit, but when snow blocked the pass she returned, just in time to find his lordship . . . engaged with her own sister. In the master bedchamber. The rumor is that Lady Teàrlag was someaught of a witch, and anyway,

110

that she burned the castle doon around them. The stories say she still walks the remains of the halls, making certain no other lass gets near her husband."

"That's terrible," Jane exclaimed, sending the crumbled stone ruins an uneasy look.

"The lesson is nae to cross a Highlands lass. Ever. There's nae a more fierce creature in the wide world."

"Oh, I can believe that," Jane said, chuckling. "And so does Lord Samston, I'll wager."

Now *that* was interesting. "Didnae ye say Winnie would be aboot here today? I thought the four of us might be oot riding together."

"I think Winnie changed her plans. I know she changed the earl's."

Hm. In the MacLawry family Bear was known as the headstrong one and Arran the clever one, but he'd spent his life navigating successfully around them and Ranulf and an infatuated lass, not to mention floods, landslides, ruined crops, and well above two hundred cotters. Something had happened between Samston and Winnie yesterday, and while at first he'd thought Winnie might have been trying too hard to cover some happy secret, now it looked as though the earl had fallen out of favor — which was splendid — but he needed to know what, precisely, had transpired. And if he'd miscalculated and needled Rowena too hard in the village. Or if Samston required a bloody nose.

"A man should know better than to step beyond what he's earned," he ventured. That seemed vague enough to suffice.

Jane blinked her pretty brown eyes at him, clearly surprised. "She told you?"

"Well, she couldnae tell her brothers," he decided.

"That's true enough. She said if they knew Lord Samston had kissed her, they would murder him even if she dealt with the silly man herself. Imagine, thinking he could compromise her into a marriage by having *me* catch them kissing. He should have known I would never tell anyone." Jane chuckled. "Honestly, I think Winnie dealt with him better even than Lord Glengask could have."

Lachlan clenched his jaw. "Aye, I'll agree with that," he forced out.

The bastard had kissed her. And he himself had been lucky that the damned earl hadn't gained her affection, or he might have lost this battle before he'd even begun it.

Whatever he was doing, he needed to stop

fumbling about. Winnie — Rowena — was barely speaking to him, and however frustrated that made him, he couldn't blame her for it. She thought he had no interest in her. Well, he would find a moment when she would listen to him and tell her that he did, and then . . .

Movement beneath the half-fallen entryway of the ruins caught his attention. In the past he would immediately have assumed the skulker was a Campbell or a Daily, looking to murder a MacLawry. It still could be, he supposed, but with the truce it was more likely a drover or someone unfamiliar with the place's reputation.

A flash of green muslin caught the sunlight. Or it could be someone who knew better than to sneak off anywhere on her own, but who was either concerned about her impressionable, chatty friend, or jealous of her. God, he hoped it was the latter.

Lachlan swung down from Beowulf. "Let me look at that stirrup of yers, lass," he drawled, approaching Jane and her mount from an angle that would let him look beyond her to the ruins. He wasn't going to make a fool of himself by ambushing a doe by mistake. "It looks a mite long fer ye."

"Thank you, Lachlan. I have to say, I adore Winnie, and she generally seems very

113

levelheaded, but she may have given up on you too soon."

"She told ye she threw me aside, did she?" he asked, frowning. This wasn't about who'd lost interest in whom, however; this was about getting a bit of information while he figured out for certain who was watching them from the ruins.

"Well, she actually said you were never hers, and she just finally realized that. Honestly, I don't know why you didn't fancy her. If I was a man, I'd want to marry her. She's splendid and funny and very, very brave."

"What if I was wrong?"

He wasn't certain he'd spoken aloud until she tilted her head at him, her expression stunned. "Beg pardon?" she squeaked.

Lachlan cleared his throat. "I mean no offense to ye, lass, because ye're a fine, bonny young lady. It's . . . Damn, I have nae idea what it is, but she's nae the bairn she was a week ago."

"Lachlan, are you interested in Winnie?" The news must have been truly earth-shattering to her, because she barely managed a whisper. And that was a good thing, considering the lass lurking in the old ruins.

Of course it was just as possible that saying such a mad thing aloud would cause the mountains to fall. "I think I am. At the least, I dunnae like the idea of Samston or one of those other Sassenach scalawags putting their hands on her."

"Goodness," she breathed. That seemed to be the lass's favorite expression. Privately, he didn't think there was anything good about it. Not at all. "I don't know what . . . You should tell her, of course."

"I tried to, yesterday, but since she came back from London, every time we begin a conversation we end with an argument." Telling her, conversing with her, using pretty words — that was the Sassenach way, anyway. And he was not a damned Sassenach.

A bit of black hair above a pert nose edged into view at one side of the fallen archway. He'd caught her spying on him enough over the years to know that the nose belonged to Winnie.

"Ye know, I think I spied some ducklings in the reeds at the near side of the pond there, Jane," he said aloud. "Would ye care fer a look? I need a moment or two to think."

"Of course." Leaning down, she put a hand on his arm. "She was very . . . disappointed in you. It may be too late."

It was not too late, because he wouldn't

accept that. All Winnie needed was a man from the Highlands to woo her. And he needed to figure out if he'd perhaps received a blow to the head, or if it had merely taken him eighteen years to sort himself out. To see her the way she truly was, and not for the child she'd been.

Had he merely been a fool? Or was there something to the saying that the forbidden fruit was the sweetest? Because just two days ago he'd renounced any claim to her. He'd set himself free. And now he'd begun to realize that by doing so he might just have made the greatest mistake of his twenty-six years.

Rowena ducked behind the old tumble of stones. She'd asked Lachlan to stay away from Jane, and yet there he was, being . . . chivalrous. And flirting. She wrinkled her nose. He'd never bothered to check whether *her* foot was in the stirrup, for heaven's sake. Once he'd even ridden off and left her when she'd claimed to have a dizzy spell.

Not that she cared, of course. Adam, Lord Samston might have played his hand and lost, but she had three Highlanders on the way just to meet her. She was no longer a girl in want of a first kiss, either. Rowena touched her fingers to her lips. It hadn't been a . . . well, a glorious kiss, but it *had* been a kiss. And if once upon a time she'd dreamed that it would be Lachlan to give her her first kiss, well, that was just stupidity. He'd made it quite clear that he wasn't interested in her, and she'd made other plans.

She'd only snuck out of the house this morning to make certain Jane was well. He'd been so unlike himself yesterday, so angry, that she needed to be certain he wouldn't seduce Jane just out of spite or something. Taking a breath, she glanced around the broken masonry again. Both horses and riders had vanished into the misty morning. Perhaps they were holding hands and exclaiming about how blue the bluebells were. She certainly didn't care.

"What the devil are ye doing in here, lass?"

Rowena squeaked, whipping her head around. Lachlan MacTier, Lord Gray, leaned against what had once been a doorway of the old fortress, his arms crossed over his chest and his expression amused. *Drat.* "I thought I saw a ghost," she lied. As she straightened, something caught at the back of her skirt, pulling her back onto her knees again.

" 'A ghost'?" he repeated. "Old Lady Teàrlag, come to find her cheating husband?"

"I don't know," she returned, twisting to tug at the back of her riding habit. The only thing worse than being discovered by stupid Lachlan was being trapped here. "It made me curious."

"Ye always have been fearless, Rowena. I'll give ye that."

She stopped tugging and faced him again. "What did you call me?"

"Rowena. It's yer name, isnae?"

A soft shiver ran down her spine at his low brogue saying her name. "You never call me Rowena. It's always 'Winnie, you have burrs in your hair,' or 'Winnie, leave me be.' " There. That was what she needed to remember — that he thought of her as a child, as a sister, and that Lord Samston had kissed her. That other men found her perfectly marriageable and attractive and a lady. And that she preferred a man who didn't detest London and the Sassennach, anyway.

He straightened, pushing away from the mossy wall and making his way closer. "I dunnae think ye saw Lady Teàrlag, lass. I think ye wanted to know what I was doing oot here with Jane Hanover."

"You were out here with Jane?" She seized on the admission.

"Ye said ye didnae care. It wasnae a secret.

But I want to know what ye're doing oot here alone. Nae a groom, nae one of yer brothers, nae one of the deerhounds in sight. That's nae wise."

"The Campbell himself will be visiting here in a fortnight. No one's going to jeopardize his plans. And now I want to remind you that she's very romantic. Jane is, I mean. Don't hurt her."

Lachlan crouched beside her. His gaze on her face, he leaned closer and slowly reached back around her. Rowena held her breath. He was just teasing, because he couldn't stand the fact that she was no longer infatuated with him, that she'd moved on to find a man worthy of her attentions and affection.

With a hard tug he freed her skirt. She started to her feet immediately, but he caught her arm and held her there, eye to eye with him. "Jane mentioned that the shiny lad, what is it? Sandstone? That he —"

"Samston," she corrected, not gazing at his mouth.

"That he kissed ye," he continued, as if she hadn't spoken.

"Damnation," she muttered, feeling her cheeks warm. "I told Jane to be quiet about it. The last thing I want is one of my brothers piling into him fists first."

"It's nae just yer brothers he needs to worry over."

"Oh, please." She yanked her arm free and scrambled awkwardly to her feet on the uneven stones. She needed something. Height. Not having him be so very close to her. Something. "You can pretend you're my brother, but I already have three. I don't need another one. And if I'm to fall in love and marry, I will need to speak with men. Dance with them, even." She put a hand to her chest. "My goodness, I might even find someone who loves me in return. Kissing might very well be involved."

"And yet I hear ye turned Samston away. After the kiss."

Blast it all. She could blame Jane for tattling about the entire incident, but Lachlan had very likely tricked the information out of her. He did that to Bear all the time. "Yes, I did. I've found several men to be . . . less than I'd hoped. You, included."

"That's nae amusing, Rowena."

"It's not meant to be." Turning, she shoved him in his rather broad, hard chest. "Go away. Leave me be. I've chased you since I could toddle about, and now I've learned the error of my ways. I was a silly child who didn't know any better. I don't want you any longer. The only thing I *do* want from you, Lachlan MacTier, is for you not to interfere with my chances at romance and happiness."

Before she could pull her hand away he grabbed her wrist again, holding her against him. "I know ye still like me, Rowena, and I know ye're only trying to make me jealous by bringing all those dainty fops to the Highlands."

"They aren't fops. They're just fashionable. Something about which you know nothing." She tugged, but his grip was like iron. Other people said Lachlan had a temper, but she'd honestly never seen it. Not directed at her. "I'm not trying to do anything to you," she continued, finally looking up to meet his lush green gaze. "Eighteen years of being ignored and laughed at is long enough. Now let me go."

"I'll nae have ye looking at me like I'm nae a man," he said in a lower tone, unmoving. "Like ye can blink yer pretty eyes and I become invisible. Ye can decide ye dunnae want me, but it'll nae be because ye've decided I dunnae exist." He glanced past her, where she'd been perched watching him flirting with Jane. "Because ye're only pretending ye dunnae like me, Rowena. And *I* know it."

With a twist of his hand he yanked her up against him. She gasped, and his hard, warm mouth closed over hers. He wasn't gentle at all, but then he was a Highlander born and bred. He wasn't gentlemanly or shiny like any of the men who'd followed her north to Glengask. Power, passion, anger — Rowena closed her eyes at the sheer force of him. Lachlan MacTier, kissing her. Devouring her. And just for that moment, she wanted to be devoured.

Abruptly he pushed her away, setting her on her feet as if she weighed no more than a feather. "Now pretend I'm invisible," he murmured, straightening.

Rowena stood there in the ruins of Castle Teàrlag and stared at him. If this had been a year ago — three months ago, even — she would have been . . . Well, it wasn't three months ago, was it? It was today, and she had other plans. Other men coming to court her.

"I see you just fine," she stated, and slapped him as hard as she could. "No, you're not invisible. And you're not nearly as charming as ye think ye are. You had your chance. Go away, Lachlan MacTier."

A red mark shaped like her hand began to appear on Lachlan's tightly clenched jaw, though he hadn't bothered acknowledging the hit. "Very well," he drawled. "But this isnae over with, Rowena." He flashed a surprising grin. "Now ye've made it interesting."

He turned on his heel, and after a moment the sounds of Lachlan and his horse faded into the mist. Around her the trees whispered, and she could almost believe the broken grounds and tragic Lady Teàrlag were speaking to her. And from what she knew of Lady Teàrlag, they were in complete agreement about the deserved fate of flirts and philanderers.

She was *not* about to fall into the same trap again. Not when she'd finally escaped it — him. Not when she had a half-dozen handsome young men of title and wealth all pursuing her, and not when her oldest brother had specifically arranged for her to meet three more, any of whom would benefit the clan. Lachlan was likely playing, anyway, angry that the puppy who'd tagged after him for so long had decided she preferred being elsewhere.

But he was correct about one thing; she was not going to be able to continue pretending that he was invisible. Not after that kiss. Not when for a bare second she'd remembered how much she'd once longed to be kissed just like that, and by him.

"Damn ye, Lachlan MacTier," she muttered, letting her own brogue loose for a moment. "It *is* over. It is."

CHAPTER FIVE

The Viscount of Cairnsgrove arrived just before sunset. He came in a coach, two younger people who looked enough like him that they had to be his brother and sister emerging after him. Rowena watched from the window of Bear's bedchamber as the trio stepped down to the drive to be greeted by Lord Glengask himself.

She always enjoyed seeing members of other clans meet Ranulf; their courtesy and occasionally their shaking hands were enough to tell her how much respect even the roughest, most fearless Highlanders had for the MacLawry, as they all referred to him.

Niall Wyatt's hand didn't shake as he held it out, but he did bow quite low. The two younger ones, both with the same blazing red hair as the viscount, looked ready to faint. Other than noting they showed Ranulf the proper respect, though, most of her attention remained on Cairnsgrove.

The clan Watson colors were blue and green and yellow, and he did wear a scarf of those colors. Other than that, though, he might have been mistaken for any ginger-haired English gentleman — beaver hat, superfine coat of dark blue, tan buckskin trousers, a blue and black waistcoat, and a fine, shiny pair of shoes.

"Well, he's a pretty one," Bear observed, stripping off his riding coat as he joined her at the window. "That's Cairnsgrove, isnae?"

"Yes. Ran wants me to meet him."

"Does he now? And how do ye feel aboot that, *piuthar*?"

"I feel . . . curious." The idea that she was gazing at a man of whom Ranulf approved — even if Lord Cairnsgrove was his second choice, overall — felt very odd. Her brother approved of almost no man when it came to the lad's suitability to be her spouse. And he'd brought in men who actually enjoyed London, or at least didn't shun the place. It was very unlike her oldest brother.

"So ye've truly thrown over Lachlan, then?"

Rowena sent her brother a glance. She could tell him that Lachlan had kissed her and that she'd slapped him, but wars had begun with less provocation. Aside from that, it was easier just to pretend it had only been the events of some last, mad daydream, the remnants of a wish she'd once carried about with her.

Lachlan didn't truly want her, anyway. It was only that she'd bruised his pride and he'd reacted like a ham-fisted brute. Yes, the kiss had rattled her, and continued to do so, but only because it had been unexpected. And because it had been so different from the chaste, passionless one she'd shared with Samston. Of course she hadn't realized that first kiss had been passionless until Lachlan had mauled her.

"Winnie? Are ye in there?"

She shook herself. "What, Bear?"

"Ye're truly finished with Lachlan?"

"Yes. Yes, I am." Taking a breath, she left the window. "Well, I suppose I should go meet our newest guests," she said, smoothing at her blue and brown muslin gown.

"Aye. And I hope ye can keep yer eyes open long enough to finish the chat."

Rowena slowed her exit. "Do you know him, then? Or are you just being contrary?"

Bear nudged her into the hallway. "A bit of both, most likely," he said with a grin, and closed his door on her.

Well, that wasn't at all helpful. Of course if he'd been keeping her in mind Ranulf had very likely selected someone who didn't share many of the same likes or hobbies as her brothers. Someone calm and safe who might actually have the time and inclination to allow her into his life, to show her affection and not decide after eighteen years of ignoring her to try to kiss her to death when she'd finally become wise enough to turn her back.

The Wyatts sat in the firelit morning room, Ranulf and Charlotte chatting with Cairnsgrove while Jane and Edith and Arnold Peabody peppered the younger two with questions about the weather in Edinburgh.

Jane sent her a curious look, but for the moment Rowena settled for smiling at her friend. They could figure out later just what had happened today. Keeping the smile on her face, she walked up to stand beside her brother.

"You must be Lord Cairnsgrove," she said, facing the viscount. "Ranulf said you were coming for the wedding."

"Yes, indeed," he answered, taking her hand and bowing over it. "Niall Wyatt, at your service."

Well, that sounded very chipper. She dipped a curtsy. "Rowena MacLawry, at yours."

Ranulf took Charlotte's hand. "Will ye two excuse us fer a moment? I need to introduce my betrothed to yer *bràthair* and *piuthar.*"

"Of course, Lord Glengask," the viscount returned. "They are both quite excited to be here. Glengask and the MacLawrys are rather mythical in Edinburgh."

Once they'd gone, Cairnsgrove faced Rowena squarely. "I hear you just returned from London. I find Town a bit tedious, I admit, but I do enjoy the theater. Were you able to attend any plays?"

He hadn't a trace of a Highlands accent, she realized. In fact, if she hadn't known he had an estate just outside of Edinburgh she would have thought him just up from London, himself. "Yes, I was," she answered, then felt a warm shiver go up her spine. When she glanced sideways she wasn't surprised to see Lachlan stroll into the room with Bear, Arran, and Mary.

Blast it, why couldn't he just stay away? Mossgreen eyes met hers and didn't look away. She did, though. He could just go attempt to mesmerize someone else.

"We were able to see *Hamlet,*" she continued, returning her attention to Cairnsgrove, "and the evening before we left London we attended the premiere of *Speed the Plow.*"

He clapped his hands together. "Splendid choices. Who was your Hamlet? The one I attended last year featured a fascinating performance by a lad — oh, what was his name — Andrew Wilsby. That was it. Such a nuanced portrayal, for a moment or two I feared he'd actually gone mad before my eyes!"

"I don't recall the name of our Hamlet," Rowena said, keeping the smile on her face. "But it was a fine performance. Do you go to London often, then?"

"Every chance I get. Theater in Edinburgh is, well, adequate, I suppose, but it's certainly not London." He laughed. "But then, what is? Oh, that's your brother, isn't it? How good to see you, Lord Arran."

Arran walked up to shake hands. "Niall. Have you met my wife? Mary, this is Niall Wyatt, Lord Cairnsgrove. Niall, Lady Mary MacLawry."

The viscount's face flushed. "Oh, you're married now? I had no idea! I — Congratulations, of course. To both of you. Lady Mary, very pleased."

As sheltered as Rowena's upbringing had been, she knew a broken heart when she saw one. And Niall Wyatt's heart had just broken. For heaven's sake. Evidently Ranulf wasn't as all-knowing as he pretended, because while Niall did favor a MacLawry, it clearly wasn't her. She took a breath, then put a hand on his arm. "Lord Cairnsgrove was just lamenting the dearth of good theater in Edinburgh," she said aloud. "I admit, as fine as some of the soirees were, I think going to the theater was perhaps my favorite part of being in London. Everyone was so . . . glittery."

Cairnsgrove visibly shook himself. "Indeed. And everyone intends on being seen coming or going, because otherwise they're left sitting in the dark in their best finery."

Lachlan chose that moment to circle around behind the viscount. Forcing a laugh, Rowena tightened her grip on their guest's arm. "Very true, my lord."

"Oh, please, do call me Niall."

"Niall it is, then."

For the next hour before dinner she pretended to flirt with a man who was clearly more interested in her brother than he was in her. And as she told him about Arran and Mary's meeting and their elopement, she became aware of two things: firstly, she actually had a great deal in common with Niall Wyatt, who'd lost his heart to someone who would never return his affections; and secondly, she was pretending to flirt only because Lachlan was present.

He'd said he wasn't finished with her, which was ridiculous because she'd stated the exact opposite thing to him the day she'd returned to Glengask. And during that conversation, which he'd initiated, the scoundrel, he'd made it very clear that he had no interest in her. What the devil had happened over the past few days to so change his mind, except for the fact that he'd seen other men take an interest in her?

It all would have been laughable, some kind of theatrical farce, except for that kiss. The kiss that had made her forget for the barest of moments that she'd sworn never to fall into her old habits again, never to become infatuated again with Lachlan Mac-Tier, because he wasn't worth the heartbreak. And that hadn't changed. It couldn't change, when he was only pretending to pursue her because now other men wanted her. Not the man whose arm she currently held, but other men.

And when he arrived tomorrow, if Lord Robert Cranach of clan Buchanan found her interesting, and not just because she was fond of the theater, then she was ready — quite ready — to fall in love with him. The sooner the better.

"Well, how many lads is Glengask pushing

at Rowena, then?" Lachlan slammed a dart into the target on the wall so hard it rattled loose his earlier bull's-eye and sent it to the floor.

"I'm nae counting that one," Bear commented, pointing at the red-tailed dart resting on the polished wooden floor. "Yer total is fer the darts in the target at the end of the round."

"I dunnae give a damn if ye count it or eat it," Lachlan growled. "Why's yer brother throwing men at yer sister? I thought he didnae mean to force her into an arranged match."

"He doesnae mean to. I dunnae think so, anyway. Ask him. Or ask Winnie. But stop trying to murder the dart board."

"Arenae ye concerned fer yerself?" Lachlan persisted, hurling his last dart only to have it dig into the paneled wall a good four inches from the board.

"Fer myself? I'm nae marrying her. Have ye gone mad?"

His jaw was beginning to ache from being clenched so hard. "I mean, Ranulf tried to marry Arran off to Deirdre Stewart, and now he's got Rowena aimed at a Watson. What's to —"

Munro barked a laugh. "Cairnsgrove

133

would rather have Arran aimed at him, I wager."

"That's beside . . . Wait. What?"

"Niall Wyatt couldnae take his eyes off Arran all night. Did ye nae notice? I'm just glad he prefers scrawny MacLawrys."

Of course he hadn't noticed; he'd been too occupied with glaring at the way Rowena hung on to his arm. And if Arran was scrawny, then he was skin and bones. Of course compared to Bear, they were all scrawny. But that didn't signify at the moment. "Cairnsgrove doesnae mean to offer fer her, then?"

Bear shrugged as he moved in front of the board. "Dunnae. He might; the Watsons could use the alliance. I suppose it depends on whether Winnie would go along with it or nae. In Ranulf's mind it might be perfect, marrying his sister off to a man who'll nae put his hands on her."

"That's idiotic."

"What're ye getting all heated up aboot, Lach? And get yer damned pitiful pieces oot of the way so I can throw."

Stalking up to the wall, Lachlan yanked his darts free, picked the fallen one up from the floor, and threw himself into the chair Munro had vacated. There were times he found Bear's blunt assessments refreshing;

clan politics could be maddeningly complex, and the youngest MacLawry brother had a keen eye for seeing through shite. This morning, though, Bear was simply being thickheaded, and Lachlan was halfway to being convinced it was intentional.

"Is Ranulf forcing Rowena into marrying, or nae?" he insisted. "Ye should take a damned interest, Bear, because ye could be next."

Bear's throw nearly caught himself in the foot. "What the devil are ye talking aboot, man?"

"Arranged marriages. Arran, Rowena, and ye. Half the clans are sending someone here to witness Glengask's wedding. Have ye nae thought he might have a lass in mind fer ye among all those guests? He's bringing in lads fer Rowena. Or one lad, anyway."

"Three lads fer Winnie, I ken," the mountain said with a frown. "Cairnsgrove's nae but the first. James MacMasters and Lord Robert Cranach are due here this afternoon."

"Clan Buchanan," Lachlan finished, recognizing the names. He hadn't met either man, but the mere fact that they had been specifically invited, presumably for Rowena's perusal, was maddening. Infuriating.

He could admit that perhaps he'd been a

bit foolish to think he could sway Rowena back to being in love with him with one kiss. The slap had told him that. Even so, with Samston out of the race he'd figured to change her mind fairly easily. But then Cairnsgrove had shown up, all pretty clothes and Oxford accent and talk of the theater.

If not for Samston being an idiot and Cairnsgrove riding sidesaddle he might have lost her twice now. His luck was not going to continue. And two more suitors, both selected by the brother Rowena adored, would be arriving today. "Where's Rowena?"

"I dunnae. She and that Jane Hanover were up nearly till dawn gabbing aboot someaught. She's likely still asleep. Who do ye think Ranulf means to send me after? Nae Bethia Peterkin, I hope."

Lachlan stood again. "I thought ye already had her in yer bed. And her sister, Flora."

"Aye. And I might have called one by the other's name, but I dunnae remember which one." Bear shuddered. "One or the other of 'em swore to stab me in the heart."

"Ye're lucky if that's all they mean to stab." He pulled open the billiards room door. "And Glengask'll likely want ye with a MacAllister, since he knows the Campbell was after an alliance with them."

"A MacAllister? Nae Gormal MacAllister, I hope. She has but one eye. And — dammit, Lach! What aboot the game?"

"I concede."

Otherwise ignoring Munro's bellowing, Lachlan strode down the hallway and up the adjoining one toward the castle's west wing where the family's bedchambers were located. Arran and Mary had moved to a larger set of rooms on the south end to give them more privacy, but with all the guests arriving both Bear and Rowena had given over their adjoining sitting rooms to be turned into additional bedchambers.

He knew all that just as he knew the layout of Glengask better than the back of his own hand — because he spent more time there than he did at his own home. Gray House was fine enough, but he much preferred loud, bustling Glengask and the MacLawry siblings to his own company. He'd sat on the floor in Rowena's bedchamber for more tea parties than he could count.

And now? Now he didn't want tea parties. He wanted her.

He stopped outside her bedchamber. If he knocked she would more than likely lock the door and tell him to go away, not necessarily in that order. Instead he quietly pushed open the door and closed it behind him again, then knocked.

The mound of blankets atop the bed stirred. Tempting as it was to go peel them away one by one to get at the treat that lay beneath, he stayed by the door. The only way to win this game was to have her want him back, and he couldn't win by frightening her.

"Who is it?" she mumbled, her head still somewhere beneath the heavy covers. "Mitchell, I asked you not to wake me."

"It's Lachlan," he answered.

The blankets stopped moving. "Go away."

"Nae."

Silence. "You're already in here, aren't you?"

"Aye." That taken care of, he went over to push open one of the sets of heavy green curtains covering the windows. The ones she'd selected because they matched his eyes, as he recalled.

On the bed one gray eye, half obscured by disheveled hair the color of raven's wings, slipped from beneath the covers. "You need to leave. Now."

The miniature tea set with which she'd once tortured him sat neatly on a shelf. Carefully he removed one of the blue and white porcelain cups. It had a small chip in the delicate curved handle. "This is the cup ye always gave to Munro," he said, "so if he broke it ye'd still have three good ones."

"Don't make me yell for help, Lachlan. Ranulf *will* ban you from the house. At least."

"Aye, he likely would." He set the blemished cup back and picked up the one on the far end of the row. "And this one was mine," he went on, turning it in his hand. "Ye thought the pattern opposite the handle looked like a valentine heart."

"And you always made a face when I said that." Her right eye appeared as well, both of them glaring at him.

"Well, ye were relentless, lass." Returning the cup to its miniature saucer, Lachlan turned back to face her and folded his arms over his chest, mostly to keep them from doing something she'd consider ungentlemanly.

"Then you should be relieved that I've set you free. You were glad on Tuesday, when I didn't argue over you telling me we would never suit."

"Ah, that. It turns oot I was wrong."

Rowena sat up, girlishly holding the blankets tucked up beneath her chin. Was she naked under there? His cock twitched at the thought. Perhaps he should have folded his hands in front of him, to keep that fellow behaving himself.

"It took me several weeks to realize how wrong I was about you," she returned, her voice perfectly steady. "How did you manage to overturn eighteen years of thought in four days?"

"I —"

"Let me guess," Rowena interrupted. "You missed having someone fawning over you. And then, to make it worse, you saw men fawning over *me.*"

He narrowed one eye. "That second bit might've been part of what struck me," honesty made him say. "But only because it made me look at ye. Nae, it made me see ye. Nae as ye were, but as ye are."

"And that's why you decided to maul me yesterday, I presume."

There he stood, telling her his true deep feelings, at least as many as he'd presently figured out, and she continued to glare at him like he had horns. And warts. Which he didn't. "That was a kiss, lass. Because I *do* care fer ye, and I *do* intend to woo ye."

Rowena burst into laughter.

"What the devil's so amusing aboot that?"

"It's just . . . We had this conversation a hundred times in my head, and it always sounded so much more romantic." She sighed. "If you're doing this because you miss my attention, then I'm sorry. There are several other young ladies here who've told me they find you handsome, though. If you're sincere, then woo away, but please realize that you're too late. I will not be wooed. Not by you."

Lachlan took a breath, frowning. This was *not* how this conversation was supposed to proceed. "I dunnae think I am too late," he returned. "And I also think ye dunnae realize what ye want. Ye saw all the pretty, mild gents in London and decided ye'd have one fer yerself, because that's what ye ken a lady does. But ye're nae an English lady, Rowena. Ye're a Highlands lass, and soft hands will never do fer ye."

Her chin lifted. "How insightful of you, Lachlan. I suppose it's a good thing, then, that Lord Cairnsgrove is present. He's not an Englishman."

He snorted. "So ye'd marry a man with a yen fer yer brother, just to spite me? I dunnae think ye're as finished with me as ye say."

From her expression she'd already realized the earl's preferences, but she wished he hadn't done so. "I'm not spiting you, Lachlan. Ranulf asked me to choose someone. I'm assessing." Her brow furrowed. "And this is *for* Ranulf, so I will not allow you to

141

ruin it." She took a breath. "You're wrong, anyway. I was born here, but I don't belong here. Not any longer."

It was even worse than he'd realized. "What, are ye English now?"

"I was always half English."

They seemed to be at an impasse. And if Ranulf had made a request rather than an order, Rowena would try to honor it. "I'll tell ye what, lass. Ye see if any of yer pretty lads stirs yer heart. I'll nae interfere, as best I'm able to restrain myself. But at the end of each day I'll come into this room and I'll kiss ye good night."

"Nae. Absolutely not." For the first time in this conversation she sounded unsettled, with her true, sweet brogue slipping into hearing.

"Nae? Then ye'd rather I stomp on toes and punch faces? As ye will, then." He took three long strides to the side of the bed. "I'm nae surrendering, Rowena. That's a fact. I'm a part of this . . . competition, I suppose it is, and I intend to win." He turned for the door.

"And if I allow you to kiss me you'll otherwise behave?"

Lachlan stopped in his tracks, waited a heartbeat, then faced her again. "I cannae promise that. I'm a Highlander, and when I see what I want, I do what needs doing to get it." He paused, knowing he needed to sweeten this arrangement a bit if he wanted her to agree to that nightly kiss — and whatever might come after. "I can promise to give ye time to chat with yer beaux, nae to kill anyone, and nae to begin any clan wars, but only if ye agree to my terms."

She stayed silent for so long he thought he might truly have missed his chance with her after all. And that . . . hurt, somewhere deep in his chest. If someone as alive and spritely as Rowena gave up on him, was she the one losing out, or was it him?

"I suppose I have no real choice then," she said finally. "One kiss each evening, in exchange for you not stepping between me and my future. And you will promise not to begin *any* fights."

"Fights with anyone?" he pursued.

Her mouth twitched. "Fights with my guests. Brawls. Fisticuffs. You will not begin one."

"Aye. I'll agree to that." Especially since *he* was her future, whether she would admit it or not. And anyone else who went in pursuit of her, well, they were beginning trouble. Not him. "Shall we shake on it?"

With a grimace she pulled her right hand from the blankets and held it out. Returning to the bed, Lachlan gripped her fingers, then lifted her hand to brush his lips against her knuckles. "I may be late to this soiree, Rowena," he murmured, reluctantly releasing her fingers, "but I know ye better than anyone."

"Only if you were paying attention. As I recall you spent most of your time trying to escape me. And even if you know what I used to like, I'd wager you don't know me now."

"We'll see aboot that, won't we?"

Once Lachlan left her bedchamber and quietly shut the door behind him, Rowena flopped backward on the bed again. However she felt about him, he certainly had a way of filling a room with his presence.

A kiss every night. She should feel annoyed and angry that he'd used her wish for a few civilized weeks against her, that because she wanted Ranulf to have a perfect wedding she had to break her own oath to stay far away from the so-called charms of Lachlan MacTier. Annoyed, though, didn't quite describe the shivering, unsettled sensation traveling through her gut and up her spine.

What he'd just said to her was the answer to a young girl's romantic dream. Her dream, until a short three months ago. She supposed it couldn't be all that surprising that hearing it now was perhaps just a little thrilling. As for the rest of it, he absolutely didn't know everything about her. How could he, when he'd done nothing more than humor her when she was little, and avoid her when she was old enough — or thought she was — to know what she wanted? And he knew nothing of London and its sophisticated amusements. That was what she truly enjoyed now.

Twenty or so minutes later, a knock sounded at the door. "Who is it?" she called, hoping it wasn't any of her brothers. She didn't feel up to the task of explaining to Ranulf why she wouldn't be marrying Cairnsgrove, or why Lachlan had abruptly decided to pursue her. To woo her.

"It's Mitchell, my lady," her maid's voice came. "Ye said nae to wake ye, but yer brother's taking some of the Sassenach lads fishing, and I thought ye'd want to know."

Oh, dear. Rowena threw off the covers and slid off the bed to her feet. "Come in!" She sat at her dressing table to brush her hair and her teeth as Mitchell went to the wardrobe to find her something suitable to wear. "Which brother?" she asked belatedly, though she could guess.

"Laird Munro. He and Laird Gray walked into the breakfast room, Cooper said, and offered ten pounds and bragging rights to whichever man of them caught the biggest trout by sunset."

"So the ladies have been left behind?"

"Some of 'em have refused to go doon to the loch, but the rest decided to have a picnic luncheon on the shore."

Mitchell held up a pretty white muslin walking dress dotted with red and black flowers. Rowena had chosen the material in London because it bore the MacLawry colors, and she nodded her approval.

"That sounds quite fun, really," she said, standing again to shed her night rail and pull on a light shift, then lifting her arms so Mitchell could slide the gown on over her head. Since Lachlan had gone directly from barging into her bedchamber to organizing a fishing expedition, she was rather surprised it sounded so . . . civilized.

"Aye. Cooper's sent a half-dozen of the footmen doon to the shore to put up a canopy and tables and chairs. I haven't seen so much bustle since the last clan gathering."

"They needn't go to so much trouble," Rowena countered with a frown. She seated herself again so Mitchell could put up her hair. "I'll tell Cooper all we need are some blankets to sit on."

"The brown-haired miss, Lady Edith, isnae? She said the ground was too wet fer sitting doon, and they must have shelter from the Scottish sun." The maid leaned closer. "What's so frightening aboot the Scottish sun? We dunnae even see it that often."

"Ladies need to protect their complexions," Rowena replied with a smile. "Men don't like a lady to have red, blotchy skin."

"I remember ye coming home burned by the sun more than once," Mitchell commented as she finished the single thick braid and began coiling it atop Rowena's head. "Ye looked fine and healthy to me, even if ye did smell a wee bit like fish."

Rowena laughed. "That doesn't sound very ladylike."

It was only since she'd visited London that she'd realized how unusual her childhood had been. Since her fifth birthday she'd been raised entirely by her brothers and her uncle Myles. As far as she'd known, young ladies all went fishing, wore trousers so they could ride astride, learned to use a pistol and a rifle and a sword, and donned very frilly gowns for tea parties.

She knew better now. And so those things

147

Lachlan claimed to know about her didn't signify as anything but a source of embarrassment. If he meant to use them against her, well, she knew a few unsavory things about him. She didn't want this to turn into a war, but neither would she ever — *ever* — waste another moment mooning after Lachlan MacTier.

In fact, just these few moments were too many. Squaring her shoulders, she pulled open her bedchamber door and strode for the stairs. She could walk daintily once she reached the main floor and her guests. Perhaps she hadn't organized today's excursion, but she *could* keep it from dissolving into MacLawry chaos.

"Ye look very determined this morning," Arran said, pausing at the top of the stairs to wait for her.

"Evidently I'm late for a fishing expedition," she returned, hurrying past him.

"The men left but five minutes ago, and the lasses are still choosing their wee parasols." The middle MacLawry brother descended the stairs behind her. "I've a wager with Bear over which lass gets blown into the loch first."

With a scowl she stopped, whipping around to look up at him. "That is not amu . . ." She trailed off as she caught sight of his easy grin. "You're teasing me."

"Aye. Ye had a serious look aboot ye. And since ye're arranging fer a horde of Highlanders to attend a gathering and a wedding, I thought ye could use someone telling ye what a fine job ye're doing of it. Because ye are doing a grand job."

Rowena caught up his uninjured arm and let him escort her the rest of the way down to the main floor. "The Highlanders are just beginning to arrive. No doubt we'll have our first brawl by dinner." And if Lachlan caused it, she wouldn't have to worry about kissing him again, and the unwelcome, fluttery feelings that came with it.

"It wouldnae be a proper wedding withoot a scuffle."

"Hopefully less of a scuffle than you went through." She sighed, hugging his good arm. "I was so worried about you, you know. You might have told me what was afoot. And angry as Ranulf was, he was twice as terrified that you would never reach Scotland alive."

"I ken that," he returned. "Before I met Mary I wouldnae have ever contemplated eloping, much less with a Campbell. Love's an odd beast, Rowena. When it catches hold of ye, ye'll do anything to keep it wrapped aboot ye, whatever the cost."

The mere fact that her clever, logical brother had fled London with Mary Campbell, knowing full well that a horde of angry Campbells was directly on his heels, was proof enough for her that love was mad. In fact, it made her decision to find a calm, cultured man to marry seem all the more sensible. "Where is your Mary, this morning?"

His warm smile returned. "Her stomach's a bit unsettled. I'm on my way to fetch some toast and peppermint tea."

Rowena kissed him on the cheek. "I'm so happy for you, Arran. You're going to make me an aunt."

"I reckon I'm happy fer myself. Give our excuses to yer friends, if ye will."

"Of course."

The moment Winnie grabbed up her own bonnet and parasol and left the house, Arran's smile dropped. "Is Glengask aboot?" he asked Cooper, as the butler sagged against the door. Having so many proper Sassenach about the house was no doubt exhausting.

"Aye, m'laird. Ye'll find him in the stable. Debny says we'll be oot of horse feed by the end of the week."

Nodding, Arran headed back into the depths of the house and then exited by the side door nearest the stable. He tolerated all these English here, but he didn't intend to spend any more time with them than he had to. Not when he had a new bride to keep company. Aside from that, he didn't want any of Winnie's friends, old or new, over-hearing his conversation.

He found the marquis standing beside the head groom as two of the other stableboys finished hitching up a wagon. Howard Howard, the one-eyed former London hack driver who'd helped Mary and him reach the Highlands, sat on the plank seat, the reins in his hands. Arran grinned. Whatever was afoot, he owed Mr. Howard a great deal.

"How are ye liking the Highlands, How-ard?" he asked, reaching up his hand.

The driver wiped his fingers off on his trousers before he shook it. "It's as fine as you described it, Lord Arran. And Glengask here has a fine stable. Very fine. I'm honored you found me employment here." He brushed a hand across his good eye. "You're fine folk, you know."

"Once we get to where we ken what the lad's saying, we'll all be happy as clams," Debny put in with a chuckle.

"Mm-hm. You just keep telling yourselves that I'm the one who talks funny." Howard sniffed. "Are we driving into the village, or aren't we?"

"Ye are," Ranulf put in, stepping back as Debny climbed onto the wagon's set beside the driver. "Dunnae let Tom MacNamara overcharge us fer grain. Remind him we keep his mill in business."

"Aye, m'laird."

"Horse feed?" Arran asked as the wagon rolled off in the direction of Mahldoen.

"Aye. Sassenach nags dunnae ken how to live on sweet Scottish grass, it seems." Ranulf sent him a sideways glance. "How's yer shoulder?"

"I'll nae be wrestling Bear fer a few days, but it's nearly healed." He shrugged to demonstrate. Considering that the ball Charles Calder, the Campbell's grandson, had put through him had been meant for his heart, he felt lucky just to be above ground.

"Good. Are ye going fishing with the rest of 'em?"

"Nae. Mary's staying in bed this morning. I mean to keep her company."

"Ye should, since ye're the one put her there." Ranulf turned back for the house, and Arran fell in beside him. As strained as their relationship had been over the past weeks, with a Campbell peace and Mary pregnant they'd been slowly repairing the

152

damage. Sometimes, though, it felt very like walking across melting ice.

"I had a glimpse of someaught this morning, and I thought ye should know aboot it," Arran said, lowering his voice below the noise of the busy stables behind them.

"I'm listening."

The deerhounds, Fergus and Una, galloped up from the stable and fell in on either side of them. He scratched Una's head, and the dog's wiry tail slapped him on the thigh. "Lachlan came strolling oot of Winnie's bedchamber. And he was grinning like the devil."

Ranulf slowed. "Did he see ye?"

"Nae. I ducked back around the door when I caught sight of him."

"Hm."

"That's all ye have to say?" Arran scowled. "I nearly throttled him right there."

"He told me a few days ago that Rowena was a sister to him, and that he'd nae offer fer her. And I've some likely lads coming in to meet her. So aye, I say 'hm.' They've nae precisely been friendly."

"I've noticed that. And a few months ago I wouldnae have batted an eye to see him there. But . . . it didnae seem a brotherly grin to me." And that was why he'd nearly assaulted Lord Gray before he decided to

153

do a bit of investigating first.

"If it wasnae Lachlan, I'd boot him oot on his arse fer being anywhere alone with her," Ranulf said after a moment. As he looked toward the loch, he narrowed his eyes against the morning sunlight. "I misstepped where ye were concerned, Arran. This time I'm inclined to be more patient."

To hear his confident oldest brother admit to being wrong about anything was rare enough. In this instance . . . Arran swallowed. "*I'll* keep an eye on Lachlan, then, but I'm inclined to think we shouldnae tell Bear."

"Aye. I agree with ye." The marquis resumed his walk to the house. "And I wish ye'd told me aboot Cairnsgrove before I invited him here."

"I would have, if ye'd told me who was on yer list." Arran lifted an eyebrow. "Anyone else I should know aboot?"

"Robert Cranach and Jimmy MacMaster."

That surprised him. "Buchanans? Ye are serious aboot finding Winnie a husband, then."

"I'll nae have her weeping over Lachlan any longer. Or going back to it, if she loses her senses again. I want her to be happy."

Arran nodded. "If ye need Cairnsgrove, ye could always set him after Bear."

Glengask snorted. "That'd be interesting."

"Aye."

CHAPTER SIX

"Nae, it'd be no imposition at all," Lachlan said, washing down a fine haggis with an appalling watered-down wine. "I'd be pleased to show ye Gray House, Lady Jane. It's nae as old as Glengask, but as it was built during the middle of a row with clan MacDonald it's a grand sturdy old fortress."

"Is it haunted?" Sarah Parker asked.

"Don't be silly, Sarah," her sister Susan admonished.

"Oh, aye, it is," he replied. "And it's nae the only one."

"Is that true?" Sarah squeaked, looking across the picnic table at Rowena. "Glengask is haunted?"

Rowena sent Lachlan an annoyed look. "There are stories, of course, but I've never seen anything."

"That's nae what ye used to say." Lachlan had given his word to avoid brawling with any of her male guests; he'd never said he would leave her be. "I recall many a stormy night when ye came running into the billiards room to say old Dougall MacLawry was striding aboot yer bedchamber, playing on his drooned pipes."

Beside him Jane shivered. "What are drooned pipes?" she whispered.

"Drowned pipes," Rowena said in her careful accent. "Dougall was my five times great-uncle. The story is that he spied the Campbells riding down on Glengask and grabbed up his bagpipes to warn the castle. A Campbell scout snuck up behind him and cut his throat and threw both Dougall and his pipes into the loch." She gestured at the wind-rippled water behind her. "His warning was heard, though, and the castle stood."

"And to this day on stormy nights he sounds his pipes to alert the castle," Lachlan finished. "So they say."

"My heavens," Sarah breathed. "That's terrifying."

"It's romantic," Jane Hanover countered. "Unless you're not a MacLawry. Which I am." She smiled. "Or I will be in a few days, anyway."

"Is he only seen in your bedchamber, Winnie?" Susan Parker put her hand over her heart.

"Yes," she answered, before Lachlan could

even open his mouth to reply in the negative. Rowena sent him another hard glare. "My bedchamber was once his," she lied.

"Oh, thank goodness."

"Is he the only spirit here?" Sarah Parker had her eyes squeezed almost shut in clear dismay.

From the opposite end of the table Bear pounded his mug against the table, though how he'd managed to obtain beer when the rest of them had to suffer through the damned Madeira, Lachlan had no idea. "I had a ghost hound sleeping across the foot of my bed just last month," he declared. "Cold as death, it was."

The ladies gasped. Except for Rowena, who looked truly dismayed. There she was, trying to make them all look civilized, and Glengask Castle itself stood against her. Lachlan gazed at her for a long moment. She adored ghost stories. He knew that for a fact. But in front of her Sassenach friends, she chose to pretend otherwise.

"Ye're daft, Bear," he heard himself say. "That was yer own wet coat, and ye know it."

Jane laughed, and the rest followed suit just like the sheep most of them seemed to be. Lachlan barely noticed, though. His attention remained on Rowena, at the surprise in her tempestuous gray eyes, and the slight curve to her lips before she hid her mouth behind a delicate napkin.

"If ye want a tale," he went on, "ye should have Owen tell ye aboot the old Jacobite tunnels below the castle."

"They're nae Jacobite tunnels," Bear corrected. "There's nae a Jacobite in 'em."

"What are they, then?"

Munro grinned at Sarah Parker. "Escape tunnels. In case the English army comes calling. If ye need to flee, head fer the kitchen pantry. Then, if ye can brave the rats and spiders and ghosts, ye'll find yerself oot in one of the canyons close by."

"But can't people get in through the tunnels? That doesn't seem very secure."

"The outside entrance isnae easy to find," Lachlan continued, glancing again at Rowena to see that she'd relaxed now that her Sassenach friends weren't being regaled with barbaric, fanciful tales. "It's impossible to find, really, unless someone's shown it to ye. Dunnae worry; even if we werenae at peace, ye'd all be safe here."

"Precisely," Rowena added. "Have you decided which games you'll have for the gathering, by the way?" she asked him.

At least she was speaking to him, if only because he'd helped her out. "Nae. Fer all yer Sass — friends here, I thought a horse race and mayhap the stone put." Considering he actually hadn't given it a moment of thought since she'd ordered him to help organize the games, that seemed fairly tame and gentle.

"May anyone enter these contests?" Samston asked, practically the first noise he'd uttered in better than a day.

"Aye," Lachlan answered. "If ye've the courage to attempt it, we're all willing to watch ye fail."

The earl's cheeks darkened. "I'd wager a hundred quid on my King against any Highlands nag." He sent a pointed glance at Rowena.

That settled that. Lachlan stood. "Oot of the tent, ye frilly fop," he growled. "Where there's more room to beat ye senseless."

"Lachlan!" Rowena said sharply. "I will not see a brawl over horse insults."

From her expression she knew precisely what had angered him, and that sent his blood boiling. She knew she'd just been insulted, and because she was pretending to be English, he was supposed to ignore it. Not bloody likely. "Dunnae trouble yerself," he snapped, striding around the table toward Samston. "I'll nae pummel him until I've dragged him oot of sight over the hill."

"This is ridiculous!" The earl jumped to his feet, but only to begin moving backward away from Lachlan's approach.

"We had a deal, Lord Gray."

Rowena's statement stopped him in his tracks. Clearly she would use this as an excuse to avoid kissing him, even if he'd only leaped to defend her honor. Taking a deep breath, he jabbed a finger into Samston's chest. "We value our horses here," he rumbled, "and we dunnae insult another man's . . . property unless we're willing to defend our idiotic commentary with our own blood. Keep that in mind, ye fool." Turning his back, he walked around the table and resumed his seat.

A long, awkward silence ensued, and of course Rowena would blame him for that, as well. This would have all been much easier if she still thought he walked on water. Even Bear looked mildly surprised, but then the mountain didn't know Samston had kissed his sister and been rebuked.

"So ye two are going to race, then, I take it?" Bear finally said. "Because if ye're putting a hundred quid on yerself, Samston, I'll take that wager. Against both of ye."

Lord Bask, one of the other Sassenach, then decided to join the race himself, though he was a bit more polite with his bragging about his Arabian, Lucifer. Half the black horses in Mayfair were evidently named Lucifer or Satan, but then Lachlan supposed it made a soft lad feel powerful, to say he rode the devil.

"Could there be a lady's race?" Lady Edith asked.

"Aye. Fair warning, though — Rowena and her Black Agnes have won at the last two games. And those were MacLawry games. We'll have half a dozen clans here, this time."

"I meant to ask you, Winnie," Jane broke in with her customary good humor, "why did you name a white mare Black Agnes?"

Rowena smiled. "She's named after Black Agnes Randolph. She held her keep against the English army even with her husband off fighting elsewhere. The Earl of Salisbury left without breaking Dunbar Castle's walls after five months of trying. Lachlan's own mother was called Agnes after her."

"So she's a heroine," Jane said with a nod. "But not a ghost."

Bear shook his head. "Two hundred years ago Parliament ordered Dunbar dismantled so nae two stones lay together. But they say Black Agnes still roams the hillside where it once stood."

"Goodness." Sarah Parker sighed with a

smile. "Perhaps I should have asked if there's anywhere in the Highlands that isn't haunted."

After that the conversation returned to fishing and the dance that Rowena was apparently arranging for tomorrow night. Lachlan hadn't heard a word about it until then, and he hadn't been invited, either, but he'd be damned if he'd miss a chance to show Rowena he could dance a jig as well as any English aristocrat.

"We have more guests arriving," Bear said, his gaze on the road that wound down by the loch before it climbed up the long hill to Glengask. "Two men, on horseback."

It wouldn't be any Campbells, then, because even with a peace between the clans none of them would dare arrive in such small numbers. And the clan MacLawry chieftains were all bringing family and whoever they'd chosen to compete in the games. Lachlan turned his gaze back to Rowena, to find her watching the figures on the road, as well.

"James MacMaster and Robert Cranach, do ye reckon?" he said quietly.

She blinked. "You know about them?" she whispered, leaning across the table toward him.

He wanted to kiss those slightly parted

lips, feel her soft breath on his face. "Aye. Do ye figure they're more like Cairnsgrove, or Samston?" he returned in the same tone.

"Hush." Rowena glanced toward the end of the table, where Cairnsgrove chatted with William Peabody. "Perhaps all I care about is that neither one is you."

Well, that cut deeper than he cared to admit. Lachlan forced a smile. "If that was true, lass, ye'd already have chosen a man. And ye havenae, so this race isnae over."

"I'm not a trophy to be won."

"Nae. Ye choose the winner. Just dunnae ferget, I'm in this race just as much as any other of yer shiny lads. And I dunnae mean to lose."

That was the complication, though — she was the MacLawry's only sister, and Ranulf had left the choice up to her. A hundred years ago, fifty years ago, even, and he would have simply stolen her away in the night, thrown her over his saddle, and found a priest to declare them handfasted.

Now, though, he was supposed to be a gentleman in a contest with other, more practiced gentlemen. And he already had a black mark against him, simply because he hadn't realized until a few days ago that she'd become a lovely, desirable young woman.

He didn't like it, at all. But unless or until he came up with a better solution, he would have to play her game. Luckily he wasn't above cheating — or anything else that would help him win.

Half an hour after the pair of riders disappeared around the side of the hill, a trio of men came walking down the path to the loch. Most of the male guests had returned to fishing, but not all of them. Not the one she most wished would go somewhere else and give her time to think.

It had to be Munro who'd told Lachlan about her newest prospective suitors. Ranulf would never have thought to do so, and Arran wouldn't on principle. Glaring at her brother's broad back as he whipped his fishing pole about wouldn't do her any good now, however. Neither would scowling at Lachlan where he sat between Jane and Edith beneath the canopy and apparently tried to learn how to embroider. Either he was a terrible student, though, or he had most of his attention on the newcomers, as well.

Dash it, why wouldn't he go back to fishing? It had all likely been his idea, anyway.

But he sat there well within hearing — likely still just causing trouble because she

165

no longer found him irresistible. That excuse, though, didn't make quite as much sense as it had before he'd kissed her at Castle Teàrlag. Before he'd grabbed her up in his arms just as she'd imagined since she'd turned fifteen and her stating she would marry him began to mean something more . . . romantic. Something sexual.

Her cheeks heated, and she took a sip of Madeira. Just because she'd had those thoughts about him didn't mean she couldn't now have them for anyone else. For heaven's sake, she'd been ready to fall in love with Samston, until she'd realized that he cared for her wealth more than he did her heart. She'd been excited and hopeful upon meeting Cairnsgrove, even if that had only lasted for ten minutes or so.

Now, she meant to be cautiously hopeful and wise. Ranulf preferred Lord Robert Cranach. Six months ago she would therefore have chosen anyone but Lord Robert — if, of course, she hadn't already been set on Lachlan. Well, she wasn't set on Lachlan any longer, and Ranulf had only asked instead of ordered.

The tall, imposing man in the middle of the other two couldn't be anyone other than the Marquis of Glengask. To his right, the man was slighter but stout, with wheat-colored hair and a wide jaw. He wasn't as handsome as Lachlan, though in all honesty few men were.

Rowena turned her attention to the man on her brother's left. The first thing she noticed was his long black riding coat and the way it flapped against the back of his worn black riding boots. Could a coat be romantic? It did seem poetical, at least.

Beneath the coat he stood taller by half a head than his cousin, his face longer and narrower and his eyes a very pleasing warm brown. He wore his dark gold hair close-cropped and neat, and his gaze moved from her to Ranulf as the men conversed.

As the trio reached the canopy, she stood, hardly noting as the rest of the ladies present did the same. What she *did* note was that she very much hoped the man in the black riding coat would be Lord Robert Cranach.

"Rowena," Ranulf said, gesturing at her to approach, "I've added two more guests to yer list. I hope ye dunnae mind, *piuthar.*"

"Of course not, *bràthair.* The more, the merrier."

"Good." He indicated the shorter man. "Then Rowena, may I introduce ye to James MacMaster? James, my sister, Rowena."

"Very pleased, Lady Rowena," he drawled

in a light Highlands accent. But then he spent time in London. Ranulf had told her both Buchanan men did.

She curtsied. "Likewise, Mr. MacMaster."

"And this is Lord Robert Cranach, younger brother to the Marquis of Helvy. Rob, my sister."

The black riding coat sketched a very elegant bow. "My Lady Rowena. Ye truly are as lovely as all the gossips say."

The Highlands touched his voice as well, but clearly he'd spent a great deal of time elsewhere. Belatedly Rowena inclined her head. "Lord Robert. I'm very pleased to meet you."

He smiled. "I'm going to be forward, because I see all these lads here looking at ye. I hear you're holding a dance tomorrow night, and I would very much like a waltz with ye, my lady."

Oh, this was much better than she'd expected. "I shall put your name on my card, then."

On Ranulf's other side, Mr. MacMaster gave a loud sigh. "I knew this would happen. A lass casts her peepers on Rob, and the rest of us may as well be goats."

Rowena laughed, aware that she likely sounded a little giddy. She certainly felt that way. "Well, if you'll each lend me an arm, I will be happy to introduce you to everyone."

They promptly complied, and with her in the middle she guided them to the group sitting the farthest from Lachlan. She intentionally hadn't looked in his direction since the men had appeared on the trail, but she was certain she could feel his gaze on her. She didn't care, of course, that he knew who they were and why they were at Glengask. At least they'd been invited. He just appeared whenever he felt like it, which seemed to be all the time.

When she couldn't put off the introduction any longer, she stopped in front of where he still sat, ankles crossed, while on either side Jane and Edith stood primly. The ladies, of course, were perfectly polite and friendly. Her jaw clenched, she met Lachlan's gaze. Such pretty green eyes, he had — and she wished them and the rest of him to the bottom of the loch.

"James, Lord Robert, this is our neighbor," she announced, putting as much social distance between herself and Lachlan as she could. "Lord Gray, James MacMaster and Lord Robert Cranach."

Slowly, almost lazily, he climbed to his feet. "MacMaster, Lord Robert," he drawled. If he felt the need to demonstrate that he was the tallest of the three, he was wasting his time. She already knew precisely how tall he was. And that had nothing to do with anything, the aggravating man.

"Gray." Lord Robert inclined his head.

"Ye didnae come all the way from Fort William on horseback, did ye?" he asked, offering his hand.

Lord Robert shook it. "No," he answered. "We've a coach a few hours behind us. I prefer to ride when I can."

"And I didn't want to be left behind," James added.

"The —"

"My brother Munro is, of course, fishing," she said quickly, before Lachlan could challenge them to an arm-wrestling match or something. "With the rest of the men. Shall we?"

"I am yours to command," Lord Robert said grandly, gesturing with his free hand.

Rowena's feet barely touched the ground as she led the two men from clan Buchanan down to the shore and made the rest of the introductions. If the next fortnight went as splendidly as the previous thirty minutes, Lachlan MacTier could shout about prizes and winning them until he was blue in the face, and it wouldn't matter a whit.

Because while he might have bullied her into a few kisses, that only made him less a gentleman. And she wanted a damned gentleman.

Lachlan straightened, watching as the yellow billiards ball rolled into the top left corner pocket — precisely where he hadn't wanted it to go. *"Ya bas,"* he grumbled at it.

"Cursing at the wee thing willnae save ye." Bear chuckled.

"I thought you were playing red," Arnold Peabody commented from one of the chairs at the side of the room.

"He was," his brother said from the adjacent chair.

"And with that, I'm off." Lachlan tossed the cue to Bear, who deftly caught it and offered it over to Jimmy MacMaster.

"I mustn't refuse, for the pride o' clan Buchanan," MacMaster said, taking the stick and helping Bear reset the table.

And just like that, I'm replaced, Lachlan thought sourly, as he pulled on his coat. "I'll see ye in the morning, Bear. Ye've nae forgotten, I hope, that ye gave yer word to help me drive yer damned cattle off the south field so I can get my wheat in the ground."

"Aye. I'll be there."

"Oh, that sounds like jolly fun," Lord Bask said, looking up from the game of faro he and Cranach and Edith's brother Victor were playing. "Count me in."

While at another time Lachlan might have had something choice to say about Sassenach riding all over his fields, tonight he had better things to do. He nodded. "As ye will."

He could spend the night at Glengask if he chose; he'd done so countless times before. But if he did so, that would rob him of his excuse for leaving the billiards room before dawn. And he had a rendezvous to keep.

The moment he was out of sight he changed directions, heading up the stairs rather than down. In the back of his mind he knew that by not telling Munro what he was about — and worse, by not correcting what had become the lie he'd told Ranulf — he was betraying MacLawry trust. They allowed him into this castle, into their lives as part of their family, and now he was sneaking about like a thief. He *was* a thief, out to steal Rowena's virtue, her heart, and her hand.

He could tell them what he intended, he supposed, if he couched it in the proper terms. After all, Glengask had *invited* men in for exactly the same purpose. But firstly he had enough pride to want to be certain he would succeed before he risked being laughed at or, worse, turned away. Secondly, if any of the MacLawry brothers realized his intentions, they'd be within their rights to bury him in his own wheat field.

Outside Rowena's doorway he slowed, looked about for servants and errant guests, then lowered the handle and slipped inside, closing the door silently behind him.

"I can't believe you actually think I'm going through with this."

Rowena sat in one of the chairs before the fireplace, an open book in her lap. She hadn't changed out of her evening gown; evidently she didn't want him seeing her in her night rail again, which was a damned shame.

"I do think ye are," he returned, walking over and dropping into the adjacent chair.

"You nearly came to blows with Lord Samston. The agreement was that you would behave yourself."

"The agreement was that I wouldnae start a fight. I didnae. He did, and I still didnae bloody his nose. Even after he insulted ye. Because ye asked me nae to do it. So give me some damned credit fer that, at least."

She shook her head. "It wasn't necessary. No one but Jane knew he was insulting me."

"I knew. And more importantly, *you*

knew," he returned, emphasizing the word. "And I imagine he'll nae do it again, so dunnae expect me to apologize."

"No, that would be too much to expect." Rowena sighed.

He leaned over and took the book from her lap. *"Culpepper's Medicine,"* he read. "So ye're a physician now? Or were ye pretending to read so I wouldnae think ye've been sitting here, thinking of me?"

Retrieving the book, she set it on the end table at her elbow. "This is silly, Lachlan. And it doesn't mean anything."

"If it doesnae mean anything, why are ye trying so hard to weasel oot of it?"

"I'm nae — not — weaseling out of anything. I'm just . . . I'm trying to tell you that a few kisses aren't going to sway me. And more than that, every time you intend to sneak in here for no good reason, you're risking your friendship with Bear and everyone else. And with me."

"That's fine. I dunnae want to be yer friend."

Her gray eyes, flecked with orange-reflected firelight, blinked. "You don't?"

He shook his head. "Nae. Friends are fer tea parties and mud throwing and games of billiards. I want more than that from ye, Rowena."

Abruptly she stood up and walked to her bed and back again. "Lord Robert's very charming."

"Of course he is," Lachlan returned, not bothering to hide his scowl. "I could be charming and ask ye to please write my name on yer wee dance card and lift my pinkie when I drink tea if all I wanted was fer ye to think me a gentleman."

A brief smile touched her mouth and then vanished again. "I would never think you a gentleman."

"I walked into that one," he conceded. "But ye used to think me a gentleman."

"That was before I knew what one was, Lach. You're too late now."

He pushed to his feet, as well. "If I'm nae a gentleman, then, there's no sense dancing aboot ye."

Rowena took a half-step backward as he advanced on her, and he immediately slowed. Whatever he wanted of her, having her turn around and scream for help wasn't any part of it. When she stopped and lifted her chin, her gaze trailing from his eyes to his mouth, he couldn't help smiling.

"This isn't amusing," she declared, her fists clenching and unclenching.

"I'm nae amused. I'm pleased."

"Pleased? Why are y—"

175

"Because ye're nervous, ye fierce lass," he murmured, and took one long step forward.

He touched his mouth to hers. Rowena kept her lips tightly closed, but instead of insisting she cooperate, he only changed tactics. Feather-light, he brushed at the corners of her mouth, advancing and retreating until her lips softened with a sigh that drove sensation all the way down to his cock.

"Rowena," he breathed, and closed on her again. Cupping her face in his hands, he teased at her mouth, the tug and pull between them almost palpable. When she slid her arms over his shoulders, he couldn't help smiling again.

"Stop that," she mumbled, kissing him back.

"Nae."

Eventually she would come to her senses and push him away. So as much as he wanted to continue touching her, with a last nibble at her lower lip he backed away. As well as he knew her, or thought he knew her, he couldn't read the expression on her face. He wanted to know what she was thinking — and more importantly, feeling — but for likely the first time ever he had no idea where even to begin.

When she shifted he tensed his muscles,

ready for either a slap or a kiss. Instead of touching him, though, she finally broke her gaze from his and walked past him. As he turned to watch she reached the door and faced him again.

"Good night, Lachlan," she said, and lowered the latch.

"That's all ye have to say?" he returned, just remembering to keep his voice down. The idea that he was sneaking about the house would still take some getting used to, apparently.

"We have an agreement, and I satisfied it. Now go, before Bear comes by and takes an axe to ye."

"I'm nae satisfied, Rowena, but I'll do as ye ask." He stopped directly in front of her. "I reckon ye'd best put my name on yer wee dance card fer tomorrow night as well, because I *will* be dancing with ye."

She swallowed. "I'll give ye a quadrille."

Lachlan put his hand over hers where she held the door handle. "I'll have a waltz."

"I promised the waltz to Rob."

" 'Rob,' is it?" he said softly. "It's yer party. Have yer fiddler play two waltzes. One of 'em's mine."

"Lachlan," she said, lowering her head.

"Yer word, lass."

Finally she blew out her breath. "Fine.

Ye'll have a waltz. Now go away."

Her words might have sounded annoyed, but her tone didn't quite match. And neither did the way her gaze lowered again to his mouth, as though she couldn't quite stop herself. And then there was the way she'd forgotten to speak like a Sassannach, something he wasn't about to point out to her. Not when he could hear her sweet brogue again.

"All right, then. *Oidche mhath.* Good night, Rowena. And dunnae ferget, I'll be back up here tomorrow night, after yer soiree." Releasing her hand, he let her pull open the door.

"You're still not a gentleman, Lachlan. And a gentleman's what I want," she whispered at his back as he slipped into the hallway.

"It isnae," he returned, and headed out for a cold, uncomfortable ride home.

CHAPTER SEVEN

"Are ye looking for someone?" Rob Cranach asked, moving through the soiree crowd to hand over a glass of tepid lemonade.

Rowena blinked, then took a long swallow of the tart liquid to give herself a moment to think. Her brothers — and Lachlan — had let her drink whisky on occasion, and she could have used a glass tonight. Last night she hadn't even fallen asleep until almost dawn, and then the next three hours had been interrupted by dreams of Lachlan dancing with her and kissing her and doing some other things that were rather hazy and nebulous, but as she recalled felt both wicked and very pleasurable.

And then all day she'd seen no sign of Lachlan at all. She knew Bear and some of the other men had ridden the two miles to Gray House to help him clear stray cattle from one of his fallow fields, but Bear was back in time to lead a ride out to Madainn Srath so he could regale everyone with the tale of Lady Teàrlag.

It was frustrating. All day she'd gone about with a retort ready on her lips, a response to his final comment last night, and then he'd failed to appear. He knew full well she would be walking with Lord Robert, that she might even have requested his help with setting up the rarely used formal ballroom at Glengask — not that he would know anything about proper soirees.

Of course Gray House was a significant property in its own right, and he had the last planting of the year to see to. But the timing, she decided, was likely intentional. He *knew* she would have something to say to him, and that if he was present he would compare unfavorably to the suave and charming Rob.

"Lady Rowena?"

Oh, and now Lachlan had her distracted again. Silently she added that to her list of grievances against him. "I'm sorry, Rob," she said aloud. "I've never organized such a large party before. It has me a bit at sea." It sounded plausible at least, though in truth she should probably be spending more time than she was worrying about the soiree.

"Well, ye have nothing to worry about, my

lady," he said with a smile. "I've been in Mayfair ballrooms that couldn't hold a candle to this one."

"Thank you for saying so."

Jane came skipping up, her older sister in tow. "Winnie, tell Charlotte we can have as many waltzes as we want."

"I didn't disagree," Charlotte said with a grin. "I only said having a dozen waltzes may see us mistaken for a bawdy house."

"This house has been a great many things," Ranulf put in, joining them, "but it's nae ever been nor is it ever going to be a bawdy house. One waltz, Rowena."

That would free her from her promise to Lachlan. Even so, she felt oddly disappointed, and that was without Lachlan even being present. "Well, now you'll have us mistaken for Parliament," she stated. "Three waltzes."

Her oldest brother looked at Charlotte. "How many times might a man dance with his betrothed in his own house, *leannan*?" he asked her.

Charlotte cleared her throat. "Three times. But only two waltzes."

Ranulf swung his head back in Rowena's direction. "Ye see, someone who gives me a straight, honest answer. Two waltzes. But ye'd best have yer fiddlers play one now."

"I shall escort you," Rob said, offering his arm.

She wrapped her hand around his sleeve. "Ranulf knows the fiddlers prefer being called violinists," she commented. "He's very stubborn, though."

"He's made a good life for his clan," Lord Robert returned. "He can call them whatever he chooses, as far as I'm concerned."

Like her brothers and Lord Cairnsgrove, Rob and James MacMaster had donned their plaid for the evening. All her female friends from London seemed to find men wearing kilts naughty and exotic, but to her this was just what Highlanders wore. She could admit that Rob and her brothers, at least, made it look very handsome, indeed. The Buchanan yellow, green, and red was bonny, but it was odd and . . . disconcerting to think that she might soon be trading the MacLawry black, white, and red for other colors, for other loyalties.

She caught the attention of one of the violinists on the overlooking balcony and requested a waltz. Then Rob led her out to the center of the floor, put his hand on her waist, and they began to dance.

The dance floor filled. Ranulf and Charlotte, Arran and Mary, Bear and — oh, dear — Jane. Nearly everyone had left their seats,

and she began to breathe a little more easily. As she was the only MacLawry female
present this was her responsibility after all,
and it would be so until Charlotte and
Ranulf were wed. And then, well, she would
be unnecessary here — except for the alliance she might secure with her own marriage.

That wasn't entirely true, of course,
because she could never feel useless or unneeded where her family was concerned.
She was the only sister of the MacLawry,
after all, and nothing separated the Mac-
Lawry siblings. Nothing.

"I wish I'd been in London to see your
debut, my lady." Rob smiled at her. "I had
business in Inverness that took longer than
it should have."

"Do you go to London often?" she asked.
A Highlander who could waltz, treat her
with deference and respect, and who didn't
view London as the lowest pit of hell. It was
marvelous, really.

"I try to go at least twice a year," he
returned. "This is the first Season in four
that I've missed."

"What was your business in Inverness, if I
may ask?"

"Sheep. Wool, actually. I oversee the sale
of raw wool to the mills on my brother's

behalf. And this year, well . . ." He paused, lowering his voice and moving a breath closer to her. "This year I negotiated a majority ownership of the two largest mills in the city for clan Buchanan."

"Well. Congratulations," she said, burying her uneasiness at the mention of sheep. Clan MacLawry didn't raise sheep, except for the handful of the Highland breed they kept for their own mills and their own use. Sheep meant cotters pushed off land to make room for grazing. It meant emptying the Highlands of her own people. And that was everything the MacLawrys stood against.

Ranulf knew the Buchanans made most of their wealth from mutton and wool, though. And he'd selected both Robert Cranach and James MacMaster as possible suitors for her. Therefore, the Buchanans had something he wanted or needed for the clan. He wouldn't be promoting an alliance, otherwise.

"Ye have a very serious look in your eyes," Rob noted, as they continued twirling about the room.

"Do I? That happens so rarely."

He chuckled. "Good."

She wasn't certain what he meant by that, but she smiled anyway. This, a lovely party with her new friends, a waltz in the arms of a handsome man who paid attention to her and complimented her — it felt perfect.

And then she saw him, and nearly stumbled over her own feet. Lachlan Mac-Tier. The rest of the Highlands men wore kilts, but not him. Not tonight. No, tonight he'd donned a long-tailed jacket of dark gray, tan buckskin breeches, and polished black Hessian-looking boots with yellow tassels. His shirt was snowy white, his waistcoat black and gray, his cravat crisp and neat. He looked . . . Rowena twisted her head to keep him in view as she wove about the dance floor.

He looked as well and properly dressed as any English gentleman present — better, in fact, than most of them. She hadn't even known that he owned Sassennach clothes, or that he would ever deign to wear them if he did.

Before Robert Cranach could question why she was staring, mouth agape, the waltz ended. Belatedly she joined in the applause, then smiled at her partner. "That was lovely. Thank you."

"Don't thank me, my lady. It was my pleasure." He glanced from her to Lachlan and back again. "A rival, I presume?"

"Lachlan? Heavens, no." She deliberately

waited until Lord Gray was in hearing before she continued. "He's always saying he's like another brother to me."

"A brotherhood of Highlanders, I reckon," Lachlan countered. "I apologize fer being late, Rowena. We planted half the south field before I realized the cattle werenae coming in through the fence. They were coming doon the stream bed and up the far side. So I've a bonny new fence along the bank, now."

She wanted to say she hadn't even noticed he wasn't there, but it sounded petty even in her own head. Aside from that, planting a field only to have it trampled and eaten could be a disaster — not just for Lachlan, but for his cotters and the miller and all the related shopkeepers and on and on. Ranulf always said the smallest of disasters could cause much larger ones.

"Well done, then," she said instead.

"It's nae as exciting as a soiree, but it couldnae wait until tomorrow." He took in the white-and-gold-decorated ballroom. "I hope I didnae miss all the good dances." Sharp green eyes met hers.

"Only the first four," Rob answered for her. "I see your brother is looking at me rather pointedly. Will ye excuse me, lass?"

"Of course."

"So Glengask was looking at him, eh?" Lachlan said, mimicking Rob's lighter accent with surprising accuracy. "I dunnae suppose Ranulf has looked at anyone else half as pointedly tonight."

Rowena turned her back and went to find Jane. She was not going to listen to him making fun of the man she was most likely going to marry. And Jane might well need her help. The only thing worse than her friend falling for Lachlan would be seeing her lose her heart to Munro. Most ladies had learned by now not to risk anything that precious where her brother was concerned.

A hand caught her arm. "One glare?" Lachlan said, moving around in front of her. "That's a wee effort, Rowena."

"Why did you dress like an Englishman?"

He glanced down at his splendid attire and straightened his coat. "English is what ye say ye like, isnae?"

"You're not English, however you decide to dress."

Lachlan gestured at Rob's retreating backside. "Neither is Lord Rob Cranach."

"No, he's a Highlander. Unlike you, though, he can discuss the theater and fashion and literature."

"So can Cairnsgrove."

"But Rob also tells me I'm pretty and

187

desirable and he doesn't argue with me over everything. He likes me."

"He likes what yer dowry can do fer the Buchanans, ye mean."

Rowena clenched her fist. "Now you've insulted both Rob and me. You deserve a slap for that."

"But ye'll nae do that, will ye, lass?" He grinned, and she involuntarily glanced at his mouth before she caught herself. "If this was a Highlands party, ye would."

He was quite possibly the most aggravating man she'd ever met, Rowena decided. "I thought you were attempting to look and act like an Englishman," she said as evenly as she could. "If that's the case, I'm afraid it's a very poor impersonation."

Moss-green eyes studied her for a long moment. "Ye wish me nae to speak what's on my mind, then," he finally murmured, "and to smile and tell ye flattering things to convince ye that I'm the lad for ye. I can manage that."

"That isn't —" With a barely stifled growl she stopped herself. She could protest that he had to mean what he said, but he would only counter that she had no way of knowing whether he — or anyone else — was being sincere or not. And then she would begin to wonder how many of Rob's compliments were calculated to win her approval. Damn it all, she couldn't help doing that now. "Don't bother," she said instead.

"Nae. I'll be a gentleman fer ye, lass." With that he offered his arm, giving her the choice of walking with him or stomping away like a madwoman from what looked like a very proper gesture.

She wrapped her hand around his sleeve. "Take me to the refreshment table."

They walked in that direction, though he seemed to be taking a rather roundabout route. "Ye see? Very proper."

"Don't talk to me."

"But then I cannae say yer hair is black and shiny as a raven's wings, or that yer eyes are the color of a stormy sky."

She dug her fingers into the cloth around his arm. "That's not flattery," she stated. "You're only making a mockery of gentlemanly behavior."

"Am I now?" He lifted an eyebrow. "How so?"

"You only picked poetical items with the correct colors, as if I'm supposed to think you think of me poetically. We both know you don't, though."

"So I should've said yer eyes glare at me like an angry wildcat's, and yer hair's as black as my own heart? I've nae heard any

Sassenach be that honest."

"Perhaps not," she admitted, refusing to be amused. "But from you, I require honesty." Rowena grimaced. "I viewed you through a rainbow's colors for far too long." She'd asked him for honesty, so she supposed she was obligated to be truthful, herself.

"Is that it, then?" he asked abruptly, lowering his arm and turning to face her squarely, looking down to meet her upturned gaze. "Ye imagined me to be some sort of Galahad, and now ye blame me because I'm nae the man that I never was?"

"That doesn't make any sense." She started past him, but he shifted to block her path.

"Aye, it does," he countered. "And ye still have that rainbow wrapped aboot ye. It colors how ye look at all these lads. Ye're fooling yerself, Rowena. And I'm the only one ye see clearly now. It scares ye, doesnae? After all that talk aboot London and gentlemen and Society, the man ye've always wanted was me. And now ye've realized I'm nae some Beau Brummell, so ye cannae admit ye still like me."

"I can't admit I still like you, because I don't," she protested, her jaw beginning to ache from being clenched so hard. "You're the worst man I know."

"I'm the only one nae pretending to be someaught I'm not," he snapped, the line of his mouth flattening.

"Ha!" she retorted. "Look at yerself, dressed like a Sassenach because ye think that's what I want."

"Aye, I did dress fancy fer ye. But now I've figured ye oot, and I willnae do it again."

"Ye dunnae have any idea aboot me! Now leave this house before I —"

"The two of ye separate. Now." Ranulf stepped between them so quickly it startled her. "Whatever the devil's got ye fighting, ye can settle it tomorrow. Lachlan, ye'd best leave."

"Nae," the viscount countered, to Rowena's surprise. Lachlan was Ranulf's closest ally. He always acted to support and enforce Glengask. Always.

"Dunnae make me ask ye a second time. Go. I'll talk with ye tomorrow."

"Rowena promised me a waltz. I mean to have it."

The heated tone of his voice surprised her. No one spoke to Ranulf like that, especially when he was being so evenhanded. But Lachlan didn't seem to care. Rather, his gaze remained fixed on her, as if nothing

191

else — no one else — existed. None of this was a jest, she realized. He did want her for himself.

Abruptly the floor seemed to fall away from beneath her, leaving her scrambling for balance, a toehold, anything to keep her from gaping at him, openmouthed. Lachlan MacTier wanted her. *Her.* For eighteen years nearly every waking and sleeping thought had centered on this man. And as she struggled to keep her expression level, she realized she truly had no idea how to react to him now. It didn't change anything, of course — it couldn't. But even so . . . If nothing had changed about what she meant to do with her life, why did she feel so . . . different, suddenly?

"I cannae have outsiders seeing MacLawrys fighting amongst ourselves, Lach. I willnae have it." Ranulf's gaze could have frozen water.

Oh, no. This was not supposed to happen. Rowena tried to bring her thoughts back into some kind of order. Lord Gray was an integral part of the clan. If something happened to change that — and it now seemed quite possible — none of them would be the better for it. And however confused she felt, she certainly didn't want Lachlan banished, anyway. "I —"

Abruptly Bear put his arm across Lachlan's shoulders. "What say we go doon to the Bonny Bruce and ye buy us a large quantity of liquor?" he rumbled.

Lachlan shrugged out of her brother's grip, then visibly shook himself. "I dunnae need ye to drink with me. I can see to it myself." With a last look at Rowena, he turned on his heel and left the ballroom.

"What the devil was that aboot?" Munro demanded, frowning at her.

"I don't have time to discuss it with you," she said, trying to sound unconcerned and gather her wits back together. "I have guests to see to."

"Rowena," Ranulf said, his tone iron.

"I don't want to cause a scene, Ranulf. Please."

His shoulders lowered. "Aye. Ten o'clock in the morning, in my office."

She nodded. "Thank you."

So now she had twelve hours to decide what to tell Ranulf, when she didn't even know what to tell herself. All she wanted was a proper, romantic life with a man who might care for her as much as she cared for him.

And now the man she'd once thought of as her knight in shining armor was acting like a madman. Everything would be simpler if Lachlan just stayed away. At the same time she couldn't rid herself of her thoughts about his scheduled visit for later tonight — not because she looked forward to his kiss, but because she worried about the trouble he might make if he decided she'd broken their bargain.

"That was . . . unsettling," Bear rumbled. "I dunnae think I've ever seen the two of them argue. Tease, aye, but nae fight."

"She always agreed with everything he uttered, before," Ranulf returned, watching as his sister and youngest sibling pasted a smile on her face and went to ask her uncle Myles to dance a quadrille with her. For a lass so interested in being married, and one with a dozen eager lads dancing attendance on her at her own soiree, Myles was a curious choice. Unless, that was, she needed a moment to shake off thoughts of someone else.

"Are ye expecting Rob Cranach to offer fer her?" Munro swung around to pin a look at the Marquis of Helvy's brother.

"Aye, I expect he will."

"Mayhap she felt the need to tell Lach that he missed his chance. Though that would likely make him happy. Could be he said that, though. I —"

"Bear, ye'll set yer brains on fire if ye keep

thinking so hard." Ranulf clapped him on the shoulder. "I reckon we'll nae decipher any of it tonight."

"Am I missing someaught?"

"I'd say that's more likely than nae," Ranulf answered, because Munro would expect some sort of insult, and he wasn't willing to raise his brother's suspicions until he'd deciphered for himself what in Saint Bridget's name was afoot.

"Ah. Ye go ahead and jest, then, and I'll remind ye that in a week ye'll be standing before God and most of the clans while ye wed a Sassenach lass."

A sliver of uneasiness went through Ranulf, not because he hesitated to wed Charlotte, but because of all the guests this wedding would attract. Through an equal measure of effort and blind luck he'd managed peace with the Campbells. With so many uncertain allies and secret rivals about to be in attendance, anything could happen.

And that was the other reason he wanted Rowena's husband chosen and her future secured. She was eighteen now, and she'd made it known that she was available and looking for a husband. The sister of the MacLawry, and the power and wealth she represented, could prove too tempting — and if someone stole her away against her will or against his wishes, that would mean war.

"I'll keep that in mind, Bear," he said aloud, "and ye remember that my wedding will be a grand time for me to find ye a wife."

"Ye're a cruel man, Glengask," Munro returned, for the first time looking somewhat concerned.

"Aye. Ye've no idea. Now go dance with someone."

Left to himself for a rare moment, Ranulf cast his gaze around the room. Charlotte stood with Arran and his Mary, the trio laughing at something or other. Rowena still danced with their Sassenach uncle, Myles Wylkie, the flush slowly fading from her cheeks. Half the room away the two Buchanans, Lord Rob and his cousin James, were deep in what looked to be a serious conversation. Rob was no fool that he could tell, and if Cranach saw Lachlan as competition for Rowena he might well decide to offer sooner rather than later. And that might be best for everyone concerned.

The Bonny Bruce tavern in Mahldoen was generally a good place to find a lad willing to throw a few punches. Tonight, though, the place was quieter than death — no doubt because the chieftains and the other clans would begin arriving tomorrow. The village would be patched and mended and everyone dressed in their Sunday best, and black eyes and split lips wouldn't be welcome.

"Another fer ye, Lord Gray?" the tavern master asked, and Lachlan nodded.

"Aye. A last one fer the road, if ye please."

"I thought ye'd be up at the castle fer Lady Winnie's dance," Tim continued, topping off the well-used mug with ale. "Ye look fancy enough fer it."

Lachlan made a dismissive gesture. "Too many Sassenach and their frills."

"Aye. They do spend a fair bit of coin, at least."

They had one redeeming quality, then. What the devil was it that Rowena admired so much about them? Talking about the theater made no sense when the nearest one was better than sixty miles away in Inverness. The same with Paris fashion. That lacy, silk nonsense wouldn't last a week out in the Highlands.

Did she truly want to leave the Highlands for good? Whatever she said, he couldn't quite believe that. This was a place that ran through a man's blood and sank into his soul. A lass, even one with education who'd seen the gaslights of London, couldn't simply decide she belonged elsewhere.

Hell, if she wanted to visit fancy places he would be happy to take her to London, whenever she wished. He'd have a theater built in An Soadh and he'd hire actors to fill it, if she wanted it.

But if the rub was about him not being English, then why had she been twirling about the dance floor with Rob Cranach? The man was a Highlander, even if he generally chose to be seen as otherwise. Lachlan frowned. Aye, that was Lord Rob — a fellow who'd wear his kilt when it was to his advantage to appear Scottish, and who in the next breath could laugh at the quaint Highlanders and say he spent most of his time elsewhere.

Scowling, Lachlan looked down at the proper Sassenach clothes he'd borrowed from Arran. Clearly he wasn't as skilled a hypocrite as some, and he knew he didn't belong in this attire. He'd thought to impress Rowena, but she'd known instantly what he was about. "Damned fool," he muttered at himself.

Tim brought over a pitcher of beer. "Are ye set on ale, m'laird? I've a fine brew Tom MacNamara the miller and I've concocted."

Two swallows emptied his mug, and Lachlan held it out. "Let's have it, then."

The tavernkeeper grinned. "I knew ye'd be game fer it. Ye're a good sort, if I do say so myself."

Tonight Tim would likely be in the minority with that opinion. In truth Lachlan felt ready for anything tonight, except that nothing offered itself. Something, though, began tickling at the back of his brain. *Game.* The games. They were set to take place over the two days before the wedding, and Bear had left the planning of it to him.

What had he told Rowena's guests? That he'd figured horse races and stone throwing would be the most . . . appropriate for them, gentle folk that they were. But these games weren't meant to impress the Sassenach. Rowena might like to think otherwise, but this was about clan MacLawry. About showing the other clans, and their own, that Glengask and his chieftains and his people were not to be trifled with. The games were about the Highlands.

Rowena loved the games. She always had, anyway, and he doubted even three months in London could change that. Lachlan grinned. She was a damned Highlander, and he would prove that only another Highlander — a true Highlander, not just a man who wore the costume from time to time — would do for her.

By his reckoning it was past three o'clock in the morning when he left the Bonny Bruce and swung up on Beowulf for the three-mile ride back to Gray House. Generally he would have had at least one of his men with him, because a MacLawry chieftain out alone in the dark could be a dangerous proposition. Tonight, though, enough anger and frustration still curled through his bones that he would welcome a bit of trouble.

Most of the lights at Glengask were out as he rounded the path by the loch, so the soiree must have been over with — or nearly so. With a frown he turned up the road toward the house. He knew precisely which windows belonged to Rowena, and they all still flickered and glowed with candlelight.

She owed him a kiss. Was she up there waiting for him in her lovely lavender gown, or was she still in the ballroom dancing about in Lord Robert's arms?

He wanted to know, and he wanted his mouth on hers. He wanted to strip the lavender silk from her soft skin and put his mouth on her, and be inside her and claim her for himself.

But he wanted her to have those same thoughts about him, feel the same . . . need that he did. And drunk or sober, he knew perfectly well that at this moment she didn't. Or rather, she'd convinced herself that he was some nebulous fairy prince of her dreams, and that London had awakened her.

"Bloody London."

It felt good to say that, so he did it again. Twice. And then with a last look at her lit windows he turned around and headed back to Gray House. Dreams and wishes and rainbows had caused all this trouble, as far as he was concerned. And so beginning tomorrow, he'd give her a look at who he truly was. And who *she* truly was. And Robert Cranach had best stay out of his damned way.

"Ye look like a steamy pile of shite," Bear said, as he walked into the Gray House breakfast room the next morning.

Lachlan nodded from his customary chair at the head of the table. His table. That seemed important today, because he wasn't entirely certain how he felt about any of the MacLawrys. "So do ye. At least I ken what happened to me. What's yer excuse?"

"Sarah Parker. That lass is nae as sweet as she looks. My back looks like I rode naked through nettles." Shaking his shaggy black hair, Munro made his way over to the sideboard and selected a generous helping of breakfast. "Did ye go doon to the Bonny Bruce withoot me?"

"Aye. It was emptier than a church on Monday, though. Naught to do but drink."

Bear took the seat opposite him and gestured at the one footman still remaining in the house for a cup of tea. "What were ye and Winnie fighting aboot?"

That was Bear, directly to the point. Finesse was for diplomats. Lachlan finished his bite of toast and washed it down with his own tea. "Rainbows."

Bear cocked an eyebrow. "Ye nearly came to blows over rainbows," he said, dumping five lumps of sugar into his teacup. "And ye expect me to believe ye, why?"

"If ye want more than that, ye'll have to ask her." He slid a piece of paper across the table. "Ye left the games to me, but I figured ye should at least know what I've decided."

Turning the paper to face him, Bear read it as he devoured a soft-boiled egg and an entire baked trout. "Ye left oot bear-baiting," he said after a moment, looking up again. "Are ye trying to get everyone killed?"

"Nae. Those are proper contests fer a proper Highlands games." He indicated the list with a free finger. "And dunnae ye want to have the Sassenach leave here feeling just a wee bit of fear?"

"So they can bring their army north and try to wipe us oot again? Those that are still standing after the caber toss, stone put, foot race, horse race — men and women — hammer throw, weight throw, sheaf toss, blunted claymores, target shooting, *maide leisg,* and greased-pig chasing, anyway."

"I wrote down the pipes, fiddles, and dancing contests on the other side." Lachlan gave a mock frown. "Do ye think I should suggest to Ranulf that we have three days fer the games? Two might nae be enough."

"Ye've gone mad, ye know."

"Nae, I havenae." He sat forward. If he couldn't convince Bear, he didn't stand a chance with Glengask. "This isnae just a gathering of clan MacLawry. All our best will be here, aye. But so will Campbells, Stewarts, Buchanans, a share of MacDonalds, MacGregors, Camerons, and Gordons. And that's nae all of them."

"Aye. They started arriving at dawn. I came to fetch ye to help me organize the tents along the loch if ye were civilized again."

"And what impression do ye want them all to return home with? That we hold a fine, civilized wedding and a few aristocratic contests that any Sassenach could win? That we're practically Sassenach ourselves, we're so gentle and gentlemanly?"

His friend frowned again. "That's how Ranulf wants the English to see us. Civilized."

"And does he want the other clans to see us as civilized? As polite knee benders who faint at the sight of blood? Because we'll have a bushel of English here, and a bloody acre of Highlanders."

Munro looked at the list again, a slow smile touching his face. "Ye're nae mad after all, Lach. In fact, I ken ye may be a genius." He slammed his fist on the table, making tea slosh from his cup. "This is a Highlands games," he rumbled, lifting the list. "And we're Highlanders."

"Aye. We are. And anyone who expects less of us is in fer a surprise. Now shall we take the list to Glengask?"

"Oh, aye. Winnie might nae like it, but I ken Ran will. Ye should do the talking."

Lachlan pushed to his feet. "Let's get on with it, then. We have some tents to pitch and some games to arrange." And a woman's heart to win.

Chapter Eight

Rowena looked down at the list. "No! No, no, no!"

"I gave my approval, Rowena," Ranulf said from the chair behind his large mahogany desk. "I'll nae have ye contradicting me."

"The games were supposed to keep everyone occupied before the wedding. This," and she shook the page in her fist, "this is . . . uncivilized!" It was also clearly written in Lachlan's neat hand. Apparently he'd decided to find another way to torment her.

"Most of my guests are uncivilized."

"But mine aren't."

"Rowena, generally I'd agree with ye. But think aboot this: I have to balance holding my ground in the Highlands with opening new avenues in London, and even abroad. If I can hold fierce games, keep them from falling into chaos, and the next day marry an English lady from a respected family in front of both Scottish and English aristocrats, I've proven myself doubly strong, and doubly formidable."

In a stupid, manly fist-bashing way, it made sense. "It's a large risk. We've seen chaos erupt out of clan MacLawry games. Here you'll have, what, a dozen clans participating?"

"Aye." He gazed at her levelly, deep blue eyes to her gray. "This is on *my* head, *piuthar.* My failure, or my success. And in my opinion, the risk is worth the reward."

"But —"

"Rowena, I'm nae accustomed to explaining myself. And nae more than once. I've decided."

She knew better than to argue with that. She'd likely have more success yelling at a stone wall. "Very well, then."

"Good. Now. Ye and Lachlan. What's amiss?"

Oh, so many things. "Nothing. It was just a silly argument."

He didn't look convinced. "Over what?"

"I truly don't wish to talk about it, Ran. It's over with, anyway." Quite possibly it was entirely over with, since Lachlan hadn't stopped by to collect his kiss last night. And that was despite the fact that she'd stayed up until nearly dawn — not because of the kiss, of course, but because she wanted to

206

finish the argument. And because she couldn't seem to become accustomed to the fact that he wasn't simply teasing.

"Ye're nae still pining over him, are ye?"

"Nae. No. Of course not. It's . . . it's just now that I'm not infatuated over every little thing he does any longer, he's quite aggravating."

"Can ye plan this gathering together, or should I remove him from the thing? Ye can have Bear, instead."

That would make things so much easier. At the same time it felt cowardly, though, and of course he would likely tell her that to her face. Nor would it resolve whatever it was between them. "I can work with him. Bear will only want games where he can throw heavy things as far as possible. At least Lachlan included races and dancing and target shooting."

After a long moment Ranulf nodded. "See to it, then. I have chieftains arriving. And MacDonalds."

Since he meant that to be amusing, she smiled, then stood and left his office. Why she continued to feel the need to protect Lachlan from her brothers she had no idea, but she'd done it yet again. And now they were organizing the gathering together.

The day had begun overcast, and over the

past few minutes light bands of rain had begun skipping across the hills. Most of her London friends had scattered for the morning, retreating to Ranulf's large library or the morning room or, from the sound of it, the billiards room and the music room. At least she didn't need to keep them entertained today, because she simply wasn't in the mood.

Cooper at the front door held out a light sealskin overcoat for her, and she slipped into it and her bad-weather walking boots — which generally saw more usage than her good-weather walking shoes. She donned one of Arran's floppy-brimmed hats over her coiled hair and stepped outside into the rain.

"Rowena."

She turned to see Ranulf descending the stairs just inside. "What is it?"

"As I said, there are Highlanders arriving today. Take Una with ye." He patted the smaller of the two massive gray deerhounds on the head. "Una. Guard Rowena."

"Come along, Una," she echoed, and with the hound padding beside her she headed down the path toward the loch.

As she topped the hill, she slowed. Yesterday this had been a rolling, heather-filled meadow. Today two dozen canvas tents were already up, along with several canopies and temporary wooden structures and rolls of cloth and wood for another three dozen or so. It looked very like the beginnings of a MacLawry clan gathering, even though she knew this event had much more significance. The MacLawry was marrying, ensuring the continuation of the MacLawry line, and all the surrounding clans meant to witness it.

For the first time she was glad all of this wasn't aimed at her. And she hoped Ranulf would have a tight hold on Charlotte when his betrothed saw the horde of Highlanders who would be filling these tents over the next few days. They all lived in such small groups these days, so isolated from each other, that now, more than ever, no one wanted to miss a gathering.

"Bear, tie it off before I get flung into the loch, will ye?"

"I am! Give me a damned minute."

She looked over at the tent currently being erected. A man, shirtless in the rain, in fact wearing nothing but a MacLawry kilt and muddy work boots, hauled backward on a long stretch of canvas to keep it tight while a handful of other lads tied the crossbeams and pounded anchors into the ground. When the piece was secured he released it, swiping rain and longish brown hair from his face as he turned around.

"Lachlan," she said aloud, taking in his well-muscled shoulders and abdomen, the light trail of hair that traveled from his chest downward to disappear beneath the band of his kilt. Her breath caught a little.

He inclined his head. His bare skin must have been warm, because she could swear steam lifted from him as he approached. "Rowena."

"Ye — Aren't you cold?" she asked, when she couldn't think of anything else to say.

"Nae. And I'd be wet throughout, regardless." He tilted his head back, closing his eyes and opening his mouth to the rain. "Fer Highlands weather, this is refreshing."

"If it doesn't knock you down, it's not weather," she returned, paraphrasing one of Arran's favorite sayings.

"True enough." He held his hand down, and Una trotted forward for a scratch. "I'm glad ye've got one of the dogs with ye. This place'll be crawling with rival clans by sunset. The Camerons've already claimed the two tents doon to the left."

"And you're concerned over my safety?"

His brow furrowed. "Of course I am. I want nae harm to come to ye, lass. Ye're precious to me."

Now he was just trying to be charming again. And he undoubtedly knew precisely how magnificent he looked standing there bare-chested and muddy. "Then we aren't arguing any longer over who sees whom more clearly?"

"I reckon proof will do us better than words," he returned, gesturing her toward one of the completed tents down the path they'd left open to the right.

Curious, she ducked inside, out of the rain. Una shook droplets everywhere, then padded to one side of the opening and lay down. No one else would join them without the hound's approval. "How do I prove that I see you clearly, then?" she pursued.

Lachlan tugged on one of the ropes, then faced her again. "First, ye owe me someaught."

Her pulse skittered. "I do not. You didn't appear at the agreed-upon time or in the agreed-upon place."

"Ye bellowed so loud I got tossed oot of yer party on my arse. And then I got drunk. I couldnae collect a kiss when I was three sheets to the wind."

"I didn't make you go drinking."

He grinned jauntily. "Aye, ye did, but I'll concede the point before it begins another argument."

Had fighting with her truly upset him that much? She hadn't slept well at all, herself, but then she'd been waiting for him to make an appearance. "Regardless," she made herself say, "the agreement was for the end of the evening, in my bedchamber. This is neither." And she had no intention of being charmed by him. Not again.

"Hang the agreement." Striding forward, he took her face in his hands and kissed her.

Electricity shot down her spine, sharp and breathtaking. Lachlan didn't settle for a chaste, close-lipped kiss like the one Samston had given her. Instead, he molded his mouth against hers, pulling and seeking until she had to respond in kind or simply expire. She clasped her hands around his wrists, keeping him close against her.

Rainbows, reality, childish daydreams — it all melted beneath the heat of his embrace. Rowena rose up on her tiptoes to meet his mouth more squarely. She wanted to run her fingers across his bare chest, and gripped his arms harder to keep her hands still. Because once she began touching him, she didn't think she would be able to make herself stop.

"Lachlan! Where'd ye get to?"

At the sound of Bear's voice just on the

other side of the heavy cloth, Rowena jerked backward. Oh, goodness. Munro could not be allowed to find them mauling each other. His gaze on her lips, Lachlan wiped the back of his hand across his mouth.

"Sweet Bridget," he murmured, then took two steps backward. "I'm in the tent," he called, "discussing the games with yer sister."

A moment later Bear ducked inside, water dripping from his long black hair and making his thin shirt cling to his muscular chest. He looked from Rowena to Lachlan and back again. "Nae slapping or kicking?"

She took a quick breath. "Ranulf agreed to your plan for the games," she offered. "Is it truly necessary to throw trees, rocks, hammers, and wheat sheaves, though? Might we substitute a rope pull or something else for one of them, at least?"

"I'd trade ye the hammers fer a good rope pull," Bear agreed. "Did he give us the third day, or are we still to manage with two?"

"We'll begin at noon on Wednesday, and you'll have until sunset on Friday," she decided, since Ranulf hadn't specified.

"Having the evening before the wedding to sober up does make some sense," Lachlan put in, "though we cannae guarantee that's how anyone'll make use of the time."

"Aye. I'm nae leaving my good word to keep the peace in the hands of the Campbells or the Camerons." Bear grimaced.

"Of course not." Rowena patted him on one large, wet shoulder. "But we can guarantee that the MacLawrys will be sober and ready to stop any trouble before it begins."

He nodded. "I ken we can do that. And I'm glad to see the two of ye talking and nae yelling. We're all friends here. We're family."

Lachlan had said he didn't want her friendship, and that kiss hadn't given her the impression they were family. That kiss had made her feel positively naked — or at the least, made her want to be touching him skin to skin. She needed to return to the house before she said or did something that would set her back three months and into her old, silly, girlish infatuation.

"We are all friends," she agreed. "And I need to get back to the house for the meeting with Father Dyce."

"I'll walk ye," Lachlan said, before she could escape.

"Just ye dunnae leave me to do all this myself, or I'll blame all the drownings on ye." With that Bear gestured them to precede him back into the rain.

From his expression Lachlan would rather

have remained with her in the tent. Because that same thought occurred to her, Rowena snapped her fingers at Una and practically ran out into the drizzle. A dozen heartbeats later, though, a tall, solid warmth moved up beside her.

"You don't need to come with me," she said, keeping her gaze on the path before her. "I have Una."

"I said I'd escort ye."

"But you're what I'm attempting to escape."

Lachlan chuckled. "I mean to dog ye like ye dog my thoughts during the day, and my dreams at night."

She risked a glance at him. "I'm not the first woman you've kissed, though."

His expression sobered. "Nae, ye are nae."

"And you didn't begin kissing other women in just the past three months."

"Ye still want me to be honest, lass?"

"I require it from you, Lachlan." She'd spent far too much time in fantasies where he was concerned. Whether that was his fault or not, she wouldn't tolerate more lies or fabrications. She couldn't. Especially now, when . . . when he said he wanted her.

"Then over the years I've kissed my share of lasses. I am eight years older than ye, Rowena."

"And you've done more than kiss them," she insisted.

He blew out his breath. "A time or two, aye."

She abruptly wanted to cry. Even the part of her that yelled it should have been her in his arms knew better, but it still hurt. "Who?"

"That, I'll nae tell ye. It doesnae just concern me."

"How is it that I never knew?" she persisted. "I knew when Bear and Arran were . . . misbehaving. And I practically lived on your heels."

"I didnae want to hurt yer feelings," Lachlan said, looking off toward the castle. "I knew ye thought ye . . . loved me, even when ye were twelve and I was twenty. So I was discreet, I suppose ye'd call it."

"Did ye love any of them?"

"Nae. I wanted to, but I didnae. In fact, I was aboot to go spend some time in Edinburgh to find a likely lass to wed when ye ran off to London."

She would have lost him anyway, even if she hadn't cured herself of her obsession with him. The notion sent brief panic through her, even though logically she knew it no longer mattered. "Will you leave after the wedding, then?"

"Nae," he said again, meeting her gaze. "Circumstances have changed."

"Yes, they have." And she needed to keep reminding herself of precisely that. It was only that their ideas of what those circumstances were seemed to be radically different. And his came with kissing.

"Why did ye stop writing me?" he asked abruptly.

"I beg your pardon?"

"When ye got to London and settled in with the Hanovers. Ye wrote me a letter every day fer better than a fortnight, and then ye stopped. Without another word. Why?"

"You never wrote me back," she returned.

"I —"

"And it occurred to me," Rowena continued, for her own sake as much as his, "that you *never* wrote me back. Poems I sent you, a million letters, notes, flower necklaces, biscuits, shells, pretty pebbles. You'd be polite and thank me, but you never reciprocated. Ever. And beginning with the first night I went to a party in London, men surrounded me. Handsome, wealthy men who sent me flowers and notes and poems. Men who were interested in me."

A few feet from the door he stopped, taking hold of her wrist to keep her beside him.

"I cannae apologize fer growing up with ye or fer seeing ye the way I did. Ye werenae the only one saying we were meant to marry, ye know. Every time ye smiled at me Bear or Arran would start in with their Lord and Lady Gray shite. And that's when ye were eight years old. It terrified me that my life had already been planned oot withoot me having a say in it, and that I was expected to wed a wee bairn."

Thunder rumbled in the distance, its echo rising and falling in the hills around them. "I never thought of it like that," she said after a long moment. As she looked at it now, she could see that she'd been rather relentless, but at the time — in her own mind, at least — the two of them together was a fact merely waiting for the right moment to happen.

"I loved having all of ye aboot me," he went on. "And I adored ye. Just nae the way ye wanted me to." Lachlan took a long look at her. "Even when ye came back. I was surprised when ye said ye were done with me. And relieved."

"Then we can both move forward." Rowena tried to pull her wrist free from his grip, but he only tightened his hold.

"I *am* moving forward. And the way I see it, ye're obligated to give me a chance."

She lifted an eyebrow. "I'm not obligated to give you anything." This was easier; arguing was easier on her insides than a heartfelt conversation was.

"Ye are," he insisted. "Ye chased me like a wildcat on a rabbit fer nearly eighteen years. Now ye can tolerate it and listen while I chase ye fer a bit." He stroked his thumb along her wrist. "And while I kiss ye and do my damnedest to woo ye into my bed."

She swallowed, his touch raising goose bumps on her arms. "And then what? Ye change yer mind again?"

His slow smile, rivulets of water running down his face and bare chest, made her shiver. "I marry ye."

Even with his recent behavior and the luscious kisses, Lachlan declaring his intention to marry her stunned Rowena down to her toes. *Sweet Bridget and all the heavenly angels.* She couldn't seem to stop staring at him. A thousand thoughts flickered through her mind, but nothing settled long enough for her to grab onto it.

"Dunnae ye have a thing to say aboot that?" he asked, tilting his head.

She pushed back against the hard pounding of her heart. "Six months ago I would have been in your arms and weeping with joy at this moment."

"But ye're nae weeping now, I notice."

He didn't look terribly flattered, but he wasn't yelling, or stomping away, at least. She needed to make him understand. It would be nice if she could also convince herself enough that she would at least stop dreaming about him. "My life has changed, Lachlan."

"Nae as much as ye'd like to think, I reckon." With a last squeeze he released her wrist. "I can be patient. And ye can remind yerself how what ye wanted from me wasnae realistic. Because what I want from ye now *is,* and I think if ye look at who we are now, ye might just agree with me."

"Fairly soon I hope *you'll* realize that I do see you for who you are," she returned. "I'm not playing hard to get, Lach. We simply aren't compatible. I don't want a simple Highlands life. Not any longer."

Lachlan smiled again, less humor in his sharp green eyes this time. "Well, then. Until we come to a point of mutual understanding, I suppose I'll keep visiting ye at night fer a kiss."

With that he walked away, fading out of sight in the misty rain as he returned down the trail toward the meadow and Loch Shinaig beyond. She wished he were as easy to dismiss from her thoughts and feelings as he was from her sight.

The front door opened. As she turned to look, Lord Robert Cranach stepped out beneath the narrow overhang on the portico. "There ye are, my lady," he said, smiling. "A group of us have gotten up the courage to play charades. I declared that ye must be on my team."

Putting the smile back on her face, she ascended the shallow front steps and went inside, handing her wet raincoat and hat to Cooper and stepping back into her proper lady's shoes. "I'd be delighted."

Now that was a proper activity for ladies — and gentlemen. Not putting up tents in the rain or dragging in cartloads of logs for caber tossing. Lachlan MacTier wasn't her elusive knight. He wasn't even a gentleman. He was a barbarian Scot in a world that had little patience for his kind any longer.

Robert Cranach was the future of the Highlands. Ranulf wanted clan MacLawry to be part of the future, as well. Her making a match with Rob could help her brother accomplish that. Aside from all that, he was handsome and sophisticated and a gentleman. As she was no longer a burrs-in-her-hair Highland lass, he was precisely what she needed. What she wanted.

He would never drag her about through

the rain or maul her in a tent. And he would take her to the theater and not argue with her at parties. Yes, he was perfect. And so it didn't matter a whit if for another day or two she allowed Lachlan to kiss her in the evenings. Hopefully that would be enough to convince them — him — that they would never suit, that a match between them had only been a silly girl's dream.

After that, he would have to listen to reason. If he didn't, she would have to tell Ranulf what was going on. And she truly did not want to do that. For all their sakes.

"And ye'd be Lord Gray, I reckon," the red-haired lass said, taking a seat in the chair next to the one Lachlan stood behind.

"Aye. And ye'd be Lady Bridget Cameron, if I'm nae mistaken."

"Och. Smart and handsome." She favored him with a broad smile. "Ye arenae mistaken. My cousin Florence is making eyes at the MacLawry's brother Munro, but I reckon ye're even more bonny than he is."

Lachlan glanced down the long table, where Rowena sat flanked by Gregory Mackles, Lord Arden, on one side, and Lord Robert Cranach on the other. Arden was one of the MacLawry chieftains and well known to be overly fond of his drink,

222

but then he wasn't the problem, anyway.

"Thank ye, lass," he said aloud, when she looked up at him and lifted a curved red eyebrow.

"So ye may be asking yerself," she went on when he declined to say anything more, "how it is that one of the Cameron's nieces, of the age one-and-twenty, remains unwed."

It hadn't occurred to him to even think the question. "And ye'd answer by saying what?"

The last of the ladies found her seat, so all of the men standing like sentinels about the table could finally seat themselves. If a fellow waited for the lasses before he sat down in some households, he'd have only scraps for dinner. Ranulf sat at the head of the impossibly long table, with Charlotte at his right elbow. His own chieftains sat scattered about the place settings, strategically placed in case of trouble.

The Cameron and his wife sat to Ranulf's left, while the MacDonald and his daughter were just beyond Charlotte. Once the Stewart and the Campbell arrived the arrangements would become more complicated, and he was glad it wasn't up to him. No, that was for Ranulf and Rowena to figure out — which brought his attention around to her again, not that it was ever far from her.

"I'd answer by saying that my uncle gave me a list of six lads to meet here at the Mac-Lawry's wedding. He said my making a match with any of them would please him."

The Cameron seemed to have only nieces — at least a dozen of them — and so far he'd managed to have them marry into at least seven different clans. Lachlan supposed that was one way to ensure that clan Cameron would never be attacked. "Did yer cousin receive the same list?"

Her spectacular brows knitted together. "Aye. And my other three unmarried female cousins. But ye dunnae want them. Their mother is Irish."

"Ah. Thank ye fer the warning."

"I likely shouldnae be telling ye such things, but ye were the one on my list I most liked the looks of."

"Well. I'm flattered, then." She was pretty, actually, and if his intentions toward Rowena hadn't reversed themselves last week he might have expressed more enthusiasm. As it was, she immediately became another obstacle between him and Rowena's bedchamber.

"I hear ye're the one arranged the games," Bridget went on, tugging at the front of her yellow gown, evidently to give him an even better view of her substantial bosom.

"I did," he returned. "With Lord Munro and Lady Rowena."

She was about as subtle as Rowena had been at age fifteen. That was when her strategy had begun to alter, as he recalled. Instead of loud pronouncements and grabbing onto him, she'd taken to sighing and feigning various injuries, sending him coy glances and pretending to be caught unawares while reading a book or arranging bouquets of flowers. She'd wanted him to notice her, and while he could say that he'd intentionally failed to do so, the clarity with which he remembered their every encounter was startling.

And of course the lack of response on his part had been deliberate. One returned glance, a kind note of thanks, or even noticing that she looked fetching, and he would have been hooked like a fish. However much he wanted her now, he had a good idea if he'd been trapped against his will he would have begun despising her before he ever discovered how truly delightful she was as a grown woman.

"I mean to enter the lady's horse race and some of the dancing. Will ye come and watch me?"

"I'll be there." Not for Bridget Cameron, though.

He looked over at Rowena again, to see her chuckling at some nonsense spewing from Lord Rob. What the devil did Ranulf think he was about, letting a Buchanan anywhere near his only sister? The MacLawrys didn't need any alliance badly enough for him to offer her up to anyone as part of a deal.

At the end of dinner Arran stood, lifting his glass. "I'd like to propose a toast," he said. "To a peaceful gathering of clans, and to Lord Glengask and his Lady Charlotte."

Everyone rose. "Glengask and Charlotte," Lachlan repeated with the rest of them, and downed the rest of his wine.

Once the ladies left the table he saw no reason to remain behind, particularly when Rob Cranach began some tale about wool prices. And there sat Glengask, who hated Cheviot sheep and all they represented, listening with a polite smile on his face. Aye, Rob could tell a story, and he had a trace of a Scots accent and a residence in Fort William. In Lachlan's opinion, none of those things made him a Highlander.

He pushed to his feet. "Excuse me," he said crisply. "I need a bit of air."

When he left the huge formal dining

room, though, he headed for the drawing room rather than the nearest door or window. He'd been half jesting when he'd told Rowena he meant to dog her footsteps, but as she never left his thoughts, she might as well not leave his sight, either.

"Ye've come to join the lasses, have ye?" Lady Bridget cooed from the open doorway. The feminine chatting and laughing beyond her sounded like a flock of dainty-voiced geese. He didn't much want to go in there, either, but Rowena was inside.

"Aye," he returned. "The lot in here are prettier than the hounds in the dining room."

Bridget laughed. "Do ye truly want to chat with a flock of hens, though, Lord Gray, or would ye rather cozy up to one bird in particular?" She tugged down on the front of her gown again, nearly exposing her breasts to his view.

"If yer gown doesnae fit ye, lass, there is a fine seamstress in An Soadh."

Reaching out, she caught hold of one of the silver buttons of his waistcoat. "Why dunnae ye take this dress off me, and we'll see how well *ye* fit?" she breathed.

Lachlan took a breath, grateful for a moment that she hadn't grabbed hold of his kilt. A few years ago he wouldn't have thought twice about agreeing to a quick tryst with her. Rowena was occupied and so wouldn't know he'd been elsewhere, and Bridget wasn't interesting enough to tax his mind or his heart. It would certainly help ease some of his frustration.

With a smile he took her hand, drawing her fingers away from his buttons. "Ye seem a bonny lass, Bridget," he drawled. "There's another lass who owns my heart, though, and I'll nae have another."

Her return smile looked forced, but Bridget Cameron nodded and stuffed what she could of her bosom back into her dress. "Ye're a handsome lad, Lord Gray. If this lass should disappoint ye, well, I'll be aboot fer a time. I'll keep my bedchamber door unlocked fer ye."

Inclining his head, Lachlan stepped past her into the drawing room — and found himself face-to-face with Rowena. *Damnation.* Had she overheard any of that conversation? With his luck, she'd heard just enough to decide he needed a swift kick in the man parts. "Rowena."

"Lachlan."

Bridget moved past them, and Rowena shifted sideways to give her room. Her gaze, though, remained fixed on his face. "The other lads are still at the table," he said, trying to calculate her mood. He always used to be able to tell what she was thinking; there was something . . . fascinating in not knowing what she might say or do next.

She nodded. "You should've gone with Bridget Cameron," she said finally, her voice low.

"Nae. Ye can decide ye dunnae like me, but I'll nae make it that simple fer ye."

"So I'm the lass who owns your heart? I can understand lust, I suppose, but now it's your heart? After one week?"

"Is that it?" he returned, moving closer to her and deciding he'd made some progress if she at least believed he wanted her. "Ye reckon I've fallen fer ye too quickly? Would ye believe Lord Rob if he said he loved ye? Ye've only known him fer three days. I've known ye since the day ye were born."

"But you never liked me until this week."

"I never thought of ye as a woman grown until this week," he corrected. "Do ye think I would've worn bonnets and drunk tea from wee cups, or let ye win foot races or teach ye to shoot a pistol or come aboot every day if I didnae like ye?"

She brushed at one eye. "You're friends with my brothers. Of course you came by."

God's sake, she was stubborn. But then, she was also worth the effort. "Lass, do ye know why I didnae answer yer letters?"

"Why not, then?"

"Because I didnae want to break yer heart." He took another step toward her. "If ye wrote me today I'd answer ye, because now I can say all the things ye wanted me to say before. I see ye now, Rowena. I truly, truly do. I've always loved ye. Now, I'm *in* love with ye."

He'd expected it to be much harder to say those words. But they came very easily, really, as though they'd been waiting in his chest, in his heart, for a very long time and they'd just dislodged themselves.

"I . . . I don't want to have this conversation right now." Rowena's cheeks had paled, and he reached out to steady her.

"Lass, are ye —"

"Don't touch me, Lachlan. I can't —"

"Lachlan!"

They both froze at the flat sound of Ranulf's voice coming up the hallway. Lachlan turned to face the marquis. It was time he stopped tiptoeing about. His intentions were honorable, after all. "Ranulf, I —"

"Enough," Glengask snapped. "That's twice ye've made her run off."

Lachlan glanced over his shoulder. Rowena was gone, disappeared somewhere into the depths of the hen-filled room. "It was just a damned conversation."

"Evidently," Ranulf continued in the same low, controlled voice, "Rowena adored ye fer so long that she doesnae know what to do with ye or any other man now. I'll nae have these antics going on with all the clans here looking fer trouble — and looking at my sister as a way to make an alliance. She's marrying Lord Robert Cranach. That should end any confusion."

A cold, deep pain settled sharply into Lachlan's chest, robbing him of breath and thought. He'd almost managed to convince her that he was sincere. Another day, two days, and he would have had her for himself. "Nae," he muttered, not certain the word was even audible.

"Aye. It's time. And it's done."

CHAPTER NINE

"Fairy tales?" Jane repeated, her brow furrowing. "Like the one with the girl in the red hood and the wolf who ate her grandmother?"

"No. Like . . . like the girl who's always loved the prince, and just after she realizes that it's silly and naïve and half-witted to love someone who doesn't even know who she is, it turns out that he *does* know who she is, and he wants her to be his princess." Rowena tried to slow down her breath, but that did nothing to slow the fast beating of her heart. If there was one person's opinion she wouldn't listen to right now, it was her own. "Could that be true?"

"Well, how does the prince know who she is? Is she a maid in his house? Because I don't think a prince would marry a maid."

"Jane, they just . . . They know each other."

"Oh. But is she a peer?"

"What does that matter, for heaven's sake?"

"You asked if the fairy tale could be true." Jane took a drink of her tea, eyeing her over the rim of the cup. "It can't be true unless the girl and the prince are at a similar level socially. Unless the girl is very rich, and the prince is very poor." She set aside her cup. "If, for instance, she's an orange girl he sees peddling her fruit as he rides about his kingdom on his magnificent stallion, then it can be a fairy tale, but it can't be true. If, on the other hand, the girl is the sister of the prince's closest friend, then I don't see why he couldn't suddenly be struck on the head and realize she's grown up to be a lovely lady of wit and virtue, and he loves her and wants to marry her."

Rowena narrowed her eyes, grinning despite herself. Jane sat on the couch beside her, a perfectly innocent expression on her face — except for the twinkle in her brown eyes and the slight upturn at the corners of her mouth. "You wretch!" she exclaimed. "Did you guess?"

Jane shook her head, her grin deepening. "I've been observing. When he looks at you, especially when you're not looking at him, he gets a very doe-eyed expression." She planted her chin on her fist and looked skyward, batting her eyes and sighing soulfully.

"If he looked like that, someone would drag him off to Bedlam," Rowena countered, chuckling and truly surprised. If Jane realized it and saw it, then she could no longer quite dismiss it.

"And he told me," Jane continued. "I got him to take me riding out to that bluebell valley, and I was trying to flirt with him, until he said you'd gotten beneath his skin, and he hoped he hadn't taken too long."

"Truly?"

"Truly."

Did Lachlan love her? Or rather, could he be *in* love with her? He'd said he was. Now, Jane seemed to think the same thing. Could she believe it, though?

She wished she'd made a drawing of every look they'd ever shared, of every time she and Lachlan had laughed over putting a frog down Bear's trousers or of when they'd fallen into a giggling heap after a snowball fight. Then she could be certain she was seeing what was there, and not just what she wanted to see.

How simple would it have been for him to declare that he was tired of her chasing after him? He could have told her, demonstrated how little regard he had for her, a thousand different times and ways over the years. Surely she hadn't been so blind that he'd tried, and she'd simply missed it.

But the first time she could ever recall him doing any such thing was last week, when he'd very clearly and very . . . gently said he wanted her to be happy, but she was a sister to him and they would never suit. And then a day or two later he'd come back to tell her he'd been wrong, that he just hadn't seen that she'd grown up.

"Ah, Rowena, someone should paint a portrait of ye."

Starting, she looked up to see Rob Cranach approaching. "I don't think I could sit still for that," she returned, too shrilly, and swallowed. If she couldn't settle herself, *she* would be the one carted off to Bedlam.

"Might I have a word with ye, my lady?" he continued, stopping in front of her and offering his hand.

"Certainly." Clearly, thinking and deciphering all of this would have to wait until tonight. Or after tonight, since Lachlan seemed determined to kiss her before bed again. And to herself she could admit that she looked forward to it. Clasping Rob's fingers, she climbed to her feet.

Rob transferred her hand to his arm, and headed them toward the door to the hallway.

"I meant to tell ye, ye should wear lavender as often as possible. It sets off yer eyes to perfection."

She bobbed her head. "Thank you." What had Lach said when she'd told him to stop trying to flatter her? That she had eyes like a spitting wildcat's? At least Lord Robert knew how to pay a lady a proper compliment.

That was what she needed to recall — that she wanted someone calm and sophisticated in her life. That she'd worked very hard to learn refinement and the proper way of speaking. Why had she finally given up on Lachlan? Because she'd finally realized that he wasn't a refined, stately gentleman. He had a clever wit and he was certainly strong and capable, but he was first, last, and middle a Highlander. A barbarian.

Rob led her just down the hallway to the orangerie, where he stopped and took both her hands in his. "I've just spoken with your brother," he said. "In fact, Glengask came to find me. He's given his permission for us to wed."

For a moment his words didn't even register. Then, as they sank in, an odd roaring sound began filling her ears. "I think I'd like to sit down," she managed, and then everything went black.

She opened her eyes abruptly, then couldn't figure out why she seemed to be staring at a strip of MacLawry plaid right at the end of her nose. Even stranger, she felt like she was moving.

"I'm falling."

"Ye're nae falling, Rowena."

Ranulf's voice was right in her ear. She blinked hard. He carried her, she realized. Ranulf was carrying her up the stairs, and the plaid was the one he wore draped over one shoulder.

"I can walk."

"Aye. I've seen ye do it." His grip didn't alter.

"Put me down, Ran. I'm nae a bairn." She blinked again as they topped the stairs and he turned them toward her bedchamber. "I mean, I'm not a bairn. A baby."

Someone else, Charlotte, moved past them and pushed open her bedchamber door. While Ranulf's betrothed went about lighting lamps and stirring up the fire in the hearth, Ranulf set Rowena down on her bed and hauled the covers up over her. Then he sat down on the mattress beside her.

"Now. Mitchell's on her way up with tea and a cool cloth fer yer head."

Rowena took a deep breath, noticing her oldest brother's very concerned expression, and Charlotte standing directly behind him with her hand on his shoulder. As she watched, he reached up to grip his betrothed's fingers. They looked so much in love, and for a moment — just a moment — she was jealous. "I'm fine," she said aloud. "I fainted, I think."

"That, ye did. And I'm sorry to say everyone knows aboot it, because Rob Cranach ran into the drawing room yelling that ye'd fainted dead away. Of happiness, apparently."

"Yes. Congratulations, by the way," Charlotte said with a smile, and tightened her grip on Ranulf's hand and shoulder.

"I mean to make certain she's got all her senses before I congratulate her, woman," he retorted, without heat.

Oh, dear. "Everyone knows?" she repeated, her mind going to a man with ruffled mahogany hair and sharp green eyes who had ten minutes earlier declared that he loved her.

"Aye. Even some of the dead, I reckon. He has a strong pair of lungs, Rob does." Ranulf sighed. "It should keep any MacDonalds or MacCullochs from trying to make off with ye, though I'd intended a slightly less magnificent way of making the announcement."

Slowly Rowena realized she still wore her shoes, and she dug beneath the blankets to pull them off and dump them onto the floor. It was far easier to focus on that, to think about how silly she must have looked wallowing about on the floor and how embarrassed she would be tomorrow when she had to admit that she'd fainted. But she couldn't tell anyone why, that it hadn't been because she was overwhelmed with happiness. That she didn't know how she felt, except for confused.

Mitchell rushed into the room, clucking, a tea tray laden with tea and smelling salts and compresses in her arms. "Oh, my dear," she kept muttering, putting the things down with a clatter on the dressing table.

"I'm fine, Mitchell. Truly." And Rowena truly wished everyone would go away and give her a moment or two to think.

"Let her see to ye, anyway. It'll make *me* feel better." Standing, Ranulf leaned over to tug on her ear. "So ye know, I told Lachlan and yer brothers before Rob dragged ye off."

"Lachlan knows?"

"Aye. And that had best solve whatever nonsense has ye snapping at each other. Now ye can be friends like ye said ye wanted to be." Taking Charlotte's hand, Ranulf headed for the door. "Now stay up here and

239

get some sleep. The games begin tomorrow, and I want to see ye and Black Agnes win the racing ribbon."

She nodded. "Good night. And thank you, Ran."

"Just dunnae do that again. Ye frightened me, *piuthar.*"

Rowena allowed Mitchell to fuss over her and help her change into her night rail, mostly because listening to the maid's nonstop chattering kept her from dwelling too much on her own thoughts. Finally she couldn't stand it any longer, and she sent the servant back downstairs for the evening.

She turned on her side, piling blankets and pillows over her head even though they did nothing to ease the turmoil of her thoughts. A man had proposed marriage to her tonight, and apparently fainting meant she'd answered in the affirmative. It was nothing like she'd imagined in all her daydreams — though of course in those, Rob Cranach wasn't the man proposing to her.

A day ago she would actually have said yes; Rob was the sophisticated man to whom she could see herself married. They would summer in London, he would take her along when he went to Inverness or Edinburgh on clan Buchanan business, he would know all the latest books and plays and operas and discuss them with her in the evenings. It *was* what she wanted. Everything she wanted.

With a quiet click, her door opened and then shut again. Her heart beat an abrupt quick tattoo in her chest, and she squeezed her eyes closed even though her head was still well beneath the blankets.

"I know ye're nae asleep," Lachlan's dry voice came. "Ye have a rumbling snore."

"I do not."

In the silence she heard him walking to her window and then the soft rustle of curtains. "Come here and cast yer eyes on this," he said after a moment. "Or do ye wish me to carry ye to the window?"

She threw off the blankets. "Other people expressed concern that I fainted, you know," she commented, slipping off the bed and walking over to stand beside him.

"Are ye well, then?" He looked down at her, his eyes shadowed in the near dark.

"Yes, I'm fine."

"Then stop yer complaining and look."

That didn't seem very nice, but as she looked out over the sloping hill at the foot of Glengask, she forgot to be annoyed at his cavalier conversation. Half a dozen bonfires burned, shadows flitting about them as some of the Highlanders danced. She leaned across Lachlan's arm and pushed open the window. The sound of bagpipes and the thump of drums drifted up the hill, mingling with the scent of wood smoke. "It looks ancient," she breathed after a long moment.

"As old as the Highlands. Aye."

With him in his ghillie brogues and her in her bare feet, the top of her head fit just beneath his chin. She'd always been surrounded by tall men, and while at times she found their height annoying, on most other occasions she appreciated the protection and comfort their formidable presence provided. Tonight Lachlan's presence, though, didn't feel all that comforting. Rather, he seemed . . . coiled, like a wolf just before it sprang.

And the next thing she said, whatever she said, would likely set him loose. Of course remaining silent wouldn't do her any good, either. Rowena took a slow breath. "After your and my official nonalliance, Ranulf suggested three likely men and asked me to choose one of them."

"I know that. Cairnsgrove, MacMaster, and Cranach," he commented, still gazing outside at the firelight.

No explosion yet, anyway. She nodded. "I didn't know he'd settled on one for me until

Rob took me aside this evening to tell me Ranulf had sought him out and given his permission for a match."

"And then ye said aye to him."

"When he told me the information about it, I'm fairly certain I told him I needed to sit down, and then I fainted."

Lachlan didn't move a muscle, but the air around him seemed charged, as if he'd come to abrupt attention. "Ye didnae tell him aye?"

"Everyone seems to think I did, so I suppose I might as well have done it."

He faced her again, green eyes glinting red in the reflected firelight. "Ye didnae tell him aye," he repeated, no longer making it a question. His voice was little but a low, harsh growl.

Why did that matter? Ranulf wanted the match, and Rob was the perfect man for her. She would agree to it, even if tonight she'd been more surprised than excited. "Not yet," she said aloud.

Lachlan put his hand on the back of her neck and pulled her forward, mashing his mouth against hers. Off balance, heat spearing through her, Rowena wrapped her hands into the lapels of his jacket and held on.

When he began nipping at her jawline, for

a handful of moments Rowena thought she might faint again. He knew just where to touch her to send shivers up and down her spine. This was no teasing good-night kiss.

"Ranulf said with this settled, you and I could be friends again," she muttered, trying to sound matter-of-fact and logical and knowing she was failing badly. "I didn't tell him that you'd already announced that you didn't want to be my friend."

"Ye're right, lass. I'm nae yer friend," he murmured back, shifting his hands to unfasten the small trio of buttons beneath her chin.

Oh, goodness. "But we are friends," she insisted, her legs beginning to feel wobbly. When he tugged her gown sideways to bare her left shoulder to his kisses, she moaned.

"So ye ken I should shake yer hand and go away then, do ye?" Returning his attention to her mouth, he began plucking pins from her hair and dropping them to the floor. "I'm nae going away. Nae tonight. Nae till I've felt yer bare skin against mine and I've kissed every inch of ye. Nae till I've made ye mine."

Her thin night rail began to feel hot and scratchy against her. This was so, so wrong — even if she hadn't quite agreed to another man's proposal, she hadn't refused him, either. The match, the alliance, *would* happen. But she'd dreamed for a lifetime about dancing in his arms, and for the past three years about something more sexual, of just this night, with just this man.

"Lachlan, we —"

"I reckon I've used enough words to try to convince ye how I feel aboot ye, Rowena," he interrupted. "So ye tell me nae right now, or put yer arms around me."

The one good thing about being in her position was that she was valued for the alliance she represented, and not for her virginity. Because at this moment she couldn't quite remember why she'd decided she didn't want Lachlan pursuing her. She couldn't quite recall anything, except how fast he made her heart beat. Rowena touched his face with her palm, then slowly slid her arms up around his shoulders, pulling herself closer against him.

Lachlan dipped, catching her up in his arms, and carried her over to her rumpled bed. She couldn't seem to stop kissing him, but that only matched his hungry mouth against hers. He set her down on the blankets, pursuing her as she lay back.

"Ye say ye dunnae care fer me any longer," he muttered, reaching for the hem of her night rail and pulling it up past her knees and then above her waist before she could even pretend modesty. "I think ye've bewitched me, Rowena MacLawry. I cannae think of anything or anyone but ye."

"Even with Lady Bridget throwing herself at ye?" she returned, aware that she'd forgotten her proper accent somewhere, and not particularly caring. Lachlan knew who she was. Or at least who she felt like, tonight.

"I'd nae have her. She wasnae who I want." He sank down, moving his mouth down her stomach, following the retreat of her night rail as he continued pushing it up her body.

She gasped as he licked one exposed breast and then the other. Digging her hands into the tangle of his hair, she arched against him. And then he slid a hand between her legs, and she gasped again. Heat and desire spun through her. Even with other women practically begging to share his bed, even with her constantly telling him they would never suit, he wanted her. Finally, he wanted her. And however she imagined her perfect future, she wanted him just as badly. Just as fiercely.

When she shoved at him, he sat back a little, and she pursued him upright to push his coat down his arms. The MacLawry colors tented at his hips, and she reached beneath the kilt to grasp his jutting cock. *Sweet Saint Bridget and all the heavenly angels.*

"Ye're nae a shy lass, are ye?" He chuckled, tilting his head back a little.

"Nae with ye."

"I hope ye didnae think I was lying to ye aboot wanting ye, Rowena. Because I do."

She could certainly see and feel the evidence of that. "I want ye, too, Lachlan."

Brief satisfaction crossed his lean features. "Lift yer arms, lass."

Reluctantly she released him to do as he asked, and he pulled the night rail off over her head. Her hair fell around her shoulders, and as Lachlan gazed at her she felt lovely and wicked and wanton — all those words she'd read about, but had never quite understood before this moment.

"Well?" she prompted, watching him as he gazed at her from knees to head and back to the middle again. "What do ye think?"

His short laugh sent warmth cascading again between her legs. "I think ye're lovelier than moonlight on water, lass, and fierce as fire at sunrise." Shifting to sit on his backside, he swiftly unknotted his ghillie brogues and set them on the floor. His cravat and shirt followed, so all he wore was his kilt.

And Lachlan MacTier looked magnificent, like one of the famed ferocious Highlanders of old, the ones who'd driven off the Romans and claimed this land back for themselves. Rowena shook off that thought, though, as he unfastened the kilt and dropped it atop the rest of his clothes. She didn't need to imagine anything tonight. And she'd made up enough tales about him over the years. Tonight he needed to be precisely who he was. Tonight, that was more than enough.

He caught hold of her again, his hair falling across one eye as he lightly pinched her nipple and then followed with his mouth, his free hand trailing to caress between her legs again. She dug her fingers into his shoulders, pulling him harder against her. His cock brushed against her thigh, and she shivered. Growing up with three brothers she knew what was what, and she wanted him inside her.

Nudging her knees apart with his own, he took her mouth in a deep, heart-stopping kiss. As their tongues tangled he pushed forward with his hips, entering her in a slow, hot slide. Abrupt pain made her stiffen, but with his wicked hands on her breasts and his lips and teeth on her mouth, she relaxed again, the sensation of him inside her, his weight across her hips, indescribably . . . satisfying.

"Ye're mine now, Rowena, my fierce lass," he murmured, lifting his face away from hers, gazing down into her eyes as he pushed deeper inside her, until she took him fully.

"Ye think so?" she asked, breathless.

Slowly he pulled out and then slid in again. "Aye." He did it again. "Aye."

Rowena kissed him again, digging her fingers into his shoulders as he moved inside her. He'd called her fierce, and tonight she felt like she was as she met him thrust for thrust, the pace increasing until with a deep, shivering groan she came. He slowed as she spasmed around him, kissing her hot and openmouthed, stifling her moans until her senses settled again a little. "Sweet Saint Bridget," she managed.

He grinned, looking breathless himself. "That's nae the end of it yet, lass. Let's see if I can do that to ye again."

Abruptly he twisted them so that he lay looking up at her while she straddled his hips, still impaled. Lachlan thrust up, putting his hands around her waist until she caught onto the rhythm of their motions. She liked this, the sense that she controlled the moment — until he put his splayed hands on her breasts, teasing and tugging.

The muscles across her abdomen began to tighten again, and she planted her hands flat on Lachlan's chest to shatter once more. He took her hips and pulled her down over him as he growled and threw back his head.

With a deep, shuddering sigh Rowena collapsed against his chest. Beneath her cheek his heart beat hard and fast. Her Lachlan. She'd wanted this — him — for so long. And just when she'd given up . . .

No. She hadn't given up. She'd altered what she wanted. She'd become wiser and decided she wanted someone more refined.

If so, though, why was she so . . . satisfied? Why did she want to do nothing as much as lie curled in his arms, precisely where she was? Perhaps the physical act of sex had not only overwhelmed her senses, but her judgment. That seemed entirely likely. After all, she couldn't even catch her breath. How was she supposed to think clearly?

"Ye're being quiet," Lachlan said, his voice rumbling beneath her cheek. "Especially fer you."

"Am I?" she returned, unmoving, wishing becoming unthinking were as simple.

"Aye. I know I hurt ye, but I willnae do so again. I swear it."

She sensed that he wasn't just talking about tonight, that he was attempting to make amends for discounting her all those years. "It doesn't matter. I'm spoken for."

His arms around her back tightened, then relaxed again. "Ye didnae tell him aye. So ye *are* spoken fer, but by me."

She lifted her head, brushing her hair out of her eyes to look down at his face. "You and I are the only ones who know about this," she said, gesturing between them, "and the fact that I didn't say yes to Rob. That I haven't *yet* said yes to Rob."

"He knows ye didnae say aye, and he lied aboot it."

"I'm not so sure he lied, Lach. He assumed I would agree to be his wife, and then I fainted."

Lachlan shifted out from under her and sat up. "Ye mean to go along with it." His green eyes practically snapped with abrupt anger.

Sitting up as well so he wouldn't tower over her while he glowered, Rowena pulled a pillow around in front of herself. Yes, he'd just seen her naked, and his mouth or his hands or both had caressed every inch of her, but without clothes on she still felt very vulnerable — inside and out. "Ranulf wants the alliance. And Robert Cranach, unlike

251

you, is very nice, and we have many of the same interests."

"Ye mean he has interests and ye've decided they're the ones a proper young English lass should have, as well." Reaching out, he yanked the pillow away from her and tossed it halfway across the room. "Ye're nae some cold-blooded miss who chats aboot the weather and the theater over tea and says her day is oh, so busy. Ye're a Highlands lass with fire in yer heart and the wind in yer hair — and I wish ye would see that aboot yerself again."

She still didn't see it, Lachlan realized. All it took was one look at her face, at the tightly closed lips and narrowed eyes, to tell him that she considered tonight to be an anomaly, a one-time indiscretion. And now that he'd made her angry, she likely wouldn't listen to him at all. Worse, she might just go find Rob Cranach and say the words she hadn't managed earlier.

"That is your opinion," she said stiffly, her lovely brogue buried again, as if she'd decided to become a completely different person and simply done it. On the outside, anyway. "I don't share it. And now I think you should leave."

Damnation. "Mayhap I'm a bit ham-fisted with my words, Rowena, but ye shoved me behind the stable and then refused to look at me again. If ye want to visit the theater I'll build ye one. I'll take ye to London every year if that's what ye want. But if ye pretend to be what ye arenae and ye marry while wearing that mask, ye cannae take it off again. I worry that ye'll be miserable." *And that I'll be miserable withoot ye,* but he didn't say that part aloud. It wouldn't help. Not now, anyway.

She shoved him in the chest. Hard. She might as well have been a wee songbird batting at him with her wings, but he shifted away and stood on the far side of the bed. Her gaze lowered to his cock before she looked up at his face again, which actually made him feel a bit better. Rowena could pretend to be proper, but she'd been free and eager enough with him when the mood struck her.

"You don't need to worry about me," she said, belatedly pulling up blankets to cover herself again. "I'm no concern of yours."

"But ye are, lass." He squatted down to retrieve his kilt and then straightened to wrap it about his hips again. That done, he shrugged into his shirt. "And ye're still obligated to do as I wish, anyway, if ye dunnae want me to misbehave."

"I am not. You won't misbehave and risk a

war, now that the clans are here."

"True enough. Ye dunnae care, though, if I tell everyone ye didnae agree to wed Cranach and that he made that part up to coddle his own pride?"

She paled a little. He knew what she must be thinking, that she could deny the rumors — and that that would likely make them even more interesting for the gossips. Or she could ignore it, in which case it would be Cranach wondering who she'd told and why.

"All I ask is that ye dunnae give Cranach yer true answer until after yer brother's wedding. Ye've spent the last three months as an Englishwoman among the English. Spend the next four days as a Highlands woman among Highlanders. Then decide who ye want to be fer the rest of yer life."

Rowena contemplated him for a long moment, while he finished dressing to give her time to consider what he'd said. Forcing her into it didn't sit well with him, but seeing her choose Robert Cranach would be even worse. Especially if she did it just to spite him — whether she would ever acknowledge that to be a reason or not.

Finally she put her hands on her hips, the blanket sagging deliciously to her waist as she did so. "And what would you suggest I say to everyone who congratulates me on my betrothal?"

Lachlan frowned. He knew what he wished she would say. Obviously, though, she wouldn't be telling anyone they could congratulate her, but they had the name of her husband wrong. "Ye tell them Robert hasnae asked fer yer hand, and ye're a Highland lass who willnae succumb until she's been asked properly and has given her answer." He tilted his head. "Or are ye going to be dragged aboot without having yer own say?"

"You think you can sway me that easily, Lach?"

"Lass," he returned, blowing out his breath, "nothing about ye is easy. In our years growing up, that's what most aggravated me aboot ye. And it's what I most adore. Yer spirit." He sat again on the edge of the bed, far enough away that she couldn't kick him if the mood struck her. "If it were easy to sway ye, I'd nae have any clothes on, and we'd still be naked together in this bed."

Her long, curling hair falling over her shoulders and half obscuring her breasts, Rowena slid off the bed and padded naked around to face him. He stood again, tapping his fingers together to keep from reaching for her. Evidently frustrated with her or not, he still desired her badly.

"Well," she noted slowly, putting out a hand to tug on his waistcoat, "I hate to admit it, but you make a good argument. No, I will not marry someone without being asked, and without giving my answer. Four days, Lachlan." She lowered her hand again. "But you will not change my mind."

"I dunnae know aboot that, lass. I'm very persuasive." Leaning down, he kissed her soft, stubborn mouth. When she kissed him back, he slid his hands around her bare, slender waist and pulled her against him. Whether she'd realized it yet or not, she needed a man who would stand his ground against her. The lass would be bored senseless by a proper gentleman.

With a last kiss she put her palms flat on his chest and pushed herself away from him a few inches. "We'll see about that. Now leave, before someone realizes you're in here."

"Aye." Taking a last glance about to be certain he hadn't forgotten anything, Lachlan walked to her door. Edging it open, he glanced into the hallway. It was empty, which he supposed was fortunate, though he wouldn't have minded an excuse to remain longer in her bedchamber. "Sleep well, Rowena, my fierce Highlands lass. And dream of me."

He knew damned well he'd be dreaming of her. He'd gotten himself four days to convince her that he knew better than she not just what she truly wanted, but what she needed. And that she and he were a perfect match.

CHAPTER TEN

Today, this part of the Highlands no longer looked empty. The vast meadow at the base of Glengask Castle had become a living carpet of sound and color and scent.

Generally the MacLawry clan gatherings saw nearly five hundred people in attendance, but the unique circumstance of Ranulf's wedding had drawn in even more — and that didn't include the other two hundred men, women, and children who arrived with the chiefs and chieftains of other clans.

"Good heavens," Charlotte breathed, as she descended the hill with Rowena and the Mayfair set.

All morning Rowena had been swinging from excitement to trepidation and back again, but the awe in Charlotte Hanover's voice made her smile. "Most of them are your clan now, Charlotte," she said. "Just remember what Ranulf told you; don't go anywhere without Owen. It's likely everyone will just be wanting to meet you, but it's always better to be a little cautious."

"Aye," Owen agreed, and patted the bulge beneath his jacket, only partly obscured by the MacLawry plaid draped over his shoulder. "Me and this blunderbuss willnae be far away."

"Ranulf has protection as well, doesn't he?" Charlotte whispered, taking Rowena's arm. "It seems he would be a more likely target for any trouble than I am."

"We've all got clansmen watching over us," she returned, warmed by her almost sister-in-law's concern even as she looked over the crowd and pretended to herself that she wasn't looking for Lachlan. He would be somewhere in the middle of everything with Bear and Ranulf this morning. And she had more pressing things to worry over right now than him. The cool mountain breeze ruffled past her, and for the thousandth time since he'd left her bedchamber the image of him naked, looking down at her from mere inches away, touched her. Dash it, why did everything make her think of Lachlan this morning?

"Ranulf has Fergus and Una with him, too," Jane put in. "I saw him leaving the house this morning with them. And Bear."

"I certainly wouldn't want to anger those dogs," Charlotte said, smiling again. "It's just . . . there are so many people. And this isn't even half the clan, from what he's said. And they all look to him."

Of course Charlotte would be more touched by this representation of Ranulf's duties as clan chief than by the size of the crowd. That was one of the reasons Rowena was so glad the two of them had found each other. Ranulf needed someone who would look after him first, and the clan second, since he'd always put himself far to the back of everything else.

Holding Mary's hand, Arran moved up beside them, a content smile on his face. "The clan is mostly farmers and fishermen, peat cutters, drovers, and cowherds," he said. "A fierce lot when riled, but they're nae riled today. And as I've been forbidden to try my hand at any of the games, I'll be close by ye, as well."

At the edge of the meadow they had to slow, with everyone wanting to curtsy or bow to Charlotte, and pay their respects to Arran and — with even more open cunosity — Mary. The clashing notes of bagpipes and hundreds of voices chatting in both English and Scottish Gaelic was nearly deafening, and it certainly didn't help Rowena collect her thoughts. If Ranulf hadn't left the house so early she might have caught him then, but she'd overslept. A small smile touched her again. At least she had a good reason for that.

Lachlan had asked her to try to be a Highlander today, but to herself she could admit that with a gathering around her it would have been difficult to be anything *but* a Highlander. In a moment she had her hands full of clootie dumpling and short-bread, and handed bits of treat around for her friends to try.

She looked about as she greeted familiar faces and welcomed new ones. Many of these people, even if they didn't share her name, shared her blood. Somewhere in the past, everyone who wore the black and gray and blood-red colors was a MacLawry, or they'd married into the clan, or more recently they'd been taken in when their own clan had cast them out to make room for sheep and grazing.

Directly to one side of the large, rough circle that had been kept clear for the first of the competitions, they set out blankets and some chairs for Charlotte's parents. Her event, the ladies' horse race, was set for late afternoon, but she'd already donned her riding attire so she wouldn't have to go back to the house and change clothes.

"Aren't you going to sit?" Jane asked, looking up at her.

"In a moment. I need a word with Ranulf, first." A few words, and they were ones he definitely wouldn't like. But if he decided to announce to everyone that his sister was betrothed, she would be caught without ever having been asked.

"I spy him," Arran said, still on his feet, as well.

"That's because you're mountain-sized," she responded, swallowing her nerves behind a smile.

"I'm nae but a hill. Munro's mountain-sized." He offered his arm. "Come along. I'll get ye to him."

That meant she would be telling all three of her brothers. *Best to get it done all at once,* she decided, mostly because she didn't have a choice, and put her hand around his sleeve. "Thank you."

"Mm-hm," he said, as they plowed around the edge of the circle. "Tell me someaught."

"What?"

"I've seen ye pretend to swoon a half-dozen times or so, generally in the hope that Lachlan would catch ye. I've nae known ye to genuinely lose yer senses. So what happened last night to unsettle ye so?"

Heavens, with everything that had happened last evening, she'd almost forgotten that it had begun with her fainting. "If you'll get me to Ranulf, I'll tell you."

"Fair enough." The middle MacLawry brother sent her a sideways glance. "Are ye nae happy aboot Cranach? Ye look a bit . . . off."

Of course if anyone noticed it would be clever Arran. "It's . . . I'm not . . ." She blew out her breath. "Stop noting things for a blasted minute, will you?"

"Aye. I can do that."

Finally they pushed through another group of spectators and emerged into the central clearing. *Wonderful.* So she'd have an audience of seven hundred or so while she spoke a private word to the man who had everyone's attention today. As she approached Ranulf another man clad in MacLawry plaid stepped into view, and she almost stumbled, warmth fluttering through her muscles. Lachlan.

Of course he would be there with Ranulf; she'd put Bear and him in charge of arranging the blasted games. But how was she supposed to tell Ranulf what she needed to say with him standing there, distracting her?

"Glengask, a word with ye," Arran called.

Ranulf met them halfway, Bear and Lach-

Ian and the two deerhounds flanking him. The MacLawry had worn his kilt, too, of course. Even if she was perhaps a bit prejudiced in their favor, in her opinion they were the finest, most bonny group of men in all of Scotland. And England.

"Aye," he said. "Make it a quick word, if ye will. If I dunnae call the games open soon, I predict a riot."

"It's nae me who wants a word. It's Winnie."

The tall men surrounded her, and she caught Lachlan's warm, encouraging gaze. Of course this was what he wanted, though — more time and opportunity to try to change her mind. She was not doing this for him, though. Rather, this was because she refused to surrender without a word given to Rob Cranach. She took a deep breath. "I didn't agree to marry Rob," she said all at once.

Ranulf stared at her for a moment. It wasn't often that she did something to genuinely surprise him — her flight to London had been the last one she could recall. But he looked startled now. "Say that again?" he finally urged, his brows plunging together.

"I'm not saying I won't agree to marry him," she continued, meeting Lachlan's gaze and daring him to contradict that. He'd suggested she speak the truth, and she meant to do so. But that didn't mean she'd decided on him.

"Ye'd best explain, *piuthar,*" Bear put in. "Sooner, rather than later."

"He — Rob — took me aside last night and announced that Ranulf had hunted him down and given his permission for us to wed."

"I wouldnae use the word 'hunted,' precisely," Ranulf countered. Then he sent his own glance at Lachlan. Did he suspect there was more to their arguing than either of them had admitted? "But that's neither here nor there, I suppose. Go on, lass."

Rowena nodded. "I — it surprised me. I mean, you did say I would be able to choose, Ranulf. And I suppose I'd had too much wine, but anyway, I fainted. He didn't actually ask me anything, and I certainly gave him no reply."

"That's nae what he went aboot telling everyone." Bear lifted his head to search the crowd. "The bastard. I'll —"

"Ye'll do naught to him," Ranulf cut in, before Munro could finish describing what sort of violence he would do to Rob. "Ye said ye had no objection to marrying Cranach, aye, Rowena?"

"Aye, but —"

"Arran, go find him. Now. He'll ask, and ye'll answer, and it'll all be settled and everything made clear."

Arran started to stride away, but Rowena grabbed his arm. "That isn't very romantic, Ranulf. For heaven's sake."

The marquis pinned her with the look that had once caused Samuel Cameron to wet himself. Rowena, though, refused to flinch or to look away, let him make what he would of that. "Give us a moment, lads," he said evenly, his gaze never leaving her face.

In a second they were alone, just the two of them, in the center of a vast circle of onlookers, not all of them wishing the best for the MacLawry family. Uneasiness settled into her stomach. Her brother or not, there was no more formidable man in the Highlands than Ranulf MacLawry. And she evidently had his complete, unwavering attention. "This can wait until tonight," she said. "There's a pending riot, as I recall."

"Nae," he said flatly. "It cannae wait. Ye do realize there are thirty or so lads oot there who would chew off their own arms to wed ye, Rowena. Some of them would woo ye, and some of them wouldn't bother with that."

"I've attended every gathering since I can

remember," she returned, frowning. "What's the difference?"

"The difference is that ye turned eighteen three months ago. The difference is that ye were nae the only one to think ye'd be wed to Lachlan. The difference is that everyone here knows by now that the two of ye have been bickering and ye'll nae have him. And that there are other men here seeking to court ye. Ye've put yerself on the block, *piuthar*. Ye're now seen as a woman grown, and an available one. And every lad who wants ye, every clan who wants an alliance, every climber who wants to join nae just clan MacLawry but the family MacLawry, is looking at ye right now with lustful, calculating eyes."

He'd never spoken to her so bluntly before. And his words hammered through her like doom. That was why he'd given his permission to Rob Cranach, why he'd asked Lachlan to tell her there would be no match between them, and why he'd likely meant to use the occasion of opening the games to announce her betrothal. To protect the family, and to protect her.

"So. If it's yer pride that's making ye hesitate, Arran will fetch Cranach and we'll see to it that he asks ye nicely. If it's someaught else, ye need to tell me. Now."

267

His hard blue gaze flicked beyond her shoulder in Charlotte's direction. "And dunnae think I've somehow lost my will because of my lass. I'll nae be embarrassed by ye, Rowena. I'll nae allow the clan to be embarrassed or endangered because now ye dunnae want what ye wanted a day ago."

She took a deep breath. Oh, dear. This didn't bode well. "I've looked at Rob Cranach, as ye asked me to. He's very gentlemanly and pleasant. I'll likely marry him. But now it's . . . It's complicated."

"Complicated . . . how?" her brother prompted.

"I may have made a mistake," she said slowly. "About Lachlan."

Ranulf turned his head to glance at Lord Gray, standing beside Bear and looking at them, clearly frustrated that he'd been uninvited from this chat. Her brother faced her again. "Nae," he said.

Rowena blinked. "But —"

"Nae. The last time ye had a sense that he didnae care fer ye as much as ye cared fer him, ye fled — alone — to London."

"Mitchell was with me."

"And she's damned lucky I didnae leave her behind in London." He took a step closer to her. "Nae, Rowena. Eighteen years is enough. I'll nae see ye heartbroken again when ye realize he's nae the man ye imagined. This is a fresh start, and it's one ye need."

"I'm not saying I wouldn't marry Rob," she tried again, attempting to figure it out in her own head at the same time she was speaking. "I just want a few more days — four more days — to decide. Aside from that, these games, this gathering is for you and Charlotte. I don't want it to be about me."

He narrowed his eyes. "Ye're a clever lass, aren't ye?"

"Perhaps, but it's also the truth. Enjoy your moment, Ran. For once."

Finally he gave a slight nod, as if to himself. "The rumors have already begun aboot ye and Robert. I'll let them stand. That's the four days ye'll have before I formally announce yer betrothal. To Rob Cranach."

"But Lachlan and I are —"

"That's enough, Rowena. The two of ye told me ye were over with, and I made plans accordingly. I'll nae be swayed again. And I'll nae have another of my siblings rewriting alliances behind my back. When Robert bends a knee and asks fer yer hand, ye'll say aye. Is that clear?"

She blinked, unexpected tears blurring her

269

vision. "But —"

"Rowena." He sighed. "I asked ye to choose, and ye did. Dunnae do this to yerself. Eighteen years of crying after a man who doesnae want ye back is enough." He took her chin in his hand and tilted up her face to gaze directly into her eyes. "Four days. Ye may nae like it now, but I reckon ye'll understand once ye see it through. I'll tell him to ask ye, and I'll tell him to make it romantic. And that is that." He searched her gaze. "Say ye understand me, and ye'll do as I ask."

Unable to speak, realizing just how deep this hole was now that she'd allowed Lachlan back into her heart again, Rowena settled for nodding. This *was* what she'd asked for. She just wasn't certain she wanted it, any longer.

"What did he say?" Lachlan asked, intercepting Rowena as she walked over to where her Sassenach friends and Lord Robert sat.

"Not now," she muttered, not looking at him.

Lachlan took her arm, trying to make it look friendly. Brotherly, if that's what everyone expected. "Aye, now, Rowena. Will he give ye — us — four days?"

Silently she shook her head. "No," she

muttered, her voice tight and quiet.

"What do ye mean, no?" he returned, exaggerating the sound of the word.

"He won't confirm the rumors for four days, but only because I said I wanted this gathering to be about him and Charlotte. He said you and I swore off each other, and he made his plans accordingly, and I will not embarrass him by rearranging his alliances."

For a long moment he stared at her as she walked beside him. Yes, he'd made a mistake in not realizing precisely who stood before him. But to not even allow them a chance . . . "But ye told him that Cranach never proposed to ye. I heard ye say it."

"Yes, and he'll encourage Rob to ask me in a proper, romantic manner. Once I'm asked, I'm to say yes. He won't hear any more excuses, and he thinks I'm still just infatuated with you and won't let go of the fantasy."

That might have been flattering, under different circumstances. Now, it sounded like the bell tolling doom. He cursed. "I dunnae accept any of this."

"You have to, Lachlan. I won't see you and my brothers fighting each other." She freed her arm. "And as I said, I never said I would choose you, anyway. It's just . . . It's

271

finished."

He stopped, watching as she returned to her friends and seated herself next to the damned interloper she meant to marry. The muscles across his shoulders held so tightly he would swear they creaked. It wasn't meant to happen like this. If he was certain of one damned thing, it was that he and Rowena were meant to be together.

"Are ye ready, Lach?" Bear asked, slapping him on the back.

He jumped. "In a minute."

Ranulf had neglected one wee corner of his grand plan to marry off his sister, anyway. Lachlan stalked the rest of the distance to where Lord Robert Cranach sat with his cousin on one side, and Rowena on the other. Rowena couldn't marry a dead man.

"Cranach," he said, stopping in front of the group, "I didnae see yer name or yer colors put up fer any of the games here."

"I'm happy to watch the expected triumph of clan MacLawry," the devil returned with a smile.

Rowena kept her gaze on her hands. "No one is being forced to participate, Lachlan. It's just for fun."

"Ye're a bonny, strapping lad, Cranach," he pressed, ignoring her halfhearted protest.

"Do ye mean to sit there, or are ye going to defend the honor of clan Buchanan and toss a caber? Just fer fun, of course."

The Marquis of Helvy's brother narrowed his eyes. "Might I have a word with ye, Lord Gray?" he asked, standing.

"Certainly." Fisticuffs would be better, but he'd settle for a word. For the moment.

Cranach rose and gestured him to walk a few feet away from the rest of Rowena's guests. "I assume this is about me marrying Winnie," he commented.

"Ye're nae marrying her. Ye have to ask her *permission* before ye can marry her, and ye've nae done a thing but let her fall to the floor in a faint. She's nae given ye a thing."

"And you want her for yourself? Are we to settle this over cabers?"

"Or the rope pull or the stone put or claymores or target shooting, or the horse race," Lachlan returned. A man could break his neck during any of those, if he wasn't careful. "I'm only speculating that the sight of ye crawling off the field with yer tail betwixt yer legs willnae impress her overmuch."

"I think I'd be using my time better by sitting beside her while you wallow about in the mud, actually, Gray."

Lachlan shrugged. "Ye're a damned cow-

273

ard. And ye're nae to propose to her until after ye speak with Glengask." It wasn't much, but if he wasn't going to be able to put a sword through the man, he could at least slow him down.

Cranach smiled. "I'll do that, then. And for your own edification, I'm fairly certain Rowena is a lady who prefers a good poetry reading to seeing a lad end-over-end a tree for no good reason."

Well, he was wrong about that. Probably. No, she hadn't asked to be rescued, and she hadn't even actually said she bore him any affection at all — the exact opposite, in fact — but Lachlan had no intention of surrendering. If he'd learned anything from a lifetime in the Highlands, it was that there were two ways of doing things: the straightforward way, and the crooked way. It seemed he'd just chosen the crooked way.

"Speak as prettily as ye like, Cranach. Ye've nae won anything, yet."

"Considering she's never even mentioned your name in my presence and that you seem to know all about me, I'm willing to take my chances." Cranach offered his hand. "Good luck to you, Lord Gray."

Lachlan clenched his jaw and shook his hand, unsurprised even to hear that Rowena wasn't the only one pretending an accent.

The only difference was that Rob was pretending to sound like a Highlander, while she was pretending she didn't sound like one. It was all nonsense as far as he was concerned. "May the best man win, then."

"What the devil was that aboot?" Bear asked, as Lachlan rejoined the men standing by the scattering of logs.

"Didnae I tell ye?" Lachlan said, taking the wide end of a caber and pushing it skyward while Munro braced the narrower end against his feet.

"Tell me what?" With a grunt Bear lifted the upright caber in both palms, bracing it against his chest and one cheek.

"I mean to marry yer sister."

Lachlan swatted his friend on the back, sending him forward. The caber wobbled, then straightened as Bear took a few running steps forward and then heaved upward, sending the log end over end. It landed at just past two o'clock from the six o'clock marked by his feet.

Bear lifted a fist into the air to acknowledge the loud cheers of the crowd. "Ye're a right bastard, ye are," he muttered as he returned to his starting position and shook out his arms.

Lachlan shoved another caber free and braced the narrow end while Bear pushed the larger end up into the air. "Aye. Remember when ye gave me the caber with black beetles crawling on it? Now we're even."

Once the log was straight up, he bent, braced his knees, and lifted it up in his clasped hands. The thing was a beast three times his height, nearly twenty feet long. Shoving air into his lungs he trotted forward and heaved, keeping the thing from twisting sideways as it launched into the air and slammed wide end down into the ground and went over again. It thudded down midway between eleven and twelve o'clock.

"Beat that, big man," he called, throwing both arms into the air as the crowd roared.

"Ye're leaking red, ye know." Bear tossed him a cloth as they stood aside to watch the rest of the competitors throw.

He glanced down at the forearm he'd scraped against the rough wood. "Now it's a games," he said with a hard grin, wiping the blood away with the cloth.

"That was what Winnie and Ran were gabbing aboot, wasnae?" Bear sent his sister a quizzical glance. "So she's decided against Cranach, after all? And Ranulf agreed?"

Lachlan shrugged. "Nae precisely," he said.

Bear moved around to face him. "And what does that mean?"

"It means naught's done until it's done. I've nae surrendered." Now that he'd tasted her, he would never give her up — though telling her brother that would not be in his best interest.

"Well, that explains why ye've been more prickly than a patch of briars, anyway." Green eyes several shades lighter than his own took in the crowd, Ranulf standing on the edge of the clearing with Charlotte on his arm, and then Rowena still seated with Cranach directly beside her. "Ran wants the Buchanan merchants in the Colonies, I reckon," he said after a moment. "I'd rather have ye sitting at Hogmanay dinner with us than Cranach, though. He's too smooth fer my taste. Whatever ye need, ye let me know."

"Ranulf willnae like it. He's set on Cranach."

Munro drew in a breath through his nose. "Ran's getting the lass he wants. Arran got the lass he wanted. Fair is fair."

Lachlan nodded, more appreciative than he could say. "Thank ye, Bear."

"Ye're welcome. And if ye break her heart again, I'll chop ye into wee pieces and feed ye to the pigs."

"I dunnae mean to let her go, this time." If he could catch hold of her.

And he would. He had to. Because the

idea of not having her there for him to kiss, to jest with, to argue with, to hold in his arms, was simply unacceptable.

He scarcely noted when he, Bear, and three large lads from other clans advanced to the next round of cabers. With a few minutes to rest — and drink a quantity of whisky — he left the clearing to go check with Debny and make certain the ladies' horse race route would remain well within sight of both the spectators and the men assigned to keep watch over Rowena.

"Move the hay bales," he instructed, gesturing. "I dunnae want them on the far side of the rock piles."

"Aye, m'laird," the Glengask head groom returned, and went to collect a handful of stableboys to assist him.

"What did you say to Rob?"

A warm shudder ran through his bones as he recognized the voice and turned to face Rowena. "I told him that ye hadn't been asked anything, and that he wasnae to ask ye until he'd spoken with Glengask. And I may have intimated that his path wasnae as uncluttered as he seemed to be assuming. Why?"

"Because he's been glaring at you all afternoon, and being very courteous to me."

Good. An enemy with his attention divided was twice as easy to defeat. "And what aboot ye? Have ye been glaring at me all afternoon?" Because his attention wasn't divided. It was set on her, and nowhere else.

Her gaze lowered to his bare chest. Her cheeks reddening, she met his eyes again. "It doesn't matter. Ranulf decided."

"Ye're nae Ranulf."

"And you are an aggravating man."

"Aye," he agreed. He cocked his head, studying her mobile expression, the pretty gown of red and white with the MacLawry tartan over one shoulder. "Ye know, ye used to agree with everything I said."

"That was when I was infatuated with you."

"I'm glad ye're nae infatuated now. I like sparring with ye, I like seeing yer eyes flash with lightning, and I like yer sharp tongue." He wanted to taste that sharp tongue of hers, but there were far too many people about for that.

"You're glad I don't like you?" she repeated, lifting an elegant eyebrow. "I mean, I suppose that does make everything —"

"But ye do like me," he interrupted. "And finally, it's nae because of what ye imagined me to be." Beyond her he caught sight of one of the Glengask footmen who'd been tasked with keeping the family safe. Good.

He didn't want her walking about on her own, even to come to see him. "It's who I truly am."

"You're trying to change the subject. I came over here to tell you to stop antagonizing Rob. I won't be the reason for a brawl, especially under these circumstances."

Lachlan took a step closer to her. "I'll stop antagonizing Cranach when I've heard ye say ye'll marry me."

"Lachlan."

"I'm nae a gentleman, my fierce lass. I'll nae play according to gentlemanly Sassenach rules of conduct. Ye are the only reason I'm in this, and I'll settle fer naught else." He took another step forward, so they were only inches apart, her sweet, stubborn face lifted so she could continue to glare at him. "Ye're nae married, yet. Ye've nae said aye to anyone. Ye keep yer door unlocked tonight, Rowena."

The quick breath she took, the rise and fall of her bosom, made his cock twitch. "And what if I lock my door?"

"I reckon I'll break it doon." Lachlan caught hold of her hand. "Ye blow hot and cold, lass, like the wind when it cannae decide on the season. I find it maddening. So if there's naught here, if ye've fer certain decided to surrender and marry Cranach because we didnae change our minds soon enough, ye need to tell me. Now. No jests, no innuendos, nothing I can interpret to mean someaught else. Tell me."

She gazed up at his face, her fingers flexing in his. "I don't know," she said finally, then pulled her hand free and walked away.

"Thank God," he muttered darkly, and with a scowl went to toss another round of cabers.

It hadn't been a rousing endorsement, but it was better than a slap in the face. Whether Rowena realized it or not, she'd just said she was giving him a chance. And he didn't mean to waste it.

CHAPTER ELEVEN

"Why do so many of these games involve throwing heavy things about?" Jane asked, holding Black Agnes's bridle as Rowena settled herself into the sidesaddle. Proper or not, today she would almost have preferred to ride astride, but as none of her English friends would ever do such a thing, she supposed it wouldn't be fair. Flora Peterkin was riding astride, and so was Lady Bridget Cameron, but neither of their ponies could match Black Agnes on her worst day. Not on a two-mile-long course.

"When the English took away our swords and guns," she said, checking to be certain her riding hat wouldn't blow off and startle any of the mounts, "the men looked for other ways to show their strength. And to show the Sassenach that we weren't finished fighting, even if we had to resort to throwing rocks."

Jane nodded, turning her head to watch a

stout, large-muscled man walk past. "It's impressive. And somewhat intimidating. Did you see how far Lord Gray threw that last caber? And the blood on his arm when he wiped his brow? It was rather . . . magnificent."

Yes, it had been, the devil. And he'd bested Bear, which almost never happened. The thought that tonight he wanted to come to see her, even with all the other lasses looking at him today, even with any hope of a match between them gone — and not knowing if she'd decided to let him in or not — left her hot and rather . . . uncomfortable. A shivery thrill ran down her spine and settled between her legs. Then she noticed Jane looking up at her expectantly and shook herself. "He did quite well, yes."

"Ah, he cheated." Bear strolled up and tugged on the saddle cinches. "Well, nae cheated, precisely, but he distracted me. I nearly put that last caber into the cook's tent."

"I saw that," Rowena returned, putting on a grin. "We would have had to eat smashed venison tonight."

"Aye. Flattened deer." He squeezed her ankle. "If ye beat that Sarah Parker, I'll purchase ye a new gown."

"Why do you want me to beat Sarah?"

"I reckon she might have it in her mind that she deserves a prize if she wins, and I'm damned tired."

Jane's face turned scarlet, but Rowena snorted. "Poor man. I'll do what I can, but I'll not make any promises."

He nodded, taking the bridle from Jane to lead Black Agnes over to the starting line. "What was that pretty-faced Buchanan chewing on yer ear aboot all morning?"

"He was reciting poetry," she returned.

"Poetry? Aboot the Highlands, at least?"

Rowena shook her head. "The latest Byron poem. It was very lyrical."

"My arse is very lyrical."

"Munro Branan MacLawry," she burst out, trying not to laugh. "You cannot go about saying such things in polite company."

"Are ye polite company now?" he returned, a crooked grin on his face. "Because I saw yer face while he was reciting at ye, *piuthar,* and I reckon ye would rather have been watching the games."

She sighed. That was the rub, wasn't it? "Today, aye. But the games are only once a year, and I like poetry."

"Then tell him to write ye some, and nae steal someone else's words."

"He's not so bad, Bear. You'll get used to him."

He tilted his shaggy head. "Ye mean *ye'll* get used to him. I'll be here, at Glengask."

Before she could spend any time contemplating that pair of rather insightful comments from her brawny brother, Arran approached, lifting a flag to one side of the line of riders.

"Are ye ready, lasses?"

"Aye," she called, wrapping her hands into the reins, the response echoed by the twelve other women on the line.

"Then ready, set, and . . . go!" He dropped the flag.

The course was marked by hay bales and stakes with ribbons tied to the tops. The course was just over two miles long, beginning along the shoreline of the loch, then winding up to the edge of the trees, back around the front of the massive piles of granite boulders, up the hill toward the castle, and then back down into the meadow.

Black Agnes lunged into the lead, with Rowena low along her back and murmuring her encouragement. She glanced over her shoulder to see Flora Peterkin and Sarah Parker directly on her heels, the rest fanned out beyond them.

Sarah's bay mare, Precious, caught them at the trees, but Rowena held Agnes in — this wasn't a sprint, and clearly Sarah was very eager about something. She grinned, the wind chilling her teeth. It would serve Bear right, but she hadn't entered this race to lose it.

At the top of the hill she gave Black Agnes her head. The mare shot forward, dirt and grass kicking into the air under her hooves. Rowena whooped, the sound echoed by the crowd of MacLawry cotters ahead at the finish line.

They drew even with Precious halfway down the hill, and Rowena caught Sarah's expression of surprised dismay as Agnes pounded into the lead. Breathless, grinning, her hair flying about her face, Rowena whooped again as they crossed the line with half a length to spare.

"Ye're a grand, bonny lass, ye are," she panted, patting Black Agnes on the withers. The mare's ears flicked forward and back, and she neighed.

The crowd closed around them, and then Lachlan was there, lifting his arms to her. Rowena kicked out of her stirrup and took hold of his shoulders. When he lifted her into the air she felt a completely different kind of breathless. This man wasn't hers, couldn't be hers, and yet . . .

What she needed to remember was that he'd had his chance. He wasn't some man she'd just met for the first time when she'd returned to Glengask. They had a past, where he'd ignored her flirting and left her to walk home when she'd pretended Black Agnes had gone lame.

But at the same time, he hadn't teased her about how she felt. He hadn't flaunted other women in front of her. In fact, as she began to see all her hounding and flirting from his point of view, she realized that he'd been . . . kind. And good-humored. And at times, indulgent.

"What is it, Rowena?" he asked, setting her feet on the ground but keeping his hands around her waist.

She moved closer, to whisper into his ear. "I won't lock my door," she murmured, then turned to receive Ranulf's congratulations before she could see how Lachlan would respond to that. She supposed she would find that out, tonight. After all, as he'd said, she hadn't been proposed to, yet.

They dined that night in the meadow, on stumps and logs and chairs, on blankets and seated on the cool grass. The Campbell had arrived late in the afternoon with two dozen of his men, and they sat mingled with Mac-Lawrys and Stewarts and MacDonalds. No one drew a dagger, no one reminded anyone else of past misdeeds or brought up old blood feuds. That, despite the fact that the hulking Dermid Gerdens, one of the men who'd nearly killed Arran and her in London, was part of the Campbell's entourage. This gathering was a new start for all the clans, though. Even the Gerdenses.

Rowena's family had done this. Ranulf had worked for most of his life to make a peace in the Highlands, and then Arran had eloped with the Campbell's granddaughter and had convinced the Campbell and the MacLawry to shake hands. It was, quite simply, remarkable.

Rowena looked over at Robert Cranach, sitting only a few feet away and downing a mug of ale. Her family had done so much for the Highlands, for their people, and Ranulf had asked her — well, ordered her now — to do one more thing. It should have been an easy thing, too; Rob was handsome, charming, and cultured.

But it wasn't that easy. Not any longer.

Lachlan was wild, and impetuous, and proud to be so. He was already an integral part of clan MacLawry, and brought with him no new alliances. He bled Highlands red, and would never be happy in London, or even in Edinburgh or Aberdeen. That didn't matter, of course — except that it did. Because whatever her mind told her, that it was settled and she was merely waiting for flowers and a man on bended knee, her heart wasn't nearly as certain.

On that cue Bear and Lachlan strolled into the small cleared area around the bonfire. Both wore sabers in scabbards on their hips. She smiled, something deep and heated running through her.

Jane took her arm. "Are they going to fight?" she whispered, concern on her face.

"No. They're going to dance."

"Dance? Did you know?"

Angus Mackles, who'd been Glengask's chief piper since before she was born, came into view and took a place on the far side of Bear. The two men unsheathed their sabers and set them on the ground, forming a pair of crosses with the scabbards.

Right hands curved up into the air and left toes pointed, they waited. Then with a wail the music began, and they stepped into the dance. Perfectly together, perfectly in unison.

"What does it mean?" Jane whispered after a moment.

"It's about power, and controlling it,"

Rowena answered, her gaze never leaving Lachlan. "They step and jump aboot the sword to all four points of the compass, crossing back and forth. If they touch a blade it's bad luck for the clan, but they get as close as they can to show they have no fear."

"Oh. It's rather splendid. Do you sword dance, Lord Robert?" her friend asked.

"No. It's a very old-fashioned dance. I do waltz, though."

It wasn't old-fashioned. It was fierce, and very difficult, especially when performed in tandem. And it was mesmerizing, in a way she'd never noticed before. The flex of strong, hard calf muscles, the flash of knees, the swirl of MacLawry plaid with the blood-red bands picking up the firelight, and the sweet, ancient sound of the lone pipes.

When they'd danced the four points each returned to his original position. They stopped, the music stopped, and they bowed in the same heartbeat. For a long moment the only sound in the clearing was the crack of the fire and the soft exhalation of the bag-pipes.

And then the gathered clans roared. Tonight, they were all fierce, free, blood-spattered Highlanders.

Rowena stood. Green eyes met hers across

the firelight. "I'm quite tired tonight," she said, her gaze still on Lachlan. "I think I'll go to bed."

Lachlan downed the mug of beer someone handed him, then nearly choked on it as another lad pounded him on the back. The sword dance had been Bear's idea, and he was still somewhat surprised that Ranulf had given his approval. But he had, and by God, they'd shown the clans that the Mac-Lawrys still remembered the old ways. Most of the other clans had already learned that the MacLawrys also embraced the new — or at the least were willing to turn it to their own advantage.

All that spun through his mind as moments of later significance. At present, he was mostly interested in watching Rowena head back up the hill toward Glengask Castle, two footmen flanking her. From her expression just before she'd left, she wanted him to join her up there. He was certainly more than willing to do so.

He could only hope this meant that she'd realized how much she valued her own culture and traditions, because he figured he had been lumped into that basket. At least tonight it was the basket she wanted. As he set down the mug and accepted another handful of congratulations he spared a moment to glance at Lord Robert Cranach. Rob still sat on the blanket where most of the Sassenach had gathered, and he was conversing again with his cousin. Smug bastard. Well, he might have won — though Lachlan wasn't yet ready to wager on that count — but he hadn't won yet.

"I'm going up to the hoose," he told Bear, who nodded at him.

No, he didn't have an excuse for leaving the party to visit another man's home, but luckily his friendship with the MacLawrys was deep enough that he didn't require one. He had no idea what he would say, anyway; admitting he was off to ravish their sister — especially now that she'd nearly been handed over to someone else — would only see him tossed into the bonfire.

Without the crowd and the several fires surrounding him, the walk up the hill was surprisingly chilly. Not that he felt the cold. Not tonight. Not when a fierce young lass waited for him.

Cooper the butler had been given leave to attend the gathering, so it was one of the underfootmen who opened the front door for him. Other than nodding at the lad, Lachlan ignored him as he headed for the stairs. He had a feeling that finding his way into Rowena's bedchamber would be a much easier proposition than escaping the house afterward, but he meant to take the risk.

Her door was shut. Lachlan rapped twice, softly, then opened the door and slipped inside. Before he could take a breath she was on him, her mouth molding against his, her hands digging into his shoulders and pulling at his tartan and shirt.

He put his arms around her waist, touching soft, warm skin. Saint Bridget, she was already naked. "I'm glad it was me, walked in here."

With a breathless chuckle, she licked at his throat, then returned to his mouth again. "So am I."

"Slow doon, lass," he murmured, his voice muffled against her. "We've nae reason to hurry."

"I want ye, Lachlan," she returned, dropping his tartan to the floor. "I don't know if ye're good for me, but I want ye."

Moving his hands to her shoulders, he held her a little away from him. "I *am* good fer ye, lass. And I dunnae mean this to be a handful of nights ye can look back on later and sigh aboot. These nights are only our first nights together, Rowena. Only our first."

For a moment he worried that he'd just pushed her too hard, and that she would try to shove him back out the door rather than admit she might be trying to think of a way out of a marriage with Lord Rob. Then she sighed and closed on him again, pulling his shirt free from his kilt and sliding her hands up his chest beneath the material. "Convince me," she breathed.

Oh, that he was quite willing to do. Once she'd yanked his shirt off over his head he unbuckled the saber and carefully set it aside, not wanting to alert anyone with its solid clank on the hard floor. Then he unwrapped his kilt and dropped it as well. He felt a bit foolish in his stockings and ghillie brogues, so he reached down to yank out the knots and then used one foot to bare the other.

As she reached up to catch his face and nibble on his ear, his eyes practically rolled back in his head. He'd hoped the dance would stir something in her — a pride, memories, realization — but lust was perfectly acceptable, too.

Turning, he pinned her against the wall, grabbing her wrists and holding her arms above her head as he devoured her mouth. She gyrated her hips, brushing against his cock, and he groaned. Whatever shyness she'd had last night, she'd clearly gotten past. Tonight she was a wildcat, pushing him to the very edge of control. He loved it.

Freeing her arms, he put his hands on her hips and lifted. "Put yer legs aboot me, my fierce lass," he said in a low voice.

She did so, and dug her fingers into his shoulders. Lachlan lowered her over his own hips, impaling her against the wall. With a gasp she bit his shoulder hard enough to leave a mark, but he didn't care. All that mattered was that Rowena was in his arms, around him. And he meant to claim her for his own. Forever.

Thrusting forward, he entered her hard and fast, her quick, moaning breaths as arousing as the rest of her. Outside the bagpipes had resumed, this time playing an old country song, "The Bonnie Lass of Fyvie." He wasn't so certain he wanted to hear a tune of unrequited love while he was inside Rowena, but he was grateful for anything that would keep the majority of the household outside in the meadow.

With another quick moaning breath she climaxed, and he slowed his movements as she shivered around him, clinging to his shoulders. Grinning, he kissed her sweet mouth. "Good God, ye feel fine to me, lass," he murmured, slipping his arms around her back to hold her and walking them over to her bed.

Still inside her, he set her onto her back and moved over her. Taking a breast into his mouth, he resumed his thrusts, slow and deep, in time with the motions of his tongue. The flex of her fingers, her obvious arousal and delight — it pushed him to the edge, and then beyond. With a low moan he climaxed, pressing against her as he came. He didn't know if she realized it or not, but he deliberately hadn't taken any precautions with her. Because he already knew that she would have his children, be his woman, whether she'd realized it yet, or not.

When he could breathe again he rolled onto his back, his heart stuttering until she turned on her side and curled against him, resting her head on his shoulder. Every time she approached him, every time she initiated contact, it felt like a gift.

"How long had you lads been practicing that dance?" she asked, running her fingers in a lazy circle around his left breast.

"We did it once," he returned. "We didnae have time fer more, and that's a thing that once ye learn it, ye cannae ferget it."

"I think you could forget it, if it didn't mean anything to ye."

He frowned. What did that mean? "It

means some-aught to me, Rowena."

"I know. And it does to me, as well, surprisingly enough. I remember when you and Bear taught me to dance it."

"Aye. The clans would be scandalized to know a wee lass danced the swords. But ye did it well, and ye knew what it meant." He paused, considering. "Is that what ye were talking aboot? That ye fergot it?"

"No. I mean, I think it would take more than one practice for me to get it right, but then women don't generally dance it. I . . . never mind."

"Ah."

She twisted her head to look up at him. " 'Ah,' what?"

"I'll nae say his name while I'm in here with ye, lass. But I assume he didnae remember the dance?"

Rowena settled against him again, her breath soft and warm on his chest. "If he ever knew it."

Did he detect a note of disdain? He could gloat, he supposed, but that didn't seem productive. It could come back to haunt him. This "being a gentleman" nonsense was just that, but he cared for her feelings, and so he altered what he wanted to say. "He's the lad yer *bràthair* wants ye to wed, Rowena. And he was chosen fer his English culture, because that's what ye say ye value. Ye cannae expect him to know the ways of the Highlands, too."

"And you only know the ways of the Highlands, I presume?"

"I know a bit more than that. I can quote ye a bit of Keats, if ye wish: 'Much have I travell'd in the realms of gold, And many goodly states and kingdoms seen.' "

She chuckled. "I had no idea."

"That's because I generally read at night, after I go back to Gray Hoose." Outside the pipes began another song, the accompanying words echoing up from the meadow.

"That's 'Flowers of the Forest,' " she commented. "Isn't that a bit somber for a celebration?"

"Ye know us Scots: Always ready to celebrate, and always remembering death's but a poorly spoken word away." He listened for a moment, then began to softly sing.

Dool and wae for the order sent oor lads
    tae the Border!
The English for ance, by guile wan the day,
The Flooers o' the Forest, that fought aye
    the foremost,
The pride o' oor land lie cauld in the clay.

Rowena turned onto her stomach, resting

her chin on her hands atop his chest to watch him. "That's what frightens me, you know," she said quietly. "Not the English — not this time, anyway — but how fragile this peace that you and Ranulf and Arran have managed for us is. What do you think would happen if I did turn Rob away? I don't mean just with him, but with clan Buchanan. And don't lie to me."

"I wouldnae lie to ye. I never have."

She lifted an eyebrow. "Nae?"

"Nae."

Rowena almost wished she hadn't asked the question, and not just because Lachlan hadn't wanted to say Rob's name while they were lying entwined and naked, on her bed. But she'd become accustomed to confiding in Lachlan, she realized. And as she recalled, he did always seem to tell her the truth, or at the least tell her that he couldn't or wouldn't discuss a certain topic with her. Arran and Ranulf would tease, Bear would distract, but Lachlan answered her questions. And if she was remembering all the times he'd failed to return her romantic interest, she supposed it was only fair that she also remember the good things about him. The good things that for three months she'd forgotten.

"Bear reckons that Ranulf wants the Buchanan merchant contacts in America," he said after a moment, his left arm draped loosely over her back. The easy possessiveness of the gesture was . . . arousing.

"And do ye agree?"

"Nae. I think Ranulf wants the wool manufacturers."

"But we don't raise sheep."

"Nae. What we do have are cotters in need of employment, though. And I think Ranulf would appreciate the irony of those who lost their lands because of sheep making their living because of 'em."

For a long moment she gazed at his face, his expression unreadable in the half dark. "You aren't helping, ye know."

He shrugged beneath her. "Ye asked me a question. I answered it."

"Then why should I marry ye? If I could, I mean."

She expected that to make him angry. In some ways, she preferred that he be angry. When they argued she found it much easier to recall his less attractive qualities. Because of course she knew them all.

His hand stroked slowly down her spine. "Ye should marry me because I adore ye, my fierce lass. I ken how stubborn ye are, how ye like all yer gowns to have lace, how ye dunnae mind spiders but roaches make ye scream."

Her heart gave a warm thud. "Go on. What else do ye know about me?"

Lachlan smiled. "I know ye like sad songs, but prefer Shakespeare's comedy — especially *The Taming of the Shrew.* Yer favorite color is lavender. And ye truly do think ye saw the ghost of old Dougall MacLawry and his pipes in this room with ye one night during a storm."

"But did ye believe me about it?"

"Aye. I saw the look on yer face, and I did believe ye. Why do ye think I ran up here with a dagger in my hand when ye came downstairs screaming?"

Her brothers had run up to her bedchamber, too, angry in a way she hadn't understood until much later. They'd thought a strange man had been in her bedchamber, though. Evidently only Lachlan was willing to admit that he believed the story she'd told. She believed it; even now, as a woman grown, she kept her eyes closed on stormy nights.

She kissed his chest. "That's nice of you to say, anyway."

He lifted an eyebrow as he tucked his free arm beneath his head. "I'm nae nice. I told ye, I dunnae lie to ye, Rowena."

"Then tell me something. Truthfully." It

would likely be wiser to stop asking questions, to stop thinking, and to simply enjoy being with him while she could. But perhaps he'd thought of a solution to this predicament even if she hadn't been able to conjure a single thing. "You know what Ranulf said. I'm to marry Lord Rob. So why do you keep talking about marrying me?"

"It's nae just me talking aboot it, Rowena. And until ye've said yer vows to another man, I'm nae giving ye up. Nae even then, truth be told."

She brushed at her eyes and the tears that threatened to overflow them. "Why is it now, after I thought to walk away from you, that I finally believe you like me?"

"Because I *do* like ye. I *love* ye, Rowena. Mayhap it took ye slapping my face to open my eyes, and mayhap ye have changed some, or I have, but I adore ye. And I willnae let ye go." His arm tightened across her back.

"Ranulf says ye will."

Lachlan sat up, pulling the sheets up over her chilled legs and shifting so he could lean back against the headboard. She moved, too, twining her fingers with his and resting her cheek against his shoulder. Why could she imagine being with him like this every night? Why could she imagine waking in his arms and listening to him sing to her in his lovely baritone? And why did London seem the silly daydream now, when she finally had it in her grasp?

"What, precisely, did Ranulf say?" he asked, brushing hair from her eyes. "Other than the bit aboot him having Cranach propose to ye properly?"

Rowena sighed. "Are ye looking for a secret passage away from this mess? Because I doubt Ranulf would allow such a thing to slip by him."

"Just tell me, lass. Unless ye are getting precisely what ye want."

"That's not fair, Lachlan. I asked him for time to choose between the two of you." Although as she considered it, she'd truly been asking for time to reconcile to letting Lachlan go. And four days wouldn't be nearly enough time. A hundred years wouldn't be enough time for her to choose to give him up. Not any longer.

For a long moment he sat silently beside her. She felt the rise and fall of his chest as he took a deep breath. "I'd say yer time is up, Rowena. Forgetting everything else, who would ye choose?"

Within the half-dozen heartbeats it took him to ask the question, she knew the answer. She'd thought it would be more difficult, and perhaps it should have been, but when it came down to nothing but a choice between civilized Lord Robert Cranach and wild Lachlan MacTier, it was very, very simple.

"I would choose you," she whispered.

He tilted her chin up and kissed her soft and slow and long. "Thank Saint Andrew fer that."

When she could breathe — and think — again, she scowled. "But it doesn't matter. Ranulf said that when Lord Rob proposes to me, I am to give my consent."

His fingers tightened around hers. "That's how he said it? When Cranach proposes, ye're to agree?"

She nodded. "Aye. What —"

"So he doesnae consider yer fainting to mean ye agreed to anything. In Glengask's eyes, ye're nae yet engaged."

"What does that —"

Lachlan straightened, turning to face her. "What if Cranach doesnae propose to ye, then?" His eyes glinted ferociously.

"Ye can't kill him!" she exclaimed, alarmed. "It would be the start of a war with the Buchanans."

"Which we would win handily," he said absently, his mind clearly spinning some plot or other. "But nae. I'd only kill him as a last resort."

"Lachlan."

"What if fer some reason he decides nae to propose to ye? Ranulf wants to announce yer betrothal at the wedding feast. If it's nae to Cranach, it'll have to be to me."

"But why would he not propose?" She flushed as he lifted an eyebrow at her. "I don't mean because I'm an irresistible siren or something. I mean because of my dowry, and whatever Ranulf has decided to grant clan Buchanan upon our wedding."

His slow, sly grin both worried and aroused her. He might not be plotting a murder, but she doubted Ranulf or anyone else would approve whatever he was thinking. She wasn't certain *she* would approve it, though if he would always look at her in that same intense, possessive way, she could likely be convinced to attempt just about anything.

"First, tell me what ye know about Cranach," he said, moving over her again with his clever mouth. "Everything ye know."

She moaned at his touch. "I thought you didn't want to talk about him while you were in bed with me," she managed, sinking backward onto the soft pillows.

"Oh, I'll talk aboot him if it gives me a

way to keep ye from him, my fierce, bonny lass."

Rowena twined her arms around his shoulders. This was going to be trouble. All her life her brothers had indulged her and spoiled her, and if Lachlan managed what he was about to attempt, she was going to terribly disappoint Ranulf. What Lachlan had said earlier continued to sink into her, though. She wasn't infatuated with him any longer. She wasn't blind to the man he truly was. And that man, the one holding her in his arms and kissing her, oh, everywhere, was turning out to be much more interesting and much more compelling than the one she'd imagined.

The idea of giving him up, even in exchange for employment for the cotters they kept taking in, didn't seem fair. It wasn't acceptable, in fact, and she meant to do what she could to keep Lachlan MacTier, the real, true Lachlan MacTier, in her life. This time, forever.

CHAPTER TWELVE

Going against Ranulf MacLawry's wishes was a risky proposition under the best of circumstances. Removing Rowena from Glengask's plans, halting an alliance with the Buchanans, and directly countermanding his orders would be something most of his clansmen, much less one of his dozen chieftains, would never even contemplate.

Lachlan, though, meant to do more than contemplate defiance. He meant to see it through and take for himself what had been promised to another man. And he now had three days in which to do it.

The morning was to begin with the men's horse race. Yawning, Lachlan oversaw Beowulf being saddled, and then trotted him the two miles to Glengask to warm him up. They likely wouldn't be winning the race, but it had to look like he'd tried.

He found Glengask's head groom in the stable yard, barking orders as a dozen geldings and stallions were led out and walked about the yard. "Good morning, Debny."

"M'laird."

"I dunnae see Prince," Lachlan commented, unwilling to waste precious time with small talk.

"Lord Robert's black? Nae, he's nae entered in the race."

"Hm. We'll see aboot that."

With that he entered the castle through one of the side doors and made his way up to the large breakfast room. Cranach sat at the table, a large plate in front of him. And he was seated beside Rowena, damn him, as if matters had already been settled. Well, they hadn't. And they wouldn't be. Not the way Cranach believed, anyway.

Rather than walking straight in to begin the game, Lachlan leaned against the door frame and watched Rowena. Long eyelashes half hid her quicksilver-gray eyes, and the smile on her oval face looked forced — which didn't surprise him. Whatever happened, she would be right in the middle of it. He would protect her, and he would stand beside her through all of it, but eventually she would have to tell her brother her own mind. It all came down to that.

This morning she also looked tired, and for that he refused to apologize. He'd stayed in bed with her until just before dawn, and had barely made it out the side door before the kitchen servants rose. For a moment or two he'd even weighed the consequences to both of them if he simply allowed himself to be caught in her bedchamber. If Ranulf wanted an alliance with the Buchanans, though, he would find a way to get it — unless Lachlan and Rowena took the opportunity out of his hands altogether.

Finally he pushed upright and strolled into the room. "Are ye certain ye should be eating so heavily before a horse race, Cranach?" he drawled.

In response a dozen pairs of eyes looked up at him, but only two of them mattered. He exchanged a glance with Rowena, then clenched his jaw and turned his gaze to Lord Robert.

"I find the quantity of bread and gravy I consume has nothing to do with my enjoyment of viewing a horse race," Cranach returned, with his customary faint, slightly condescending smile.

"Oh," Rowena said, then covered her mouth and looked down again.

Lachlan hid his own grin. She was in it with him, his Rowena. Before dawn he'd been certain, but they'd been on different paths for so long that for a moment he'd had his doubts that she would go through with it now that the sun was up and she couldn't blame any madness on a dream. But she was still with him, by God. "What's amiss, lass?" he asked, in case Lord Robert didn't bother to inquire.

"Nothing, of course. I . . . Oh, it's silly."

"What's silly, Winnie?" Robert finally queried. "Ye must tell us."

"It's just that after I won the ladies' race, I mentioned to Jane and Edith that we — you and I, Rob — would be a triumphant duo once you won the men's race. I didn't know I was going to be the only one competing."

Oh, well done, lass, Lachlan thought silently. "Well, perhaps he can recite poetry to ye while *I* win the prize, Rowena."

"I'm going to be watching the race," she returned, real excitement touching her voice. "Not listening to poetry."

"A pity it's too late for me to enter, then," Rob commented, his smile fading a little.

"Oh, it's nae too late, m'laird." This time it was Owen, Glengask's head footman and London butler, who spoke up. "I'll run oot myself and tell 'em to saddle yer pony if ye wish it."

"Grand!" Rowena exclaimed, then subsided again, but not before she sent Lachlan a glance that warmed him to his bones. "I mean, it would be grand. It's up to you of course, Rob. As I said, it's all for fun."

Cranach inclined his head. "I suppose I'm racing, then."

"I'll see ye at the starting line. And ye'd best stop piling on that gravy."

By the time they all lined up at the start, there were twenty-six horses entered, everything from shaggy mountain ponies to Lord Samston's black Thoroughbred. That was good; the more confusion and muddle, the better. The men's course was twice the length of the ladies', and it wound behind boulders and into the tree line in several places.

Bear and his big gray stallion, Saturn, were in the mix, as well, though, and that could be a problem. Munro had said he supported a match between Rowena and him, but Lachlan wasn't certain how close his friend would be willing to get to directly defying Ranulf. Even if that wasn't precisely what they were doing, it was close enough.

"I talked to Ranulf last night, after ye left," Bear said in his version of a low voice, reining up beside Lachlan and Beowulf. "He wants Winnie happy and married and nae sighing over ye any longer, Lach."

"And I want Rowena happy and married

311

to me," he returned, settling into the saddle as Arran appeared with the flag. "And I want her here, in the Highlands, and not at Fort William or in London for most of the year and nae wearing another clan's colors. Nearly the same thing."

"Aye, if dirt and water are the same."

Lachlan took a breath. "I know what Ranulf wants. And I think I know what Rowena wants. All I ask is that ye keep what I said to yerself, and ye dunnae interfere, Munro."

"I reckon I'll wait and see a bit before I decide that."

"Fair enough." Lachlan nodded. It wasn't a rousing endorsement, but Glengask hadn't appeared with a rifle in his hands, so it would have to do. For now, anyway.

"Gentlemen!" Arran called in a carrying voice. "And Scotsmen!" That elicited some laughter, and the middle MacLawry brother grinned. "On yer mark. Set. Go!" And he lowered the flag.

The course all across the meadow was lined with spectators, so Lachlan settled in a length or so behind Prince and waited. Samston and his Devil or Satan or whatever the black's name was sprinted into the lead. The Sassenach could gallop all the way back to London, for all Lachlan cared. It wasn't the earl who concerned him.

The second he was out of sight of the spectators and into the trees, Lachlan kicked Beowulf in the ribs. With no noticeable effort the bay closed on Prince. They drew even, and then pulled half a length ahead. Lachlan shifted right in the saddle. In response, Beowulf veered hard to the left. Prince saw them coming and edged left as well, sending Cranach whipping into the low-hanging branches at the edge of the trail.

"Whoa, boy, none o' that!" Lachlan yelled, straightening and making a show of tightening up on the reins. They fell back again as the course rounded out to the edge of the meadow.

"What the devil was that?" Bear asked, coming up hard on his right.

"What?"

"I've seen ye ride, Lach."

Lachlan scowled. "It was a Highlands hello. Ye said ye'd stand back."

"And if ye do it again he'll know it wasnae an accident. So *ye* stand back."

Damn, damn, damn. He had three bloody days, now. If Bear tried to step on everything he meant to attempt, he would have to either admit defeat and watch Rowena walk up the church aisle and on to another man's bed, or he would have to grab her and make a run for it. And she would never do that to Ranulf. He would consider it, but he was a MacLawry chieftain. Moving directly in opposition to the MacLawry's orders troubled him to his bones.

The riders pounded onto the narrowest part of the course, between the huge boulders and the standing rain from the last storm. And he watched as Cranach kept Prince steady in the center of the path. And he cursed.

Munro and Saturn pushed past him and up on Cranach's left. "I dunnae mean to lose my own damned race!" Bear bellowed, staying to the middle as he and the big bay shoved past a pair of riders and then shouldered hard into Prince.

The wiry black stumbled. Then he righted himself. Cursing again, Lachlan settled low on Beowulf's neck. "Go, lad," he muttered. The bay's ears flicked back at him, and then they were off. "I'm nae losing ten quid to ye, Bear!"

This time Prince stumbled into the mud, missed a step, and balked. Lachlan only had a second to glimpse Cranach's green-faced expression before the man went head-first into the mud and Prince resumed the race without his rider.

Back onto the flat meadow again, Beowulf edged up on Saturn. They both passed Devil/Satan, who looked ready to toss his own rider. "Thank ye, Bear," Lachlan panted.

"Ye owe me. Dunnae ferget that."

"I willnae."

Duncan Lenox, one of the MacLawry chieftains, passed Donald MacAllister at the last turn and flashed across the finish line on his chestnut gelding, Bruce. Lachlan and Bear finished fourth and fifth, though as far as Lachlan was concerned, twenty-fifth would have been fine. Because Lord Robert Cranach didn't even finish twenty-sixth.

As soon as the rest of the horses cleared the trail he turned Beowulf back up toward the boulders at a walk. No sense hurrying, after all. When Cranach came into sight, Lachlan didn't even bother hiding his grin. No one else, would, either. "Cranach, are ye injured?"

The six-foot pile of mud swore at him. "You bloody did that on purpose."

"I've taken a mud bath a time or two myself. They say it's good fer the skin. I dunnae ken aboot yer fancy riding clothes, though."

"Give me a ride back, at least."

Lachlan backed Beowulf out of Cranach's

reach. "Nae. Ye'll have me all dirty."

"I'll see you with a bloody nose, I will."

"Ye can try. The next event's the rope pull. I'll sign ye up." He turned the bay back toward the crowd.

"She's going to be mine, you know."

"Aye? Then welcome to the family." Kneeing his bay, Lachlan left Cranach behind to walk the rest of the way back to the tents. Once he'd dismounted and handed his mount off to a groom, he went to find Rowena.

She stood with the Hanover sisters, Charlotte and Jane. At least Ranulf wasn't there. He wished he knew how far she would be willing to go — because he would meet her there. "Lasses," he drawled, brushing grass and dirt from his kilt.

"Lord Gray," Jane said, offering him a smile and a curtsy that was purely Sassenach. A rare pleasant one, she was, but English without a doubt. "I see you trounced Lord Samston."

"Aye. I dunnae reckon he means to pay up on his wager, though." He shrugged. "I didnae win the race, so I'll nae press him on it."

"That's very generous of you," Jane returned. "Under the circumstances I don't think I'd be so magnanimous."

Her sister's brow furrowed at that. "Under what circumstances, pray tell?"

Jane forced a laugh. "Oh, it's nothing. We — Rowena and I — discovered Samston only pretended to be infatuated with Winnie because he wanted her dowry."

"Ah." Ranulf's betrothed turned her gaze on Lachlan. "And you knew about this?"

Ranulf wouldn't have fallen for a thick-headed lass. He therefore needed to tread carefully. "I figured it oot," he said, folding his arms over his chest and straightening. She was a tall lass, but that still meant she barely came to his chin. "Rowena gave him a piece of her mind and sent him scuttling away, so I didnae feel the need to bloody him over it."

Charlotte nodded. "Good, then. I'm glad it's been handled. I imagine Ranulf would have preferred to know, but he's had several other things on his mind this week." She grinned, excitement lighting her hazel eyes nearly to green.

"As do y— Oh, my," Jane exclaimed, her attention on something beyond Lachlan's left shoulder. "What happened to Lord Rob?"

They all turned to look, and Lachlan took the moment to brush the tips of his fingers against Rowena's. "He claims he'll have ye,

317

whatever I say aboot it," he breathed, standing as close to her as he dared. "I bade him welcome to the family."

"Oh, dear," she muttered back, as the rest of the crowd caught sight of the muddy scarecrow figure. "Perhaps I should try talking to him. He's been nothing but polite so far, after all."

"Ye know, he only pretends to sound like a Highlander," he returned. "Oot of yer hearing he says 'verily' and 'jolly good.' "

A laugh burst from her chest. "I seem to be pretending an accent as well, Lach. I cannae hold that against him."

"He's a good man, then." Clenching his jaw, he lowered his head toward hers. "Why should ye nae marry him?"

Her gray eyes practically sparked. "Because there's another man I want," she stated, thankfully keeping her voice down. "For a time I thought only one of us had grown up, and then I wondered if we were simply destined never to want the same thing at the same time. But no one knows me as well as he does. No one means to me what he does." She lowered her head to give him a sly glance from beneath her long lashes. "And I daresay I'm the only lass who knows what the wee scar on the left side of yer arse is from."

Lachlan snorted, far more content and optimistic than he likely should have been. After all, they were attempting to bend the orders of the most formidable man he'd ever met, and the stakes were the happiness of a woman who'd always been precious to him, and who over the past few days had become vital to his own survival.

"If I have my way, Rowena, ye'll be the only lass who ever knows yer mountain of a brother put a fish hook through my hind-quarters. Now, go talk to Lord Rob, and dunnae let him get ye anywhere alone." For a bare, mad moment he nearly kissed her right there in front of all the clans.

She nodded, clearly not realizing how close she'd come to a public disaster. "You'll just have to trust me."

"I do, lass. That, I do."

Ranulf had discovered some time ago that good haggis tasted, for all intents and purposes, the same. He shoveled in another mouthful, smiled, chewed, and swallowed. "That's glorious, Mrs. Meason," he proclaimed, and moved on to the next offering.

Why the devil anyone cared for his opinion as to who cooked the best haggis, he had no idea. But someone had handed him three ribbons and asked him to choose his three favorite dishes, and so he would. As he nodded and smiled over the next plate he caught sight of a mud-covered Lord Robert Cranach stalking through the crowd toward the house.

Immediately he looked about for Rowena. A moment later he found her standing a few steps behind Charlotte and Jane, in deep conversation with Lachlan. The first two were looking at Cranach, as was most everyone else at the gathering. The second two were looking at each other.

Their fingers brushed, quickly, and then parted again. Lachlan said something, his expression serious, and Rowena nodded. Then she smiled. Only then did she incline her head and go walking after Cranach.

"Ye've three more left to sample, m'laird," Mrs. Forrest, his head cook and the lass Rowena had asked to oversee the food competitions, commented. "Do ye wish another beer?"

"Aye, Mrs. Forrest. I need to rinse my gullet."

He downed half the beer Peter Gilling fetched for him, and resumed his stroll along the table, dividing his attention between the haggis and his sister. Rowena might have gone to get herself proposed to, but Cranach didn't look in the mood to bend down on one knee and say something a young lass eager for love would find romantic.

Aside from that, she hadn't been happy about his pronouncement yesterday. Today, she looked . . . excited. What, then, had changed? A night of reflection, perhaps — after all, he'd gone to a great deal of effort to find a man who met the requirements that she'd deemed most important. But Lachlan looked happy, as well. And that, he couldn't quite find a reason for.

A few weeks ago, aye. He would have expected Lord Gray to be relieved that Rowena had found another man on whom to lavish her attention. Why, then, was Lachlan presently gazing after Rowena and wearing a supremely unbrotherly smile?

He took his last mouthful of haggis, choked it down with more beer, and handed out the three ribbons. Charlotte, he decided, owed him a grand favor for keeping her away from the Scottish treat — and he had several ideas how he would collect. With a grin of his own he whistled Fergus and Una to his heel and strolled through the pockets of boisterous guests toward where Arran supervised the laying out of the stout pull rope. The contest was to be among clan MacLawry, as they represented the majority present, and all comers.

The rope spanned the narrow stream that crossed one edge of the meadow on its way to Loch Shinaig. A bright red ribbon marked its center point, directly over the middle of the water. "Who are ye putting in the front on our side?" he asked.

"Lach volunteered," Arran returned, "which is only fair considering he and Bear are supposed to be the ones organizing the damned games."

"They couldnae lower the flag fer a race they were in."

"Aye. I ken that it makes sense fer me to help oot, with my maimed wing."

"But?" Ranulf prompted, half his attention on where Rowena and muddy Cranach stood talking, Jane Hanover now with them.

"It's naught ye need to worry over," Arran said with a grimace, making a dismissive gesture with one hand. "Ye've enough in yer brain, what with getting married day after tomorrow."

A low, excited . . . satisfaction flowed through his veins at the thought of it. Charlotte was his, and always would be, but he wanted everyone to see it. Saint Andrew, he wanted to bellow it to the sky. Ranulf shook himself. If something troubled clever Arran, he needed to know what it was. "Oot with it."

"I dunnae ken what it is." His brother shrugged. "Someaught's afoot."

"Trouble?" The MacDonalds were the most likely source, but there was no love lost between the Gerdenses and the Mac-Lawrys — and the Gerdenses answered to the Campbells. "What have ye seen?"

"Naught in particular. It's just . . ." He shrugged. "Lachlan scheduled all the contests, had it doon on paper to keep it organized. This morning he went and changed everything, so there's nae a man who knows where he's supposed to be when. And he added Lord Robert's name to most of the competitions. And then he went off and left me with the mess." Arran scowled. "I dunnae mind it, truly. I'm nae complaining aboot that. It was just . . . the hairs on the back of my neck pricked."

With a nod, Ranulf looked across the meadow again. "I know the feeling."

"Mayhap I'm just expecting trouble," his younger brother continued. "We've had only three fights since we put up the tents. It's unsettling."

Perhaps that was it, after all. After so many years of conflict, it *was* unsettling to see Campbells sitting with MacLawrys, and

323

Camerons with Stewarts. "Who's at the front of the other side of the rope?"

"It's supposed to be none of the MacLawry's affair, but it's Lord Rob's name on the list." Arran stood there for a moment. "Do ye want me to change it?"

"Nae. Leave it. If he doesnae like it, he can change it himself."

Whatever was afoot, Lachlan, Rowena, and Rob Cranach seemed to be at the center of it. He'd told Rowena in no uncertain terms what he expected of her. She knew there would be consequences if she defied him. He had even less tolerance where Lachlan was concerned. Lord Gray had no right, and no reason, to make trouble now. For God's sake, they'd both had eighteen years, and had failed miserably to do what he'd hoped and expected. If they were up to something now, and he had more than a suspicion they were, he was willing to give either or both of them enough rope with which to hang themselves.

"But how did Lord Gray make you fall off your horse?" Jane asked, then took a step back as Rob gestured and mud flew off his arm and spattered the grass.

"He shoved me off the trail," Rob snapped. "He and your brother, both, Lady

Winnie. And that was after he tried to push me into a tree."

Why hadn't she noticed before how his voice went up an octave when he was indignant? Perhaps because she'd never seen him unsettled before. But then she'd known Lachlan for all of her eighteen years, and that couldn't possibly compare with four days of a fellow on his best behavior. Until this moment, of course.

"It *was* a Highlands race, if ye'll recall," she said, for the first time in three months not trying to hide her accent in front of a . . . beau. Or former beau, whether he knew it yet or not. In fact, she intentionally exaggerated her brogue. "Ye have to expect some shoving aboot. Ye didnae lose any blood, did ye?"

Rob and Jane both blinked at her. "I've a few scratches, yes," he answered.

"Well, that's a sign of yer bravery, then."

Jane clasped her arm. "Why are you talking like that?" she muttered.

Rowena giggled, covering her mouth with her free hand. "It's how I talk," she exclaimed, hoping she sounded apologetic. "I suppose it's the gathering and having all my people aboot. I am a Highlands lass, ye know."

And a few months ago she would never

have said such a thing. It wasn't only Lachlan's influence, though; seeing all the clan around her, hearing the songs, realizing how proud and pleased and supportive all these people were to see the MacLawry, their chief, about to be married — it touched her deeply.

They — some of them barely scraping by, others refugees from neighboring clans who'd been lucky enough to make it to MacLawry land with their families intact — had such pride about who they were, and there she was with her fine gowns and a fine, warm house to live in, pretending to be someone else. Whether she truly belonged in the Highlands or not, whether she could be happy there or not, she still wasn't entirely certain. But she wanted Lachlan. The rest she would have to figure out later. She only hoped she had the time to do so.

"If you ladies will excuse me, I think I've had my fill of the games for today."

"But I just talked to Lachlan," Rowena countered, "and he said you'd challenged him to the rope pull."

"He's mistaken."

Blast it all. They needed Rob to continue his involvement. If he vanished for the next day, he would have time to gather his thoughts. He would have time to be logical.

And that would never do. She put her hand on Jane's and squeezed. If she flirted with Lord Rob, it could set the plan to dissuade him from proposing to her backward again, and they only had three days left as it was.

"But Lord Robert," Jane blurted out. "Lord Gray said you would turn tail, and I wagered him two pounds that you wouldn't. And he's so . . . arrogant, already."

He turned around, looking at the two of them with his right eye, and still blinking mud out of his left. "You wagered in my favor, Lady Jane?"

She bobbed her head, blond ringlets bouncing. "Of course I did."

"And you, Lady Winnie?"

Rowena lifted her chin. "I cannae wager against my own clan." Or against the man she'd begun to favor above everything and everyone else in the world.

"Well. I suppose I cannot disappoint a supporter," he commented, sending a pointed glance at Rowena.

Jane, though, freed her hands to clap. "Hurray!"

Rob inclined his head. "I need to summon my valet and change into something less brown. If you should see Lord Gray, please tell him I look forward to our next meeting."

They watched him out of sight over the hill. "Oh, thank goodness," Rowena breathed, fighting the urge to sag to the ground. "Thank ye so much, Jane."

"You're welcome, of course, but I wish you'd tell me what the devil is going on. I thought you'd be furious with Lord Gray for embarrassing Lord Rob."

Rowena pulled her friend a little farther away from the MacLawry men who always surrounded her in public. "You must promise not to say anything to Ranulf."

"I'm not bringing anything to your brother that might make him angry." Jane shuddered. "He's far too fierce for me. So what are you doing? Is this because Lord Gray decided he likes you?"

She sighed. "Yes. And if Rob proposes to me, I have to marry him," she whispered, hoping the noise around them and the small distance she'd managed away from her sentries would keep anyone else from hearing. "Those are Ranulf's orders."

Jane looked at her. "I do like fairy tales, you know, but if you mean to defy Lord Glengask, you need to be certain this is more than wishful thinking. Lord Rob is the most sophisticated Highlander you've ever met. You told me that three days ago."

"I know I did. It's complicated."

"Lachlan is the reason you ran off to London, Winnie. You said you were finished with him."

Evidently she'd said quite a few things she was now rethinking. "We've . . . come to a mutual understanding," she said slowly. "I'm glad I left. If I hadn't, I don't think I ever would have seen that Lachlan's nae a daydream. And he wouldnae have seen me as anything other than the MacLawry's only sister."

"But are you certain, Winnie?" Jane pressed, her generally effusive smile buried beneath clear concern. "I'll be very upset with both of you if he's just teasing and you get your heart broken. Again."

"I was angry with him when I was in London. I only told you bad things about him. I think now, for the first time, I'm finally seeing who he truly is. And I like him. Very much." "Like" wasn't the correct word, though. But the word she felt in her heart, the one she wanted to use, needed to be said to Lachlan. "We argue now," she continued. "And he likes that I don't . . . worship at his feet."

"That's good. It's . . . it's wonderful. Can't you tell Lord Glengask, then?" Jane persisted, shaking her out of her thoughts.

"I tried to. I think he's decided he's heard

enough about Lachlan and me."

Jane's look was easy to read — it said that perhaps she should be listening to her family and friends since clearly she couldn't trust herself where Lachlan MacTier was concerned. She knew that wasn't so any longer, but proving it to anyone else was something she simply didn't have time for. Not now. Now when she had less than three days to avoid one marriage, see that another one went forward, and clear the path to the future she wanted for herself.

But having Jane on her side would drastically improve her own odds of success, so she took a breath. "In London I told you that I'd never seen Lachlan clearly. He was perfect, a young girl's daydream come to life. And I didn't really know any other men except for my brothers, so I had no basis for comparison. Now I do."

"I seem to remember that you wrote Lachlan every day for a fortnight and he never wrote you back. And he gave you riding boots for your eighteenth birthday."

"I know. I haven't forgotten." Though a few weeks ago the idea of her defending Lachlan's character would have been laughable, she had a very good idea of how important it was that she be able to convince Jane. For heaven's sake, if her friend didn't believe it, how was she supposed to convince Ranulf? Much less herself. "I realized that however *I* saw us, *he* saw us as friends. And he saw me as a wee girl. But he's nae just a handsome face. We've been chatting, and he listens to me. I like talking with him. Last night, he sang for me." She smiled at the memory.

"Last night?" Jane repeated. "I thought you went to bed early."

Rowena leaned even closer, her grin deepening. "I did. I just didn't go alone."

Jane's mouth opened. *"What?"*

CHAPTER THIRTEEN

"Hush, Jane," Rowena said, unable to keep the excited amusement from her voice. Jane was likely the only person in the world to whom she could confide such a thing. It was still a risk, but all morning she'd wanted to burst into song herself. This would all be settled for the best. It had to be, because while as a girl she hadn't been able to imagine a life with anyone but her flawless prince, today she couldn't imagine spending her days without amusing, witty, stubborn, maddening, handsome Lachlan Mac-Tier. The idea of any man but him kissing her, touching her, holding her, made her feel ill.

"Speak of the devil," Jane muttered, and Rowena looked up to see Lachlan approaching. The plan had been for them to keep their distance from each other today, but her heart gave a happy thump nonetheless.

"And how's our dirty Lord Rob?" he

asked, falling in beside her as they headed back toward the cluster of tents and canopies.

"He's convinced ye tried to kill him."

"Nae. If I'd tried to kill him, he'd be dead." He glanced past her at Jane. "Are ye still an ally, then?"

"Of course I am."

"It's all right, Lach. I told her everything." Rowena grimaced. "Almost everything." And Jane had helped without knowing what was going on. She'd waited her entire life for a friend like Jane. Perhaps *that* had been the best part about London. Making a true friend, and having some time to reflect on not just what she wanted, but who she was.

Lachlan gave Jane an assessing look. To her credit, the younger Hanover sister met his gaze without flinching. Finally he smiled. "I think ye might be part Scottish, Jane."

"By my sister's marriage, at least."

"So, in that case," he said after a moment, moving between them and offering each an arm, "will Cranach be joining us fer the rope pull?"

"Aye. Jane told him she'd wagered ye two pounds on whether he'd have the courage to appear or not."

"Then I owe ye my thanks, my lady."

Jane blushed. "I was helping Winnie. She

seems to be smitten with you."

Lachlan's warm, slow smile heated Rowena all the way to her bones. "I'm glad to hear that. I know I'm smitten with her."

Putting her free hand on her hip, Jane eyed him with obvious skepticism. "And you're certain now? You won't change your mind?"

"I'm a chieftain of clan MacLawry," Lachlan said brusquely. "I grew up with Rowena's brothers as my own family. I'm risking both my friendships and my place in the clan by going up against the MacLawry's orders. So if I dunnae look certain to ye, Lady Jane, look again. And I've enough to answer fer withoot ye biting at me, too."

This time Jane opened her mouth and closed it again before she nodded. "Now I believe you."

"Ye've some spleen, lass. I'm trusting ye because Rowena does."

Rowena forgot sometimes that he had a temper. She saw it so rarely that it was an easy thing to discount, though she knew that once when he and Munro had gotten into a fight, her brother had ended with a broken nose and a black eye. Bear said that Lachlan's temper was akin to a cannon with a very long fuse. His reaction to Jane's questioning his sincerity made her wonder just how long the fuse had been burning — and how much powder was packed into the cannon.

"What do we do now?" she asked. "Arran's already pushing back the crowd aboot the rope pull, and Rob's still with his valet."

"I'll worry aboot the rope pull," he returned. "A nice bagpipe duel should serve. Ranulf's judging puddings now, but he'll nae be so distracted in a few minutes. I dunnae trust him nae to realize someaught's afoot, so try to keep yer distance from him if ye're able. I've put Cranach's name up fer the stone put and the sheaf toss."

"Sheep toss?" Jane took up, her eyes widening. "I know the MacLawrys don't care for sheep, but —"

"Sheaf," Rowena corrected, laughing. "With an *f*. Twenty pounds of straw bound inside a sack. The men heave it with a pitchfork over a pair of posts with a pole laid across the top of them, and they raise the center pole higher each time." She formed an *H* with her hands, trying to explain.

"Well, thank goodness. I didn't relish seeing sheep being thrown about."

Lifting an eyebrow, Lachlan chuckled. "That might nae be a poor idea. Fer next year's gathering, of course." As they reached the circle of bustling tents and Highlanders, he edged closer. "Bear knows I'm after ye, but I dunnae think he knows all the circumstances. And it'd be wiser if he didnae."

There wasn't much more she could tell Bear even if she wanted to, Rowena reflected. Mostly because of her unwillingness to outright defy Ranulf, all they had was a vague plan to rattle and annoy Lord Rob enough that her dowry and an alliance with the MacLawrys wouldn't be worth the trouble of having to marry her. If given free rein Lachlan would likely have settled matters by now, but the two of them would also likely have been forced to flee the Highlands.

Yes, she was willing to step right up to the edge, but she still wasn't certain she could move beyond that line when it came to Ranulf. Not only was he the clan chief, but he was also her oldest brother — and the one who'd stepped up to raise her after the murder of their father and the suicide of their mother. He'd done everything for her, beginning when he'd only been fifteen years old. Three years younger than she was, now. And now it was this, the one thing he'd ever really asked of her, that she couldn't do.

"Lass," Lachlan said softly, his breath warm against her cheek, "dunnae ye fret.

Yer brothers are my brothers. I'll do anything I can nae to ruin that. But I'll nae lose ye."

She wanted to step into his arms, to rest her head against his shoulder and hear his heart beating. "I know that, Lach. This isn't a lark to me, either. And I do trust ye."

When they caught Ranulf glancing in their direction, Lachlan parted from them and headed over toward where Bear was about to win the stone put. The entire mad scheme seemed more plausible with him at her side, and she held Jane's hand a little more tightly once he vanished into the crowd.

"What can I do to help?" her friend asked. "Other than to cajole Lord Rob to participate in the competition your Lachlan means to drag him into."

Her Lachlan. She liked the sound of that. "I've desperately wanted to confide in ye for days, Jane. Believe me, ye're already helping. A great deal."

"Yes, but lending an ear isn't very heroic. What else do you need?"

For a moment Rowena considered. "After I fainted last night, Ranulf said he would see to it that Lord Rob proposed to me in a proper and romantic fashion. So don't leave my side when Rob comes about. Whatever I say."

"Oh, I excel at being persistent and annoying. Just ask Charlotte. Or Arran." Jane grinned. "I am now your shadow."

Rowena hugged her friend. "I'm so glad to have met ye," she said, tears pushing at her.

"Don't be silly. I never had any adventures before I met you," Jane returned. "And in two days we'll be sisters."

Yes, they would. In a few short months Rowena had gone from being the only lass in a household of men to being one of at least three ladies. She had one sister-in-law, Mary, who would make her an aunt sometime in the spring. And on Saturday she would have Charlotte, with Jane as a bonus. Then only Bear would need to find a lass, and the game would be tilted in the lasses' favor. She grinned. That would be something to see.

If she married Rob, that would change, though. She would no longer be a Mac-Lawry. She wouldn't be living two scant miles from where she'd grown up. Even more than that, she would lose the man who'd been such a large part of her life for so long she couldn't even imagine not seeing him every day. She couldn't imagine not being able to kiss him and touch him and chat with him whenever she wanted. It was almost startling how easily he'd gone from being a part of her life to being the most important person in her life. If she couldn't be with him . . .

No, she didn't want to think about that. She'd fled Glengask once because he'd refused to notice her — or so she'd thought. The idea that she might have to flee again to keep him terrified her, but every minute she spent with him only added to her determination not to lose him again. She just hoped she wouldn't have to choose between him and her brothers.

Please don't let it come that, she thought, sending the prayer to Saint Andrew and Saint Bridget and any other helpful soul who might be listening. *Please.*

The moment Rob Cranach came into view, Lachlan motioned for the MacLawry drums and pipers to finish up their piece. He couldn't afford to give Cranach time to consider precisely what was afoot and how much better off he'd be simply to keep his distance.

Arran had been glaring at Lachlan for the past twenty minutes, more or less, except for the time he'd devoted to gazing long-ingly at his wife — presently seated beside her grandfather, the Duke of Alkirk. A few weeks ago having any Campbells present, much less the chief of the clan, would have been what caught everyone's attention.

Now, though, Lachlan needed to do three things, simultaneously if possible: beat down Rob Cranach, avoid the eyes and attention of the chief of his own clan, and see and touch Rowena MacLawry whenever possible just to be certain he hadn't dreamed up the whole thing.

He knew precisely where she was — kneeling in front of a loom at the weavers' tent and showing Jane Hanover how they went about making the MacLawry plaid. If for no other reason than her importance to and popularity with her own clan, his lass needed to remain a MacLawry. No yellow Buchanan colors would ever suit her, no matter how hard anyone tried to make it so. Not even if the MacLawry himself favored the match.

"For the devil's sake, Lach, either take hold of the damned rope or forfeit the contest so I can go see Mary," Arran finally growled at him.

"Ye're nae worried over her being with the Campbell, are ye?" Lachlan returned, guilt pushing at him. He wasn't the only one with his heart in the mix today.

"I'm worried he'll have her naming my

firstborn Campbell MacLawry or someaught." A swift smile pulled at Arran's mouth. "That's too much weight fer any bairn to bear."

"Then go ask the Campbell to judge the contest, why dunnae?"

Arran cocked his head. "I knew ye were a smart one, Lach. But now I cannae ken how ye stay aboot Bear." With a swift nod he strode over to the well-appointed canopy where the Campbell and his kin had set their chairs.

A moment later the Duke of Alkirk, together with the half-dozen brawny lads whose sworn duty it was to protect their chief, walked up to where they'd laid the rope. "Thank ye fer starting us off, Yer Grace," Lachlan said, motioning the Mac-Lawry lads behind him to take hold of the rope.

Across the stream a good number of Camerons picked up their end of the rope at the very back of the pull, smart lads that they were. That left the MacDonalds and Campbells in the middle — always a risky proposition — and several Buchanans at the front. They, of course, gave Lord Rob Cranach the lead and worst position, directly across the water and mud from Lachlan.

Stomping his feet to create a base he could

brace himself against, Lachlan took a firm grip of the rope. He didn't much care whether the MacLawrys won or lost; his only goal was to see Cranach fall into the mud-edged stream. If he cracked his head in the process, even better.

"Take hold, lads," Alkirk instructed, keeping a watchful eye on the ribbon suspended over the water to make certain it didn't shift one way or the other. "Steady, steady . . . Pull!"

The rope snapped taut, water droplets flinging into the air. On one side a rainbow of plaid kilts dug into the ground and hauled backward, while on the other side the uniform black and white and red of MacLawry refused to give ground.

"Hold, lads!" Lachlan bellowed, one foot slipping before he could dig in again. "On three! One, two, three!"

As one they heaved backward, churning up the grassy ground. The ribbon granted them two inches, then lost one as the other side regained their footing. It felt like pulling against a mountain.

Lord Robert checked over his shoulder at the heaving, grunting Highlanders behind him. Evidently following Lachlan's lead, he began counting. As he reached two, Lachlan barked out the order to pull again. This time they gained four inches. The noise from the mostly MacLawry spectators around them drowned out what he was certain was a curse from Cranach.

"And three!" he yelled again, not feeling the least bit ashamed of his strategy.

The MacLawrys pulled, dragging a scrambling Cranach up to the muddy edge of the creek. Lachlan's arms were beginning to ache, but he refused to shift his grip. He had three days to convince the faux Scotsman to detest the Highlands and the idea of marrying into a family firmly rooted there. Every second, every word, mattered.

They lost an inch to the Buchanans, then reclaimed it. "Come on, lads!" Lachlan grunted. "For the MacLawry and his bride! Pull!"

Cranach's feet went out from under him. Slow as a dream he slid forward into the water, one hand now clinging to the rope as he tried to keep his kilt from going all the way up his backside. Ha. A true Highlander didn't care about such nonsense.

Lachlan pulled so hard he went down onto his rump and had to lie nearly flat to keep the tension on the rope. Cranach's cousin, MacMaster, went over head-first, dumping both men into the churned-up mess.

■ ■ ■ ■

The Campbell lowered his hand away from the Buchanans. "MacLawry wins!" he called, likely the first time he'd ever uttered those words. If Lachlan had needed any proof that miracles could happen, that provided it. Now he only needed one more.

Cranach came tearing up the bank on all fours, like a rabid dog. Dropping the rope, Lachlan shoved to his feet. He hadn't expected a fight — not yet, anyway — but the idea of putting a fist into Lord Robert's dainty jaw didn't trouble him in the least.

"You did this!" Robert sputtered, swiping mud and water from his face.

"Aye," Lachlan answered, deliberately grinning. "Me and fourteen of my kin. Do ye mean to pummel all of us, or just me? Because I'm happy to oblige, whatever ye decide."

Abruptly Ranulf stood between them, a solid, immovable wall. "I think all these lads deserve a beer," he said in a carrying voice. "And then I think we could stand some dancing!"

"That —"

"Come have a word with me, Lord Robert," Ranulf interrupted over the sound of the stampede toward the tents holding the beer and ale and whisky, and began to put his arm across Cranach's muddy, sticky shoulders before he evidently rethought the wisdom of that.

The brief glance Glengask sent at Lachlan barely lasted a heartbeat, but it chilled him to the bone. Then the marquis led the dripping Buchanan up toward the castle, a handful of men and the two deerhounds in tow.

Damnation. How far did Ranulf intend to go in placating the poor excuse for a Highlander? Just what did he want from the Buchanans that made him willing to soothe an idiot's pride for something as half-witted as losing a fair contest? If Ranulf simply added more concessions to Rowena's dowry every time Cranach sneezed, this plan of theirs was not going to work.

Cursing again, Lachlan wiped his sore hands on his kilt. It could just as easily have been him in the water. He'd certainly been willing to risk it. Hiding his frown, he walked through the crowd bent on congratulating him and hoped he hadn't just lost the war.

Adam James, the Earl of Samston, looked from Lady Rowena MacLawry, seated at one of the scattered tables placed across the meadow, to the Marquis of Glengask. The MacLawry, as they called him, seemed in a hurry to apologize to Lord Robert Cranach for somehow permitting that fellow to be yanked into the mud.

Though Robert had barely spared him a look in four days, no doubt because he was intent on securing his own fortune, the two of them were actually acquainted. Not as well as he'd thought, apparently, since he hadn't even known Cranach was a Highlander, but they were both members of the Society Club and White's. Evidently everyone was playing games here, and not just the burly, underdressed fellows on the field.

When Winnie had invited him to Glengask, for instance, he'd thought his nearly three-month courtship of her had finally begun to see results. Glengask had miles of property in Scotland, and a great deal of gold in addition to the land. As a bonus, Winnie was pretty, if a touch too sure of herself.

He'd done it all correctly, fluttering and flirting with her, being the pleasant, socially connected man she'd seemed to prefer. Perhaps he had rushed a bit in kissing her, but he wasn't one to miss an opportunity — and that had seemed a good one. Why she'd decided his behavior was cause for ridicule and insult, he had no idea. That was how the game was played.

Now, though, seeing her pushed at a man with no title and a penchant for poor wagering simply because he'd been born north of Hadrian's Wall, it all seemed ridiculous. And her family likely had no idea she was plotting and whispering and laughing behind everyone's backs with that brutish Lord Gray. Was Cranach simply the next man to be lifted up and then cast aside for amusement? Or did Cranach win the prize because he'd remembered to say "ye" instead of "you"?

He took another drink from his quaint, chipped mug, turning his gaze toward where the Duke of Alkirk held court. From what he'd been able to glean, the Campbell and the MacLawry had been deadly enemies until a few short weeks ago. Now they were in-laws, which seemed to make them allies, if not friends.

But not everyone in Alkirk's circle looked pleased by that circumstance. His gaze went to the broad-shouldered barrel of a man who stood behind the duke and sent a baleful gaze in Lord Arran MacLawry's direction. Generally he didn't bother to converse with a fellow who could barely count without using his fingers, but he'd made an exception for Dermid Gerdens. After all, they had something in common.

Standing, Adam strolled by the gathered Campbells and made a show of chatting with several of the young ladies there — though with those accents, he could hardly understand more than every third or fourth word they spoke. When Dermid glanced in his direction, Samston canted his chin in the direction of the loch and then moved off again. With all these Scotsmen present he'd half expected to find scores of them bathing in Loch Shinaig — but that would assume they bathed.

As it was, a few short minutes of heading north along the shoreline found him alone amid a stand of stunted pine trees. Leaning back against one of them, he gazed at the vast, flat mirror reflecting the scattered clouds and the opposite shoreline. It would have been lovely, if it had been closer to London and civilization.

"I'm here," a thick brogue announced from behind him, sooner and more quietly than he expected.

"You move very quietly for such a strapping fellow," he noted, turning his head as Dermid Gerdens walked past him, bent down to pick up a stone, and threw it what seemed like half the distance across the loch.

"I like sneaking."

"You're proficient at it." Adam waited to see if that merited a response. When it didn't, he folded his arms across his chest. "Have you heard from your brother?"

The shaggy red-haired head shook from side to side. "I told ye the Campbell sent him to Canada."

"Ah, yes. And that was because of his run-in with the MacLawrys, you said?"

"Aye. I was there, with my pistol, but George said it was Donald's fault. He said Donald lied aboot what happened, and that my brother was trying to start up a war between the Campbells and the MacLawrys."

Adam already knew all of this — practically everyone in London knew within hours after it happened that Donald Gerdens, the Earl of Berling, had gone after Glengask and had nearly shot both Arran and Winnie MacLawry over some insult or other. No one seemed to know precisely what had sparked the feud, but Highlanders frequently seemed to have little or no idea why they were killing each other. "It would take quite the heroic deed to earn your brother's return from Canada, then, wouldn't it?"

Dermid hurled another stone. "Aye."

"And you've been able to send word to your friends?"

"I said I would, and I did. So if ye know someaught that'll make the Campbell let my brother come home, ye tell me what it is."

A sliver of uneasiness whispered down Adam's spine. This man could likely break him in two, if he had half a mind to do so. And half a mind seemed a fair description for Dermid Gerdens. Evidently it was his brother the earl who had the intelligence, though even that could likely be disputed given Donald Gerdens's present residence somewhere in Canada. "Glengask wants his sister, Winnie, to marry Lord Robert Cranach."

"I already heard the Campbell talking aboot that. He said the MacLawry would see the rest of us poor and begging by the end of the decade."

"But only if he married Winnie off to a Buchanan. What if . . ." With someone else he would have given the opportunity for a man to come to his own conclusions — which would lessen his share of any blame later — but Dermid had likely never had a complete thought in his entire life. "What if that money for her dowry, and the alliance her marriage will make, could assure the

Campbells and Gerdenses had a very large share of MacLawry wealth?"

"We're nae allied to the Buchanans."

Oh, good God. "I mean to say, what if Winnie married you, instead of Cranach?"

The heavy brow furrowed. "She doesnae like me."

Adam began to feel like the lone shepherd in a land of sheep. "Does that matter?" he persisted. "I've heard stories of brave Highlanders stealing their brides out from under the noses of their enemies. Campbell and MacLawry are practically allies now. It would be very simple, I would think. And since she's the MacLawry's only sister, not only will her dowry be enormous, but you'll be nearly as powerful as the Campbell, himself. He would *have* to allow Lord Berling to come home."

A slow smile touched Dermid's face. "They would write a song about me, I reckon. And I could live with Donald again, and I wouldn't have to do everything the Campbell tells me."

"Exactly."

The mountainous man strode forward and stuck out his hand, so swiftly it made Adam flinch before he realized it was a friendly gesture. He shook Dermid's ham-sized appendage. "You need to act quickly and carefully. If anyone realizes what you're doing they'll try to stop you. They all want the MacLawry wealth and power for themselves."

Dermid smiled again. "I like to sneak."

And Adam liked to see that no half-civilized, mouthy chit made him look like a fool. This might be the Scottish Highlands, but no one insulted and embarrassed an English lord. Not this lord, anyway.

CHAPTER FOURTEEN

Lord Rob Cranach didn't participate in the sheaf toss. Lachlan didn't even have the opportunity to cajole or bully him into it, because Cranach didn't move from Ranulf's side all afternoon.

Rowena tried to enjoy watching the competition, tried to be sincerely pleased when Tom MacNamara, the miller at An Soadh, tossed a sheaf up over a bar set at nearly three times his height to win. Every thought she had, though, every prayer, centered on finding a new solution for her to avoid being proposed to by Rob for the next two and a half days.

And since the plan had been to make him not *want* to marry her, to not even attempt to ask for her hand, she was at a complete loss. And then it got worse.

"He's smiling," Jane muttered, as workers removed hay and poles and rakes from the clearing in preparation for the evening's dancing.

"He's a damned coward," Lachlan took up, standing a few feet behind her and ostensibly chatting with Bear. "Going aboot like Glengask's lapdog so I cannae get close enough to say a word to him."

"Ranulf agreed to give him Fen Darach," Bear said, his voice lower and more dour than Rowena was accustomed to hearing from him. "The old mansion and five hundred acres. As a wedding gift."

"I thought Arran would take Fen Darach." Cold anger, at herself, at Ranulf, and at Cranach, burrowed toward her heart. "So he means to punish me by hurting Arran? That's . . . It's awful."

"It's effective." Lachlan slammed his fist into his thigh. "He knows ye'll nae risk anyone else's happiness, even fer yer own."

She closed her eyes for a long moment, still trying to see a path through what was rapidly becoming an endless field of nettles. "In the back of my mind I thought this might be his idea of a test, to see how far you and I were willing to go to prove to him that we belonged together. But it isn't a test, is it? He decided that we should have realized what we wanted two days before we did, and now he doesn't care that we've changed our minds."

Lachlan's hand brushed the back of her arm, then dropped away again. "This is only over if ye surrender, Rowena."

"And what do we do next, then?" she demanded, standing up and whipping around to face him. "What's the next plan? Do ye murder Rob Cranach? Do ye kill Ranulf?" She shuddered.

"Rowe —"

"Nae! That's how high he's pushed the stakes, because he knows we'll never do such a thing. I want ye, Lachlan. My heart . . . My heart is breaking." She drew in a sob. "But what can we do? Please tell me, because I cannae think of a thing."

"We could run," he said, very quietly.

For a dozen heartbeats she considered it. "We would have to go all the way to America. Even then he'd likely find us. And if we married, he'd disown me. He'd banish both of us. We'd have no clan."

"I'd still have Gray House and the land, and enough money to take us anywhere."

Running would mean she might be able to keep Lachlan, but at the same time she would lose her brothers, her clan, the only home she'd ever known in the only land she'd ever known. They would never be able to return.

"Ye cannot sell Gray House," she said

aloud. "I wouldn't allow it."

"Oh, ye wouldn't?" He lifted an eyebrow.

"No, I wouldn't. But we couldn't live two miles from him. Someone would die over it, Lachlan. And it might be you." She shook her head, unmindful of the tears running down her face and who might see her weeping. Ranulf knew he'd won; seeing evidence of that fact would hardly surprise him.

"We've two days, my fierce lass. Dunnae give up yet."

" 'Yet,' " she repeated, hearing the bitterness and the defeat in her own voice. With a deep, shuddering sigh she held out one hand. He would never stop. Not until he was dead or Cranach was dead or Ranulf was dead. So she had to make him stop. "Walk with me."

He took her hand, but she couldn't look at his face. If she did, her resolve would crumble. She would break into a thousand pieces and never be whole again.

They walked to the edge of the clearing, beyond the rock tumble to the trees. She heard the low murmur of voices close behind her, and turned around. "Go away," she ordered the trio of large men.

Owen looked down at his feet. "We cannae, Lady Winnie. We're to watch over ye."

"Lachlan can watch over me."

"My l—"

"At least wait by the boulders, Owen. We'll be right here."

After a moment he nodded, then gestured at the two other MacLawry men with him. "I can give ye five minutes, my lady."

As angry and frustrated as she was, as badly as she wanted to sprout wings and fly far, far away, this wasn't Owen's fault. She inclined her head. "Thank ye."

The moment the trio disappeared behind one of the boulders, Lachlan grabbed her by the shoulders. It wasn't a kiss; it was far too desperate and hungry for something as simple and pure as a kiss. Rowena sank into him, clawing at his arms and his shoulders, wanting to disappear inside him.

"Dunnae quit," he finally murmured, the raw hurt in his voice tearing at her all over again.

Finally she met his gaze, to find green eyes as bleak and haunted as winter. He knew. He was as stubborn as she was, and of course he'd thought through every twist, every angle, every trick — and more options that likely had never occurred to her. And he knew. They'd run out of luck. And time. And hope. Rowena took a ragged breath, pressing her forehead to his. "I love you, Lachlan MacTier, with every ounce of me. I'll nae love another. Not ever." She drew her fingers along his jaw, feeling the hard, clenched muscles there.

"Dunnae say it," he whispered. "Pl—"

He lurched forward, pushing her hard away from him. Stumbling backward, she caught sight of red just below his left shoulder, and then a blade pushing out through his shirt.

Before she could pull air into her lungs to scream, something hammered against her skull from behind. Everything went white and then black.

Lachlan coughed. The taste and smell of blood and grass flooded his nostrils, and he forced open his eyes. "Rowena," he rasped, his chest burning.

Silence answered him. Grunting in pain, he shoved his hands beneath him and pushed away from the ground. A few feet in front of him, something blue caught his gaze, and he crawled toward it. A shoe.

"Rowena!" he called again, louder this time. "Owen!"

Grabbing the shoe, he twisted to sit on his backside. His shoulder throbbed, and warm wet ran down his chest and his back. They'd evidently missed his heart, but not by much, the bastards. What they had done, though, was even worse.

"Owen!" This time he bellowed, and then began coughing again.

The footman trotted into view, then sped into a run. "Laird Gray! What's —"

"Someone stabbed me," he growled. "And Rowena's gone. Get Ranulf. Now."

"Saint Bridget," the servant breathed, his face going gray.

Motioning one of the other men to stay behind, Owen ran back toward the meadow. Holding up his right hand, Lachlan clutched the shoe to him with the other. "Help me up, Ben."

The servant pulled him to his feet. All his blood seemed to have gone, leaving him cold and dizzy, but Lachlan shook himself. He would collapse later. Now, he had work to do. "There were at least two men," he muttered, moving forward into his own footsteps. Grass didn't hold prints well, but he'd spent his life tracking animals. He knew where Rowena had been standing, and he knew she hadn't matted the grass down while he'd been talking to her. She'd fallen — or been pushed.

Black fury thudded into him, followed swiftly by fear. But they wouldn't kill her, he reminded himself. Rowena MacLawry was of far greater value alive. Unless it was only MacLawry blood they wanted. "Bloody, bloody damnation," he grunted.

Who would dare? He staggered, putting a hand to his shoulder. Forcing himself to straighten, he looked about, not with the gaze of a worried lover, but a hunter. That's what she needed, now. For him to find her. Forest to his left, the loch a short distance behind him, the boulders ahead of him, and the meadow with a thousand Scotsmen to his right. He started into the trees, keeping his gaze down, searching for sign.

"Lachlan!"

Ranulf's bellow stopped him. As much as he wanted to do this on his own and make whoever had taken her wish they'd never been born, he was wounded. And he was one man. Ranulf commanded an army. He turned around. "Stop!" he ordered, putting out his right hand, only then noticing the blood dripping down his palm.

The marquis and his hounds, both his brothers, their Sassenach uncle, and twenty other men ranged behind them skidded to a halt. Most of them were armed — however peaceful the gathering had been, of course Ranulf would plan for the worst. And now the worst had happened.

"We were standing there," he said, pointing at the ground a few feet in front of Glengask. "I got hit from behind, and I'm certain I saw someone moving up on Rowena as I fell."

"At least two, then," Ranulf said, his voice clipped and precise. "Debny, Peter, look fer sign. The rest of ye, fan oot into the trees. Keep in sight of each other, and yell oot if ye see anything. *Anything*."

With a chorus of "aye, m'laird" sounding behind him, Ranulf stalked forward. He avoided the ground where the two men now squatted, searching, but didn't stop until he stood a foot from Lachlan.

"Why didnae ye see men coming up aboot ye?" he asked, his voice dropping even further.

Lachlan straightened as best he could. "Because I was kissing Rowena, and we were occupied with trying to figure oot how to stay together." Dissembling now would only be a waste of time, and that was one thing they didn't have. Aside from that, nothing Ranulf said or did could possibly matter to him as much as finding Rowena. His Rowena, whether anyone else wanted him to have her, or not.

Ranulf curled his fist and swung. The blow to Lachlan's jaw staggered his already uncertain balance, and he went down on one knee. Blinking, he shoved back to his feet. "Ye may as well hit me again," he growled, "because I'll nae step aside from her as long as I'm breathing."

"Dunnae tempt me," Ranulf returned.

Sending his brother a frown, Munro stepped between them. "Can ye nae see Lach's been stabbed? Do ye think he would've allowed this if he could've prevented it?"

Ranulf strode around them, making for the trees. "He *could* have prevented it, if he'd stayed away from her. Ye gave me yer word, Gray."

"Ye knew what was happening," Lachlan shot back. "Ye could've prevented this, if ye'd stopped stomping yer foot aboot Buchanan wool and listened to her fer a damned minute. Listened to either of us."

Glengask's back stiffened, but he kept walking. Now that Lachlan had said what he needed to say, worry swept in to replace his anger. Light-headed, Lachlan sagged. Bear put a hand under his good arm. "Ye need a doctor," he said, starting them back toward the meadow.

If it had only been pain, he would have refused to go. But he needed his feet under him if he meant to do any good here. "Ye can track her, Bear," he said. "Go find Rowena. Ben'll help me get patched up."

The servant nodded, and Bear handed Lachlan off. "This is my fault, I reckon," Rowena's brother said darkly, touching Rowena's shoe where Lachlan still clasped it. "I could have said someaught to Ran, and I didnae."

"Just go. We'll argue over whose fault this is when she's safe."

"Aye." Bear trotted off.

Any of them could have said something, done something, to change the course of events, but Lachlan remained fairly certain he still would have found himself at the edge of the trees, kissing Rowena. But who else knew that? Who had taken her, and why had they chosen this moment?

Leaning more heavily on Ben than he cared to acknowledge, he made his way back to the thick of the gathering. With such close quarters everyone seemed to know already that Rowena had gone missing. Before four hundred men could go tramping off through the trees, he stepped up on a tree stump.

"Lads, let Glengask and his trackers see if they can find a trail," he said with as much volume as he could manage. "The best any of ye can do right now is to look aboot ye. Is anyone missing? Did ye hear anything odd that makes some sense now?" He looked about the crowd — not for a friendly face, necessarily, but for one he could trust. Most of Ranulf's closest allies and friends were already in the forest. And he didn't know if he still qualified as one of those, or not.

"If ye ken someaught," he continued, "even if ye think it may nae be important, speak to Lady Charlotte or Lady Mary Mac-Lawry."

Grim-faced and clearly worried, the two ladies nodded. "We'll be at the Campbell tent," Mary stated in a carrying voice. "Don't delay; if you know something, please come forward."

That done, Lachlan finally allowed the blackness at the edge of his vision to wash over him again and envelop him in darkness. Someone was looking for her. And they would find her — he would find her — because the alternative was simply unthinkable.

Rowena couldn't catch her breath. She couldn't feel her hands, either. When she forced her eyes open, all she could see was a brownish filtered glow too close for her to focus on. And she was being bounced about madly, her head aching with each thud.

Gradually she figured out she was face-down across someone's saddle, her arms bound behind her, a sack over her head, and a cloth tied across her mouth. And then everything else flooded back — Lachlan trying to push her away, the blade emerging from his chest . . .

She drew in a rackety sob. No. Not his chest. It had been his shoulder. Squeezing her eyes closed, she forced herself to think logically before pain and grief could overwhelm her. She'd grown up with four men in her life. They'd taught her to shoot, and how to use a sword. Though they'd tried to make it a game, they'd taught her how to defend herself — though not against cowards who struck from behind. But she knew where to find a man's heart, and she knew — *she knew* — that blade had been high.

Therefore, Lachlan was still alive. It was nonsense to consider anything else. And because he was still alive, he would be able to tell her brothers what had happened. All of them — all of the MacLawrys — could be following them even now. Rowena shifted a little, trying to ease the pressure of the saddle against her lungs.

"She's awake," a deep male voice said from close above her.

"Club 'er again. We dunnae want her giving us away. But nae so hard this time. Ye nearly killed her, before."

She stifled the urge to flinch. Even if Lachlan . . . Even if he was unconscious, she forced her mind to amend, staying well away from any other possibility, Owen and his men had been close by. Ranulf would know she'd been taken. Bear and Arran would know. Lachlan knew. All she need do was slow her captors down and give her clan time to catch them.

She kicked out. Her feet were bound together, she realized belatedly, so she arched as best she could and then rammed her knees down. Hard. The horse beneath her sidestepped. Twisting onto her side while someone cursed and grabbed at her shoulder, Rowena kicked again. With a sickening slide she went down headfirst. Curling as tightly as she could, she landed hard on one shoulder. Thank God her brothers had also taught her how to fall.

Bouncing and rolling, she finally came to a stop. And then she made herself stay limp and still. The scent of heather mixed with the onion smell of the sack; they were in a meadow of some sort, she would guess. And it was still day, or she wouldn't be seeing any light through the sack. What else did she know?

From the earlier discussion over clubbing her, there were at least two men, both with horses. On the tail of that thought hooves stopped just beyond her, and then bootsteps approached. Two? Or three pairs of feet? With her head still throbbing and her ears ringing, she couldn't be certain.

"Is she dead?"

"She'd better nae be dead, or we'll be hanged fer certain. Why didnae ye tie her doon?"

"Because she was oot cold," the deeper, slower voice answered. "If she's dead, I'll nae get her dowry."

Her dowry? Whoever this man was, he thought to marry her? And stabbing men and kidnapping women didn't trouble him in the slightest, evidently. It occurred to her that she should likely be afraid — a young lady dragged off by at least two strangers to God knew where — but she wasn't. She was angry. No, she hadn't liked what Ranulf was forcing her into, and yes, she'd been weighing the consequences of fleeing the country to be with Lachlan. But they'd hurt the man she loved, and they'd dragged her away from her family. That would not be allowed to stand.

Lachlan had called her his fierce lass. While she hadn't felt terribly fierce, being pushed into a marriage she didn't want and not doing anything more than pouting about it, at this moment and until she stopped these men, she was fury in the flesh. No one took a MacLawry and got away with it. No one.

A foot pushed her onto her back, hurting both her wrists. The sack jerked off her head, but she kept her eyes closed. Even when her head bounced painfully back to the ground, she didn't flinch. She felt someone kneeling heavily on the edge of her dress. And she kept still.

"She's nae moving," the slow voice said.

"Well, poke her or someaught. See if she's breathing."

The cloth binding her mouth was pulled down to her neck. Breath touched her cheek as he leaned over her. He smelled of beer and haggis. Someone from the gathering? Well, she would see to it that he couldn't return there. Not without being known. Snapping her eyes open, at the same instant she pushed up with her hands and bent her knees, shooting into a sitting position. The side of his face directly in front of her, she stretched out and bit down as hard as she could.

With a howl he stumbled onto his backside, holding his left cheek as blood spurted from between his fingers. Rowena spat the sick taste of blood out of her mouth. "I know ye," she snarled, lurching at the red-haired behemoth again. "Dermid Gerdens. I know ye." She turned her attention to the thinner man holding the horses. "And I know ye, Arnold Haws. Ye're damned Campbells, and I'll see ye hung fer this!"

A third pair of boots with a slight limp came into view. When she looked up, for the first time a wisp of fear tangled in with her anger. *Oh, no.*

"And ye know me, don't ye, Winnie Mac-Lawry?" he said, gazing at her with black eyes, his accent faded from a life spent mostly away from the Highlands. Not far enough away for her taste, though.

"Aye, I know ye," she returned, working to keep her voice steady. She tugged at her wrists, but the knots didn't budge. "Ye're Charles Calder. Ye shot my brother Arran."

"Aye." He nodded, his black eyes and his slicked-back black hair lending him the appearance of something . . . evil. And she hadn't heard anything about him to dispute that description.

"Ye werenae invited to the gathering. And ye've no right to be on MacLawry land."

He smiled. "Well, it seems I've a taste now for spilling MacLawry blood." Calder lunged at her, grabbing her by the back of the neck before she could twist enough to find him with her teeth. He yanked the gag back into place, then tightened it so she could only breathe through her nose. "Stop bleating and give me the sack, Dermid."

"She bit me."

"It'll heal."

"She said she'll see us hanged," the big man stated in his ponderous voice. "But she cannae if she's dead."

"Dermid, don't ye know a thing about the law?" Calder returned, shoving the onion-smelling sack back over her head. "A wife cannot testify against her husband. Not even if she wants to. And since I stuck Gray in the heart, she's our only witness."

Rowena shuddered. In the shoulder. The blade had missed his heart. Silently she repeated it to herself, over and over, willing it to be true. Lachlan was alive. And he would come for her.

"Is that true, Arnold?" the big man asked. "She cannae say anything against us?"

"I reckon it is."

A large hand grabbed her by the front of the dress and hauled her to her feet with no noticeable effort. "Ye cannae say a word against us, Lady Winnie. Because we'll be married."

He slapped her. The blow stunned her, mostly because she couldn't see it coming,

370

the coward. She staggered and would have fallen, but he still held her up by the neck of her gown. And then he laughed and threw her back over someone's saddle.

It was likely a good thing they'd gagged her again. Otherwise they might have done more than hit her. They could say whatever they wished, and hit her if they chose. Rowena meant to remember all of it. She would testify against them, because she would be marrying Lachlan MacTier — not Dermid Gerdens. Only Lachlan would do for her, no matter who wanted a mill or ships or merchants or anything else. She meant to survive this, and when she did, no one had best get in her way.

This time they tied her to the saddle. Rather than waste her strength fighting to move she lay still — as still as she could with the horse pushing the breath out of her with every step — and listened. From her glimpse at the sky before they'd covered her eyes again, it had been nearly evening, which meant they'd dragged her off hours before she'd regained her senses enough to know what had happened. From the direction of the sun they were headed roughly south and east — toward the wildest parts of the Highlands.

Lachlan had taught her to know and

notice those things. Lachlan and her brothers. And he'd also taught her other things that were much more pleasurable. He'd told her that at heart she was a Highlands lass with a Highlands heart, and at this moment that was precisely who she was. She was not some well-read, theater-loving, sophisticated debutante. She was a MacLawry of the clan MacLawry, and someone was trying to drag her away from her family and her love.

They would not succeed, no matter who they were. She had a wedding to attend in two days. And she had a man to apologize to, because she'd very nearly given up on the two of them. She would not do so again.

CHAPTER FIFTEEN

Downing another swallow of whisky, Lachlan strode toward the Campbell tent. Three MacTier men followed a yard or two behind him; however certain he was that Rowena had been the one and only aim of whoever took her, he wasn't about to allow someone else to finish the job they'd started. Not until Rowena was safely back at Glengask again.

"Have ye learned anything, lasses?" he asked in a low voice, stopping in front of Charlotte and Mary.

"Everyone suspects everyone else," Charlotte said, her mouth tight. For someone who'd only recently become familiar with clan politics, the deep-seated suspicions and old grudges were likely bloody aggravating.

Mary nodded. "Even your septs are accusing each other. The Camerons think the Mackles might be angling for more power by a marriage to the MacLawry's sister, and the Stewarts are angry because Arran married me instead of Deirdre Stewart." She scowled. "I heard that one quite a bit."

"I'm sorry to put all this on ye, lasses," he said, not surprised to hear any of it — or that no true suspects had been uncovered. Clan was clan, no matter what a cousin or cousin's cousin might have done.

"Don't apologize, for heaven's sake, Lachlan," Charlotte stated, grabbing his hand. "If I knew this territory any better, I would be out there looking for her myself."

"Ranulf wouldnae like that, my lady." He had his own quarrel with Glengask, but the marquis's main goal had always been to keep his family safe. He couldn't forget that, no matter how angry, furious, he was. "I've nae heard anything from any of the lads. Have ye?"

"No. Not a word. Just torches in the trees."

They were still looking for tracks, then. That didn't bode well. He inclined his head. "If ye'll excuse me then, I have something I need to see to."

Charlotte tightened her hold on his hand. "Whatever is between you and Winnie, you —"

"I love her, Charlotte. That's what's between us. So dunnae tell me I need to sit doon or rest or let Ranulf see to it." He glanced beyond her to see Lord Robert Cranach sitting with his cousin, both of them dining on prime venison. "And keep that *amadan*," he muttered, jabbing his finger in Rob's direction, "well away from me and mine."

She released his hand. "Go find her, Lachlan."

Turning away, he nodded. "I mean to."

One of the grooms brought Beowulf down to the edge of the meadow, and stiffly he swung up on the big bay. The motion pulled at the fresh stitches in his shoulder, and he winced. Once he reached the forest he didn't know which way to go, and that bothered him more than a stab wound. If he had any idea who'd taken her he would have a clue where to begin looking, but as hard as he tried all he could remember was a pair of boots. And trousers. No kilt. That meant no clan colors.

The men who'd grabbed her might not even have been at the gathering. They could be anyone, though given who they'd come after and the timing of the attack, he would have been willing to wager that they were Scotsmen.

"Gray."

He pulled Beowulf up by the last of the tents. The man who stepped partway out of the shadows surprised him to his bones. Short-cropped steel-gray hair, a straight spine, and piercing gray eyes. He was one of those men in the Highlands who could never be mistaken for anyone but himself — the Campbell. "Yer Grace."

The Duke of Alkirk inclined his head. "I wasnae aboot to tell two lasses, even my own granddaughter, aboot clan affairs," he said, his voice low. For once the half-dozen men who generally accompanied him were nowhere to be seen.

"I'm nae a lass."

"Ye're a MacLawry chieftain, though. This doesnae sit well with me. A clan settles its own business."

"I'm looking fer Rowena MacLawry," Lachlan replied. "I dunnae care if it was the devil himself who took her. She's mine, and I'll have her back by my side."

"That, I like," Alkirk commented. "It means the MacLawry willnae have his alliance with the Buchanans."

"Then what can ye do to help me with it?" Unexpected or not, he wasn't about to turn down any help that could get him pointed toward Rowena.

"I sent Berling to Canada," the duke said after a moment. "After that mess in London I didnae want him stirring up more trouble."

"So it wasnae Berling." He glanced toward the trees and the widely scattered torches. "Thank ye, then."

"I brought his brother to Alkirk. The lad's nae fit to chew his own food, but I thought . . . to help him stay clear of trouble. If a man's born a fool, then ye have to expect him to be foolish."

"Yer Grace, I've nae time fer family tales aboot people I dunnae care fer."

"I brought him here, one of the lads to keep a watch over me and mine. I've nae seen him since luncheon."

Dread settled into Lachlan's gut. He didn't know Dermid Gerdens — he didn't make a habit of becoming acquainted with any men of clan Campbell. But he'd heard a few things. Mostly they concerned Dermid playing the muscle for his rat of a brother, and that he liked brawling even more than Bear did. That didn't sound like a man who could arrange a kidnapping in the middle of a clan gathering and two days before the MacLawry's marriage. "Is anyone else missing?" he asked, reining Beowulf back in when the bay tried to sidestep.

"That sounded somewhat accusatory, lad," the duke returned coolly. "I'm nae in the habit of being doubted. I told ye what I know. I've nae involvement in it. As far as

I'm concerned, do whatever ye will with Gerdens. I've had my fill of that damned part of the clan."

"If that's so, then I reckon ye'd be happy to tell me where Dermid would most likely go to ground if he knew a set of angry MacLawrys was on his heels," Lachlan pressed.

The Campbell sent him a speculative look. "I dunnae make a habit of charting bolt-holes, lad."

"It wouldnae be Sholbray, I would guess," Lachlan continued, mentally reviewing the map of the territory. Sholbray was the Earl of Berling's closest estate, but it was only two hours from Glengask, south along the river Dee. It was likely too obvious a risk for a slow-witted man fleeing with a woman who wasn't his.

"Berling has another estate, half a day northwest of Fort William," Alkirk said after a moment. "Denune Castle. It's hardly more than an old ruin and a pond, but there's nae much around it. Except fer the parish church and a handful of drovers' huts and cottages."

Lachlan nodded, his heart wrenching again. Glengask was two days from Fort William, and there was a large space of nothing in between. Rowena would be on her own, with at least one brute who'd already struck her. He wanted to go. Now. But the more information he had, the more successful he was likely to be. "I have the feeling Dermid would nae do this on his own. What's yer opinion on that?"

"Ye ask too many questions, lad. We may nae be fighting, but I'm nae yer ally."

"This isnae aboot me, Alkirk. And if ye know someaught that could help me find Rowena MacLawry, the odds of ye and the MacLawry *becoming* allies would be a mite improved."

"And if I dunnae help ye, we'll all be at sword points again, I assume?" The duke blew out his breath. "No, I dunnae think Dermid could manage this on his own. He might stab ye or club ye, but Glengask would have tracked him doon by now. As fer who he's with, I dunnae have any idea. I left half my nephews and grandsons well away from here, to avoid any trouble."

Lachlan nodded. "Thank ye, Yer Grace."

The duke faded back into the darkness of the tent, and Lachlan headed up the slope toward the trees. Torches and lanterns ranged for a mile north and south of where he and Rowena had been attacked. The fact that some of the Highlands' best trackers still hadn't found any sign of where Rowena and her attacker had gone meant his suspicion was likely correct. Dermid Gerdens hadn't done this on his own.

"Where's Glengask?" he barked, reaching the glade. It had been hours. Rowena could be miles away by now. She could be hurt. *Damnation.*

"I'm here." Ranulf strode into the firelight. "Are ye patched up?"

"Aye. Well enough." Lachlan didn't know why he'd bothered to ask; they were only allies until Rowena was safe. "The Campbell found me," he said brusquely. "He says Dermid Gerdens has gone missing."

The marquis's stark expression paled a little. "Dermid Gerdens. I knew that lout would be trouble. I figured it was his brother leading him aboot by the nose, though. Bloody hell."

"Someone must still be leading him aboot, dunnae ye think?" Lachlan pursued. "Nae that I expect ye to name all yer enemies. We dunnae have that long."

"I didnae do this, Gray. Owen said she sent her men away so she could talk to ye. This is on yer head. And I swear, if —"

"Stow it, Glengask. If she's hurt, I'll kill every man who had a hand in this. If . . ." He swallowed, his mind refusing to travel that path. "Alkirk suggested they might be headed to Denune Castle, half a day northwest of Fort William. It's one of Berling's holdings."

"Berling," Ranulf growled. "I'll kill him this time."

"The Campbell exiled him to Canada. If ye want him dead, ye'll have quite the voyage." He gathered up the reins. "Me, I'm headed fer Denune Castle."

The marquis took a step closer, reaching out as if to snag the bay's reins. Lachlan backed him out of the way. "Ye're in no shape to ride anywhere, Lachlan." Glengask scowled.

"I'm in no shape to stay sitting on my arse looking fer a trail when I've an idea where she's headed." He patted the rifle strapped beside his saddle. "I have what I need. And just so ye know, yer future brother-in-law is doon at the tents dining on a fine venison. That's who ye're giving her to." With that he kicked Beowulf in the ribs, and they set off south at a gallop.

Dermid and whoever else rode with him would have to know that MacLawrys wouldn't be far behind them. They would therefore be in a hurry. He cut across the valley beyond the loch, heading for the nearest open road going in the correct direction. It was the first time he'd ever felt grateful to that damned Irishman General George

381

Wade. The man's obsession with building roads in the Highlands might have led to the English overrunning Scotland, but tonight all he cared about was that Wade's road south was the only easy path through the mountains.

His shoulder ached, but with every pounding footfall it only reminded him how much danger Rowena could be in. It would likely have been wiser to slow his pace in the dark, but he knew this part of the Highlands as well as he knew his own fields. He would have to be more cautious later, but at the moment he preferred speed.

"Lachlan!"

The loud bellow echoed through the hills around him. With a curse he slowed, but didn't stop. A moment later hoofbeats rode up on him, and he rolled his good shoulder as he turned. "I'm nae going back."

"I dunnae expect ye to," Bear returned. "How certain are ye that it's Dermid, and that he's headed fer Denune?"

"I've nae better idea, and the lot of ye spent three hours looking fer tracks and didnae come up with a damned thing."

"Then ye can say we all fell on our arses today, I suppose. I'm here because she's my little sister, Lach. She's the best of us, and I'll nae sit back and pound my chest while she's oot there. And I brought them" — he jerked his chin toward the three riders with him — "because I reckon that improves the odds of at least one of us getting to her."

Lachlan nodded. "As ye say. Let's go, then."

"It's done," Arran said, walking into Ranulf's office. "There's nae a cotter's shack or a duck blind for a hundred miles that doesnae have a MacLawry man on his way to search it."

Ranulf nodded. "Close the door."

His brother complied, but stayed close by it, as though he was ready to charge into action should any news arrive. They both were; the entire household was. Everything had stopped. The tents down in the meadow were nearly silent, the dozen bonfires of the night before reduced to two. No pipes sounded into the still night, no one sang, no one even seemed to be speaking.

He picked up his accounting book and flipped it open, then snapped it shut again. With a growl he hurled it into the opposite wall. "Why the devil am I standing here?" he demanded, hoping Arran could give him an answer. "Why am I nae oot there with Munro and Lachlan?"

"Because ye're the MacLawry," Arran

answered. "Because when someaught's amiss, yer clan looks to ye."

"My sister is looking to me. To help her." His voice caught on the words.

"In all honesty, Ran," his brother said, his tone cautious and very worried, "that's yer guilt talking. Because I'm fairly certain Winnie's looking fer Lachlan."

"It doesnae matter," the marquis said dismissively. "Nae as long as she's found."

The one time he'd let himself be distracted — by Charlotte, by a wedding that now would not be taking place until Rowena was safe and home again, by arranging for employment for more of his cotters and trying to see Rowena happy and safe from further heartache — he'd lost her. The lass he looked on not only as his sister, the warm light of Glengask, but almost as a daughter. She had been solely his responsibility since she'd turned five and their mother had swallowed poison, with him just eighteen. The age she was now.

"They'll find her," Arran was saying, though it sounded as if he was trying to convince himself. "There's nae a place in the Highlands any man could hide from ye." His grim smile held more anger than amusement. "I considered that very thing a few weeks ago, and I came to the conclusion that the only place Mary and I could hide from ye would be in an American forest somewhere."

That snagged his attention — and better yet, drew his thoughts away from Lachlan's parting words. "I know we werenae . . . I was damned furious with ye, Arran, but did ye truly think I would harm ye? Because I wouldnae. I couldnae."

"Now's nae the time to debate that, Ran. Suffice it to say both ye and all the Campbells were after us, and I didnae mean to be separated from Mary. By anyone."

Slowly Ranulf nodded. He knew he was supremely sure of himself; a man couldn't be weak-willed and still see to the well-being of three thousand men, women, and children. But he'd made a mistake with Arran, and it had nearly cost him a brother. "Did ye find Lord Rob?" he made himself ask.

"Aye. Eating a fine venison at the Buchanan tent. I refrained from cracking him in the jaw, but it was a close thing." Arran eyed him. "I ken that a man has to eat. But we havenae taken the time fer it, and neither did Munro."

Or Lachlan. Arran didn't say that, but it hung there in the air between them, anyway. The viscount had been stabbed back to front, and a few short hours later he was riding across some of the wildest parts of Scotland on a hunch. In the dark. "Rob's known Rowena fer only a few days," he said aloud.

"And she's money and land and an estate to him. She's nae something precious. Nae something that cannae be replaced."

Ranulf slammed his fist on the desktop, and Arran jumped. "He ignored her fer eighteen bloody years!" Of course they both knew who "he" was. "All she did was follow him aboot, until she finally realized he wasnae the only man in the world."

"If I say someaught else, are ye going to throttle me?" Arran asked.

"I may feel like doing just that, but nae. Ye know I value yer opinion. Even when ye're wrong."

"Well, thank ye fer that." Arran refused to sit, but he did cross his arms over his chest. "Ye made no secret of the fact that ye favored a match between them."

"I wouldnae have allowed her to be aboot him so much if I didnae."

"And so every day from his eighth birthday on, Lachlan knew his future. And she was a wee, clinging bairn."

"He doesnae look at her that way now."

"Because ye took the yoke off his shoulders, I imagine. Ye stopped trying to force them together."

Ranulf narrowed his eyes. "So in yer opinion, all this is my fault?" he asked stiffly.

"I wouldnae accuse ye of any such thing." Arran scowled. "All I'm even suggesting is that ye look at who defied ye to go after her, and who didnae bother to volunteer." He lowered his hands again. "And now I think I'll take a ride aboot the loch, just in case we missed someaught."

Ranulf motioned at him. "Go. But take Fergus with ye. Rowena may nae be the end of it, and Charles Calder put a ball through ye once already." He paused, ice forcing its way into his chest.

Across from him, Arran abruptly swore. "Ye dunnae think —"

"Ye go riding," Ranulf ordered, striding for the door. "I'm going to have a word with the Campbell."

Arran pulled open the door and fell in behind him. "Nae. I'm going with ye. I'll nae breathe again until I hear that Calder's in Canada with his damned cousin."

Taking the stairs two at a time, cursing himself with every step, Ranulf made for the front door. He'd offered the Campbell a fine bedchamber, but evidently Alkirk didn't feel comfortable enough to rest his head beneath a MacLawry roof. What that meant now was that he wouldn't just be speaking to one man; he would be asking some hard questions about a difficult subject in front of all the Campbells who'd arrived for the wedding.

The wedding. Damnation, he was supposed to be married the day after tomorrow. "Where's Lady Charlotte?" he barked at Cooper as they reached the foyer.

"I'm in here," her sweet voice called back from the morning room, before the butler could answer.

Changing directions, he walked into the quaint, comfortable room. It didn't feel so comfortable at the moment, though. Charlotte, her sister, their parents, and Arran's wife Mary sat huddled close together near the door, while his own Sassenach uncle, Myles Wylkie, stood still as a statue, his gaze fixed out the window.

Charlotte rose as he entered, walking up to him with her hands outstretched. He stopped her at arm's length, though, not wanting her embrace. With her in his arms he couldn't be as angry, as sharp, as ready to strike as he needed to be right now.

"We've sent men to every building fer a hundred miles," he said, to the room in general. "Lachlan's headed toward Fort William with Bear, to an old holding of Lord

388

Berling's."

Charlotte gasped. "Berling?"

"It may be his brother who's taken Rowena."

Myles finally turned around. "Then send everyone," the viscount stated, his voice unsteady and his hands clenched. "You command a damned army, Ranulf. Send them all. Get her back."

Ranulf shook his head. "If our suspicions are wrong, we've wasted two days there and back. Bear took Peter Gilling and two others with him. They're nae alone oot there."

Jane made a broken, sobbing sound. "Winnie's all alone," she whispered, and dropped her head into her hands.

He didn't want to think about that now. He couldn't. Everything he had, everything he was, looked for a way to rescue his sister. The rest he put aside for later. "I need a word with ye, Charlotte."

"Of course."

She followed him into the far corner of the room. "I'm sorry, *leannan*," he murmured. "This isnae anything that I . . ." He trailed off.

Charlotte put a hand on his sleeve before he could say anything else. "Find Winnie," she said quietly. "Everything else can wait." She reached up her free hand and cupped his cheek. "I'm not going anywhere."

"I'm nae accustomed to hearing how a lass might react to having her wedding postponed," he returned, fighting the urge to simply be with her and let the rest of the world fade away, "though I imagine it's generally more full of yelling. But ye're nae any common lass, are ye?"

She shook her head. "No, I'm not."

"I love ye, Charlotte, in case I dunnae say it often enough."

"And I love you, Ranulf. Do what you need to do."

He kissed her, hard and without caring that her parents were watching. Then he nodded. "Ye'd best nae go anywhere. Because I do mean to marry ye."

"I'm nae going to do anything while ye have this sack over my head," Rowena stated, trying not to stagger as pins and needles pricked up and down her legs now that blood and feeling returned to them. "I dunnae trust a one of ye to keep yer word."

"Put her back on the horse, then," Calder's voice said, flat and annoyed.

"I dunnae want her pissing on me," the highest-pitched of the voices, Arnold Haws, she knew, complained.

She worked her jaw again, lowering the

gag down her chin just a little more. "I will, too," she assured them. "Take the sack off my head, and untie my hands. Where do ye think I'll go?"

The sack was pulled off her head, and she blinked, sucking in the cool, damp air of the Highlands night. Thankfully it was a mostly clear evening, with a three-quarters moon just sinking past the sharp peaks to the west. The cold breeze had gone past chilling her, but she'd been cold before. She'd even been lost before, though not since she'd been ten years old. Ranulf had been frantic, she remembered, and refused to let her leave the house for three days after that.

A large face with a blood-streaked cheek loomed in front of her. "I'll untie ye, and we'll nae look while ye piss, and ye'll behave yerself."

Rowena returned his gaze levelly. She had no qualms at all about giving her word and then breaking it. Not to these men. They had no honor, and she wouldn't be held back by her own. "I'll behave myself," she agreed.

After a minute of increasingly painful fumbling, the rope about her wrists loosened. She held in a gasp as sensation flooded back into her fingers. Then she sent them each a glare. "Face away from me," she ordered. "Make a triangle or someaught so I can't get past ye without ye seeing."

One by one they complied, Calder of course, turning his back last. They stood in a broken meadow, covered here and there with heather and thistle and bluebells. It was likely lovely in daylight, but she was more interested in the rough boulders that poked up among the flowers.

Squatting, she relieved herself, at the same time reaching all about her for something, anything, she could use as a weapon. Her fingers touched a half-buried rock, but when she dug it out, it was too small to even be an annoyance.

"Are ye finished yet?" Dermid asked, shifting.

"I can barely feel my legs and arms," she retorted. "Give me a blasted minute, ye heathens."

Aside from the weapon, this was all about slowing them down. Annoying them, confusing them, turning them against each other — only the first seemed plausible, but every second she could keep them from riding was a second Lachlan could use to catch up to her.

Her fingers found another rock, and she tugged, trying not to lose her balance. It came free, a nice, fist-sized specimen. Straightening slowly and quietly so the men wouldn't hear her skirts rustling, she looked at each of them. She could hurt one of them, but that would only get her slapped and thrown back onto a horse again. No time gained at all.

Rowena then turned her attention to the horses. They all had their heads down, grazing. And because this was only a momentary stop, none of them were hobbled or tethered.

Drawing as much air into her bruised lungs as she could, she cocked her arm, just as her brothers and Lachlan had taught her. She'd once killed a rabbit with a well-thrown stone, and they'd had it for dinner that night.

Not daring to wait any longer, she screamed — as loudly and fiercely as she could. As the men jumped, whirling around to face her, she stepped forward and hurled the rock. The nearest horse reared, screeching as the rock caught it squarely on the nose. It bolted, the other two following at a gallop.

Someone, Calder, she thought, cuffed her on the back of the head, and she went down onto her hands and knees. "Get the damned horses," he snarled.

Cursing, the other two ran off into the dark, whistling. If the animals were as well trained as those at Glengask, they wouldn't run far, and they would return when called. But that didn't matter, as long as it took time.

"It's a shame ye have to look pretty when we show ye to the parson," Calder continued, yanking the gag back up and this time tying it so tightly that she couldn't close her mouth around it.

Her hands and feet were still free, though. And he'd been shot in the leg by his own grandfather, Arran had told her. Flinching forward, she turned to face him and kicked — wishing she'd been wearing the riding boots Lachlan had given her for her eighteenth birthday instead of one stupid blue walking shoe.

He stumbled, cursing, then threw himself on her before she could dart away. They fell to the ground with him at her back. "Wrong leg," he hissed into her ear.

She flailed, kicking and punching at him, trying to twist beneath him so she could hit harder. He was both larger and heavier than she, though, and he was certainly meaner. Grabbing hold of her left arm, he twisted it up behind her, shoving her own hand into the small of her back.

"I'll break it," he panted. "Stop fighting."

If she'd had any doubt that he was bluffing, she wouldn't have given in. With a broken arm she would be lucky to remain conscious across the back of a horse, though, much less able to think and plot her escape. Rowena stopped hitting at him, but she wasn't about to relax.

"Don't move," Calder ordered, and grabbed her free hand, pulling it back with the other one. "Some men might prefer a lass with spirit," he went on, binding her wrists again. "I don't. I like her to lie quietly and whimper while she spreads her legs for me." He yanked the knots tighter. "Maybe I'll let Dermid have ye first. That should take the fight out of ye."

The idea of either man touching her so intimately frightened and disgusted her, but that was precisely what he'd meant to do, she was certain. Keep her quiet and cowed so they could hurry on their way, and then do whatever awful thing they thought of, later. Paralyze her with fear so she couldn't think, and therefore let her be the instrument of her own doom. Devil take all of them.

She wasn't some soft English lady. She was a Highlands lass. More than that, she was a MacLawry. And no MacLawry, man or woman, surrendered without a fight.

Even with no easy way to judge the time, by her best estimate at least half an hour passed before the other two men trotted up, the third horse in tow. "The damned things crossed the road and were halfway to Loch Garry," Arnold Haws said, jumping to the ground.

They were all the way to Loch Garry already? Good heavens, they'd made better time than she'd expected. Either that, or she'd been unconscious for longer than she'd realized. Either way, they were definitely headed for Fort William. And far away from Glengask.

The two men stood her upright, and slipped the damned sack over her head again. She knew who they were, and she knew roughly in which direction they were riding, so she didn't know why they bothered — unless it was to further frighten her.

Rather than being afraid, though, the moment they'd hidden her face she began chewing on the gag pulled tight through her mouth. They had their plans, but so did she. And whatever they tried to convince her, she wasn't alone.

She knew that, as well as she knew the color of her own hair. Lachlan MacTier was coming. And the MacLawrys were riding with him.

CHAPTER SIXTEEN

Lachlan reined in. "Did ye hear that?"

Beside him, Bear's face was as angry and worried as he'd ever seen it. "I heard someaught."

"It was Rowena," Lachlan said, certain down to his bones. Was she trying to let any pursuers know where she was? Or was she crying out in fear or pain?

Clenching his jaw, he kicked Beowulf again. The last words he and Rowena had said to each other would not be the last words they spoke. Ranulf would not keep them apart. Dermid Gerdens and whoever rode with him would not keep them apart. He'd been swearing that to himself, repeating it over and over, for the past eight hours.

"Slow doon, Lach," Munro called from behind him. "We dunnae want to overrun them in the dark."

"That scream was well ahead of us," he countered. "And I'll nae lose ground to them because ye want to be cautious."

"I'm nae being cautious. They'll nae be directly on the road, and ye know it. I ken ye want her back. So do I."

"I want to be close enough to keep them moving. Because if they're running, they cannae be hurting her."

Fresh anger jolted through him, as it did every time he imagined what she must be going through. She'd tried so hard to convince herself — and everyone else — that she was a proper, sophisticated English lady. He'd tried to remind her that she should be proud to be a Highlander, and she'd been listening. He knew that.

And now a Highlander had taken her. Who could blame her if she never wanted to see Scotland again after this? Or if she wanted nothing further to do with him? Lachlan cursed again.

By coming back to Glengask from London, she'd lost everything. If Ranulf had his way she would leave Glengask and clan MacLawry altogether to become a Buchanan. If he had *his* way she would remain a MacLawry, but only until the chief banished him from the clan. In addition, she would lose her dream of residing in London with a husband who enjoyed poetry and the theater and sitting about doing nothing. If

Gerdens had his way — devil take it, he didn't know what Gerdens wanted of her, but it wouldn't be anything she would choose.

Was he the least of three or four evils for her, or was he not even that? She'd said she loved him — finally, the words still tearing through his heart — but whatever he told himself, he knew she'd been about to concede to Ranulf's demands.

That would all matter later. Now, he just needed to find her. And make certain the men who'd taken her would never attempt such a thing again. Ever.

Lachlan wanted to shout back, to answer her and let her know that someone was coming. That he was coming. While he wanted her captors to keep moving, though, it would be foolish to let them know just how close he was. And he couldn't afford to be foolish.

He shook himself. However far behind Rowena they were, he needed to pay attention to what was around them. Bear kept pace beside him, and he could practically feel the big man's sideways glances. If Rowena's brother didn't like the way the pursuit was proceeding, he was welcome to conduct his own chase. Lachlan had no intention of stopping.

"Peter!" Munro finally called. "Ye and Aulay move oot to the left and keep pace with us. Eòin, head to the right with me. Spread oot. That'll give us a better chance of seeing any sign of riders."

It made sense. The road was the most likely route from Glengask to Fort William but that didn't mean Rowena was actually on it. They could be flanking it on either side, or paralleling it from the hills to the east. But they were headed this way. He supposed he owed the Campbell thanks for that. Without the duke's help, he might still be trying to figure out who'd taken Rowena, much less riding to rescue her.

He tried to ease the strain on his shoulder as best he could, but the ache and warm wet slowly staining his shirt told him he likely shouldn't be riding anywhere. Lachlan ignored the warnings, though; he could get himself patched up again later.

As his companions fanned out on either side of the road, it almost felt like he was riding alone in the pre-dawn dark. Beyond the sound of hoofbeats and Beowulf's breathing and the creak of leather, he kept listening. The scream didn't repeat, and he could only hope it wasn't because she was unable to make a sound.

Just after sunrise they rode up to a roadside inn brandishing a wooden sign with THE BRUCE INN carved into it in large, ornate letters. Half the inns and taverns in the Highlands carried that name, so it wasn't much help in telling him how far south they'd come. The green and blue and white plaid painted on the door, though, *did* give him more information.

"Gerdens plaid," he muttered, as they trotted into the stable yard.

"Aye," Bear seconded. "We stay just long enough to water the horses and get a quick bite of breakfast."

"I'm nae —"

"Ye've lost blood, and ye've nae had anything in yer gullet fer better than twelve hours." Munro swung down from Saturn and stalked over to catch Beowulf's bridle. "And neither have any of us."

"I dunnae like it." Frowning, unwilling to ride down his friend, Lachlan dismounted — and staggered as his boots touched the ground.

Bear caught him with an arm under his good shoulder. "I dunnae like it, either," he muttered. "Ye're nae the only man who'd give his life fer Winnie. Get someaught to eat. I'll nae have ye slowing us doon."

Lachlan took a breath. "I ken that, Bear. I've nae intention of holding ye back. But this — I — I should've protected her. However I feel aboot her, I shouldnae have forgotten the first rule at Glengask: always protect Rowena."

Peter Gilling took charge of the horses and instructed that they be watered and wiped down, and ready to travel in twenty minutes. The rest of them walked into the inn, to find it already crowded with drovers and farmers and travelers. A few months ago a group of MacLawry men in MacLawry plaid setting foot in a Gerdens tavern would have been enough to begin bloodshed. Today, except for a handful of baleful looks, they were left to themselves.

"I suppose we owe Arran thanks fer marrying a Campbell," Bear commented under his breath, as they took seats at a rough-hewn table and benches close by the door.

"I'm nae so certain of that," Lachlan returned. "Withoot peace, no Campbell or Gerdens would've been able to get within a mile of Rowena."

"Aye. But if they *had* managed to get to her, they might've killed her instead of dragging her off."

That idea chilled Lachlan all over again. Bear made a good point. With no truce, the MacLawrys and Campbells and all their septs and allies had been killing each other for centuries. Both Rowena and he could well have been just another pair of casualties. "Ye terrify me sometimes, Bear."

The youngest MacLawry brother gave their breakfast request to the innkeeper before he favored Lachlan with a grim smile. "Ye're just saying that to be nice."

Peter Gilling joined them, and set a well-worn map on the table. "I paid one of the grooms a shilling fer this," he muttered.

Lachlan nodded his thanks. Peter Gilling had known Rowena for her entire life, too. As Bear had said, he wasn't the only man here willing to lay down his life for her. He needed to remember that. However desperate he was to find her, he wasn't alone.

"Where the devil are we, then?" Bear grunted, turning the map to face him.

"Ye know I cannae read those scratches," Peter returned, frowning. "And neither could young Gilbert the groom."

"Ye're here." A hand reached over Peter's shoulder, and a long forefinger indicated a spot about thirty miles north of Fort William, just off the north road.

Following the finger back up to its owner, Lachlan shoved to his feet, swearing. Munro was even faster. The tall, lean man didn't move, and instead stood regarding them with cool hazel eyes. Reddish-brown hair hung across the right side of his face, partly obscuring the faint scar that ran from just beneath his ear and down to the right side of his mouth, giving him a permanently cynical expression.

"George Gerdens-Daily." Bear clenched his fists. "I should've known ye'd be a part of this. Ye're a dead man."

Gerdens-Daily lifted his right eyebrow, the motion pulling at his scar and lifting the corner of his mouth. "I'm nae certain what it is I'm in the middle of, but I'm pleased to see ye, Lord Munro MacLawry. How's yer shoulder?"

With a roar Bear threw himself across the table.

Damnation. "Bear, nae!" Lachlan grabbed his friend by the coat and hauled backward. The movement jarred his shoulder again, but bloody hell, they couldn't afford the time for a brawl. Not when they were so badly outnumbered, and not when their first — only — task was to rescue Rowena.

"He took Winnie! Do ye nae see that?"

"Do ye think he'd be here if he did?" Lachlan pressed.

On the far side of the table, Gerdens-Daily cocked his head. "What's this?" He motioned at the men leaving their breakfasts and hurrying forward to join the fight.

"Easy, lads. This is personal between me and the giant."

"Ye ken what it is!" Bear straightened, but that didn't stop him from pointing and bellowing.

"If I'd done someaught to a MacLawry, I'd nae be shy aboot admitting it," the other man drawled. "Shooting ye, fer instance. That's been what, four years ago now?"

"Aye," Munro returned. "And I've been looking forward to returning the favor ever since."

"Well. Here I am." Gerdens-Daily spread his arms.

Lachlan wouldn't have wagered a penny that the Campbell man was unarmed. Bear would know it, as well, but that didn't stop him from making another lunge. This time Lachlan shoved him sideways, wincing as the motion tore loose some of his stitches. "Nae. There's only one Gerdens we're after now. And it's nae him."

Finally Bear subsided, sitting again. "Aye."

Gerdens-Daily, though, glanced from one of them to the other. "Berling's somewhere in Canada, if he's who ye're after. That, I'd nae blame ye fer. In fact, I might help ye bury him."

"We dunnae want him. Nae today." Bear continued glaring at the man across the table. "It's his brother I mean to put under the ground."

"Dermid?" To Lachlan's surprise, George Gerdens-Daily took a seat at one end of the bench, just beyond Peter Gilling. Whatever his other faults the man wasn't a coward, and that was for damned certain. "What did that big ox do to ye?"

Lachlan drew in a short breath, for a moment wishing Munro was elsewhere. They didn't need a short-tempered brawler for this conversation. The tangled history between the MacLawrys and this Gerdens had begun with fathers being murdered, shootings, and fights. In the past few months, however, while no one would say the animosity was finished, tensions had . . . lessened. This was not the time to renew old grudges.

"Dermid came to Glengask with the Campbell," he said, being as succinct as he could with Munro glowering at him. "Last afternoon I was stabbed and Rowena Mac-Lawry was taken. And now Dermid's nowhere to be found."

Gerdens-Daily gazed at him for a moment. "Let's see," he finally said.

"See what? I dunnae have time fer riddles."

"Ye said, 'I was stabbed,' nae 'Dermid

stabbed me.' So either ye didnae see who did it, or ye're lying. So let's see it."

Scowling, Lachlan pulled his coat away from his left shoulder. He didn't bother looking himself, but from his companions' expressions he knew he was bleeding again. "It looks the same in the back," he said, releasing the coat again.

Rubbing his chin with one hand, Gerdens-Daily nodded. "Why dunnae ye join me at my table?" he suggested, and rose to walk away to a lone table at the back of the inn.

Lachlan started to his feet, but Bear didn't budge. "I'm nae wasting time flapping my jaw with a Gerdens," the big man muttered. "Especially that one."

"Then stay here. Today I dunnae care aboot yer pride, Munro. I'd clean his boots if he can give us any information aboot Dermid."

Bear grabbed his arm. "Ye ken ye cannae trust him."

"Aye. But I can listen. Eat yer eggs. Ye gave me yer word we'd be gone from here in ten more minutes."

Rowena's brother cursed, then picked up his mug and stalked toward the back of the inn's common room. Lachlan wasn't certain whether Gerdens-Daily truly had something to tell them that required more privacy than their front table provided, or if he already knew what Dermid had done and he meant to delay the pursuit. At the moment he was willing to take the risk of the latter in exchange for a chance of the former.

He seated himself opposite Gerdens-Daily. His companions, though, remained standing, a solid wall of angry Highlanders. Dermid and his cronies had been fools to cross the MacLawrys. And if he had his way, by noon they would all be dead fools.

"Do ye have some insight fer us, or do ye mean to gloat? I've nae time fer one, and nae patience fer the other."

The innkeeper brought their breakfast of eggs and mutton, and Gerdens-Daily remained silent until the old man left again. Then he took a swallow of what smelled like American coffee. "Dermid's nae a wee man, but how did he manage to stick ye and carry off the lass and get away withoot being shot a dozen times?"

"I got hit from behind. A second man grabbed her." Lachlan put his hands flat on the table. "What do ye care, anyway?"

"So ye didnae see him," the man continued, ignoring Lachlan's question. "The Campbell told ye he'd gone missing then, I'd wager."

"Aye, he told us," Munro grumbled,

managing somehow to keep his voice down. "And he said he was damned tired of the Gerdeneses, and we could put Dermid's head on a pike, fer all he cared."

That wasn't precisely the conversation. It wasn't precisely a lie, either, so Lachlan decided not to correct his friend. Instead he gazed at Gerdens-Daily levelly. "If yer curiosity's been satisfied, why don't ye tell us something useful? Unless ye're only to keep us here."

"Ye're MacLawrys on Gerdens land. How far do ye think ye'll get? And what in the devil's name makes ye think ye'll be able to find one man here?"

Swallowing a last bite of egg and drowning it with ale, Lachlan pushed back the bench and stood again. "We've an idea or two. The Campbell wants to keep this peace."

"I dunnae care aboot the damned peace," Gerdens-Daily returned, emotion touching his voice for the first time. "Alkirk didnae lose his father to a MacLawry." He shoved his own plate away. "The MacLawrys *did* lose their *seannair* to a Gerdens, though."

"Ye h—"

"I'll nae stand by and let ye lose yer only sister to a Gerdens, too." Gerdens-Daily stood. "I've a notion he'll head fer an old ruin of a hoose called Denune Castle. I'll take ye there, if ye'll let me."

Lachlan stared at him, as surprised by the offer as he was at the fact that both the Campbell and Gerdens-Daily had named the same property. That boded well for them — and for Rowena. If neither of them had an ulterior motive, that was. "Dermid's yer cousin," he said aloud. "Ye're nae doing him any favors by talking to us."

"Aye. Hence me keeping my voice doon. I'll help ye if I can, but I've nae wish to be murdered by my own clan fer it."

Gerdens-Daily knew the land here much better than they did, and that was for damned certain. In addition, a few weeks ago he'd stopped his clan from dragging a Sassenach bride away from Duncan Lenox — and her husband was a MacLawry chieftain. Whatever Gerdens-Daily's game, he seemed to have his own sense of morality. And at the moment that would have to be enough.

Lachlan nodded. If he could help, he was welcome to do so. If he meant trouble, he was dead. Rescuing Rowena came before clan rivalries and old grudges. Even old murders. "Let's be off, then. To Denune Castle."

■ ■ ■ ■

The horses slowed to a trot, and Rowena tensed her muscles against the hard hammering. A trot meant they'd slowed their flight, but that wasn't necessarily a good thing. Either they were no longer worried about pursuit, or they were near their destination.

"I'll go up to the village and get us some breakfast," Charles Calder said, in a voice she'd already come to loathe. "And I'll see if I can locate the parson."

"Dunnae make a stink about it, though, Charles; we don't want anyone curious."

"Just me appearing there'll make them curious, Arnold," Calder returned dryly. "I'll tell them I'm with some drovers, just over the hill." A moment later hoofbeats headed away from them and then faded behind the sound of birds and wind across the grass.

"How's yer passenger, Dermid?" Haws's voice came a moment later.

A hand came down sharply across her backside, and she winced before she could stop herself. "Alive," the big brute said. "Dunnae ye worry, lass. We're nearly there."

So that was supposed to make her feel better? Rowena stifled a retort. They had no idea she'd chewed through her gag, and she meant to make the most of that when the opportunity came. Perhaps Dermid's other cheek. Or Haws's ear. It didn't matter to her, as long as no one would be able to look at either man without knowing that something untoward had happened.

Briefly she wondered what would happen if Lachlan and her brothers never found her. Her breath caught. No. He *would* find her, because nothing else was acceptable. They'd been through too much to reach these last few days, and she would not allow anything to destroy what they'd finally and mutually realized — that they were in love, and they were supposed to be together. He would do everything he could to see that happen, and so would she. Dermid Gerdens wouldn't stop them, and neither would Ranulf Mac-Lawry.

As sore and uncomfortable as she was, her stomach rumbled, and she hoped that Charles Calder would be returning with breakfast for her, as well. It seemed like ages since she'd eaten, or had as much as a sip of water. In the torrid romance tales Jane favored, young ladies were always being kidnapped, and they never ate. They refused to eat until they were rescued. Evidently being dainty and helpless and fainting from hunger was the approved reaction to being taken against one's will.

Pish on that.

The horses clattered onto what sounded like cobbles, then came to a stop. Before she could even take a deep, welcome breath, Dermid dropped her sideways, this time thankfully feet first. Even so she landed hard, her legs giving way. She collapsed in a sack-covered heap.

"The lass seems to have quieted doon some," Dermid noted, and she could hear the amusement in his voice. "Shame, that."

"I doubt she's finished making trouble," Arnold Haws returned dryly.

"I dunnae mind the wiggling. She bites me again, though, and I'll break her jaw. Ye hear that, Lady Winnie? I'll break yer bloody jaw."

She was supposedly still gagged, so she kept silent. Instead she worked on flexing her leg muscles, trying to bring feeling back into them. Reaching out with her fingertips she did feel cobblestones, and they were broken and covered with dirt. Wherever they were, it wasn't anywhere nice.

And now that they'd evidently reached their destination, the fact that these were no gentlemen who'd taken her began to make her even more uneasy. Several times during the long, bruising night they'd made crude comments about her. Then, it had been to keep her from fighting back — though that hadn't worked. Now, she wasn't so certain.

A hand under her arm dragged her to her feet. "Inside with ye, my lady MacLawry."

"Aye," Arnold put in. "We'll get ye a feather bed and a nice hot bath."

Dermid chuckled, a dull, cruel sound that made her shiver inside. "And roast mutton and mincemeat pie," he added. "And . . . And fresh strawberries." He laughed again.

Rowena tensed, waiting for him to untie her feet, but instead he grabbed her around the thighs and hefted her over his shoulder like a sack of potatoes. *Damnation.* Once she was anywhere inside, she would be much harder to find. With her legs bound together, her hands tied behind her back, and a sack over her head, she had no idea how to stop them, though.

"Does the storage room still have a lock?" Haws asked, from directly behind them.

"Aye, last I saw."

"Put her in there so we can eat in some damned peace."

She straightened, raising up hard. The back of her head slammed into something. Haws whumphed.

"Damn it all!" he cursed. A hand slapped her shoulder and one ear, but it lacked any real force.

"Dunnae bruise her face," Dermid complained. "I dunnae like a bruised face on a lass. And Parson Nicholas willnae like it, either, even if she is a MacLawry."

He dumped her onto a hard floor. A moment later a door shut, and she heard a key turn. Then, silence. For a moment Rowena lay still anyway, listening. Her left shoulder was already sore from her fall last night, though, and so she turned onto her back and dug her heels into the floor. Then she scooted down, bending her legs, until the sack slipped off over her head.

Being able to see didn't change her circumstances much, but it did make her feel better. The floor was stone, covered with dust and rat droppings. They'd called it a storage room, but other than a chair missing its seat and an overturned barrel — and her — it was empty.

No window gave her a view of the outside, though she wouldn't have been able to reach it, anyway. The only light came from a horizontal crack high up on one wall — probably where the rats were coming from.

Turning onto her right side, she squirmed her way over to the broken chair. Where the seat had caved in a single iron nail had been exposed. Hopefully that would be enough. With her head and her feet she tipped the dirty old chair over, catching it across her thigh before it could hit the floor.

Charles Calder had gone for breakfast, but she had no idea how long that would take, or whether he would return with boiled eggs for her as well, or with a parson in tow. Not in a million years would she agree to marry anyone but Lachlan, and these men had to know she meant to make trouble. Evidently she only had to appear uninjured for the deed to be done. Therefore, she couldn't be here when Calder returned.

It took some effort, but she managed to maneuver herself around so she could rub her wrist bindings against the end of the nail. She kept poking herself with the sharp point, but that didn't matter. A thousand years ago, even a hundred years ago, rival clans kidnapping women to force alliances or secure power or begin wars wasn't terribly uncommon. Dermid probably only wanted to get his hands on her dowry. He was likely to be killed before he could receive anything, but then someone would avenge him, and the Campbells and Mac-Lawrys would be battling again.

And to think, yesterday she'd been about to surrender Lachlan because she couldn't disobey Ranulf. If — when — she escaped this, nothing would part her from the man she loved. Because while she knew her brothers were in pursuit, it wasn't them whose image she kept in her heart, comforting her and reminding her that this horror was only temporary.

She wanted him there, wanted to hear his voice and feel his touch. Everything else — the theater, dances in stuffy rooms, drinking tea with her pinkie lifted — it was all like a pretty dress. It looked nice, and she felt elegant while she wore it, but it didn't make her happy. Lachlan made her happy. As for being proper and English, she didn't think she would survive this if that were all she was.

The rope about her wrists parted. Rowena gasped, her hands shaking as she carefully sat up and rested them for a moment in her lap. Bruises, cuts, rope burns — her fingers were swollen and clumsy, but she didn't have time to coddle herself. The second she could flex them again, she went to work on the bindings around her ankles.

She stood, grabbing onto the chair to steady herself, and hobbled to the door. Very carefully and slowly she pushed down on the rusted handle. It didn't give. With a silent curse in Scottish Gaelic she let it go again. For a moment she leaned there, trying to will feeling and coordination back into her arms and legs.

Then she made her way to the cracked wall, reaching her fingers up into the narrow opening. She pushed, then pulled, shoving at it as hard as she could. The stone didn't budge. *Bloody, bloody hell.* All the vulgar curses she ever heard her brothers utter wanted to spill out of her. She wanted to scream, to make Lachlan hear her.

Instead she had to wait in this tiny, filthy room, while some stupid man arrived to be bullied into marrying her to an even more stupid, cruel man, while two more intelligent, crueler men looked on. It was insufferable.

Rowena took a deep breath, trying to calm her wild thoughts down to something manageable and helpful. She might not have a weapon, but she had her wits. What could she do, then, to slow them down?

Taking another look around the room, she tiptoed back to the door. When she pressed her ear to it she could hear the muffled sound of men conversing, but she couldn't tell if it was two, or three, or four — or twenty. The door opened in toward her, which would have been a good thing if she had something with which to block it.

They'd entered the building and walked down a corridor and a shallow set of stairs before they'd dumped her into this room. A sudden thought struck her, and her breath caught. They were still in the Highlands. And Highlanders in castles made prominent targets for the Sassenach and any rival clans. Glengask had an escape tunnel entrance in the kitchen pantry and another in the corner of the morning room. Gray House had a secret exit behind the kitchen pantry. The tunnels frequently originated in out-of-the-way rooms from where the home's occupants could slip away undetected.

Still moving as quietly as she could, she went to the far corner of the room and started surveying the floor. A few wood planks remained, but the rest had either rotted away or been relocated to more public rooms. At the edge of the overturned barrel she found . . . something. She knocked on the floor with her knuckle, and it didn't sound as solid. Her heart skittered. *Oh, thank goodness.* Finally some luck.

The barrel was empty, but still weighed a great deal. She flinched with every skid and bump of the old wood as she slowly pushed it sideways. Then, going onto her hands and knees, she cleared away dust and bits of wood until she found a slight gap in the mortar. Sending up a quick prayer, she dug her fingers in and lifted.

With far too loud a creak, a section of the floor pulled up on one side. The opening was only a foot or so square, but perhaps whoever had once lived here were small-boned. None of her brothers would have fit.

She shook herself. Yes, thinking of her family, and mostly of Lachlan, gave her courage, but she had no time to waste. The hole beneath her was black as pitch, but with a deep breath she hung her legs over, grabbed the small metal ring on the bottom of the trapdoor, and dropped.

Her feet hit the floor before she even had the door closed. For a second she held it up, using the scant amount of light to try to get her bearings. The tunnel was dirt and stone with a few wood braces here and there, crumbling and ancient-looking. It headed off to her left, but she could only see about four feet in. With a last look at the gloom, she pulled the door the rest of the way closed.

Once the Gerdenses came into the storage room and found her missing, Dermid wouldn't be able to come after her. Both Haws and Calder would, and that troubled her. Best, then, not to be trapped in the tunnels. She began hunching her way forward, feeling with her hands, feeling the ground with one foot before she set her weight on it. If the tunnel was caved in anywhere, or if it ended in an oubliette meant to trap any strangers — and either was utterly likely — she would have to return to the trapdoor, or wait there in the dark to see if they came after her or simply put the barrel back over the door and left her there to rot.

That thought unsettled her more than the idea of crawling through the dark. She'd wanted to remain out in the open, somewhere Lachlan could find her. Now she was below ground, alone and in the dark. All she could give him was time, and all she could do now was pray that she'd given him enough.

CHAPTER SEVENTEEN

"That's Denune?" Lachlan stopped at the bend in the road to gaze at the tumbled old rock pile.

It must have been impressive once, up at the edge of a cliff and overlooking the entire valley. At the back the sheer wall fell for two hundred feet, eaten away by the river running fast at its base. The only way to approach was from the front, a gentle slope with only a few rocks and a low, stunted tree for cover.

"Aye," George Gerdens-Daily returned, looking up at the old structure. "I remember it being more impressive." He spat onto the rocky ground. "My father, and Dermid's, was born here. It's a shame Berling's across the Atlantic. I'd nae mind having a word with him aboot how he keeps up his properties."

Generally Lachlan would have been very interested in hearing about any tensions between the Gerdens cousins. Today he had only one concern. "Surprise seems to be oot," he commented, as a pair of horses by the doors whinnied at them. "Ye lead us in. Dermid'll nae shoot ye, I presume."

"He'll nae shoot me. But I'll nae shoot him, either. Nae over a MacLawry lass. I've done what I said."

"Aye," Bear replied. "Ye've done what any hound on a scent could do. And now ye turn tail when ye have a chance to be someaught more."

Gerdens-Daily gave a cynical smile. "I dunnae give a bloody damn what ye think, Munro MacLawry. I'm nae yer friend. But ye are welcome to come and find me if ye ever want to settle the matter of that hole in yer shoulder." With a nod at Lachlan he turned his horse and trotted back down the road.

"I could encourage him to help us, I reckon," Peter Gilling said, hefting his blunderbuss.

"Nae," Lachlan returned. "We'd still be searching fer Denune if he hadnae led us here. And I'm nae inclined to debate with him today." He kicked his heels into Beowulf's ribs. "It's Dermid I want," he said, as they lurched into a gallop.

As soon as he came in range of the mostly

intact upstairs windows he expected to be shot, but nothing stirred. Had the Campbell been wrong? Did the horses belong to some stray travelers? Had Gerdens-Daily led them to Denune because it was better than a day here and back to Glengask? At the front door he dismounted, not waiting for Bear to join him before he shoved at the sturdy oak.

It opened more easily than he expected, and he pushed inside, his pistol in his right hand. The entire north wing of the castle had collapsed, leaving the building exposed to the weather and the elements. Paint peeled in the main hallway, and any carpet had been removed, leaving behind an uneven stone floor.

"Calder!" a voice called from farther into the house. "We're in the kitchen. Did ye find the parson?"

He and Bear exchanged a glance. "Aye," Lachlan returned, muffling his voice behind the sleeve of his coat.

"Calder?" Munro whispered. "Charles Calder? Damnation."

Charles Calder. That would be another of Dermid's cousins. The one who'd shot Arran a few weeks ago. All the nice people were here, evidently. "Steady, Bear. We're here for Rowena."

"And if Calder's had his hands on her, he'll lose 'em both."

If Charles Calder had touched her, he would lose more than his hands, as far as Lachlan was concerned. He'd been diplomatic with both the Campbell and with George Gerdens-Daily, because they'd had information he found useful. After nearly twenty-four hours of pursuit, his ability to be levelheaded had just expired. He motioned for Eòin to remain close by the front door. The last thing they needed was for Charles Calder to come up behind them.

Moving as swiftly as he dared, Lachlan eased his way to the rear of the castle's main wing. Gaping holes showed in the ceiling where the roof had caved in, and as they passed, a dozen brown and tan whinchats took flight from what had once been the library. The men were expecting a parson. To Lachlan that meant one of them intended to marry Rowena — which for their sakes had best mean she was still alive and well.

This would be a temporary stop, then, he assumed. No man in his right mind would choose to live here, and even if Dermid was stupid enough to snatch Rowena Mac-Lawry, he must have had a further destination in mind.

The kitchen door stood open, and with a deep breath he straightened and stepped around the corner and into the room. "Good afternoon, lads," he snarled, leveling his pistol.

A worn table scattered with boiled eggs and buttered bread wobbled in the center of the room. Two chairs stood back from it — and both of them were empty. That could only mean one thing.

Instinctively Lachlan ducked. As he did so a claymore swung over his head and bit into the doorframe. Still advancing, he slammed up on the wielder's elbow, separating him from the weapon, then pressed the muzzle of his pistol against Dermid Gerdens's temple before the big man could regain his balance. "Enough," he growled.

Bear stepped around the two of them and shoved the second man backward into one of the chairs. "Well, well. All the rats have come north. I know ye, Arnold Haws. And I hope ye've said yer farewells to yer family, because ye'll nae set eyes on 'em again."

"Bear MacLawry," the second man returned. "I've never done a thing to ye."

"Except try to hunt doon and kill my brother Arran."

"I was only doing as Lord Fendarrow ordered. If ye have a complaint, take it up with him."

The Marquis of Fendarrow, Arran's new father-in-law, hadn't been invited to Ranulf's wedding. But then, neither had Arnold Haws. "Ye're a mite more convenient. Where's my sister?"

"Did ye lose her?" Dermid took up with a loose grin.

"Where's Rowena?" Lachlan demanded, his attention on Dermid as the big man's gaze flicked toward the short hallway beyond. "Rowena!"

Edging around, he caught sight of a closed door — likely an old butler's pantry. Not a sound came from within. His heart hammering, he called her name again. Still nothing. Motioning for Peter Gilling to take his place, Lachlan strode into the hallway and down to the doorway. He turned the key in the rusted lock and pushed it open.

"Row . . ." He trailed off. Other than a tipped-over chair and an old barrel, the room was empty. It smelled musty and unused, but as he inhaled, a faint, familiar scent touched him. Rowena's violet perfume. He was certain of it.

"She's nae in there," he said, returning to the kitchen.

"Who are ye looking for?" Haws asked, furrowing his brow. "And what are Mac-

Lawrys doing on Gerdens land? Armed, I might add?"

Bear yanked him to his feet by the collar and then shoved him at the old stove. "Ye know damned well who we're looking fer, ye rat. Ye tell us. Now."

Arnold glanced at his cousin. "Do ye know who they're looking for?"

The big man shook his head. "I dunnae."

Lachlan narrowed his eyes, then stalked up to Dermid and yanked down the bandage covering his cheek. Clear teeth marks bit into the skin, leaving an angry, bloody mess behind. "Ye didnae bite yerself."

"That?" Haws snorted. "Dermid got a bit too friendly with a lass at the local tavern. Didn't ye, Dermid?"

"Aye. I got too friendly with a lass."

Clearly they weren't going to get any answers with Arnold Haws speaking for the two men. "Bear. Take Haws fer a walk. Off the cliff."

Munro grinned, an expression that chilled even Lachlan. He hadn't precisely been jesting, but his friend had never been good at holding back his anger. And that had been boiling for the past day, with some additional help from Gerdens-Daily. "I owe Arran a wedding gift," the youngest Mac-Lawry brother growled.

For the first time Arnold looked uneasy. "Ye can't murder me. I haven't done anything!"

"One of ye Campbells shot my brother. Another shot me, and now Lach's been stabbed. I reckon that's enough." Bear tilted his head. "Even if I'm at the wrong place, as ye say I am, I'm nae leaving here empty-handed." Grabbing Haws by the arm, he shoved him hard at the hallway door.

"Dermid!"

Gerdens stirred, but with Peter Gilling's blunderbuss aimed at his midsection, there wasn't anywhere he could go. "This'll mean war," he rumbled. "The Campbell willnae —"

"The Campbell told us where to find ye," Lachlan cut in. "Ye've no protection at all. It's just the two of ye. I doubt anyone'll even weep fer ye, *amadan*. Ye're looking at yer one chance to stay alive, and if ye cannae prove to me that Rowena MacLawry is alive and unhurt, I've nae reason to show ye any kindness at all." He glanced at Arnold Haws, clinging to the door frame with his fingers as Bear shoved at him again. "Either of ye."

The two Campbells exchanged a glance. "She's in there!" Haws finally hissed, indicating the storage room.

"Do ye take me fer a fool?"

"She was," he insisted. "We went in there to check on her, and she was gone. We heard you coming and straightened it up."

" 'Straightened it up,' " Lachlan repeated, heading back into the room. "How?"

"Look in the barrel."

His heart froze. "Aulay, bring me a lantern or a torch."

The stableboy rifled through the old sideboard and came up with a broken candle in its holder. He lit it in the kitchen fire and brought it into the storage room. "Here ye are, m'laird."

Lachlan had never wanted so badly to not look. If she was in that barrel, hadn't made a sound in minutes . . . No. That wasn't how this was going to end. He would find her, she would be safe, and then he would marry her. They would have children and a happy life. Together.

Please, he thought to himself, and walked over to the barrel. With a hard swallow, trying to steady himself, he lifted the candle and looked inside. Abruptly his heart started beating again. Some frayed rope, a sack, bits of cloth. And that was all. "You bound her."

"She bit me!" Dermid retorted, as if that had been Rowena's fault.

Lachlan strode back into the kitchen and

cuffed Gerdens across the head with the
butt of his pistol. He wanted to keep hitting
Dermid, to grind him into dust. But that
wouldn't help him find Rowena. And she
was all that mattered. "Where is she?" he
asked very slowly, his voice low and flat and
as angry as he felt.

Dermid spat blood onto the floor. "Look
closer. Ye dunnae frighten me, Gray. In a
fair fight, ye're no match fer a Gerdens. If
ye had nae gotten here so quick, we'd have
been ready fer ye."

"If ye thought ye could take me in a fair
fight, why did ye stick a knife through my
back?" Lachlan retorted.

"That wasnae me."

Lachlan sent a look at Haws. "Thank ye
fer that, anyway."

Back inside the room he took a closer
look. With the candle he could now make
out a large section of floor in the middle of
the room where the dust and dirt had been
disturbed, and he laid his palm on the stone.
She'd been here, and not long ago. But
where had she gone, and why hadn't
Gerdens or Haws followed her?

A nail stuck out from the broken seat of
the chair, and when he crouched down he
saw the droplets of blood clinging to it.
Deep, cold fury ran through him. Of course

she'd tried to free herself, and she'd been hurt in the process. Which told him she was desperate to get away from these men. But there were no windows, and no other doors.

He paused, looking at the barrel again. Unless there was another door.

"Lach?"

"Aulay, watch Haws. Bear, give me a hand."

A heartbeat later Bear stood in the doorway of the storage room, swearing. "They locked her in here? In the dark? The wh—"

"Shove over that barrel, will ye?" Lachlan interrupted, crouching beside it. The dirt was disturbed there, as well, and he was certain he could make out her delicate fingertips in the dust.

Munro overturned the barrel with no noticeable effort, then crouched down beside him. "An escape tunnel?"

"I reckon so."

Lachlan dug his fingers into the small opening and pulled. With a creak the door lifted. She'd gone in there. Into the dark. Alone.

"They set that barrel on top," Bear said slowly, his face growing pale. "She'd nae have been able to get oot again."

"She may be oot the other side by now." Lachlan handed him the candle and then with some effort squeezed through the small opening and dropped to the floor. "Go see what ye can find. Or ask one of those lads if they know where the tunnel exits."

Nodding, Bear handed the candle down to him. "Ye find my sister," he said, his voice breaking. "I'll see to these bastards."

The tunnel was about three feet tall and the same wide, a dark hole lined with whatever had been to hand when some Gerdens ancestor had dug it out. Even with the candlelight he had almost no visibility; the tunnel twisted and turned sharply, likely around the huge boulders that poked up above the surface.

As he moved forward it looked like there were additional tunnels splitting off to different parts of the house. They all emptied into the main tunnel, but he didn't know precisely which one that was. Everything to the right seemed nothing more than piles of rubble, but he had to check each intersection to be certain. To try to figure this labyrinth out in absolute darkness — she could be anywhere. She could be trapped, or suffocated. Part of the low ceiling might have collapsed on her.

"Rowena!" he called, bending onto his hands and knees to look at the dirt floor of the tunnel. The ground was disturbed, but he couldn't tell if she'd been coming or going when she'd passed this way. "Rowena!"

"Lachlan?"

The voice was distant and muted and thready, but it set his heart beating all over again.

"I'm here, lass! Where are ye?"

"I don't know!" her voice returned, still thready. "I stayed to the left, but I don't know how many times I turned."

"Do ye see my light?"

A pause. "Nae."

The air down in the tunnels was thin and musty and old. He had no idea how much of it was even breathable. The candle flame flickered and faded, growing dimmer the farther in he ventured. How long had she been down there before the two men had decided to check on her?

If the light went out, he needed to be able to get both of them out. Drawing the knife from his boot, he dug it into the wall on his left, making an inch-deep arrow pointing back the way he'd come. Then, alternating between crawling and crouching, he continued forward, pausing every few feet to make another mark.

"Rowena? Talk to me, my fierce lass."

"I thought Calder killed ye," she said, the

435

pain in her voice wounding him all over again.

"I'm nae dead."

"That's what I started telling myself. Because I almost made another mistake, and we couldn't end that way."

"What mistake did ye almost make?" The tunnel branched off. She'd said she'd stayed left, so he went that way, as well.

"I almost let ye go, Lachlan." She made a sobbing sound. "How could I do that?"

"Because ye're a lass who loves yer brother. I wouldnae have let ye get away from me, though, so ye've naught to worry over."

"Ye're all I could think aboot. I knew ye'd come after me. I knew ye'd find me."

"Seems to me ye did a fair job of rescuing yerself, my lass."

The candle went out. Stifling his curse, he continued on, still stopping to carve the arrows. If she could make her way through this inky black, then so could he. The crawling and crouching sent pain from his shoulder all the way down to his fingers, but he clenched his jaw and kept going.

"I bit Dermid." This time brief humor touched her voice.

"I saw that. He'll nae be taking another lass against her will, I reckon."

Silence. "I'm very tired, Lach."

He grimaced. "We've poor air in here. I'm almost to ye. Keep talking, Rowena."

"I still don't see yer light."

Her voice did sound closer, now. The tunnel he was in veered sharply right, then left again. "The light's oot," he had to admit, hoping that wouldn't make her panic. "Ye just stay where ye are. I'll come to ye."

"Who's with ye?" she asked after a moment.

"Bear, but he couldnae fit doon the hole. And Peter, and two of the stableboys. Ranulf has the rest of the clan searching fer ye all across the northwest."

"How did ye know where to look fer me?"

"The Campbell. He told us Dermid had vanished from the gathering, and where he was likely headed with ye."

"The Campbell helped us?"

She sounded close enough to touch, now. Nearly bumping his head as the tunnel turned hard to the left again, he slowed. "Lass?"

Warm arms flung around his head, then lowered to his shoulders. *Thank God. Thank God,* he kept repeating to himself, as he found her mouth and kissed her. It felt like far longer than a day since he'd last touched her. And he swore to himself that no one would ever come between them again, Gerdens, Buchanan, Campbell, or Mac-Lawry.

"Lachlan," she whispered, holding him tightly. "I knew ye'd find me. I knew it. I just had to give ye enough time."

For a long moment he just held her. His Rowena. How could he ever have thought he would find some other lass? None could match her. None. And he was hers, as much as she was his. "I'd go to Hades itself to find ye," he murmured, stroking her long, disheveled hair. "And now let's get ye back into the sunlight, my fierce lass."

"Do ye know the way oot?"

"I marked the wall with arrows. On the right side, a few inches from the ceiling. Follow 'em until ye see the light from the open trapdoor."

"I'll follow ye, if ye dunnae mind."

He kissed her again. "Nae. I dunnae mind."

They started back with her close behind him, touching a foot or his back. He still couldn't see her, but he could feel her warm presence there with him. A man could live on that and her kisses.

He couldn't even imagine what she'd been through over the last day. Being dragged off somewhere, after seeing a man stab him.

She'd thought him dead.

Something skittered in front of him. In the deep dark, shadows flitted across his vision, but he knew it couldn't be anything he was actually seeing. It was likely a rat, but he didn't relish the idea of being bitten or scratched in the face. As he felt for the next arrow, he paused. What had Rowena said? "Did ye see who stabbed me, lass?" he asked aloud.

"Nae. But Calder said he did it."

Calder. "Charles Calder?"

"Aye. The one who shot Arran. He went to get breakfast for the other two, and I was worried what he might do when he returned."

They'd had their breakfast on the table. But there hadn't been any sign of Charles Calder. "Lass, do ye have a weapon with ye?"

"I have a rock in one hand."

He pulled his knife again. "Keep it handy. I think we may have company doon h—"

With a gasp she ripped backward, deeper into the dark. "Lach—"

At her shriek he was already scrambling back the way they'd come. A second later he touched her flailing hand, then launched past her. He hit a solid, clothed shape, then thudded into the wall with his injured

439

shoulder. The sudden pain drove the air from his lungs. He jabbed forward, and caught something with the knife.

"Rowena, find the arrows," he hissed, following up the stab with his fist.

He struck wall, and cursed. Even so, he was thankful — very thankful — that he'd managed to put himself between Rowena and Calder. Of course the coward had gone after her, but he meant to make certain that Dermid's cousin didn't have a second chance to hurt her.

He heard sound beyond him again, and scooped up a handful of dirt, hurling it in that direction. Once he heard it strike, he lunged. "Keep going, Rowena," he grunted over his shoulder. Calder would not be getting past him. Not this time.

Grabbing hold of a leg, he jabbed with the knife again, feeling a blade graze his own cheek. Lachlan shoved his good shoulder hard into Calder's ribs, knocking them into a wider tunnel intersection. "Why is it," Calder panted, swinging and hitting Lachlan in the elbow, "you MacLawrys never die when you're supposed to?"

"Because ye're nae very good at trying to kill us, I'd imagine," Lachlan returned, estimating where Calder's head was as he finished speaking and shoving it hard into the wall. Then he did it again. And again.

Finally Charles collapsed bonelessly to the ground. Lachlan didn't know if he was dead or unconscious, but he didn't much care. Favoring his shoulder, he turned back in the direction he'd sent Rowena — and felt a rock hurl by his head. "It's me, lass, damn it all," he grated, reaching out for her.

"Oh, I'm sorry!"

"I told ye to keep moving, lass."

"I wasn't leaving ye. Did I hurt ye?"

He blew out his breath. Of course she hadn't intended to go anywhere. "Ye missed me. And I should've called oot to ye." Lachlan took hold of her hand. "Let's go. Ye lead the way, this time."

"Is he dead?"

"I dunnae. Ye can go back and kick him in the man parts if ye like."

He couldn't see it, of course, but he was fairly certain she smiled as he followed her forward and to the right, along the line of arrows. Finally, after what seemed like hours, he caught the faint glow of light ahead of them.

"I can see a little," she whispered at the same moment.

"Aye. We're nearly there."

"Lachlan?" Bear's rumbling voice came. "Rowena?"

"We're here. She's safe."

"Calder may be doon there with ye!"

"He found us." Lachlan helped her straighten. "Here. Give her yer hand, Bear."

Half walking up the wall, with her hand clutched in Munro's, Rowena climbed out of the tunnel. The second she was free, she turned and reached into the opening again. "Up with ye, Lachlan."

Bear took his good hand, and she grabbed his coat, and together they hauled him up to the pantry floor. And then Rowena threw herself on him, putting him flat on his back as she kissed him over and over. Lachlan wrapped his arms around her and kissed her back. Beyond them, though, her brother sucked in his breath. Lachlan sat up, shifting her to his lap, ready to attack again if Calder appeared in the tunnel opening.

Her brother, though, was looking at his sister. Frowning, Lachlan held her back from him a little. And then he began cursing. "Why didnae ye say ye were hurt, Rowena?" he murmured, brushing hair back from her face to expose the angry black bruise on her cheek and around one eye.

"I'll heal," she said, holding out her wrists to reveal more cuts and bruises where she'd clearly been bound. "Now, I'll heal."

"I cannae say the same fer Calder and his

friends," he growled, rubbing a thumb gently along the bruises on her arms. "I say we close that door again and put the barrel back over it."

"We could put Haws in there, too," Bear agreed. "But Dermid wouldnae fit." He stood. "There's someaught else ye should hear, though. Dermid's surprisingly talkative when ye put a pistol to his head."

"What about Calder, though?" Rowena asked, uneasiness touching her voice. "He might know the way oot."

"The way oot's caved in," Bear returned, helping her and then Lachlan upright. "I dunnae want to think what might've happened if we hadnae found ye, Winnie."

"We did find her," Lachlan said sternly. "Let's send Eòin and Aulay back in there with more lights and some rope. We'll drag Calder oot, and I'll hand all of them over to Ranulf to deal with. I'm done with the lot."

He took Rowena's hand in his, and the two of them followed Munro into the front room with most of its roof and two broken windows. They sent the two stableboys to collect Calder, and then Bear walked up to smack Dermid on the back of the head. "Tell my friend what ye told me," he ordered.

Dermid sent him a baleful glare. "I said

this wasnae my idea. He said I'd be gaining a fortune in money and land, and that the Campbell would bring my brother back from Canada."

"Who said that to ye?" Bear prompted.

"The Sassenach. The one with the shiny yellow hair. Samston."

CHAPTER EIGHTEEN

Rowena glanced over her shoulder again. The two stableboys brought up the rear of the little troupe, but the two horses they'd placed between the young lads and Peter Gilling were what most concerned her. On one Dermid sat facing backward, his hands tied behind him and a sack over his head. On the other, Calder and Haws lay facedown across the saddle, every step from the horse knocking them into each other. They, too, had their hands tied behind them and sacks over their heads. And that was Highlands justice, as far as she was concerned.

She rode astride Calder's rather fine chestnut gelding. In polite company she never would have dared do such a thing, especially in a walking dress. Or rather, previous to the past few days she would have been mortified to be caught at it. Now, it felt important that she return to Glengask on her own two feet, so to speak.

"They're nae going anywhere," Lachlan said from beside her.

"I know. It's . . . satisfying to see them like that. I only wish we could gallop more. And trot. Trotting was the worst."

He reached over and touched her cheek. He did that frequently, touching her, as if he still couldn't quite believe he'd caught up in time and managed to rescue her. She'd known all along that he would reach her, but at this moment she felt so tired that sometimes she wondered if she was still Dermid's prisoner and she was dreaming that she'd already been saved.

Bear had left them about an hour ago to ride ahead and tell Ranulf they'd rescued her. She expected all her brothers would ride out to meet them, and so likely would the Campbell — if Ranulf bothered to tell him what his grandchildren and grandnephews had been up to this time.

Abruptly she sucked in her breath. "Damnation!"

"What?" Lachlan asked, looking alarmed.

"Ranulf was supposed to marry Charlotte yesterday. I completely forgot!"

"That's understandable. Dunnae trouble yerself."

"But —"

"He said they would wait until ye were

446

home safe. Now ye're safe, and ye're nearly home."

Yes, she was nearly home. She wasn't so certain that would be the end of her troubles, though. Because if Ran still meant for her to marry Lord Rob, she wouldn't be staying. She would be with Lachlan, wherever they had to go. Whatever they had to do. Compared to being kidnapped and spending hours in a pitch-dark tunnel with rats and a man who wouldn't have blinked at killing her, she could damned well speak her mind to her brother. Nor would she be cowed by him again.

They rounded the road where it ran along the loch, then started up the hill toward the castle. As she looked up, anxious to see the Scottish flag and the Glengask coat of arms floating above the roof, she drew in the chestnut. A relieved sob broke from her chest.

Ranulf strode down the hill toward her. Arran flanked him, and Bear was directly behind them with Mary and Charlotte on either arm. Jane hurried alongside Uncle Myles, a damp smile on her face. A hand touched her foot, and she jumped.

Lachlan had already dismounted, and with a grin he held up his arms to her. She wasn't riding sidesaddle, and she could climb down from the horse on her own, except that she suddenly felt wobbly. "Dunnae think too much aboot it, lass," he murmured, lifting her to the ground. "They're happy to see ye home safe."

Yes. That was all it was. Not that her brother and his betrothed had delayed their wedding to wait for her, or that her family had likely been worried out of their minds for three days. She was home.

Ranulf didn't stop his approach until he enfolded her in his arms, holding her hard against his chest. For a moment she felt like the little girl she'd once been, needing her oldest brother to hug her and tell her everything was fine. But nothing was that simple any longer. And it wasn't just her brothers she needed close to her.

"Are ye well, *piuthar*?" he asked, his hands around her shaking just a little.

"I have a few cuts and bruises, but naught that willnae heal," she returned, reaching out to squeeze Jane's hand.

"That's what Munro told us," Ranulf said, finally releasing her. "I still wanted to hear it with my own ears. And see ye with my own eyes."

Now Arran had to hug her. "Bear said ye put up quite a fight, Winnie."

"Of course I did," she agreed. "I wanted

to come home."

"We snuck oot here the back way," he continued. "The gathered clans and the entire household are waiting to welcome ye home, but Ran figured ye'd want a moment to breathe first."

She nodded. "Aye. But I have something I need to say to Ran, in case he doesn't wish to celebrate me coming back, after all."

Arran looked down at her. "He hasnae slept in three days, *piuthar.* Dunnae begin an argument if ye can avoid one."

Why did it all have to be so complicated? Of course she didn't want to fight with Ranulf. She didn't want to disappoint him, either. But neither was she willing to let Lachlan go. Deliberately she turned around, to find Lachlan speaking to Ranulf and Myles, the three of them taking turns glancing at their unwilling travel companions.

Perhaps Arran was correct. Perhaps she could wait until after Ranulf and Charlotte married. Whether it was her fault or not, her absence had caused them to delay their wedding. With a sigh she walked over to hug Charlotte. "I'm so sorry this nonsense ruined things," she said feelingly.

"*That* is nonsense," her almost sister-in-law commented. "I sincerely doubt that anyone has a single complaint about staying

449

on at Glengask for an additional day or two. And whether your brother and I are married or not, we are . . . together." Her cheeks darkened. "I mean to say —"

"Ye love him, and he loves ye, and the ceremony is for everyone else. The two of ye already know."

Charlotte gave her a slow smile. "Yes. We already know."

She looked over her shoulder at Lachlan again. "So do I."

After everyone had their turn hugging her and asking her if she was well, Peter Gilling and the two stableboys led the horses and the Gerdenses out of sight in the direction of the stable. Ranulf took her arm and headed them toward the rear of the grand house. "I'd rather nae sneak ye into yer own house, but Lachlan wants a chance to chat with Samston before he figures oot ye're safe."

She nodded. "We talked aboot it."

He glanced down at her. "Nae to rile ye up, but I'm glad to hear yer sweet voice with yer natural brogue again."

"I'm a Highlands lass. I bit a man in the face, stampeded horses, chewed through a gag, loosed my own bonds, and hid in a five-centuries-old escape tunnel. I like London. I like dancing, and I like going to the theater. But I'm nae a Sassenach. Nor do I want to be one."

His smile both pleased her and made her feel more than a little guilty. She'd put her brothers through a great deal, well before her kidnapping. And for heaven's sake, she'd put Lachlan through even more. She wanted to be with him, to fall asleep in his arms. But first they had to get through the rest of the day.

Inside the house Ranulf walked her upstairs to her bedchamber, as if he thought she might disappear again. "Come doon when ye're ready," he said, kissing her on the forehead.

"I'll only be twenty minutes or so."

To her surprise, he grinned. "It'll take ye that long to get Mitchell to stop weeping."

With a return smile she pushed open the door and went in to assure her maid that she was indeed alive, and that yes, she could wear a gown even with her bruised shoulder and bandages on her wrists.

Lachlan had put those bandages on her, and the . . . rage in his eyes made her worry whether the Gerdenses would live long enough to be turned over to Ranulf. She'd grown up with scraped knees and bruises, and while he'd generally been sympathetic, they all knew she'd earned them by willingly clambering about with boys. These, though — they'd been done to her.

"Och," Mitchell clucked, as she brushed out Rowena's hair. "Ye've burrs and grass and most likely birds' nests in yer lovely hair, my lady."

"I did some rolling about in the dirt." She smiled as she spoke; evidently she was still a lass with burrs in her hair.

"Yer brother the marquis sent lads to every cotter's shack and hunter's blind and inn fer a hundred miles, looking fer a sign of ye," the maid went on. "MacLawry men came in from every corner of the Highlands to help find ye. Lord Arran wanted to follow Lord Munro and Lord Gray, but the MacLawry said we couldnae put all our lads chasing after one possibility."

"I knew someone would find me," Rowena returned. She'd also known it would be Lachlan, even after she'd seen him stabbed. She'd needed to believe that *he* would be there — not Bear, or Arran, or even Ranulf. And she wondered where he was now, because she wanted him. Heat tugged down her spine, settling between her legs.

Someone rapped on her door. While she doubted that Lord Samston would dare come calling, particularly since he wasn't supposed to know yet that she was home,

452

she sent Mitchell to answer the door. The maid opened the door, curtsied, and stepped back as Lachlan strolled in.

"I was supposed to go home and change clothes," he said, gesturing at his dirty kilt, stained white shirt, and muddy boots. "I couldnae make myself leave the house withoot ye."

"Mitchell said I had burrs in my hair," she announced, rising from the dressing table.

"I cannae say I'm surprised," he returned with a grin. "Ye look very fine, now. A proper lady."

For a moment she studied his expression. "I am a proper lady. And I'm a Highlands lass."

"Aye, that ye are." He reached out, taking both of her hands in his. "Ye know I love ye, Rowena."

She nodded. "I do. And I love ye too, Lachlan." She'd tried to fall in love with someone, anyone, else, but it had never happened. It had always and only been Lachlan MacTier.

Lachlan took a breath. "I should likely be circumspect and sly, and wait to see the lay of the land before I ask yer brother's permission to wed ye. But firstly I'm nae certain he'll give his permission, and secondly, I dunnae want to be circumspect." He sank down on one knee.

Oh, goodness. Suddenly she couldn't breathe. All she could hear was the hard pounding of her heart in her own ears, and Mitchell's gasp somewhere behind her. Of course he wanted the maid there — they might require a witness. "Lachlan," she murmured.

"We've been friends since ye were born, Rowena. Sometimes I think we were too close as friends, because fer a time I couldnae see ye as anything else. But I see ye now. I see how beautiful ye are, and how fierce and kind and witty. I dunnae want to waste any more time we could be spending together. I love ye. I adore ye. Say ye'll be my wife, Rowena."

A tear ran down her cheek. For a long moment she looked down at him. "When I was a wee lass," she said slowly, "I imagined ye proposing to me. Ye'd be on a grand white horse, and the wind would be in yer hair. Ye'd say, 'ye're mine, lass,' scoop me onto the horse with ye, and we'd ride away. But ye're nae that man."

He gave a slight frown. "Wh—"

"Hush. I'm speaking. Ye're nae some imaginary lord with lightning shooting from his eyes. Ye're Lachlan. Ye're brave, and stubborn, and maddening, and oh, so handsome, and kind and warm and . . . Ye're everything. And I love ye. And aye, I'll be yer wife."

With a rush he stood again, swinging her up in his arms and kissing her all at the same time. Rowena laughed. This was so much better than being carted off on a white horse by some perfect, imaginary man. She threw her arms around his shoulders, being careful of his injured one, and sank down against him.

"Oh, my!" Mitchell exclaimed, jumping up and down and clapping her hands.

Slowly Lachlan settled her back on the floor again. "Ye'll never regret it, my fierce lass. Ye can show me London, and the parties, and the theater. I'll nae keep that from ye."

"I will enjoy showing you London," she returned, "but only to visit. I'm a Highlands lass, after all."

He grinned down at her. "Ye're so much more than that, I ken." Lachlan glanced over at the maid. "Nae a word aboot this, Mitchell. We'll tell the family when the moment arrives."

"Of course, my lord. Of course."

Taking one of her hands again, he led Rowena to the door. "Are ye ready?"

She nodded, but knew he could feel the tremor in her fingers. For God's sake, she'd had a harrowing twenty-four hours if she said so herself, followed by a tiring ride back north with her three captors only feet away from her. All of which made her wish Ranulf had decided to be a little less subtle. Bear had commented several times during the ride back to Glengask that a claymore just above the shoulders would end Lord Samston — and the other three — much more quickly and efficiently. Evidently she wasn't that much of a Highlands lass, though, because just the idea made her shiver.

Neither she nor Lachlan had spoken about Lord Rob Cranach, but she knew he had to be thinking about it. Or more likely, he was wondering if Ranulf would continue pressing the suit. He'd had her all but wed just a few days ago, after all. And yes, she would be marrying, but not a Buchanan. She was spoken for.

The rest of the family stood in the foyer, and Lachlan squeezed her fingers before he released her as they descended the stairs. The sooner they dealt with Samston and the Gerdenses, the sooner they could inform Glengask that Lachlan had proposed and she'd accepted. And that whatever the marquis's plans, they had their own.

Ranulf offered his arm, and she wrapped her fingers around his sleeve. "Ye should be walking with Charlotte," she said, as Cooper pulled open the front door.

"Today this is aboot ye," he returned. "And making certain ye're safe from anyone deciding to meddle in clan affairs."

The group started down the hill. Once they were in sight of the gathering, she had to be ready for whatever might happen. And while she might be fierce, a part of her wished her brothers and Lachlan would see to Samston and the other three and leave her out of it. Today had become the happiest day of her life, and she wanted a few damned minutes to enjoy it, to share the news with her family and friends. Instead she had to hide it, because her brother wanted something different for her than she wanted for herself.

The marquis glanced down at her. "Ye havenae asked after Lord Rob," he said.

However sharp-witted he was, not even the MacLawry could read minds. She was fairly certain of that. "He wasnae there to greet me earlier," she returned. "I . . . I forgot about him, really."

"Had a different lad in yer mind, did ye?" he replied.

Before she could comment on that, they

topped the rise. Good heavens. Mitchell hadn't exaggerated when she'd said Ranulf had every MacLawry male out looking for her, because they were all here now — along with their wives and children. There had been nearly seven hundred people in the meadow when she'd left just over three days ago. Now, there seemed to be twice that. And they were all swarming toward her, cheering.

Lachlan stood back a little as the gathered clans closed on Ranulf and Rowena. He and her brothers had told her that she was the darling of clan MacLawry, and if she didn't believe it today, she never would. They adored her, both because she was a MacLawry, and because of the good works she did for the poorest of them. Ranulf had concentrated on education and employment, but Rowena had made certain they were all fed and had roofs over their heads.

Samston and the others who'd settled down for luncheon at the so-called Sassenach tent joined the throng, but Bear and Arran would be watching Samston. Lachlan was looking for another man — Lord Robert Cranach. The man deserved to be flattened on principle. If nothing else, a lass had gone missing, and he hadn't bothered to let that fact disturb his dinner. But it was worse than that. She and Cranach were — had been — practically betrothed. The bastard didn't deserve to wish her well, because he'd never bothered to worry over her absence.

Perhaps, though, he did have some sense, because Lachlan couldn't find him — or any sign of a Buchanan, for that matter. Well, then. He would pound Lord Rob on another occasion. Now, it was Samston's turn.

With a nod at Arran, he headed into the crowd, making his way to just behind the earl's left, while the middle MacLawry brother moved to the right. Bear had volunteered to be his second, but then Samston would never make it to the front of the gathering, and Bear would end in prison.

At the same moment they each took one of the earl's arms and led him forward. "What's this?" Samston asked, scowling.

"Ranulf and Winnie want a word with ye," Arran said. "They'll never manage to get to ye, so we're bringing ye to them."

"I can walk on my own, then. And why do they want to see me? Winnie has made her feelings toward me quite clear."

"Aye," Lachlan took up. "Aye. And ye've done the same toward her."

Samston began to pull against their hold.

Together he and Arran could hold Bear down, though, so the bony earl didn't have a chance of escaping. In a moment they stood directly in front of the MacLawry and his exquisite sister, just as Bear arrived with the Campbell beside him.

As a Sassenach, the earl likely didn't have a true sense of what a precarious and vomit-inducing position he was in, being faced with two chiefs of the most powerful clans in the Highlands. He would know in a minute, though.

"Ah, Samston," Ranulf drawled, his blue eyes icy. "I've heard a tale or two, and I wanted yer opinion on them."

"What tales?"

"Well, firstly that ye kissed my sister and then seemed to want to use that to press her into marriage."

"That's nonsense. You never heard such a thing from me."

"Aye. It's a fortunate thing fer ye that I didnae."

Samston tried again to yank an arm free, but Lachlan didn't budge. He and Arran both had damaged wings, but the day they couldn't hold their own against a man like Adam James was the day they put themselves out to pasture. "I'm your guest, Lord Glengask. I will not be held against my will."

"Interesting choice of words, Samston." Ranulf turned his head. "Peter!" he yelled.

A widening circle had formed around them. Everyone clearly wanted to see and hear what was afoot, but likewise none of them wanted to be close enough to be caught up in whatever this was. Lachlan sent an encouraging smile to Rowena, and when she smiled back at him he felt warm to his cockles.

This had to be much harder on her than on him. All he had to attempt to manage was a growing, seething anger. She was facing the man who'd encouraged her kidnapping. He tightened his grip. Lord Samston wasn't going anywhere.

Peter Gilling appeared from the direction of the stable. Behind him, shackled and tethered like dogs, stumbled Charles Calder, Arnold Haws, and Dermid Gerdens. A half-dozen MacLawry men surrounded them, all of them armed to the teeth.

"Thank ye, Peter," Ranulf said coolly. "Dermid Gerdens. Step up here and have a word with the Campbell."

The big man's face, swollen from being battered over the past days, paled. He limped forward, two grooms holding his tethers. "Yer Grace, I —"

"Tell me aboot the conversation ye had

461

with this Sassenach, Dermid," the Campbell interrupted. "I'll nae hear anything else from ye."

"Aye, Yer Grace. He said ye'd been wrong to banish my brother, and that I needed enough power and wealth to make ye bring him back. He said if I took Winnie Mac-Lawry, Glengask would have to pay me her dowry and give me land, like when the Highlanders used to take the women they wanted."

The duke nodded. "How did Calder and Haws end up involved with this? They werenae invited to this gathering."

"Grandfather," Calder began, trying to pull forward. "I can explain."

"Aye, I imagine ye could, Charles. That's why I want to hear it from Dermid. He's no use fer fancy words and complicated lies."

"We . . ." Dermid swallowed. "Charles said he wasnae finished with Arran Mac-Lawry, so he and Arnold were waiting close by. I told them what Lord Samston told me, and we decided to take her."

All three of these men were grandsons of the Campbell. Ranulf was taking a risk by allowing the Duke of Alkirk to conduct the questioning, and by having him present to hear any decision about these men. The peace was only a few weeks old. By historical standards, it was likely the longest between the Campbells and the MacLawrys in three hundred years.

And then Ranulf surprised Lachlan again. "Yer Grace," the marquis said, "they're yer men. What do ye say?"

For a long moment the duke looked at his grandsons. Cold gray eyes, a stiff spine, and close-cropped gray hair — he looked like precisely who he was, the longtime leader of a very powerful clan. Finally he looked back at Glengask. "Ye didnae have to give them over to me, MacLawry. It means someaught to me that ye did. Dermid wants his brother. I reckon all three of them can join Berling in Canada. I'll nae have them walking on the same land that I am. If that's agreeable to ye, as the wronged party."

Today was full of miracles. Lachlan hoped there was space for one more.

Ranulf nodded. "Aye. It's more than agreeable to me. Thank ye, Campbell."

That left Samston. Ranulf started forward, but Rowena put out a hand and stopped him. Instead, she walked up to the earl, who now stood gray-faced. If Lachlan and Arran hadn't been holding him, he would likely have collapsed. That might have been fun, but it would also leave him free to attempt something. And that wouldn't happen.

She stopped two feet in front of Samston. "I liked ye," she said simply. Then she slapped him across the face. Hard. "Now ye can leave the Highlands. If I ever set eyes on ye, ye're done. If I ever hear of ye coming north of Hadrian's Wall for any reason, ye're done. Ye have five minutes to gather yer things. Whatever ye leave behind, I'm throwing into the fire." She glanced over her shoulder. "Did ye have something ye wanted to add, *bràthair*?"

"Nae. That should do it."

Lachlan shoved the earl to the ground. And then they all walked away from him.

Within an hour Ranulf managed to take Rowena around to everyone he especially wanted her to thank, and they were able to return to the house. "Charlotte," the marquis said, leading the way into the morning room, "I mean to marry ye tomorrow. Do ye have any objection to that?"

"I do not," she returned, smiling. "We're all where we're supposed to be. I require nothing more than that."

"And I require nothing but ye," he returned, then looked at the rest of them. "Because all my manly nerves are frayed, I'd appreciate if the rest of ye stayed in the hoose fer the rest of the day. Ye as well, Lach; I sent Owen fer yer formal attire. It's in the bedchamber across from Bear's."

That worked well, as Lachlan had no intention of leaving without having a moment — or several of them — with Rowena. "As ye wish."

"Good. I've a few things to see to, but I'll be aboot." He turned on his heel.

"Where's Rob Cranach?" Lachlan said, before Ranulf could exit the room.

Rowena sent him a sharp glance. Yes, she wanted to wait until after the wedding, but Ranulf had been making decisions for them with such swiftness that he was fairly certain they couldn't afford to wait that long. She was his. And the sooner everyone realized that, the less chance of more difficulties later.

Ranulf turned around. "Cranach's most of the way home by now, I reckon."

"He is?" Rowena blurted. "Why?"

"Do ye want him, lass? I had the impression ye didnae."

"No, I don't want him. But why is he on his way home?"

Her brother stepped deeper into the morning room again and shut the door behind him. "Because I didnae like the way he ate," he said succinctly.

Now Bear was frowning. "What?"

"When Rowena went missing, Cranach

and his cousin sat doon to have dinner. As I'd just agreed to give him something most precious to me, this caused me some concern as to how he viewed her." He gazed steadily at Lachlan. "Ye pointed it oot to me, as I recall."

"Aye. I did."

"Ye also mentioned someaught aboot Rowena being the heart of this clan, and what would happen to the lot of us if she wasnae a MacLawry."

An odd, hopeful thud began beating somewhere in the region of Lachlan's heart. Ranulf was a damned stubborn man, accustomed, and with good reason, to his word being law. Unless he was completely misreading the signs, though, he liked what Ranulf was saying.

"I did mention that," he returned. "And I stand by it."

"And yet ye said ye wouldnae have Rowena."

Hope crashed again. "I made a mistake. What I say now is that I'll nae have anyone *but* Rowena."

"Hm." The marquis turned his attention to his sister, standing a few feet away. "Ye've made it fairly clear, lass, that ye have some strong opinions aboot who ye'll wed. Where does Lachlan fall in that list?"

"There is no list," she returned. "I'll have Lachlan, or I'll nae have anyone."

"If ye two are so set on each other, why have ye nae proposed, Lach?"

Lachlan took a deep breath. "I have proposed."

"Did ye, now? When ye thought she was to marry another man?"

He looked at Rowena, at her profile as she tried to figure out her brother. "*Ye* may have thought she was marrying another man, Glengask, but I didnae. I wouldnae allow it. She's marrying me, whether ye like it or nae."

Ranulf folded his arms across his chest. "What did ye say when he proposed to ye, *piuthar*?"

"I said aye. I don't want to disappoint ye, Ranulf. Ye're my brother, and I love ye. I'd do anything for ye. Anything but marry a man I dunnae love when the man I adore is standing beside me."

Slowly Ranulf blew out his breath, his shoulders lowering as he dropped his hands again. "Fer God's sake, the two of ye have spun us around. I ken that some of that was my fault. I made assumptions, and didnae give ye the chance to figure things oot fer yerselves."

"Ran, ye did what ye thought was best. Ye

always do," Rowena said, walking up to put a hand on one of his arms.

He cupped her cheek with his free hand. "Ye have my blessing, Rowena. Go kiss the lad before he combusts."

With a happy shout Lachlan strode forward and grabbed her, spinning her around to plant a sound kiss on her mouth. Eighteen years of being on different paths, and they'd finally reached the same destination at the same time. Together. She flung her arms around his shoulders and kissed him back, laughing.

"It's aboot damned time!" Bear roared, clapping him so hard on the back that he nearly fell over on Rowena.

Lachlan lifted his head. "What changed yer mind, Ran?" he asked, though he likely should have kept his mouth closed. It hadn't only been him seeing that Cranach wasn't the one for her, though. Something had finally turned Ranulf back toward him.

"Ye got stabbed, through and through," Ranulf answered, walking forward to offer his hand. "Ye wouldnae stay behind, even when ye should have. Ye pushed at me and put me in my place, and then ye rode fer nearly twenty-four hours and ye found her. Ye'll look after her. Ye cherish her. That's what she deserves."

"I do cherish her," he breathed, and kissed her again, more softly this time, ignoring the congratulations being delivered around them. "I cherish ye."

With a sigh she leaned her lithe body along his. "Ye'd better, Lachlan," she murmured back, a smile in her voice. "I'm a fierce Highlands lass, and I'll nae accept anything less."

He chuckled. "I love ye, Rowena. I'll nae give ye anything less than that."

ABOUT THE AUTHOR

Suzanne Enoch grew up In Southern California, where she still balances her love for the Regency romances of Georgette Heyer and classic romantic comedies with her obsession for anything *Star Wars.* Given her love of food and comfy chairs, she may in fact be a Hobbit. She has written more than 35 romance novels, Including traditional Regencies, Historical Romance, and contemporary Romantic Suspense. When she isn't working on her next book she is trying to learn to cook, and wishes she had an English accent. She is the bestselling author of *The Scandalous Brides* series, *The Scandalous Highlanders* series, and *One Hot Scot.*

The employees of Thorndike Press hope you have enjoyed this Large Print book. All our Thorndike, Wheeler, and Kennebec Large Print titles are designed for easy reading, and all our books are made to last. Other Thorndike Press Large Print books are available at your library, through selected bookstores, or directly from us.

For information about titles, please call:
(800) 223-1244

or visit our Web site at:
http://gale.cengage.com/thorndike

To share your comments, please write:
Publisher
Thorndike Press
10 Water St., Suite 310
Waterville, ME 04901